'As cosy as it is compulsive, Sauers brings t[...] the Southern Highlands to life. Despite the [...] newcomer—and accidental amateur sleut[...] she moves to her dream cottage in the countryside, I wanted to nestle in, myself. A highly recommended, vivid read!'

JACQUELINE BUBLITZ, author of *Before You Knew My Name*

'I couldn't put this book down! From the breathtaking first page to the spine-tingling finale, *Echo Lake* held me entranced. This masterful debut combines the gripping menace of a thriller with the humour and heart of a cosy mystery, reflecting the rich character, history and beauty of the enigmatic Southern Highlands. Perfect for fireside reading, particularly if paired with a rich red and some quality chocolate!'

NINA D. CAMPBELL, author of *Daughters of Eve*

'Move over Miss Marple. With its indefatigable heroine, mist-shrouded setting, cast of quirky characters and as many trips to the pub as there are mysteries to solve, *Echo Lake* is cosy crime at its dynamic, atmospheric best—and Sauers is certainly a writer to watch.'

ANNA DOWNES, author of *The Shadow House*

'Set in the scenic Southern Highlands of New South Wales, Joan Sauers' *Echo Lake* is full of atmosphere; the very landscape echoes both freedom and foreboding. Rose McHugh, middle-aged and newly single, is a convincing, compelling and intelligent protagonist who stumbles onto a mystery and won't let it go. In her search for a killer, she finds her place in her new world as well, which gives this pacy thriller a warm heart.'

VIKKI PETRAITIS, author of *The Unbelieved*

'*Echo Lake* is a crime novel that casts its net wide. Not just a whodunnit, it also contemplates what makes for a good life, reminds the reader of the importance of historical truth and throws in a ghost story for good measure.'

MARYROSE CUSKELLY, author of *The Cane*

ECHO LAKE

JOAN SAUERS

ALLEN&UNWIN
SYDNEY·MELBOURNE·AUCKLAND·LONDON

First published in 2023

Allen & Unwin
Cammeraygal Country
83 Alexander Street
Crows Nest NSW 2065
Australia
Phone: (61 2) 8425 0100
Email: info@allenandunwin.com
Web: www.allenandunwin.com

Allen & Unwin acknowledges the Traditional Owners of the Country on which we live and work. We pay our respects to all Aboriginal and Torres Strait Islander Elders, past and present.

A catalogue record for this book is available from the National Library of Australia

ISBN 978 1 76106 759 4

Map by Aleksander Potočnik
Set in 12.5/17.5 pt Granjon by Midland Typesetters, Australia
Printed and bound in Australia by the Opus Group

10 9 8 7 6 5 4 3 2 1

MIX
Paper | Supporting responsible forestry
FSC® C001695

The paper in this book is FSC® certified. FSC® promotes environmentally responsible, socially beneficial and economically viable management of the world's forests.

For Martha

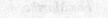

As all historians know, the past is a great darkness, and filled with echoes.

Margaret Atwood

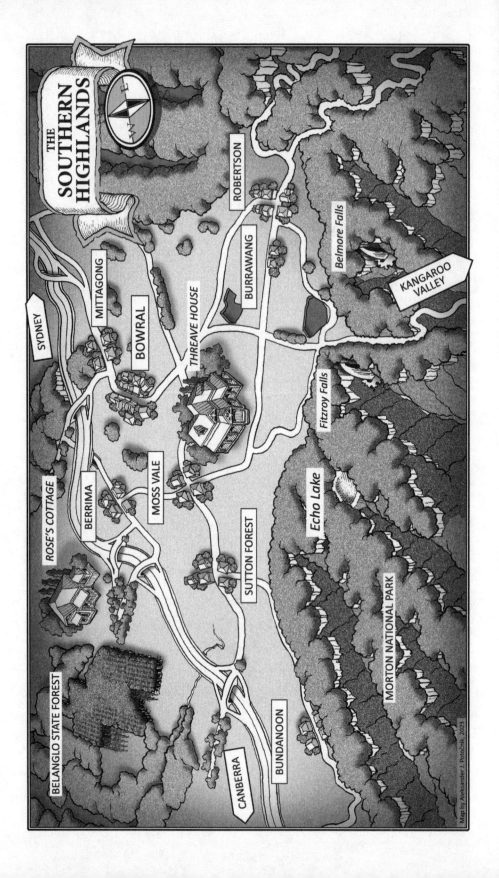

THE SOUTHERN HIGHLANDS

SYDNEY

MITTAGONG

BOWRAL

THREAVE HOUSE

ROSE'S COTTAGE

BERRIMA

MOSS VALE

BELANGLO STATE FOREST

SUTTON FOREST

CANBERRA

BUNDANOON

ROBERTSON

BURRAWANG

Belmore Falls

KANGAROO VALLEY

Fitzroy Falls

Echo Lake

MORTON NATIONAL PARK

Map by Aleksander I Potočnik, 2023

PROLOGUE

Rose runs deeper into the forest as the fierce wind makes the leaves shudder in the trees. She's never run so fast, zigzagging around trunks and fallen branches, slipping on moss-covered rocks.

Her coat gets snagged on a branch, so she peels out of it. There's barely any light and she gets tangled in vines, stumbling in her high-heeled boots. She stops, looks behind her. She can't hear anything over the trees groaning in the wind. She pulls off her boots and keeps running.

Branches rake her face, tear at her silk shirt as she trembles with adrenaline and the cold. Behind a broad gum tree, she slows to catch her breath. She touches a hand to her cheek and finds it wet with tears and blood. She stumbles on.

She fights through scrub, a tight cluster of banksia, and suddenly the ground drops away beneath her and she is falling.

She hits the ground hard.

Dragging air into her lungs, her knees throbbing, she gets to her feet and looks around. The light is nearly gone now but she recognises this place. She's been here before. Echo Lake.

The shadow descends, the sick feeling.

Then, behind her, his voice.

PROLOGUE

ONE

Six months earlier . . .

Rose looks out the window and gasps.

Kim rushes in. 'What?!'

'It's . . . *perfect*,' says Rose.

Kim looks over her sister's shoulder at the uncut grass, scrappy shrubs and scruffy trees. A towering gum is shedding its bark in ragged sheets, and the rickety garden shed looks like it would blow over in the first strong gust of wind.

'Looks like a shitload of work.'

But Rose sees what the garden might have looked like in the past—and what it could look like again.

Near the shed, red and green parrots are eating pomegranate seeds from the fruit hanging off the tree.

'King parrots!' Rose says. 'You never see those in Sydney.'

'I saw some at the zoo once.'

Rose looks around the small bedroom. 'It's just right.'

And it's true. Ever since her first trip to the Southern Highlands as a child, Rose has imagined living in a little wooden cottage by a creek, surrounded by bushland and birdsong.

She pictures where her bed might go, deciding it should run alongside the window. On cold mornings, she can bring her cup of tea back to bed, climb under the doona, and watch the birds.

Kim attempts to break the spell. 'Listen, Rose. I am the voice of reason. This house is small. It's dark. It's remote. It needs a ton of work.'

'So do I, Kim. But I have charm.' Rose grins at her own joke.

'And it's nearly two hours from Sydney.'

'Which is why I can afford it!'

'It's in the *country*, for Chrissake.'

'I love the country.'

'No, you don't. You love the *idea* of the country. You know, there's a serial killer around here.'

'He died years ago.'

Rose looks at the walls, figuring out where she'll hang her engravings. 'And it's not that dark,' she says. 'With my bedside lamps, it'll be super cosy.'

A big, brown rescue dog of uncertain breed comes in and nuzzles Rose. She scratches him behind the ears.

'What do you say, Bob: dream house or what?'

'Any questions, ladies?' Dave, the Irish real estate agent, in jeans, blazer and R.M. Williams boots, comes to stand in the doorway.

'Yeah,' Kim says. 'Why did I bother to come if she'd already made up her mind?'

Dave smiles. 'I think Rose wanted you here for your practical perspective.'

'Not if she already drank the Kool-Aid.'

The agent laughs.

Rose leaves the bedroom, tape measure at the ready, and Kim and Dave follow.

'Why is the owner selling?' Kim asks Dave.

'She's a younger woman; I think she wants to be in town, where the action is.'

'She sounds highly intelligent,' Kim says pointedly.

In the lounge room, the sun is shining through two sash windows with deep sills onto wide floorboards that reflect warm light onto the faded yellow tongue-in-groove walls. A bare light bulb dangles from a ceiling pendant.

Rose measures the length of one wall. 'The bookcase will fit perfectly.'

In fact, with the pot-bellied stove in the corner, every one of Rose's boxes is ticked. She takes out her phone and taps the compass app. She nods at the windows. 'That's north, so this room gets sun all day.' She looks at Kim as if to say: told you so.

Kim nudges a discoloured floorboard with the toe of her designer shoe. 'That looks like termites.'

'The floorboards are original but they're in good shape,' Dave says in that accent which makes you think he cannot tell a lie. 'The house has been treated and it's absolutely sound. I'll send you the survey but, of course, you're welcome to do your own.'

'Did you hear that, Rose?' Kim asks. 'Are you listening?'

'Doesn't it have a good feeling?' Rose counters.

Kim rolls her eyes. 'Here we go—you and your feelings.'

'Even you must be able to sense it. This has been a happy house. A happy home.' Ever since Rose was little, she felt that she could tune into places and get a sense of their past. She thinks of it as hearing their echoes.

Kim looks around and shrugs. 'Yeah, well, I guess it has an okay vibe.'

Rose opens the door of the stove and looks inside. 'I'm gonna save so much on heating.'

'And with all those falling tree branches you'll never run out of kindling,' says Kim. 'Don't they call them widow makers?'

Dave smiles but ignores her question. 'So, Rose, are you thinking of buying the house?'

Rose grins. 'Oh no, Dave ... I'm *buying* the house—I'm *thinking* about where to put the Christmas tree.'

Kim throws up her hands in defeat.

TWO

Rose wakes up to the fluting call of a magpie. She opens her eyes.

She's facing the window that looks out onto the back garden, where the green leaves of summer have turned a deep, rich red. Bright blue sky shows through bare branches where another tree is shedding its leaves. She intends to find out what every tree is called and how to look after it. In the city, she had a few potted succulents that needed little more than an occasional splash of water. But she wants to nurture what's hers, at least for the time she's here.

Today is Rose's first day properly living in her Southern Highlands cottage, three months after deciding to buy it. After all the paperwork and admin, packing up her city life and booking removalists, and then the process of moving in, being surrounded by boxes and tripping over pictures leaning against walls, waiting to be hung, it is done. She folded up the last box last night, and she's excited to be settled in time to enjoy the peak of autumn. Finally, she is living her dream.

For as long as she can remember, Rose has been in love with the Southern Highlands. When the weather turned cool, their mum and dad would pack her and Kim into the car, and they'd make the pilgrimage south-west of Sydney to this area of

mountains, woodland and rolling farmland dotted with pictur-
esque towns and villages. They'd pass through Mittagong and
Bowral, admiring the elms, maples and oaks whose leaves flamed
yellow, orange and red in the bracing air. Then they'd drive
further and stop in one of the smaller villages, such as Berrima,
Bundanoon or Robertson, and find a cafe that served high tea.

The most exciting part of these trips was when they'd enter
one of the state forests or national parks that crept up to the edges
of the towns, a little dangerous in their wildness. Hiking along
some deserted trail, she'd pretend she was in the real Scottish
Highlands, and swore that one day she would live here.

Unlike her older sister Kim, who loves the warmth and
beach life of Sydney, Rose prefers the Highlands' colder weather,
shrouding mists, meandering rivers and shady gorges. The
romance of the setting is like a drug to her. And it feels more
connected to history in a way that's been erased in the city. With
its colonial-era sandstone buildings, quaint gift shops and cafes,
Berrima was always Rose's favourite stop, and when she found
a real estate listing for this 1930s cottage not too far outside the
village, it was like finding the missing piece of a puzzle.

The ad alone was enough to hook her, but it was nothing
compared to her first sight of the real thing. She had driven past
Berrima, then turned off the main highway into a one-lane road
shaded by pin oaks and paperbark trees. After continuing on
through thick woodland for a bit, not seeing another house, she
came around a bend and there it was—pale yellow weatherboard
walls holding up an old tin roof, a stone chimney tilting slightly
under the tall trees.

Rose had stopped the car and turned off the engine to take it
in, and all she could hear was the gentle flow of a nearby stream
and the chatter of birds.

It was love at first sight.

Rose brought Kim along as a witness when she went to sign the contract on the cottage. Just as she was about to put pen to paper, Kim asked, 'Are you a hundred per cent sure?'

Rose looked up in surprise. 'Of course.'

Kim hesitated, then said, 'I'm just afraid you're doing this for the wrong reasons. I'm afraid you're running away.'

Rose was taken aback by the suggestion and denied it vigorously. But later she thought about what Kim had said and realised her sister was partly right.

The year before last, Rose's marriage of twenty-plus years had ended. She and her husband Peter had met during Rose's first year at Sydney University, where he was a professor of history. Relationships between teachers and students were discouraged, to say the least, but Rose and Peter didn't care. They also ignored the fact that he was nearly twenty years older than her. No one seemed to think this was a problem—or if they did, they didn't say as much publicly. As the distinguished author of a best-selling book about social systems in ancient Greece, as well as a number of widely used textbooks, Peter seemed to float above the rules that applied to others.

Rose's plan had been to become a social historian who wrote fascinating tomes about the way women lived in the past. Maybe she'd become a professor herself. But by her second year of uni she was pregnant with their son Sam, and it took her four more years to finish her degree. Ever since then, she'd worked freelance from home as a historical researcher for other writers of fascinating tomes, and looked after Peter, Sam, the house and a succession of rescue dogs. She had wanted another child but Peter thought he was too old, so she contented herself with one.

Occasionally Rose would regret not having tried to write her own books, but she was mostly satisfied with what she did and what she had. She loved doing research, even if it was in the service of someone else's work—or, more frequently now, a television show or documentary. But, more than digging through articles and archives and writing up the reports at the end, she loved talking to people and finding out their stories. Rose had gained a reputation for eliciting surprising details from interview subjects and archives. People were compelled to tell her things they hadn't told anyone else, and more than one librarian bent over backwards and even broke the rules to help Rose find some nugget in their collections, encouraged by her natural curiosity and excitement for the hunt.

Over the years, Rose was kept busy. After the school drop-off, she'd walk the family dog, do the grocery shopping and housework and put in a few hours on her current research project, then it would be time to pick up Sam and help him with his homework before making a start on dinner. When Peter got home they would open a bottle of wine while Peter regaled her with tales of the latest campus politics or scandal, neither of which she missed. After dinner, they would do the dishes together and Peter would praise her cooking, though she was hardly a contender for *MasterChef*. But of course, with all his university and publishing commitments, Peter wasn't always home for dinner.

One of the things Rose liked about her marriage was that she had so much time alone. In retrospect, she realises she probably ignored signs of trouble because she'd cherished the solitude. Even as a child she'd liked being alone, reading or drawing, or playing outside in the bush. She loved spending time with Sam, Kim and Peter, of course, and she had kept a few friends from university, but she didn't sustain many more relationships than that. She usually craved even more time on her own than she had, to connect with ideas, places, nature. She liked people, but in small doses.

Rose believed she was happy for most of those years—or, if not happy, at least content. But the year before last, when Sam moved to England to pursue a master's degree in archaeology, she decided to start doing research for her own book about the female druids and judges in ancient Celtic society. Her plan was to surprise Peter at work and take him to lunch to see what he thought of the idea.

It wasn't a classic case of in flagrante delicto, but from the moment Rose opened the door to his office and saw him with a young female student, everything was clear. He was touching the girl's arm in the intimate way of a lover, not a friend, and certainly not a teacher, and the look on his face when he saw Rose confirmed what she hoped wasn't true. Suddenly, her image of all those evening lectures, book tours and weekend conferences he simply *had* to attend morphed into a tawdry cliché.

Later, he tried to defend himself. He said it meant nothing, that he and Rose could go on as they had been—so happy for so many years. But something had stirred in Rose. Something had woken up. She realised she didn't want to go back to the way they were. In her mid-forties, facing the rest of her life, Rose decided she wanted something more.

They divorced and sold the family home, a Victorian terrace house in Glebe, near the university, that she had loved and tended for decades, and that had skyrocketed in value. She walked away with enough money to buy her little cottage outright and still have something left over to live on while expanding her research business so she could become self-sufficient. She put the idea of writing her book about female druids on the proverbial backburner.

In the meantime, Peter and the student—whom Kim privately referred to as his 'child bride'—married and bought an old house in Redfern, which they were in the process of renovating (which apparently meant stripping it of its history and charm). To top it off, Child Bride was pregnant. So, Peter wasn't too old after all.

When Kim asked Rose if she was running away, Rose didn't want to admit that she was, because that's not *all* she was doing. It was true she didn't want to bump into the happy family, or pass the old terrace that she had loved as much as you can love a house. But moving to the Highlands wasn't just an act of escape; it was an act of reinvention. Of rebirth. Rose wanted to live out a dream she'd always had, but she'd never dared entertain when she was entrenched in a marriage and life in the city—a dream of living in the country, near a creek, surrounded by birdsong.

Sam was overseas now, and thanks to digitised archives and fast internet, she could still work for historians, writers and TV producers in the city while living in the country.

Now, as she gets out of bed in her Highlands cottage, Rose realises that for the first time she can remember—maybe ever—she feels completely at home.

She pulls on her fluffy dressing-gown and steps into her new fleece-lined slippers. They were a bit of a splurge, but you can't be happy if your feet are cold.

She walks into the lounge room and feels the stove. It's still warm from last night's fire, and the rich scent of wood smoke lingers in the air. Her old bookcase stretches the length of one wall, the books organised in categories—history, biography and mystery novels, all wedged in tightly. She realises she'll have to get some new shelves for her fast-growing collection of Australian mysteries alone.

In the kitchen, Bob is waiting by the back door, already used to the new routine. Rose lets him out, shocked by the blast of cold air and pleasantly surprised that the old house's insulation is doing its job.

She turns on the kettle and tunes in to the ABC's classical music station, relieved to be greeted by the voice of the breakfast presenter whose soft Edinburgh lilt completes the illusion that she's somewhere not far from Loch Lomond. She prefers him to some of the guest presenters, and although she doesn't begrudge him the odd day off, he really should stay where he belongs, chatting away as if she's the only person listening. She smiles, wondering if he has any idea how attached listeners can get, and suspects that he's all too aware, and probably has restraining orders out on dozens of them.

Rose makes a cup of tea, brings it back to her bedroom, and climbs back under the doona, from where she can watch Bob sniffing his way around the garden.

After a shower—the water pressure's not great, but at least it's hot—Rose opens her wardrobe and decides what to wear. It's a running joke between her and the well-dressed Kim, who teases Rose about her 'uniform'. As usual, Rose picks out a black turtleneck and faded blue jeans. It's so easy, and now that she's stopped colouring her brown hair, she likes the way the grey streaks look against black. At least, that's her excuse. On the other hand, maybe she's just lazy. She sees other women in print dresses and colourful skirts and thinks how pretty they are, but she's more comfortable in pants. And anyway, working from home, she doesn't have to impress anyone. Thank God.

She slips into her old work boots and looks in the mirror on the wardrobe door. At forty-five, Rose would like to think she looks closer to forty, but it doesn't keep her up at night. She's not a great beauty, but her green eyes make up for it, especially when she smiles. She'd like to lose a few kilos, but now that she's discovered Berrima's Gumnut Patisserie, there's little chance of that. Kim tells her she's gorgeous no matter what, but Rose always feels underdressed and ill-groomed next to her sister. Even though she's eight years older, Kim looks closer to Rose's age, and has no qualms about spending her hard-earned money on clothes, manicures and hair treatments, so no grey for her. Rose worries that Kim's teacher's salary isn't enough to cover the cost of all this maintenance, but whenever she brings it up, her sister says she has no children and no pets, so she can afford it.

Rose gives Bob his breakfast, then buttons up her navy duffel coat and they head out for their first trip to the dog park.

Dave O'Neill, the real estate agent, had told Rose about the locally famous Moss Vale dog park—a huge expanse of high hills and tall trees where dogs of all persuasions can run around off leash. She was reassured by the fact that it's completely fenced. Bob is pretty good at staying close, but if he catches the scent of something as interesting as a fox or deer, there's no holding him back. And with the thousands of acres of wilderness around, Rose doesn't want to risk losing him.

She drives past postcard-perfect dairy farms, stock and station agents, and something called Horseland. Rose loves that she now lives in a place that caters as much to horses as people.

Along the route, the sun, which had shone brightly just moments ago, becomes watery and vague in a thickening mist, forcing Rose to turn on her headlights and slow down. Huge trucks rise suddenly behind her in the fog before barrelling past. She fights down a flutter of panic and glances at Bob in the rear-view mirror.

'How can they drive that fast on a narrow two-lane road? In the fog?!'

Sitting up on the back seat, Bob seems bewildered, as if wondering where his view of the cows went.

Rose realises she's holding the steering wheel in a death grip, and tries to relax.

As she drives into Moss Vale, the fog blurs the contours of the low buildings and makes it hard to read the road signs. Luckily, she had a look at the map on her phone before she left home.

She drives down a winding road, glimpsing cottages made of stone and wood with tall, tapered chimneys and small-paned windows under deep eaves among trees whose leaves of gold, orange and blood-red are luminous in the mist. The bushland thickens before she sees a clearing with a few parked cars. She pulls in and parks, relieved to have arrived in one piece.

As if sensing the marvels that await, Bob bounds out of the car and follows a dirt trail that leads to a gate in a chain-wire fence. When Rose catches up, she can make out vague shapes of assorted dogs and their owners, loping up and down the hills. Somewhere nearby, a loud bark is swallowed in the fog.

Rose opens the gate and Bob bolts into the park, which seems to stretch on for miles. She smiles, not minding the mist or the cold or the slightly muddy ground, or the smell of decaying leaves. This is what she came for.

She follows Bob up a vast hill and finds him at the top, sniffing an elegant whippet with a pink suede collar. On the other side of a wooden fence, a dozen black-and-white cows are standing as still as a painting, while a loose flock of corellas whirl overhead.

A honking note rings out. Then another, and another, until they gradually form a tune played on the bagpipes.

Rose looks around, trying to see who's playing, but the piper is hidden in the mist.

'Very atmospheric, isn't it?'

Rose turns to see a man in his late seventies with clear blue eyes and an open smile, wearing a black beret at a rakish angle. On someone else it could look silly or pretentious, but somehow he pulls it off. He also sports a dapper camel's hair coat and magenta corduroy pants. Rose is deeply impressed.

'Incredible!' she says. 'I love the bagpipes. I just can't believe someone is here playing them.'

'He comes every day—except, presumably, in the driving rain.' His accent is English, upper crust. Or a convincing facsimile.

'I'm a bit of a sucker for anything Scottish,' Rose confesses.

The whippet runs to the man, who takes a treat out of his pocket and gives it to her. Bob charges up, expecting one too.

'Bob! Stop that!'

'It's fine.'

The man produces another treat for Bob.

'Thank you,' Rose says. 'He's probably part lab, so he's always ravenous. Either that or he's just very badly behaved.'

'We all are sometimes.'

'Speak for yourself.'

He laughs.

The whippet wanders up to Rose.

'She's beautiful,' Rose observes. 'And will forever be thin, lucky girl.'

'That's Cordelia.'

Rose strokes the whippet's sleek coat. 'Cordelia, hey? Shakespeare or P.D. James?'

The man smiles. 'The latter. My late wife was a big fan of detective fiction.'

'Me too. I loved that in *An Unsuitable Job for a Woman* P.D. James made Cordelia an actual working detective, not just a meddling old lady.'

'Yes, but did you know that the first female detective was created in the 1860s? She exhibited all the deductive brilliance of Sherlock Holmes, who wasn't created until twenty years later!'

'I did not know that. I'll have to find the book.'

'I could lend it to you.'

'Thank you!' Rose is both happy and surprised to have made a connection with someone so quickly. Sometimes people just click. Thinking about making fast friends, she says, 'Cordelia is Bob's first new friend here. We just moved from Sydney.'

'Ah, welcome to the Highlands! I'm George.'

'I'm Rose. I'm so glad we heard about this park. I was—'

She sees the white shape coming towards her too late and is knocked off her feet, landing on her arse in the mud. The big white dog tears away towards a muscular man with a shaved head and no coat. The dog pauses to snap at a shih tzu, whose owner scoops it up out of the way. The coatless man whistles and the white dog follows him out of the park.

George helps Rose to her feet and she brushes herself off.

'Are you all right?' George asks.

'I'm fine.' Rose is more embarrassed at falling in the mud than injured.

'That dog shouldn't be allowed in here,' George says. 'There have been complaints. And his owner is just as unpleasant. Are you sure you're not hurt?'

'Positive.' Rose smiles, grateful for his kindness. 'And I don't blame the poor dog. It's owners who make dogs antisocial.'

'Indeed. Well, I'm afraid the cold is getting into my old bones. Cordelia?'

The whippet comes straight to him. He attaches a lead to her suede collar. Rose is as impressed with the dog as she is with her owner.

'In spite of the unfriendly welcome, I hope to see you here again,' George says. 'And I'll bring that book.'

'In that case, we'll definitely be back,' Rose assures him.

George touches his beret in a farewell salute then heads down the hill, Cordelia trotting dutifully by his side.

'See, Bob? That's how it's done.'

Bob is distracted by a low-flying cockatoo and bounds after it. Rose follows, wandering through the park with its views of far-off escarpments that seem to float above the mist.

She listens to the bagpipes as Bob play-wrestles with a frisky cattle dog, but after a while, she's aware of the dampness where she fell, and yearns for her heated car seat. When she found that the second-hand Honda she was looking at before the move had heated seats, the deal was sealed.

'Come on, Bob, let's go.'

By the time Rose leaves the dog park, the mist has thinned and she finally sees the piper, playing beneath a giant red oak. She half-expected him to be wearing a kilt, but he's in a rather unromantic blue puffer jacket and saggy sweatpants. She nods at him as they pass, but he's lost in a ragged rendition of 'The King of the Highlands'.

She grabs a towel from the boot of the car and spreads it on the back seat. Bob hops in and curls up. Rose brushes some mud off her pants, then slips into the driver's seat and turns on the heater, which starts to work almost instantly.

She is excited to start researching the local coffee scene. The process of selecting her new morning coffee spot must be undertaken methodically, but also with her senses wide open. Rose wants a cafe with a good vibe, but she also wants strong coffee and outdoor tables, so Bob can sit with her as she reads a book or watches the world go by.

As she approaches the first cafe on her list, Rose slows to a stop behind a car that's idling in the middle of the street. At first it's not clear why the driver has stopped, then she sees through his rear window that he's talking on his phone. She sighs—clearly he hasn't realised that she's waiting behind him. Suddenly a white dog's head pops up from the back seat, and Rose realises the driver is the man from the park.

His rear lights come on and he starts to back up. He's reversing into the space next to her, but he hasn't signalled or checked his mirror.

She beeps her horn to warn him, but he ignores her and keeps coming—and backs right into her front bumper.

The man springs out of his car. He's still wearing no coat but, amazingly, there are no goosebumps on his bare, muscled arms. He's in his mid-thirties and wears a chunky, expensive-looking watch. He walks up to her closed window and leans in close.

'What the fuck, lady?' He's angry, sure of himself.

'You backed into me,' Rose protests.

'I don't fucking think so.' He glances at Bob in the back seat and suddenly Rose feels protective.

'Yes you did,' she says. 'I was waiting behind you and I don't think you saw me. You were talking on your—'

A horn blares behind them.

The man gets back in his car and drives a bit further down the street, pulling over in a loading zone. Rose pulls in behind him. Clutching her phone, she gets out to approach him.

He's inspecting the rear of his car. It looks new, the blue-and-white BMW logo gleaming on the pristine boot. There's no damage that Rose can see. The white dog stares at her from the back seat. Rose feels sorry for him. She looks at the front of her Honda. It's a bit scratched, but that's probably nothing new. Or nothing worth mentioning.

A stooped woman with a flowered plastic shopping trolley has stopped to watch. Rose catches her eye. The woman scurries away with surprising speed. So much for a helpful eyewitness.

'You're gonna pay for this,' the man says, his voice ice cold.

'But it doesn't look like there's any damage.' Rose is trying to be reasonable, but there's something nasty in his eyes. She takes out her phone. 'Maybe we should take pictures.'

Rose realises her hand is shaking as she takes a picture of her own car.

Bob's face appears in the window. 'It's okay, Bob,' she reassures him.

She takes a picture of the BMW.

'Lemme see your licence,' the man demands.

Rose takes her driver's licence out of her wallet and gives it to him. He holds it up and takes a picture on his phone, hands it back.

'I'd better take yours too,' Rose says.

The man takes his licence from his wallet and holds it inches from her face. As Rose steps back to take a picture, the man looks at Bob and says, 'Ugly fucking dog. He's gonna be sorry too.'

And then, with Rose staring after him in shock, he gets into his car and drives away.

THREE

Rose returns to her car and sits for a moment, trying to calm her racing heart. Bob pokes his head over the front seat and rests it on her shoulder. She's grateful for the comfort, but it disarms her and her eyes suddenly fill with tears.

'Stop it,' she orders herself, blinking. She holds up her phone and looks at the picture she took of the man's driver's licence. Ray Mullin. His photo looks like the mug shot of a psychopath—but then again, so does hers. They tell you not to smile. Why do they do that?

She's about to drive off when her phone rings. It's Kim. Rose leaves it for a few rings and then answers brightly. 'Hi there!'

'How's it going? Moving back yet?'

'Ha ha,' Rose says flatly.

'Still drowning in boxes?'

'No, finally settled in. It's so beautiful. The leaves are incredible.'

'Just don't ask me to rake them.'

Rose laughs. 'Wouldn't dare.'

'I'll come down for a drunken weekend soon.'

'That would be fantastic.' Her voice betrays a hint of need, and Kim's radar twitches.

'Everything okay?'

'I'm—something weird just happened.'

'What?'

Rose tells her about the exchange with Ray Mullin. 'I think I'm more upset that he called Bob ugly than the implied threat to me.'

'You have to go to the police,' Kim says.

'Don't be ridiculous.'

'Remember that mother of four who was stabbed to death by the road rager? She bled out right in front of the kids.'

'But this guy drove off,' Rose reminds her. 'I'm sure when he cools down he'll realise he was at fault.'

'He doesn't sound like someone who examines his faults too closely.'

'I don't know. The police?' Rose sighs.

'What if he claims whiplash and sues and you lose the house and become homeless and a meth junkie?'

'You paint such a vivid word picture.'

'Comes from teaching kids.'

'The cops will laugh at me.'

'Who cares? You'll sleep better. And so will I.'

Rose gives in. 'All right.'

'Call me after.'

'Love you.'

'Love you too.'

Rose pulls into the car park next to the Southern Highlands police station, a modern grey-brick building that looks reassuringly ordinary. She opens the windows of the car a crack so she can leave Bob inside, and enters the building through the sliding glass doors.

A large, clean waiting area contains two long wooden benches. On one of them sits a young man with a face bloated from drink or drugs or a fight—or all three. He sees Rose staring and she looks away, pretending to be engrossed in a poster about domestic violence that's yellowing on the wall. She's reminded that the Highlands aren't only about antique shops and cellar doors and stud farms. Like any rural area, there is long-term unemployment, poverty, alcoholism and drug abuse.

Rose approaches the reception desk, which is protected by a shield of perspex. She catches sight of the insignia of the New South Wales Police Force—a wedge-tailed eagle and the Latin motto *Culpam poena premit comes*, which she manages to translate as 'Punishment swiftly follows crime'. It occurs to Rose that, in her case, no crime was committed. Not really. She's about to leave when a young police constable emerges from a side door.

'Can I help you?' the constable asks Rose from the other side of the desk.

She has intelligent eyes and her black hair is pulled back in the regulation ponytail. She looks about sixteen. According to her name badge, she's Constable Tran.

Rose approaches. 'Hi,' she says. 'It's probably nothing. I wasn't even going to come, but my sister thought I should.'

'Sisters . . .' Constable Tran says, as if she knows only too well.

'Yes.'

'Can't live with 'em, can't shoot 'em.'

Rose smiles, then describes the incident with the BMW driver.

'Can I see your licence?' the constable asks. 'And the photos?'

Rose takes out her licence and opens her phone, and passes them to the young woman, who swipes through the images.

'I don't want to file a complaint or anything,' Rose says. 'But I thought I should report it, in case he tries to blame me.'

Constable Tran stops at the picture of Mullin's licence. Her face darkens.

'Ray Mullin.'

'Yes. He was very . . . threatening.'

'Wait here,' the constable instructs.

Rose shrugs. 'Okay.'

Constable Tran disappears through the side door.

Rose suddenly feels guilty. For what, she doesn't know, but she will always assume she's done something wrong when a policeman tells her to 'wait here'.

Rose glances back at the man on the bench. Now he's staring at her.

'Rose McHugh?'

Rose turns to see a tall man with broad shoulders who dwarfs Constable Tran.

'I'm Detective Inspector Blackmore.' He's in his late forties, with olive skin, dark brown eyes, prematurely grey hair, a smart suit, and a deep husky voice, like a Hemsworth after a big night. Rose imagines he's very good at intimidating people just by showing up.

'Hello, Detective—er, Inspector.' She isn't sure how to address him.

'You say this just happened?'

'Yes.'

'How long will you be staying in the Highlands?'

'I live in Berrima. Well, a bit outside the village.'

'Your licence has a Sydney address.'

'I just moved.'

She recites the new address and Constable Tran writes it down.

'Come down for the autumn foliage?' Blackmore asks. She can't tell if he's merely being polite or a little sarcastic.

24

'Among other things,' Rose says defensively, not wanting to be predictable.

He searches her face. What's he looking at? Rose wonders. Why is he staring? She touches her face self-consciously.

'Do you have ties to the Highlands? Family here?'

'No. But we used to come down for—'

'The autumn foliage.'

Definitely a touch of sarcasm. Maybe he thinks that because he's handsome, he can get away with it. What a jerk. It was a mistake, coming here.

'Ray Mullin is well known to us,' Blackmore tells her.

'Shit,' Rose says, before she can stop herself. 'What is he known *for*?'

'Call us if he bothers you in any way,' the detective says, without answering her question. 'Do not under any circumstances approach him yourself.'

The constable cuts in, wide-eyed, 'He's really bad news.'

'Thank you, Constable Tran.' Blackmore gives her a look.

She busies herself with some paperwork.

Rose feels slightly ill.

'Even though there was no damage, you should report this to your insurance company,' Blackmore adds.

'I will. Thank you.'

'And update the address on your licence.'

'Yes, Detective. I mean Inspector.'

Blackmore turns and goes back through an office door.

Constable Tran is looking at Rose sympathetically. 'Try to stay out of his way.'

'I will.'

Rose exits through the sliding doors, not sure if the constable meant for her to stay out of Mullin's way, or DI Blackmore's.

As she heads to the car park, it suddenly occurs to her that Mullin might have followed her and done something to Bob. Terrified, she runs to the car and looks in.

Bob is sound asleep on the back seat.

When Rose gets home, she calls her insurance company and then does an internet search of Ray Mullin. Her heart sinks when a number of local news reports come up.

VICTIM OF ONE-PUNCH ATTACK RECOVERS SLOWLY IN HOSPITAL is the first headline she reads, from a story that appeared in the *Southern Highland News* twelve years ago. Ray Mullin features as the man who threw the punch. He was later convicted of 'assault occasioning actual bodily harm' and sentenced to two years in jail. One year into his term, three months were added to Mullin's sentence after he beat up a member of a bikie gang who was also serving time for assault. Since then, there were two arrests: one for assault and another for malicious damage to property.

When Rose tries to take a deep breath, she's hit by a wave of nausea and just makes it to the bathroom before losing her breakfast.

Rose slowly drinks a cup of peppermint tea with honey as she sits at her little kitchen table scrolling through Instagram. She knows social media is full of fakery and evil, but it's also a source of information and comfort. She mostly follows history and art accounts, as well as her newspapers and weeklies, but the best thing about it is having a small window into Sam's world.

Rose and Sam have video catch-ups once a week or so, but he posts pictures and stories on Instagram almost every day, and Rose's heart lifts whenever she sees his account pop up. It was thanks to Instagram that Rose found out he had a new boyfriend, a sweet-looking young man and fellow archaeology student. Rose is thrilled for Sam. She's known that he was gay ever since he was a little boy, and he confirmed it for her when he was in his early teens. She and Peter were always fine about it, but there had been some all-too-predictable bullying at school and, to this day, Rose feels a bit protective.

Today, Sam has posted a picture of a decomposing skull with a set of surprisingly white teeth. His caption reads: *Sinking my teeth into the dental non-metric workshop today*. Rose smiles. Sam is leaning towards forensic archaeology as a career, but he's still young, so who knows? She taps the photo to like it but doesn't comment. She's learned that children don't like parents to comment on their posts, and the last thing Rose wants to do is overstep boundaries.

She's reading a post from one of her favourite accounts, @historycoolkids, when Kim calls.

Rose doesn't tell her about Mullin's criminal history, and is careful not to mention his full name in case Kim does what she did and googles him. There's no point feeding her sister's dim view of country people.

Instead, Rose tells her about the dapper, bookish George and his elegant whippet, and the man playing bagpipes under the tree.

'It's very civilised down here. Very arty and sophisticated.'

'In public, but in private they're having sex with the livestock.'

Rose chuckles. 'That's not funny.'

'You laughed. Listen, I'll come down and stay for the weekend soon and we'll sort them out.'

'Great. The spare room is ready with your fancy linen sheets on the bed.'

'They were meant for *you*, Rosie!'

'I actually prefer my old cotton ones.'

Kim sighs. 'Good God, woman, all my hard work for nothing.'

Rose smiles, but she's exhausted from the eventful morning and doesn't want to have a long heart-to-heart. 'I should go,' she says. 'I have work to do and the day has got away from me.'

'Okay, love you!'

'Love you too.'

Rose hangs up, torn by the conflicting emotions that her sister often provokes in her. On the one hand, she's grateful that Kim cares so much. On the other hand, she's relieved to say goodbye. Sometimes all that love can be suffocating.

Rose has had a deeply complicated relationship with her sister ever since their parents died. Kim was twenty-two and Rose was fourteen when Kim took on the parenting duties. For better or worse, she has never really stopped. Being eight years apart, they weren't very close as children, but all that changed in a terrible instant.

Their parents were coming home from one of their rare date nights at the cinema—they had been to a revival of *The Godfather,* running time two hours and fifty-five minutes— when they were hit head-on by a drunk driver. Their father died instantly, but their mother lingered in an induced coma for three days before she too died. Rose used to torture herself with the thought that they'd still be alive if they'd seen a shorter movie, one that finished before the man left the pub. It nearly drove her mad for a while, but she eventually accepted that if they'd left the cinema earlier, they might have gone for a bite and still been on the road when the drunk got behind the wheel. And she was almost glad they had both died. They were so devoted, she couldn't imagine one living without the other.

At the time, Kim was in her first year as a primary school teacher and Rose was in high school nearby, and they made it work. Kim was there for Rose in the aftermath of their parents' deaths and, more recently, through the discovery of Peter's affair and the divorce. But sometimes Rose worries that Kim needs her more than she needs Kim, who has drifted in and out of relationships and never had children. Kim says being a schoolteacher has inoculated her against motherhood, and as far as a relationship goes, she's never wanted to spend her spare time picking up someone else's socks.

Instead, Kim lavishes all her attention on her nephew and her little sister, which is one reason Rose has to make this move to the Highlands work. She needs some distance. And to prove that she can stand on her own two feet, without a husband or her sister to support her. That she owns her own life. That she's not just running away.

FOUR

Over the next week, Rose spends most of her days on a research job, enjoying working in the guest bedroom which doubles as her home office, with her desk under a window overlooking the leafy front garden. Behind her is a comfy bed on which she sometimes takes a nap after lunch. She feels less guilty having a nap in here than she would in her own bed, then reminds herself that she shouldn't feel guilty at all.

Unlike some of her work assignments, this one is riveting. For his book about family life in early colonial Sydney, one of Peter's colleagues asked her to research the backgrounds of the children who came with the First Fleet. Rose hadn't realised there *were* children on the First Fleet.

Drawn by a strong connection to her own Irish and English roots, she had focused on the early Celtic inhabitants of Great Britain at university. Despite growing up in Australia, she still knew too little of its history. What she studied in school merely covered white history, back then described as 'settlement' rather than invasion.

When she dug through the archives, including first-hand accounts from First Fleet travellers, Rose was intrigued to find that nearly fifty children came on the ships that sailed from London to Sydney in 1788. Some were children of the soldiers who came to police the convicts, some were children of convicts, and others were convicts themselves. This last group comprised mostly petty thieves, sentenced to transportation to a land thousands of miles from their homes and families, if they had any.

Rose found herself going down a rabbit hole when she discovered that the youngest convict on the First Fleet was a 'sometimes chimney sweeper' named John Hudson, who was sentenced to transportation at the age of nine. He had spent three years imprisoned on the hulks—the decrepit ships that sat in the Thames and served as jails—and was twelve years old when he eventually arrived in Sydney. Even if John's name never made it into the book, Rose believed it was important for her to know it, to say it out loud. That was the point of history, she thought—to bring the past to life so we can understand who we are and hopefully learn and improve the way we do things, the way we treat each other.

Rose is looking forward to writing her report once she finishes her research, so she can give Peter's colleague extra detail that he hadn't asked for, but that might capture his imagination and make its way into his book. She glances up at the illustration of a young chimney sweep around John Hudson's age that she'd printed and blu-tacked to the wall next to the window. It's there to remind her that history is about everyday people whose names we usually never know.

Rose takes a picture on her phone of the chimney sweep and posts it to Instagram with a précis of John Hudson's story. She doesn't have many followers, and sometimes it's just Sam, Kim and a few history nerds who like her posts, but it's Rose's small way of putting people's stories out there in case anyone is interested. Realising that social media has been her only social life recently, she feels a stab of loneliness.

She looks through the trees across the road at a little sandstone cottage in the distance. The couple who own it have been overseas since she moved in. Theirs is the only house Rose can see from her own, and she hopes when they return that she gets along with them. She likes the relative isolation of her new home, but it would be nice to know that friendly neighbours are within earshot.

Every morning, Rose has gone back to the dog park, but she hasn't seen George and Cordelia again. Maybe they're away too. She's surprised at how much she had been looking forward to borrowing that book George mentioned. Oh well, sometimes people make promises they don't keep, she reminds herself.

She'd thought she might get to know some locals once she found her coffee spot, but although she's tried several, she hasn't yet found exactly the right cafe. One was on the main road, and her cup rattled in its saucer when big trucks zoomed by and spat out their dirty exhaust. Another was on a quiet, tree-lined side street and had beautifully worn wooden tables, but the coffee was weak and the barista seemed to resent her for ordering a cup. She has to admit she was expecting a little more small-town warmth, but she knows it will take time to make a new friend or two and to find her niche. At least she hasn't run into Ray Mullin or his white dog again.

It's late afternoon and the temperature is dropping, so she decides to light a fire in the wood stove and run a deep, hot bath.

She draws the curtains, turns on the lights in the lounge room and puts some kindling in the stove to make a fire. Kim's prediction had proved right—so many branches have been falling from her own trees that she hasn't had to buy any firewood. But so far, thank God, no widow makers. She pours herself a glass of red wine. Might as well go all out. It's one of the nice things about living alone: there's no one to tell you that Tuesday is not a night to party.

She takes the wine to the bathroom and chucks a handful of the French lavender bath salts Kim gave her for her birthday into the steaming water, turns on the radio and smiles when she hears the first soaring notes of *The Lark Ascending*.

After her bath, Rose pulls the plug and dries herself before stepping into her fluffy dressing-gown. She's wiping the condensation from the mirror over the sink when she realises that her feet are wet. She looks down and sees a pool of water gathering on the floor and soaking through the bath mat, which is starting to float at the edges. At first, she thinks the old bath tub must have leaked, but its base and sides are dry. She checks the sink and toilet. They're not the problem either.

Rose grabs a couple of towels and tries to soak up the water from the floor. There's a lot of it. She runs to get more towels.

When the floor is more or less dry, she phones a local plumber, who says he'll come in the morning. She hopes he doesn't find some hugely expensive problem. She can't afford it. At Kim's insistence, she did have a survey done, and no horrors were unearthed, but with old houses, you never knew what secrets they might be keeping.

'You'd better take a look at this.'

The plumber, Mike, had arrived promptly the next morning and Rose had left him to his investigations. Now, as she follows him through the back door into the garden, she can't believe her eyes.

There's a fresh trench running right through the middle of the yard and along the side of the house.

'My God,' she utters.

'Yeah, sorry. Only way to find the blockage.'

Rose is on the verge of suggesting he might have told her what he was planning to do when he says, 'Check this out.'

Mike leads her to the side of the house and stops under a window, where white PVC pipes run from the ground, up the wall and into the bathroom. He has removed a section of pipe and holds it out to her.

'Someone stuffed your pipes.'

'Excuse me?'

He puts on thick rubber gloves and picks up a large, wet wad of something from the ground.

'This was in your pipes here. Looks like newspaper. And there was more of it that got pushed down the line by the water draining from your bath.' He nods at the trench in the garden. 'But it started here, which is why the water came up through the floor plate in the bathroom.'

'But . . . how did it happen?'

'Someone did this on purpose. You got any enemies in town?'

'I moved in less than a month ago.'

'That's gotta be some kind of record.'

Rose stares at him. 'It must have been an accident. Maybe the paper got washed into the drain somehow. It must have got stuck a while ago and only just came loose.'

'Nah, this was no accident. Someone went to a fair bit of trouble to open your pipe here and stuff it with newspaper.'

Rose takes the newspaper and peels the wadded-up newsprint away in sheets until she finds a piece with the top of the page. As she reads the date, her heart sinks. 'This is from last week.'

34

'Somebody wanted to mess you up.'

'But who would—'And before she can finish the question, Rose knows the answer. She looks at the plumber. 'Can you fix it?'

'Sure, but it's not gonna be cheap. I'll probably be here most of the day.'

'I don't have much choice, do I?'

As Mike gets to work, Rose heads back into the house to find her phone.

The call made, she goes to her bedroom and changes into her good black turtleneck—the one without the pills on the sleeves. She does question herself briefly as to why she feels the need to change into a nicer top just because that detective is coming, but puts it down to the fact that he will probably be wearing a suit and she doesn't want to seem like a slob in comparison. She doesn't for a moment entertain the idea that, in spite of their unpromising encounter the week before, she had felt a spark of attraction.

When she moved to the Highlands, one of the things that crossed Rose's mind was the possibility of meeting someone new. There had been no one since Peter, and while she wasn't sure she was ready, there was another, less intellectual part of herself that felt excited at the prospect of romance. Kim had said she should try to snag a member of the local landed gentry, but so far Rose's only truly remarkable interaction had been with a convicted criminal.

She is standing by the window, watching Mike shake a clump of wet newspaper out of a bend in the pipe when there's a knock at the front door.

Bob beats her down the hall and is waiting when she opens the door to reveal Detective Inspector Blackmore.

'Hi,' says Blackmore.

'Thank you for coming, Detective.'

Bob licks Blackmore's hand. Rose pulls him back. 'No, Bob. Leave him alone.'

'That's okay.' The detective scratches Bob behind the ear.

Bob responds with more licking.

'I'm afraid you've made a friend for life.'

'Let's see what you found,' the detective suggests, reminding her that this is not a social call.

'Yes, of course.'

Rose leads Blackmore through the cottage. She realises, too late, that she could have taken him around the outside, but for some reason she likes the idea of him coming through her house. What has got into her? He's not at all her type; she usually goes for slender, subtle, academic. She puts it down to being starved for company and hopes he doesn't notice the unnecessary detour.

Out in the back garden, wet strips of the *Southern Highland News* have been laid on the grass. Nearby, Mike is reinserting a section of pipe.

'G'day, Mike,' says Blackmore.

'Afternoon, Joe. Looks like someone has it in for this nice lady.'

'Looks like it,' Blackmore agrees. He crouches down and scans the faded but legible newsprint. He looks up at Rose. 'So there's no one else, other than our friend, who might have any reason to do this?'

'It may surprise you, but I don't think I have a *lot* of enemies.'

Mike chuckles and Blackmore concedes the point. 'No. I'll see if I can get any prints that aren't Mike's.' He lowers his voice. 'But this guy isn't stupid, and my guess is he used gloves.'

'But how did he even find me? My new address wasn't on my licence.'

'He could have followed you at some point.'

'Oh, God.'

'You're sure you didn't hear anything?'

'No. Do you think he came at night?' She puts a hand to her mouth as the realisation hits her. 'I might have been sleeping a few metres away. Surely Bob would have heard him. He'd have barked.'

'He didn't bark when I arrived,' the detective pointed out. 'Or maybe he waited until he saw you and Bob drive off somewhere.'

'Jesus.'

'What about your neighbours?'

'The people who own that house through the trees have been away.'

Blackmore nods. 'It might be worth getting some security cameras.'

Rose sighs. 'I thought life in the country would be safe.'

Mike laughs.

Rose frowns.

Blackmore looks at her closely with that probing stare. 'It is pretty isolated here. You're sure you wouldn't be happier living in town? I mean, it's none of my business . . .'

'No. It's none of your business.'

'I'm sorry.'

Rose can see that he means it and she's torn between attraction and irritation.

Blackmore takes a fingerprint kit out of his pocket. 'Leave it with me. Even if we don't get any prints, I'll pay our friend a visit.'

'But won't that make him madder? I looked him up. It's probably enough that he stuck me with a fat plumbing bill.'

'I want him to know that I know he was here.'

'Okay.'

'Thank you, Rose.' Blackmore heads off towards the bathroom window.

Rose notices that he didn't call her Ms McHugh. She liked the way 'Rose' sounded in that deep, husky voice. She could get used to that voice—if he weren't a bit of a dickhead.

She goes inside to research security cameras.

Rose is exploring the Byzantine world of home security systems when her phone chimes with the FaceTime ringtone. She smiles before she even sees his name on the screen, knowing it will be Sam. She hits 'accept' and his happy face, framed by his shaggy brown hair with streaks of gold like his father's, appears on screen. Along with the green eyes he inherited from her, and in spite of his slightly lopsided smile, Rose thinks he's the most beautiful young man she's ever seen.

'Hello, sweetheart!' Rose says.

'Hey, Mum.'

'It must be late there. Or early.'

'Early. Get this—the owner of a big fancy house was having his garden dug up to build a wedding venue, and they found a belt buckle that might be Viking!' Sam can't contain his excitement, and Rose is pleased that he's never tried to be cool about what he loves.

'That's amazing!'

'It could be the start of a major historical find, like when they found Richard the Third buried under the council car park.'

'You never know,' Rose says.

Both she and Sam, who was only nine at the time, were riveted by the discovery of the skeleton of Richard III. The last ruler of the Plantagenet dynasty, King Richard had been killed six centuries earlier during the War of the Roses, but the location of his grave was unknown. And there it was the whole time, driven over by people coming to get council permission to build an extension on their kitchen.

'Make sure you take lots of pictures,' Rose says.

'Absolutely. So what's this about you and some road rager?'

'Did Kim call you?'

'She likes to know we're all on the case.'

'It was no big deal,' Rose lies, watching Mike go out to his truck to get more equipment to clear her plumbing.

'Good. So, are you loving it down there?'

'I am! Of course, Kim thinks I've made a tragic mistake. You don't think so, do you?'

'Mum, how many times did you bring me down to the Highlands to look at the leaves and the waterfalls and the cute little towns? This is your dream. This is *your* time.'

'You're right. I can't wait for you to come home at Christmas and see it all!'

There's a fleeting look of something in his eyes. Something he hasn't told her. 'What?' she asks. 'You *are* still coming?' She tries to keep the neediness out of her voice.

'I'm not a hundred per cent sure.'

She can see this is hard for him to say. He knows what Christmas means to her. Especially the first Christmas in her new cottage. She waits for him to go on.

'There's a dig with this famous archaeologist—they made a documentary about her. But it's in Wales, and if the ground is frozen we couldn't dig anyway.'

'Well, of course, if it's something like that, you should stay!'

'I'm sure I'll wanna come home by then.'

'This is big, Sam. You have to go where the opportunity is, right? Anyway, let me know.'

Rose can hear someone calling him.

'I've gotta go, Mum. No more run-ins with morons, okay?'

Rose chuckles. 'I promise. Give my love to the Vikings!'

'Love you!'

Rose says, 'Love you too,' but he's already hung up.

She thinks about the possibility of Sam not coming home for Christmas and why it bothers her so much. For her, the day isn't about the birth of Christ or even pagan observation of the solstice, which was where the giving of gifts, hanging stockings, carolling and decorating trees all started. For Rose, Christmas is about loved ones gathered together at home, the rooms ringing with the sound of their laughter and the beat of their hearts.

Surely it'll be too cold in Wales for a December dig? Fingers crossed.

Later that day, Rose inspects the back garden while Bob sniffs the recently disturbed earth. Mike had put back most of the dirt he dug up, but on the side of the house there are dark smudges where Blackmore dusted for fingerprints. It's ugly and it makes her angry—at Blackmore, at Ray Mullin, at Kim for predicting disaster if Rose moved to the Highlands.

A gust of cold wind from the south rattles the leaves. Rose decides to tackle the clean-up tomorrow.

She's about to go inside when she notices that Mike must have uprooted a camellia at the edge of the yard. She decides to replant it where she can see it from her bedroom.

As she opens the door to the old wooden shed, the whole thing wobbles precariously. She really must reinforce it. Or tear it down. Kim called it a death trap and she can't let her sister be right. She finds her trowel and goes out to pick a good spot for the shrub.

Bob circles her, excited, as she plunges the trowel into the ground and scoops out some soil. She smiles as he sniffs the growing pile of dirt with interest.

She has dug a hole around ten centimetres deep when the trowel hits something.

'Shit.' Rose hopes she hasn't put a new hole in one of the pipes.

But when she brushes the dirt aside with her fingers, Rose sees something small, hard, black.

She carefully extracts a small black plastic cylinder—a thirty-five-millimetre film cannister. She used to have these around all the time, back when she used real film in her camera. She unscrews the lid and a roll of film with a green and white label drops into her hand. There's no tail showing, so the roll must have pictures on it, waiting to be developed.

'Why would someone bury a roll of film in the garden?' Rose asks Bob.

She'll have to tell Sam about this, she decides; he'd love the mystery.

FIVE

The next morning she is once again at the dog park. It's cold and the sky is a hard, dazzling blue as Rose gazes across the fields. She can't get over how different the landscape looks, depending on the weather. The distant escarpments are now rooted firmly in thick forest at the edge of farmland, and the cows are all in motion as if a film director called out *Action!*

'Hello, Bob!'

Rose turns to see Bob running up to George, who digs into his pocket for a treat. Cordelia comes over to say hello to Rose, who strokes her silky coat. 'Hello, gorgeous,' Rose says before greeting the whippet's owner. 'Hello there!'

'What a fantastic day!' George replies. He's wearing his beret, the camel's hair coat and dark green velvet pants. She can imagine him in London in the swinging sixties, and she hopes she'll get to hear some of his stories.

'Isn't it?!'

'We are very happy to be home.' George explains that he and Cordelia had been visiting George's daughter in the city for a week, and he'd counted the hours until he could leave. As much as he loves her, his daughter's idea of an early dinner is eight-thirty, and he prefers to dine at six. He asks Rose what she's been up to since he saw her last, and she tells him everything—Ray Mullin, the police, the plumbing. George is riveted.

'And there's another mystery,' Rose adds.

'I am desperate to hear more,' George says, as a blast of southerly wind hits them like a punch, 'but I am cold in my bones. I don't suppose you feel like getting a coffee?'

'I'd love to! I've been looking for the perfect cafe, but I'm not sure I've found it.'

'Ah, insider knowledge is the key.'

They call Bob and Cordelia, and head for their cars.

Minutes later, Rose and George are sitting at a table at Manna—a hidden sandstone courtyard cafe lined with gardenia bushes and equipped with a water bowl for the dogs. Bob and Cordelia have collapsed, weary but happy, under the hand-hewn table. A tall oil burner blasts heat their way. Heidi, the heavily pregnant owner of the cafe, gives them each a soft woollen blanket before going inside to fill their orders. Rose looks through the window and can see a cosy room with sepia-toned photographs of old Moss Vale, and tables filled with customers enjoying the warmth from an open fireplace.

Rose laughs as she drapes the blanket across her lap. 'This is fantastic. I love the name of this place—Manna—miracle food! And if the coffee's any good I may have to move in.' She glances down at the dogs. 'It looks like Lady and the Tramp already have.'

'I'm sorry you wasted your time at lesser cafes.'

'I actually don't mind doing the research. It's fun exploring, discovering both good and bad.' Rose explains that she's a historian, and that she makes her living doing research for various academic and entertainment projects.

Heidi brings their coffees, and Rose takes a sip of hers. She sighs, smiling. 'It's official—I'm moving in.'

As they sip their coffees and begin to warm up, Rose asks George what he does for a living.

George smiles. 'I'm flattered you think I still do anything at my age. I'm retired. I used to work in book publishing back in the day. Which reminds me . . .' He reaches into the pocket of his overcoat and takes out an old leather-bound copy of *The Female Detective* by Andrew Forrester Jr. He hands it to her. 'As promised.'

Rose feels the soft, worn leather binding. 'This isn't a first edition, is it?'

'Yes, I'm afraid collecting them is a weakness.'

'Oh, I couldn't borrow this.'

'Nonsense. Books are meant to be read.'

'Thank you. I'll take good care of it. And I'll return it. I believe people who fail to return borrowed books should burn in hell for a very long time.'

George laughs. 'I knew you were a kindred spirit. But now I want to hear about your mystery.'

Rose puts the first edition into her bag and takes out the film cannister. She sits it on the table between them.

'I found this buried in my back garden.'

She opens the black cannister and takes out the roll of film.

George's face lights up. 'Buried?'

Rose nods. 'There's no tail of film sticking out so the pictures must never have been developed.'

'Waiting for your next move.'

Rose grins. 'I guess I should return it to the previous owner of the house.'

'Who was that?'

'A woman named Anna Taradash.'

'Ah, you bought Anna's old place! I know her a little bit. I've been to her shows—she's a sculptor, you know. Works in iron.'

'No, I didn't know. We never actually met.'

'I hear it's a charming cottage. I think she found it a bit remote, though.'

With a small note of defiance, Rose says, 'Well, it's perfect for me. So . . . what do you think I should do?'

'Well, if Anna buried it, she doesn't want it, right?'

'Right. But then why not just throw it away?'

They mull this over. Bob lifts his head to make sure Rose is still nearby. She gives him a scratch behind the ear.

George has a glint in his eye. 'There used to be a place in Mittagong that developed film.'

Rose smiles. 'It still does. I looked it up.'

'Well, I hope you're planning to go straight there after we've finished our coffee.'

'I'm afraid my curiosity will allow for no other course of action.'

'And I hope you'll share the results with me.'

'Of course—we're in this together.'

They beam at each other, warming their hands on their coffee cups.

It's a short drive to Mittagong, one of the bigger towns in the Highlands, and Rose finds the photo shop in a large mall. With its Aldi, KFC and H&R Block, it could be anywhere in Australia or, indeed, the world. It has no history—no soul—and she can't wait to get out of there. She orders two sets of prints—which she has always done, because the second set is only a dollar extra—and is told they'll be ready in two days' time.

She and George had speculated about what might be on the film—wedding photos of a marriage that didn't last? Holiday snaps that show nothing but rain? Some of the artist's work that she decided she didn't like? Or maybe she buried the film as a time capsule with a record of her life in the house. Rose knew the film couldn't be more than fifteen years old; she'd discovered online that that's when the logo on the roll of film was introduced.

There might be nothing there at all. Or something very mundane. Although to Rose, even the most mundane records of people's lives hold a certain fascination.

On her way home, she starts to feel guilty that she hasn't tried to return the film. It could have fallen out of Anna's pocket accidentally when she was gardening. Rose decides to stop at the real estate agency to see Irish Dave, who sold her the house. The least she can do is give Anna a set of prints. Unless they contain something horribly compromising.

She feels another twinge of guilt for hoping they do.

Rose enters the office, where agents sit in cubicles on their phones or staring at their computer screens. She's happy that she never had to work in the dubious social experiment known as the open-plan office.

Dave sees her and comes to greet her with his beguiling accent. 'Rose! Lovely to see you. I hope you're settling in.'

'Yes, I love it.'

'What can I do for you?'

'I wanted to get in touch with Anna Taradash. I found a roll of film she may have left behind.'

'A roll of film? I could pass it on, if you like—she lives right here in Moss Vale.'

'Actually, I wouldn't mind chatting to her myself.'

'Sure, I'll get her a message. But I think her studio details are online—save you some time.'

Rose smiles. 'Thanks, Dave.'

As she walks away, she wonders briefly if Dave is single, or if being friendly goes with being a real estate agent.

Back in her car, Rose looks up Anna Taradash on her phone, and sure enough, there's a website for Taradash Studio with a phone number and address. She looks it up on Google Maps and discovers it's only five minutes away. But Rose isn't sure about dropping in on someone she has never met. She herself hates it when people stop by unannounced. And it might be weird to admit she had the film developed without asking first.

She decides to wait and see what's on the film before approaching Anna.

That afternoon, Rose is deep in the world of the children of the First Fleet when her mobile rings. It's a landline number she doesn't recognise. She answers.

'Hello?'

'Hi, Rose—Joe Blackmore here.'

'Hello, Detective.'

'Ray Mullin's fingerprints weren't at the scene, but I paid him a visit.'

'Oh, yes?'

'He denied going to your house.'

'There's a surprise.'

'He did say that when you ran into him with your car, you were very aggressive, sort of unhinged, but he wasn't going to press charges because'—the detective clears his throat—'he said you were probably menopausal.'

Rose is speechless.

'Rose?'

'Sorry. I'm flabbergasted.'

'Don't worry, I didn't believe him.'

'Gee, thanks.'

'That'll probably be the end of it, but call me if anything happens, or if you run into him—I mean *see* him—again.'

'Goodbye, Detective.'

Rose hangs up, hoping that Blackmore picked up the note of sarcasm in her 'Gee, thanks'. On the other hand, what a piss-weak response 'Gee, thanks' was. She thinks about all the things she should have said, like, 'What's wrong with being menopausal?' or 'I'm a bit young for menopause' or 'Well, *I* won't press charges because he's probably a psychopath.'

She hopes that someday she can say what she means on the spot, not later, when there's no one listening.

Two days later, Rose is back in the mall as soon as the photo shop opens. She pays for the prints, then hurries back to the car where she opens the envelope.

She looks at the first picture.

It's a view of the bush.

She's disappointed. 'Trees,' she says to Bob, who is utterly uninterested, sprawled on the back seat.

She flicks through the rest. More trees. Birds. Trees again.

Just when Rose is about to accept the fact that there is nothing mysterious about her buried roll of film, she comes to a photo of a young woman with long, dark-blonde hair and wide brown eyes. She's standing on a trail in the bush in a blue denim jacket and black jeans. She is smiling directly into the lens and her expression is openly seductive.

Rose wonders if it's Anna Taradash.

She flicks through the rest of the prints. Most are views of wilderness, all taken on the same grey day—trees, trees and more trees, a black cockatoo on a branch, and a few more snaps of the woman with brown eyes. Rose thinks she's incredibly beautiful.

She finds her phone and scrolls to George's number in her contacts. She was happy he wanted to exchange numbers. It looks like she has her first friend in the Highlands, and she isn't really surprised he's so much older than she is. Rose has always been drawn to older people, interested in their long histories and accumulated wisdom. She now feels connected to this place through another human being—no longer drifting, untethered, isolated. Moving to a new town has felt a bit like starting at a new school in the middle of term.

George picks up on the second ring. 'Did you get the photos?'

Rose laughs. 'You're as bad as I am.'

'Probably much worse.'

'Have you had a coffee yet?'

'Yes, but where is it written that I can't have a second?'

'Meet you at Manna in ten.'

Rose waits until the dogs have their water and Heidi has brought their coffees. The thick envelope of prints sits on the table between her and George. Rose takes a sip of her flat white, enjoying his impatience.

Finally, she pulls the stack of pictures out of the envelope and lays them in front of him.

He looks at the top one, then the next.

His face falls. 'Trees.'

'Keep going.'

He looks at the next picture and the next. Finally, he comes to the one of the woman.

Rose leans forward. 'Is that Anna Taradash?'

George blinks. He looks at Rose, and then back to the photo. He shakes his head slowly. 'No. No, it isn't Anna.' All the gleeful curiosity has vanished from his face.

'Do you know who it is?' Rose persists, alerted by his sombre expression.

George inclines his head. 'Yes. It's Maria. Maria Aboud.' He pauses, still staring at the beautiful woman in the photo. 'She's been missing for six years.'

SIX

Rose and George agreed that Rose should take the pictures to the police. As she drives to the police station, she reviews everything he told her.

Maria was a local woman in her late twenties, and a friend of Anna Taradash. She was the wife of Nick Aboud, a wine grower from nearby Sutton Forest. They'd been married for several years when he reported her missing. She'd last been seen driving down the main road in Bundanoon. Her car was later found at the train station, but security footage never placed her on a train.

The rumour mill went into overdrive. Some people speculated that she had been unhappy in the marriage and had left him, but her husband didn't believe it—or didn't *want* to believe it. Others ghoulishly insisted that Nick had killed Maria in a rage when she said she was leaving him, but there was no evidence of what the police called 'foul play', and there had never been any hints of violence in the marriage. Her friends told police that while it was true she had been considering a divorce, they found it hard to believe that Maria would leave the area for good without telling them. Rose wondered, though, whether Maria might have been tempted to just disappear.

Sometimes it's easier to reinvent yourself and start fresh if you're completely free of baggage.

For the second time in as many weeks, Rose enters the Southern Highlands police station. In the waiting room, what looks like a large family is spread over the two benches, in the midst of an argument. Three people are talking at once to Constable Tran at reception. One of them, a man around fifty, has a black eye.

Rose digs into her bag and finds the card Blackmore gave her. She rings the mobile number.

'DI Blackmore speaking.'

'It's Rose McHugh, Detective. I wonder if you're free? I'm in the waiting room.'

Moments later, Blackmore emerges and ushers Rose back into the inner sanctum. He smells nice. Not perfumed—just clean in a pleasant, manly way. And his shirt's been ironed. He must have a partner, but he doesn't wear a ring. Maybe he irons his own shirts, Rose reasons. Maybe he's gay. She tells herself that she's just doing what she always does: assembling details to create a fuller picture of someone, an occupational hazard.

'In here,' he says, leading her into a small, windowless interview room with a takeaway cup on a table sticky with something brown. Blackmore moves the cup out of the way and asks her to take a seat. 'Has our friend been back?'

'No,' Rose says as she takes out the envelope, which now contains just one set of prints. 'At least . . . not that I know of.' She hands the envelope to Blackmore. 'I found a roll of film buried in the garden. Not where Mike had been digging, on the other side of the yard. The ground hadn't been disturbed. I was planting a shrub when I found it.'

Blackmore holds the envelope without opening it. 'You say you found a roll of film?'

'Yes, I was curious . . .' Rose realises now how weird it must sound. 'I had it developed.'

Blackmore raises his eyebrows just slightly.

'I showed the prints to a friend, and he thinks the woman in the pictures is Maria Aboud. There's no one else in the pictures.'

Now Blackmore opens the envelope and looks through the prints, stopping at the one of Maria on the trail. He looks up at Rose, then back at the pictures. 'May I keep these?'

'Yes, of course. Apparently, she was a friend of Anna Taradash—the woman I bought the cottage from.'

Blackmore is nodding. 'I'm afraid I'll have to come back to your place to take a look.'

Rose stands at her kitchen window watching Blackmore supervise two younger police—a male and a female—excavating her garden, one square of earth at a time. Unlike Mike, he asked her permission before he started digging. He said they needed to be thorough. Nick Aboud calls the station every month, asking whether they have any leads on the whereabouts of his wife, and they want to make sure no stone, or clod of earth, is left unturned. Rose told him they should do what they had to do.

As she watches them, she's reminded of archaeologists digging for artefacts of ancient civilisations. Like them, cops are really historians, searching for clues to explain what happened in the past.

Blackmore seems to be good at his job, communicating clearly with that deep voice and closely inspecting every tiny thing the other police dig up.

He glances up and she backs away from the window. But why shouldn't she be watching them? It's her house. She steps back towards the window and sees them unceremoniously uproot her rhododendron and toss it aside.

Rose goes outside. 'Please try not to kill the plants.'

The team looks up at her.

'Sorry,' Blackmore says, 'I should have said something.' He turns to his team. 'Don't cut any roots if you can help it, okay?'

The cops grunt and get back to the job.

Suddenly this all feels very invasive, and Rose doesn't want to spend the rest of the day peering through the curtains. She tells Blackmore she's going out and heads off, forcing herself not to look back to see if he's watching her.

The brisk walk with Bob up and down the hills at the dog park was just what Rose needed. It's a calm, grey day and there's only one other dog, whose owner is an older, very beautiful woman with a long, silver plait down her back. Rose thinks she looks like the artist Georgia O'Keeffe. They smile at each other without speaking as their dogs circle and sniff.

Rose is reminded of how much strength there is in the company of women, and she realises that all this business with the buried film and the prints happened the wrong way around. She should have gone to see Anna as soon as George told her she was a friend of the woman in the pictures. Anna should have seen the pictures before the police.

Rose calls to Bob and they head back to the car, where she looks up Anna's address again.

It doesn't take her long to reach it. Turning off the main road, she finds herself in a residential street with brightly painted wooden cottages, their chimneys puffing smoke into the chilly late-autumn air. She ignores an unexpected flicker of envy for the close proximity of neighbours (presuming they're friendly) and parks outside Anna's house.

Rose is enchanted from the moment she walks through the wooden gate covered in vines. The front garden is filled with lush grasses and shrubs, and in the centre is a sculpture of a tree. Planted at its base is a climbing vine, just starting to grow up through the finely wrought iron tendrils. Rose tears herself away from the garden and walks up a few steps onto the wooden verandah with a comfy old couch and, next to it, a twisting, coiling iron sculpture with ornate botanical trinkets dangling from its branches.

Rose is staring at the piece when the door opens to reveal a woman with wild black hair and ice-blue eyes. She looks to be in her mid-thirties and is wearing a lemon-yellow vintage dress and black cowboy boots.

'Can I help you?' she asks.

The smell of something baking wafts from the house.

'Hello,' Rose says. 'Sorry, I was mesmerised by this sculpture. Is it yours? I mean, did you make it?'

'Yes . . . who are you?'

'Sorry,' Rose says again. 'I'm Rose McHugh—and if you're Anna Taradash, I bought your cottage.'

Anna smiles warmly. 'Oh, Rose, it's nice to meet you. Is there a problem with the house?'

'Not at all, I love it. But something has come up and I wonder if you have a few minutes.'

Anna hesitates.

'It's actually sort of important,' Rose says. 'But I can come back another time if now isn't convenient.'

'No, it's fine. Come in.'

Anna leads her through a cosily cluttered lounge room with colourful paintings, Moroccan cushions and lanterns, into a sunny kitchen at the back of the house filled with the smell of ginger.

'I'm baking gingerbread for my nieces,' Anna explains. 'Would you like a cup of tea?'

'Love one,' Rose says as she sits at an old wooden refectory table.

Anna puts the kettle on and scoops tea into a blue-striped teapot as Rose looks around. The kitchen is painted a burnt orange, and on the walls is a jumble of black-and-white photographs of the bush. The decor and furnishings appear to have been thoughtfully chosen, but the overall effect is relaxed, homey.

'This house has such a nice feel,' Rose says.

'Thanks. It took a while getting used to having neighbours so close, but I like it now. It feels . . . safe.'

'Did anything happen at the cottage to make you feel *un*safe?'

Anna looks at her. 'No. But I tend to get spooked easily. I have an overactive imagination.' She places two mugs on the table, in the centre of which is an extraordinary sculpture—a pyramid around twenty centimetres high, made of tiny pieces of wood fitted together in an unusual geometric pattern. 'Did you make this?' Rose asks.

'No, that's by another local artist—a guy by the name of Ned Petrovic.'

'It's fantastic,' Rose says. 'It's kind of begging to be touched.'

Anna smiles. 'Go ahead.'

Rose picks up the small sculpture and feels the wooden pieces shifting slightly in her fingers, as if it's a living thing. Rose sets the pyramid back on the table.

'I don't want to take up much of your time,' says Rose, coming to the point, 'but I thought you should have these.' She takes the envelope with the spare set of photos from her bag and puts it on the table. 'I think they must be yours.'

Anna sits down and looks at the envelope with the green and white logo. 'Did I leave them in a cupboard or something?' She opens the envelope and takes the photos out.

'Not exactly. I was doing some planting in the back garden and found a roll of film.'

Anna is looking through the photos of trees, birds, trails.

'It looked like it had been dropped,' Rose adds. 'Or buried.'

'And you had them developed?' Anna asks, surprised.

'Yes, I'm naturally curious. I'm a historical researcher and—' Rose stops.

Anna's face has gone white. She's staring at the picture of Maria.

After a moment, she races through the rest of the prints, but when she reaches the end she seems dissatisfied, disappointed. She flips through the pictures again from the beginning, then puts them down. 'These aren't mine.'

The kettle has boiled and clicked off. The room suddenly feels cold.

'I showed them to a friend,' Rose says. 'He thought you knew this woman.'

'She's a friend. Or was . . .'

'I heard she's been gone for—'

'Six years.'

'That's why I've given the police a set of prints.'

57

Anna looks at her sharply.

'They might want to talk to you,' Rose says. 'Since they were found on your property.' Rose glances at the kettle, steam wafting pointlessly from its spout.

Anna looks out the window, gazing into space. There's something in her eyes, her face. Rose isn't sure, but it might be a look of betrayal.

'The film must have belonged to Maria,' Anna says. The missing woman's name hangs in the air. 'She stayed at my place every once in a while. When we'd had too much to drink.'

'And you haven't heard from her since she . . . left?'

Anna is frowning at Rose as if she's decided she no longer wants her there. Standing up abruptly, she says, 'I'm sorry, I should . . . I have things to do.'

Taking the cue, Rose gets to her feet. She feels bad for having come at all. 'Of course. Shall I leave these for you?'

Anna doesn't look at the pictures. 'No.'

Rose scoops them up and Anna walks quickly to the front door, clearly anxious to get rid of her.

'If you'd like to talk,' Rose says, 'here's my number.' She tears off a piece of the photo envelope and, finding a pen in her bag, writes her number on it. She holds it out. 'I'd like to help if I can.'

Anna takes it, then closes the door.

Rose returns to the car, where Bob greets her from the back seat with a yawn. She feels guilty for having stirred up painful memories for Anna. Rose doesn't quite know what to make of her reaction. Was it betrayal? There seemed to be a note of anger, but also longing in her face. Did Anna simply miss her old friend? Was she angry that Maria left without saying goodbye? Or did Anna have something to do with Maria's disappearance? Did she know something she never told the police? At least she knows the pictures have been unearthed, so Rose doesn't have to feel guilty for keeping them from her. Now, if the police dig up something else, it won't come as a surprise.

But the police don't dig up a thing, except Rose's garden.

SEVEN

The next day, Rose stares at the aftermath.

Uprooted camellias, rhododendrons and rosebushes have been dumped near the shed, their leaves curling, roots drying out in the sun and wind.

Even though the police left her with a big job, Rose doesn't really mind. She was the one who found the film and brought them the pictures, after all. And now she can put each plant where she wants it.

Rose picks up the rhododendron and carries it to a corner of the yard where she'll be able to see its purple blossoms from her bedroom when spring comes. She breathes on her cold hands—she's never liked wearing gardening gloves. She likes to feel the dirt under her fingers.

'Wrong spot.'

Rose spins around.

'Sorry,' Blackmore says. 'Didn't mean to scare you.'

Rose's hand goes to her hair—she must look a mess. 'No, I just wasn't expecting anyone.'

The detective is in casual gear—a fleece-lined jacket and jeans, slightly muddy boots. He seems to be completely unaware of how good he looks as he pulls a pair of gardening gloves out of his back pocket. 'Figured I'd better help you fix this before you sue for damages.'

Rose smiles. 'I wouldn't do that.'

'Glad to hear it.'

That voice. Rose wonders if he's a smoker or if his voice just came out like that.

He surveys the garden. 'Looks like I got here just in time. That rhododendron won't like it there. Not enough sun.'

'But it's in direct sun.'

'Now it is, but that's an ash above it. Lost its leaves about a month ago, yeah? Red ones?'

'Yes.'

'So next summer the branches will be longer and those thick, dark leaves will completely block out the light. Your poor rhododendron won't flower.'

'Oh,' Rose says. She realises she should be grateful for the advice, but she can't quite bring herself to thank him and admit she was wrong. With a slightly challenging tone, she says, 'Where do you suggest I put it?'

Blackmore picks up the rhododendron and looks around. The wind ruffles his hair, which she sees now is more silver than grey, glinting in the sun. He turns and catches Rose staring.

'How about near the shed?' she blurts out.

He carries the shrub over and places it a metre or so from the old wooden structure. He looks up at the sky. 'Yeah, good. Just the right balance of sun and shade. But not too close to the shed, so it drains well.' He nods, satisfied. 'Chuck me that trowel?'

Rose looks at the trowel in her hands. 'I *can* do this myself, you know.'

'I know, but I owe you.'

'Do you?'

'Yeah. Those pictures are the first lead we've had in years, especially if we can figure out where exactly they were taken—and who took them.'

Rose watches him dig a hole and then, reluctant to have him catch her staring again, she goes over to inspect the other plants. Spying a droopy camellia, more tree than shrub, she lifts it by its thick trunk and staggers across the garden, determined to show Blackmore she's a strong, independent woman who doesn't need his help.

'Here, let me.' He takes it from her and easily places it in the perfect spot as she catches her breath. He feels its thick leaves. 'You know, you can make tea out of the leaves of this variety.'

'I'd heard that.' She hadn't, and she wonders why she's pretending to know more than she does. 'Where'd you learn so much about plants?'

He starts to dig a hole. 'My mum.'

Oh God, Rose thinks, he's close to his mum. He's too good to be true. Probably a psychopath.

'Eventually you'll figure out what thrives in this climate and where. It's not just the cold winters you have to prepare for, though they can be pretty intense; we had snow a few years back. It's the scorching summers. Dry as hell, and when the westerlies start blowing . . .'

'You know, I didn't move down here with zero knowledge of the natural world.'

'Sorry.'

Then she feels bad and decides to admit she knows nothing. 'I watched that gardening show once—with the guy with the beard.'

They both laugh. It's the first time she's seen him laugh. It's a nice laugh. Husky, like his voice. Rose says a silent 'shit' to herself—she's officially into this guy. But why not? Maybe he feels a spark too. Surely he wouldn't have come here on his day off to help her replant her garden if he wasn't interested?

Her phone rings inside the house. She glances at Blackmore, who is obviously capable of getting on with things on his own. She goes inside.

She doesn't recognise the number. 'Hello?' she says cautiously.

'Hi, Rose. It's Anna Taradash. I wonder if we could talk?'

'Yes, of course.' Rose sits down at the kitchen table.

'Not on the phone. Maybe we could meet for coffee. Are you free tomorrow?'

'Sure. Where and when?'

'Do you know a cafe called Manna?'

'Yes.'

'Ten o'clock?'

'Perfect. See you then.'

Rose hangs up and goes back outside, wondering what Anna wants to talk about—and whether or not she should mention it to Blackmore.

Still on his hands and knees in the garden, Blackmore looks up at her. 'Everything okay?' It seems he's as naturally curious as she is.

'Fine.' She decides to keep Anna's call to herself. Maybe in future she'll be telling Blackmore everything, but not yet. Rose suddenly imagines what Peter would think of her getting involved with a country cop, and she smiles. He'd be horrified.

She goes to the plants, picks out a dormant rose with bare, thorny stems—and realises she has no idea where it should go. She's about to ask Blackmore, but he speaks first.

'We paid a visit to Anna Taradash after we left here,' he says.

Rose is caught off guard. 'Oh yes?'

'She said you'd already been there and showed her the pictures.'

'Well, I—'

'You should let us handle this, Rose.'

'I know. But it didn't seem right not to return something that was probably hers in the first place.'

'But they weren't.'

'No.'

Blackmore is carefully patting the soil around the camellia. 'I just don't want you to go all . . . Miss Marple on me.'

Rose suddenly decides she isn't into him at all. In fact, she actively dislikes him. 'Well, I found the film on my property, so technically it's mine and I can do what I want with it.'

'Technically, yes. But a woman has been missing for six years. Her husband, her brother, her parents—they're still hoping she'll walk through the door someday.'

Rose's righteous indignation evaporates. 'Of course. I'm sorry. I just want to do the right thing by everyone.'

'So do I.'

Rose doesn't know what else to say, so she takes the trowel he's discarded and starts digging. And does not mention to Blackmore that she has made plans to meet with Anna the next day. Not everything is police business.

That night, Rose is sitting in front of a low fire with a glass of red in hand, on the phone with Kim. Bob is asleep next to her on the couch.

'He called you Miss Marple?!'

'To my face.'

'What an arsehole.'

'He's not really,' she hears herself saying. 'He's actually very nice. He knows all about plants.'

'Oh. My. God,' Kim says with slow-dawning horror. 'You have a crush on a *cop*!'

'No, I don't!'

'Yes, you do. I can see we're going to have to watch *Deliverance* again, and *Wolf Creek*.'

Rose laughs. 'They're not about cops.'

'They're about country people. People who marry farm animals. And anyway, a cop's a cop. You're a *historian*, for Chrissake.'

'Don't be a snob.' Rose yawns.

'I'm a realist.'

'I'm hanging up, Kim.'

'But—'

'See you Saturday.'

'I'll bring some bread from Bourke Street Bakery.'

'We have bakeries here, Kim.'

'But—'

'Night!'

Rose hangs up and looks into the fire. She pictures Kim in her chic apartment in a modern building in the crowded, noisy city and feels sorry for her. Then she remembers that Kim probably feels sorry for her, living alone in the middle of the sticks, surrounded by killers and rednecks.

Rose decides to call Sam to fill him in on all the excitement, but he doesn't answer. She texts him and says to call her when he's free. *Nothing urgent*, she adds.

She scratches Bob behind the ear and, as much as she loves her dog, she allows herself a brief flight of imagination.

She pictures what it would be like to share the fire, the wine, her cosy cottage, with a human. Maybe even a cop. A country cop. But as she stares into the dying fire, it's Maria's face that floats in front of her.

EIGHT

The next day, Rose is waiting at the cafe at the appointed hour, but there's no sign of Anna. She checks her phone, but by twenty past ten there have been no calls or messages. Anna must be running late.

While she's waiting, Rose opens Instagram and her heart makes a little leap when she sees that Sam has posted a video of other archaeologists brushing away tiny amounts of soil around what looks like a long wooden structure. He narrates over the action before he turns the camera onto his own smiling face and signs off. She re-watches the video and is happy to note that he looks healthy and well fed, roses in his cheeks. What did mothers do before social media? Probably worry about their children a lot less.

When George and Cordelia show up, Rose invites them to join her until Anna arrives.

She fills George in on all the developments—or lack thereof. How the police dug up her garden but came up with zilch. She's afraid they'll never know any more than they know now about what happened to Maria Aboud.

George's face lights up when a woman in her late forties with flame-red hair, wearing a striking purple woollen coat, approaches the table. 'Grace!' George says. 'It's been ages!'

The woman leans down to give him a hug. 'Georgie—way too long.'

'Grace, I'd like you to meet Rose. Rose just moved to the Highlands, to our great benefit.'

'Fabulous. We need more good people—can't let the dickheads win.'

She gives Rose a warm handshake, and Rose likes her right away. The word that comes to mind is 'dynamic'. And there's a trace of an accent.

'Would you like to join us?' Rose asks.

'I'd love to, but I phoned ahead for takeaway. One of my drivers called in sick.'

'Grace runs the local Meals on Wheels,' George explains.

'Oh, wow,' Rose says.

Heidi comes out and hands Grace a coffee.

'Great to meet you, Rose,' Grace says. 'We'll get George to spring for cinnamon buns next time.'

'Now you're talking,' Rose says.

'I thought you two would get along,' George says as Grace flits off.

'She seems lovely.'

'She's married to a local detective. Maybe you've met him in your encounters with the local constabulary?'

And before he can say his name, Rose knows. 'DI Blackmore?'

'Joe, yes. Have you found him all right to deal with?'

Rose swallows. 'Yes, in fact he was the one who came to replant my garden.' Why don't all married men wear rings, she thinks to herself with a sinking heart. How are the rest of us expected not to make fools of ourselves?

'That'd be right,' George says. 'He's apparently something of a botanical savant. His mother runs the nursery in Berrima, not far from you. The family has been in the area for generations. Very well respected.'

Rose tries to stifle her disappointment by taking a big swig of coffee, but it's too hot and she chokes, sputtering awkwardly.

'Oh dear, are you okay?' George asks.

Rose grins through the pain as her eyes water. 'Yes, excuse me, I was greedy.' Deflecting, she asks where Grace is from.

'Glasgow, I think.'

Rose bites her lip. Damn, so Grace is Scottish. If she didn't already have a crush on Blackmore, she'd have one on his wife. Talk about mixed feelings.

She lifts herself out of her momentary stumble into self-pity and looks at her watch. It's nearly eleven o'clock.

'I'd better try calling Anna.'

She dials Anna's number but it rings out and goes to voice-mail. Rose leaves a message asking her to call. She assumes Anna probably got cold feet and decided against sharing personal information about a missing woman with a total stranger.

When she gets up to leave half an hour later, George invites her to his house for Sunday lunch and she accepts. Rose is buoyed by the fact that George is prepared to welcome her into his home; we take these little things for granted, but they mean so much. They mean as much as being left out, as *not* being invited, and she laughs at the twinge she still feels as she remembers the time when, in year nine, she wasn't invited to the popular girl's birthday party. She must have very thin skin. Or maybe she's just human.

Feeling restless, Rose decides not to go straight home. She turns on the radio and smiles as the reassuring voice of her favourite presenter introduces a work by Hildegard of Bingen, a visionary composer of the Middle Ages whom she loves. When Rose listens to her haunting music, she can imagine having visions too. As she turns up the volume, she sees a sign for Fitzroy Falls and, on a whim, takes the turn. She hasn't visited the falls for years and has been meaning to go. She feels guilty, though. She left Bob at home in case Anna wasn't a dog person, and he would love an outing like this. But what he doesn't know won't hurt him.

Rose drives along winding roads through rolling pastures, vineyards, guesthouses, horse farms and even a llama farm.

As she enters the Morton National Park, the bush thickens dramatically. Giant tree ferns, eucalypts and thick pines block out the day and she has to turn on her headlights. She loses the ABC to static and turns off the radio as she slows her pace.

She remembers coming through here on her way to Kangaroo Valley many years ago, but the magic of the bush takes her by surprise. She's some distance from the visitors centre when she notices an unmarked turn-off leading into what looks like an enchanted forest. There's no sign indicating that it's private, so, feeling up for an adventure, she takes it. She drives along the gravel road that twists through the bush until it runs out and narrows to a dirt path.

Rose parks the car and gets out.

The air is alive with birdsong, the hum of insects and wind in the trees. After the man-made sounds of the car and the radio, the sounds of nature are a relief. Suddenly, Rose feels like she's the only person on the planet—not in a creepy, post-apocalyptic way, but as if she's a bold explorer. She chuckles to herself; she certainly doesn't see herself as bold. But she is hungry for life, for the natural world. She realises she always was, but she suppressed her hunger for years. With Peter, in the city, she realises only now that she had 'settled'. She tells herself that she won't settle again.

She locks the car, puts her phone and keys in the back pockets of her jeans and sets off down the dirt trail.

As she walks through the bush, she realises she's not doing this just to get some fresh air. Ever since she saw the photos of Maria, she has wanted to figure out where they were taken. There are thousands of acres of bushland in the Southern Highlands, and even with local knowledge it might be impossible to pinpoint the location. But there's no harm in trying.

Rose has never seen such ancient-looking trees. Not just tall but also wide, they are majestic. Queens of the forest. She wishes she knew the names of all the trees. Joe Blackmore probably does. Damn. She must stop thinking about him, especially as the memory of his gorgeous, red-haired, meals-on-wheels-delivering Scottish wife makes her blush with shame.

Rose takes pictures on her phone of trees, rocks, the blue sky through the canopy. Her eye is caught by a smaller trail leading off the main one and, feeling the call of the wild, she takes it. It's soon almost impassable, overgrown with gnarled banksia and bottlebrush. She's about to turn around when she sees what looks like a clearing up ahead.

Rose pushes through the undergrowth and emerges in a wide, round clearing. There's a low sandstone escarpment around part of it and a thick stand of trees around the rest. It's beautiful. At least, it *should* be beautiful—all the elements are right. But something is wrong.

She looks around, searching for the source of a growing sense of dread.

It's dead quiet. Nothing is moving—not a leaf, not a blade of grass. There is no birdsong, no buzzing insects. Even though the sky is clear, a shadow like a mist falls in front of her eyes and a foul smell fills her nostrils. She feels a surge of nausea.

71

Rose starts to gag. The nausea is overwhelming. And the fear. She thinks that if she doesn't get out of here, she will die.

She tries to figure out where she entered the clearing, but it all looks the same—dense banksia, thorny scrub, high grass, bottlebrush, all forming a natural barrier to escape. She's starting to panic when she thinks of Bob. If she dies out here, he won't get fed.

She pulls herself together, forcing herself to picture where the escarpment was when she entered the clearing—on the opposite side, she remembers. She faces what she thinks is the right way, then reels with another wave of nausea. She looks down. Pine needles litter the ground. She looks for her footsteps. Finally, she finds her tracks and pushes through the bush, back to the thread of a trail.

Rose runs, branches slapping her face. As she puts some distance between herself and the clearing, the nausea fades. The shadow lifts. The awful smell evaporates and she can hear a currawong call. Then insects, and then the wind. She can breathe again.

She gets back to the car, grateful, relieved, and vows never again to follow a trail that isn't marked. At least not alone. What an idiot—she could have fallen and no one would ever find her. No one knew she was there. She needs to get back to Bob and her little cottage.

Rose starts the car and peels out of the gravel road at speed. As she drives, she goes over possible explanations for what just happened. There might have been a dead animal nearby—something that gave off that horrible smell. But she didn't think that was it. It was almost as if the smell was in her head rather than the air, and she's reminded of feelings she's had in the past when visiting a place where something bad had happened.

It was never this intense, but she does remember a vague feeling of dread inside a small church in Cornwall, in England, where it turned out worshippers had died in a fire hundreds of years before. She wonders what terrible thing might have happened in the clearing she just left.

As she emerges from the park into farmland, she turns on the radio and takes a deep breath, Debussy's soothing *Reverie* filling the car.

Her phone pings with a message.

She glances at the screen—there's a voicemail from Blackmore. She had put his name in her contacts when she thought they might be calling each other socially. As Sam would say, epic fail. She could wait until she gets home, but instead she pulls over and listens to the message.

'*It's Joe Blackmore. Call me as soon as you can.*'

Rose wonders if Ray Mullin has burned her house down. She feels a twitch of anxiety, remembering that she left Bob asleep on the couch. With a trembling finger, she presses the button to return the detective's call.

'Rose. Where are you?'

'I'm on my way home. Did something happen?'

'Did you speak to Anna Taradash yesterday?'

'Yes. We were supposed to meet for coffee this morning but she never showed up.'

There's a pause.

'Why?' Rose asks. 'What's happened?'

The detective's voice is heavy as he says, 'She was found this morning . . . Rose, Anna Taradash is dead.'

NINE

'Rose? Are you there?'

She can hear Blackmore's voice, but she can't respond—
she can't find any words that make sense. Finally she mumbles,
'I'm here.'

'We have her phone,' he says. 'It looks like you were the last
person she called. You'd better come in for a chat.'

Rose doesn't remember driving to the police station, but somehow she gets there.

Blackmore is waiting for her on the steps. He takes her gently
by the arm through the sliding doors, and this time into a small
office he shares with another detective, who leaves when they
enter. The one grimy window looks out over the car park.

Rose sits down and, within moments, Constable Tran appears
with a cup of sweet, milky tea. It's just what Rose needs, but she's
embarrassed when she hears herself slurping it down. Blackmore
waits. The constable is beside him, notepad at the ready.

'Thank you, Constable Tran,' Rose says, still trying to recover
her equilibrium.

'Call me Deb.'

Blackmore gives Deb a look, but she's focused on Rose. 'More tea?'

'No, I'm good, thank you,' Rose says. 'Are you sure it's Anna?' But the moment she asks, she realises that of course they are.

'I'm afraid so,' Blackmore says. 'Can you tell me what you talked about when she called?'

'Nothing. I gave her my phone number when I took the photos around, but I didn't think she'd call. She did, though, and said she wanted to meet.'

Blackmore doesn't say anything, but he doesn't take his eyes off Rose, waiting for her to continue.

'We agreed to meet at Manna, the cafe, this morning at ten. I went, but she didn't show up. I called her and left a message. I figured she'd changed her mind.'

'When you went to see her at her house, what did you talk about?'

'Nothing much. I said I liked her work. She was baking gingerbread.' Rose feels a sudden rush of sadness recalling the fondness in Anna's voice when she mentioned her little nieces. 'Has her family been told?'

'Yes,' says Blackmore. 'What else did you talk about?'

Rose thinks. 'I told her I'd found the film and showed her the prints. When she saw the picture of Maria she said the film must have been hers. She said Maria used to stay at the cottage every once in a while.'

She looks between Blackmore and Deb. They seem to want more.

'She said she hasn't heard from Maria for six years. Then she . . . she didn't want to talk anymore, so I gave her my number and left. That was it.'

Blackmore leans forward slightly, his wide shoulders blocking out the grey light from the window. He raises his hand and points to her hair. 'What's that?'

Rose reaches up and finds a small tuft of white bottlebrush stuck in her hair. She pulls it out. 'Sorry, I must look a mess. I went for a bushwalk and, um, I got a bit lost.'

Deb is scribbling notes furiously, but Rose can't imagine what's so interesting about her bushwalk.

Blackmore is watching her, his voice low and even. 'Where was that, Rose?'

'Out in the park, on the way to Fitzroy Falls.'

Blackmore is staring at her, so she finds herself rushing to fill the silence.

'In fact, I had a really weird experience. I found myself in this clearing and I suddenly felt sick to my stomach. And I had the strongest feeling—you'll think I'm crazy—that something bad was going to happen . . . or already had.'

'Do you think you could show us on a map?'

'I can try.'

She sees the detective exchange a look with Deb.

'What?' Rose asks, scared. 'Is that where Anna was found?'

Blackmore opens his laptop and finds a satellite picture of the area. He turns it towards Rose. 'Were you somewhere around here?'

Rose manipulates the image with the keypad, searching for where she turned off. She zooms in on the area. 'This might be it.'

Blackmore looks at the image. 'That's a fire road.'

'Oh, right,' Rose tries to keep the growing panic out of her voice. Surely they don't think she had something to do with Anna's death?

'And where was this clearing?'

Rose moves the image around, zooming in and back, and then sees an area that looks treeless, dead. There's an escarpment on one side.

She points. 'I think that might be it.'

Blackmore and Deb exchange a glance.

Dreading the answer, she asks, 'Is that where Anna was found?'

'No,' he says.

Deb clears her throat noisily. Blackmore gives her a look that shuts her up.

'Was she nearby?' asks Rose.

Blackmore seems to arrive at some conclusion. 'No. She was found in the park, but not near there.'

Rose looks between him and Deb, not sure how to ask the question. 'Am I . . . a suspect?'

'We don't know how she died,' the detective says, 'so no one is a suspect.' The 'yet' hangs, implicit, in the air. He looks at Deb. 'Constable, would you show Ms McHugh out?'

Back to 'Ms', she notes—not Rose anymore.

'Yes, boss.'

Deb gets up and Rose follows, a little unsteady on her feet.

'One more thing,' Blackmore says. 'Do you have any idea what Anna wanted to talk about?'

Rose thinks carefully about her answer. 'I'd be guessing. It could have been something about the cottage. But if that were the case, why wouldn't she tell me over the phone?' The conclusion seems obvious. 'I think she must have wanted to talk about Maria.'

Deb walks her to the exit, and Rose is surprised when the constable follows her outside.

'It's called Echo Lake.'

Rose stops. 'What is?'

Deb glances back over her shoulder, lowers her voice. 'The clearing, where you felt sick. That's Echo Lake.'

Rose frowns, confused. 'But there wasn't any water.'

'There used to be . . . a long time ago.'

'Did something happen there?'

Deb seems reluctant to go on.

'Please,' Rose urges. 'Tell me.'

Deb relents. 'There are loads of stories . . . That some white guy killed an Aboriginal family back in the 1800s. There was a rumour that Ivan Milat buried hitchhikers there. Nothing's ever been found. But there used to be water. And then it just . . . dried up.'

When Rose gets back to her car, she glances up and sees Blackmore watching her from his window, his expression giving nothing away.

That afternoon, Rose is sitting in her back garden at the little outdoor table she found in a junk shop, while Bob wrestles with a stick. Even in the autumn sun, Rose can sense that winter is coming, and she's glad for the woollen scarf wrapped around her neck and up over her chin.

She is also happy to see that the rhododendron has perked up in its new spot, and the rest of the plants seem to have survived. She's grateful to be in such a beautiful spot, but deeply aware that her place in this country has been secured by the white colonists who came before her. Partly out of curiosity and partly out of a need to distract herself from Anna's death, she opens her laptop to see what she can find about the history of Echo Lake.

But to her frustration she can't locate any historical records referring to Echo Lake or events that might have unfolded there. However, there is an intriguing snippet in an 1889 edition of the *Southern Mail*. An article describes in colourful terms an excursion into the wilderness near Fitzroy Falls during which 'the gentlemen and ladies stopped to bathe in a small lake with an escarpment that bounced echoes of their laughter across the water'. Perhaps that was how it got its colonial name. No doubt the original Gundungurra or Dharawal people had their own name for the lake, and she would try to find out what it was. Rose imagines that they might have set fish traps in a stream that fed the lake, but when white settlers needed to irrigate their thirsty crops, they might have diverted the stream, preventing the lake from filling. She vows to find out more if she can.

Rose is back home and curled up on the couch with Bob, watching the local news, when the story comes on. She's been waiting for it, but it's still shocking.

A photo of Anna looking happy and glamorous at one of her exhibitions flashes on the screen, the newsreader describing how the body of a local artist had been found early that morning by a hiker at the bottom of an escarpment in the Morton National Park. He goes on to say solemnly that, as yet, the cause of death is unknown, but police hadn't ruled out foul play.

Rose thinks about that strange phrase, 'foul play', and how inadequate it is to describe the unthinkable things that people do to each other.

Her phone chimes and she jumps. Glancing at the caller ID, she sees Sam's name.

'Hi, sweetheart!'

'Hey, Mum. Sorry I haven't called—we've been out in the middle of nowhere with no reception.'

'That's all right.' Even to her own ears her voice sounds strained.

'Is everything okay? You sound weird.'

Rose swallows. 'Well, a woman I met a couple days ago was found dead this morning.'

'Jesus, Mum, what happened?'

Rose tells him what she knows.

'Should I come home?'

'No! I'm fine. It's nothing to do with me. It's just very, very sad.'

'I didn't think anything ever happened in the Highlands.'

'Yeah, well . . . Let's talk about something more pleasant. Did you find a Viking hoard?'

'We found a few old coins. Nothing like what we hoped for. But we're still digging.'

'Well good luck, and keep me posted.'

'You too, Mum. I love you.' He says it with feeling, and Rose feels her heart fill like a cup.

'I love you too.'

They hang up. Some people assume that once your children have grown up and moved away, you don't worry about them anymore—they've taken charge of their own lives. But Rose knows that as long as she lives, she'll be thinking and worrying about Sam, as if the umbilical cord has stretched all the way from here to England, and was never cut at all.

'Maybe it was suicide,' Kim says on the phone a little while later. 'Maybe Anna was in love with this Maria person, and when you showed her the photos it stirred up feelings of loss that she couldn't live with anymore.'

'You're drawing an awfully long bow, Kim, but if it's true, then I'm partly to blame. *Largely* to blame.'

'Nuh-uh. The cops would have shown her the pictures if you hadn't.'

'Yes, but—'

'But nothing. It's not your fault.'

'And before I heard about Anna, I got lost in the bush.'

'Where Anna was found?'

'The same park, but not close, and I found myself in this awful place—'

'My God, you're a suspect. Were you alone?'

'Yes.'

'That's it. I'm coming down a day early. You need me to keep you out of the slammer.'

'The slammer? Who are you, Humphrey Bogart?'

'I just watched *The Big Sleep* again. Never gets old. Worth it just for Lauren Bacall's clothes.'

They say goodnight and hang up.

In spite of Kim's overly dramatic commentary, Rose is grateful that her sister will be here soon.

Thunk.

Rose wakes abruptly, a loud noise still vibrating in the air. She holds her breath, listening. What the hell was that? She reaches for her phone on the bedside table: 2.37 am. She peers over the top of the doona. The room is nearly pitch-black. She looks out the window.

It's a clear night, the stars bright pinpoints, the trees black silhouettes, swaying in the breeze.

She waits, listening.

A scraping sound. It's coming from the roof.

Her heart is thumping. She finds Blackmore's number in her phone and is about to call when there's another loud thunk, and the sound of tiny footsteps galloping across the corrugated iron.

Possums.

Rose sighs and puts her phone back on the bedside table. Sometimes the possums dropped from the trees and made an almighty racket as they scurried over the roof. She gets out of bed and goes to the lounge room, where Bob is wide awake on the couch. The possum must have woken him too.

'Come on, Bob.'

He follows Rose into her bedroom and, when she pats the space near her feet on the doona, he hops up. 'Don't get used to this,' she says. 'It's just for when I'm scared shitless.'

He drapes his head over her legs and she gives him a scratch under the chin.

Rose cringes when she imagines Blackmore coming all the way out here in the middle of the night to save her from possums. She tries to think of happy daytime scenes with the sun shining, but as she drifts off to sleep, her dreams fill instead with something hovering in the shadows at the edge of Echo Lake.

TEN

Kim is suitably impressed when she sees what Rose has done to the cottage in such a short time. Before she moved in, Rose painted the rooms a creamy white and stripped back the window and doorframes, staining the wood so it now gleamed a rich golden brown. She found an antique marbled-glass light fitting for the living room pendant, and filmy white curtains for the windows. With her rumpled but comfy furniture in place and her pictures hung, it truly felt like home.

'It looks like you've lived here forever!' Kim says. 'I've been in my place for six years and still can't figure out where the couch looks right.'

'Thank you,' Rose says, as she shows Kim around the cottage. 'So does that mean you think I made the right move?'

'I wouldn't go that far,' Kim teases. 'I mean, you're a murder suspect, but the place looks great.'

Rose ignores Kim's joke, and beams proudly as they settle on the couch and she pours them a glass of the fancy wine Kim had brought. It's delicious, but Rose doesn't think it's that much better than the cleanskin Rose usually buys.

'I'm sorry to drag you to Anna's funeral tomorrow.'

'Are you kidding?' says Kim, excited. 'I can't wait to meet the whole cast of characters.'

Rose frowns. 'This isn't a movie, Kim, it's the real world. It's my life.'

Kim looks abashed. 'Sorry.'

'I only met Anna once, but she was so . . . vivid. Her sculptures were fantastic. At least, I thought so.'

'And a lot more valuable this week than last.'

Rose frowns at her sister again.

'Sorry,' Kim says. 'I'll behave.'

'I want to pay my respects.'

'Of course. And I want to get a look at your hot detective.'

'Oh God, he's not hot and—'

'Then why does your voice go all funny when you talk about him?'

'It doesn't. Anyway, it's all over before it started. He's married.'

'Fuck.'

'And his wife is stunning. And *nice*!'

'I hate her.'

'And she's Scottish.'

'God, no, the trifecta.'

Rose was surprised to learn that Anna's funeral was to be at St Francis Xavier's, the Catholic church in Berrima. She hadn't picked Anna for a Catholic—but, then again, so was Rose at one time. Anna was young and probably hadn't made funeral plans. No one expects to die in her mid-thirties. No doubt her family made the decision for her.

Rose had looked into the church's history and discovered that the small but perfectly formed Gothic structure was built out of sandstone in 1849, its architect having also worked on the design for the Houses of Parliament in London. When she and Kim arrive, she's moved by its simple, timeless beauty.

Inside, the church feels both intimate and grand, all stone and wood, with the only bright colours coming from three tall, narrow, stained-glass windows behind the altar. It brings back mostly fond memories of going to church with her mum, dad and Kim on Sunday mornings as a child, when Rose enjoyed being swept up in the theatre and melodrama of the Catholic mass. She remembers especially liking the so-called 'holy days of obligation', when the priests would walk up and down the aisles swinging their censers, sending fragrant incense into the air to purify their souls. Rose had gone along with it all until she was old enough to learn about the rapacious history of the Church, her disillusionment leading to a complete loss of faith shortly before her parents died. At the time, Rose felt guilty that she couldn't mourn them within the bosom of the religion they loved and believed in. Only later did she recognise the irony—that even after she stopped believing, she would carry the burden of Catholic guilt to her grave.

But Rose is glad that Anna is being farewelled here and not in some soulless, suburban box. Even though she's rejected its dogma, Rose is still drawn to the works of art and architecture created in the name of the Church throughout its corrupt and bloody reign.

She and Kim sit at the back and watch as the church fills up.

Although most people are wearing black, there are splashes of colour worn by people who Rose suspects are Anna's artist friends. A couple in their sixties, who could be Anna's parents, walk with dignity, holding each other's hands, and sit in the front pew.

When Blackmore enters with Grace, her red hair magnificent against a black coat with shawl collar, Rose leans close to Kim and whispers, 'The detective and his wife.' Kim follows Rose's eyes and whispers back, 'Very attractive couple.' Rose sighs.

Constable Tran is here too, looking even younger in civilian clothes, followed by Irish Dave in a dark suit and his signature R.M. Williams boots. He sees Rose and nods hello. She nods discreetly back, and notes that's he's alone, wondering again if he's single, then reprimanding herself for letting her mind go there at a funeral.

Once the church is full, the organ starts to play a traditional hymn Rose remembers from her childhood, and everyone stands as the coffin is carried in. With his untamed black hair and pale blue eyes, Rose is sure one of the pallbearers is Anna's brother, and his silent tears make her heart lurch. Rose knows that it's only a matter of time before she'll be crying. She may have met Anna only once, but she feels the devastation left in the wake of her death.

That afternoon, on Kim's insistence, they drive into the nearby town of Bowral, where members of the Highlands upper crust—which includes local gentry, film stars and tech billion-aires—converge to spend their money. Rose always feels a little inadequate in Bowral, where even at the growers market blonde women in pearl earrings and recently manicured nails wear pristine riding boots that have probably never seen a horse. Rose is in her duffel coat and an old black dress she dug out for the funeral, while Kim is in something casually elegant; with her expensive haircut and Burberry boots, she fits right in.

They wander through Dirty Jane's, an enormous warehouse crammed with antique treasures and vintage curios. Rose watches as her sister inspects linens, shoes, jewellery, tables and chairs, none of which seem to be quite right. Kim wonders whether a zinc-topped bench would fit in her kitchen.

'Would it work with your fifties breakfast bar?' Rose asks, sceptical.

'You're right—no, it's totally wrong.'

They move on.

In a dim corner, Rose finds a dusty stall with old framed maps—the first items to excite her. She loves the yellowed paper, the fine pen-and-ink work, the hints of faded watercolour to indicate a river or stream. But she's also intrigued by the idea that a map is a historical moment frozen in time, indicating roads and settlements and even forests that may no longer be there.

Most of the maps are of Sydney or Canberra, but she unearths one of the Southern Highlands. She finds Berrima and the little stream near her cottage that runs off the Wingecarribee River. At the south-east edge of the map are the Fitzroy Falls, and just to their west, small and barely outlined, is Echo Lake. She gasps.

'What?' Kim is at her side.

'Echo Lake.' Rose points it out. She can't find the date the map was made, but judging by the style and the place names, she thinks it must have been drawn in the late nineteenth century.

'You should buy it.'

'I think I will.'

As they make their way back through the labyrinth of stalls, Kim spies a pair of Chinese ceramic lamps and decides she needs them, although Rose suspects she just felt left out after Rose found something for herself. When she sees the price tag, she looks at Kim. 'Seriously? I paid less for my first car. How old are they?'

'Well, I'm guessing from the price they're eleventh century,' Kim says, joking. 'But they're beautiful and I love them.'

87

Rose smiles, shaking her head.

Leaving Dirty Jane's with their map and lamps, they pass through a small gift shop, and Rose sees something on a shelf that catches her eye. She stops.

It's a small sculpture, around twenty centimetres high. A cube made of inlaid wood in a distinctive, geometric pattern. It resembles the pyramid on Anna's kitchen table, and was obviously made by the same artist. Rose asks the shop assistant if she can inspect the piece and, sure enough, when she holds the wooden cube it moves in the same way Anna's pyramid had.

'The artist is a real eccentric,' the saleswoman says. 'He used to sell his work out of his studio but hated dealing with customers. And he doesn't like parting with the things he makes. He acts as if we're *stealing* them!'

Rose turns the wooden cube over—it feels almost liquid. There's something about it that she wants to know, wants to keep. 'I can understand why he wouldn't want to part with a thing like this that he made with his own hands.'

Although she can't remember the last time she bought two things she didn't absolutely need on the same day, Rose buys Ned Petrovic's enigmatic wooden cube.

They can hear the fiddle and drum from the end of the street.

Rose had organised to meet George at the Irish pub in Berrima for a night out, and after a whisky at home, she and Kim are both feeling happy. Rose knows that their high spirits are partly a reaction to the terrible sadness they felt at Anna's funeral. Kim seemed to be as moved as Rose was, her wisecracking muted in the face of tragedy.

Inside the pub, they find George at a table with a view of the band—three young women, one on lead vocals, one on fiddle and one pounding the drum and singing back-up. According to the chalkboard nearby, they are the Girls from Galway. The place is packed.

Rose shouts introductions over 'The Rocky Road to Dublin' and volunteers to get wine and snacks.

She has to fight through the crowd and is surprised to see the pallbearer who looks so much like Anna Taradash behind the bar. She orders, and when he brings the bottle and three glasses, she says she's sorry for his loss. Some people find that comment a hollow cliché, but Rose believes it's not if it's heartfelt. The bartender seems touched, and thanks her before moving on to the next customer.

Back at their table, Rose pours the wine just as the Girls from Galway decide to take a break.

'Thank goodness,' George says. 'As much as I love the music, I want to be able to hear you both!'

'My God,' Kim says. 'A man who likes to listen?!'

'My sister is prone to sweeping generalisations,' Rose says.

'I find women have more to say,' George says.

'That's it, George—I'm in love,' Kim says.

'Do you know if the bartender is related to Anna?' Rose asks.

George spots him through a gap in the crowd. 'That's her brother Brett. It's a wonder he's working tonight.'

'He needs to keep busy,' Kim says. 'It can help.'

Rose looks at her sister and realises how easy it is to forget that, in spite of her breezy cynicism, Kim was as devastated by their parents' death as she was. Her need to be so much a part of Rose's life is undoubtedly rooted in her own sense of loss and yearning.

They talk about Anna's death, but with no updates from the police, it's all guesswork. Rose wonders if Anna had a boyfriend.

'Actually,' George says, 'I believe she had girlfriends. But I don't know if there was anyone current.'

'Maybe my theory about her and Maria was right,' says Kim.

'Do you know if she and Maria were ever involved?' Rose asks George.

He shakes his head. 'I've no idea.'

'Anna said Maria stayed at the cottage every once in a while. When they'd been drinking. But it doesn't explain how that roll of film ended up in the garden.'

'Could Anna have been the one who took the pictures?' Kim asks.

'I don't think so,' Rose says. 'They took her by surprise. I'd say someone else was walking in the bush with Maria that day.'

'Well, the cops will have shown the pictures to Maria's husband by now . . .' Kim says.

'Nick,' George says. 'Yes, I'm sure they would have.'

'Was he at Anna's funeral?' Rose asks.

'I didn't see him,' George says.

'I wonder if that means anything.'

A waiter brings chips, fried calamari and chicken wings, and refills their glasses.

'Ah, health food,' Kim says, reaching for a chip. 'You need to ask your boyfriend, the hot detective, if there's any progress.'

Rose can't believe that Kim has just outed her. Aghast, she turns to George, and sees he is smiling in sympathy.

'My sister has a big mouth,' Rose says. 'I admit I *did* have a small crush, but that, like so many dreams, has died.'

'Well, that's fucking depressing,' Kim says.

'Don't worry,' George tells Rose. 'Your secret's safe with me. Anyway, he's a very attractive man. And that voice!'

Kim's eyes widen. 'Ooh, a sexy voice—you didn't say. I'd have a crush too.'

'My crush is dead.'

'Oh, come on,' Kim says. 'You can't fool George. Anyway, I'm sure he's had a secret crush or two.'

George raises his glass to Kim in acknowledgement. 'Guilty as charged.'

Keen to move the conversation along, Rose asks George, 'Have you ever met Nick Aboud?'

'Once or twice,' George says. 'He has a small vineyard out near Sutton Forest. Works day and night, which I guess is true with any kind of farming. I've heard he's never got over Maria's disappearance. And he doesn't think the police did enough to find her.'

'Poor man,' Rose says.

'Hey, isn't that Irish Dave?' asks Kim.

Rose sees the real estate agent carrying a few beers towards another table amid the throng.

Kim is eyeing him speculatively. 'So is Irish Dave married?' she asks.

'Kim,' Rose says in half-hearted warning.

'Divorced,' George says.

'Interesting!' Kim turns to Rose. 'He's got that great Black Irish colouring—dark hair and pale skin. And, of course, there's the accent. Why do certain accents make someone more desirable?'

'A question for the ages. Anyway, I'm not interested. I have George,' Rose says, patting his hand.

George looks wistfully into his drink, and Rose realises too late that even though he's nearly eighty, George is still a man and she has just made a joke out of him.

'Oh, George, I didn't mean—'

'No. It's okay.' He smiles. 'There are worse things than being seen as a harmless old man.'

'You?!' Kim says. 'You're about as harmless as a rattlesnake.' And they all laugh, high spirits restored.

They're polishing off their second bottle of wine as the Girls from Galway begin their next set, striking up a stirring reel and inspiring some revellers to take to the makeshift dance floor in front of the small stage. The rhythm is infectious, and suddenly Kim gets up and turns to George. 'Come on, Georgie! Let's show 'em how it's done.'

Rose thinks George will turn Kim down, but to her surprise, he lets himself be led onto the floor. Delighted, Rose claps along as George twirls Kim in an impressive spin; it's clear he knows what he's doing. His wife, Stella, has been dead for nearly ten years, but he told Rose that they used to love to dance. It looks like he's having the time of his life. When he extends his arm, opening a gap between him and Kim, Rose has a view of the bar. Her heart almost stops when she recognises the figure standing there. But George and her sister come together again, and Rose isn't sure if it was really him.

George and Kim sway apart once more, and this time Rose sees him clearly. Staring at her.

Ray Mullin.

Rose feels the colour drain from her face. She watches Mullin place his order at the bar. While he's waiting for his drink, he turns around and stares at her again.

She looks away, her eyes searching for Kim in the crowd. Finally, Kim glances her way and catches her sister's eye, sees the look on Rose's face. She pushes her way through the dancers, followed by George. They sit down. George, winded, is relieved, unaware that something's wrong.

'That was wonderful,' he says. 'But I am glad we stopped when we did.'

'Rose?' Kim asks.

Rose turns to look at Mullin, who's now sipping his beer as he watches them, expressionless. Kim follows Rose's gaze.

'Who is that?' Kim shouts over the music.

Rose says into Kim's ear, 'That's the guy—the one who backed into me.' And messed up her plumbing, which Rose had finally told Kim about, reluctantly.

Kim looks back at Mullin and then, to Rose's horror, she gets up and heads straight for him.

Rose springs to her feet and goes after her sister.

'Kim!' Rose yells, but Kim doesn't hear her above the music. Rose fights her way through the crowd of drinkers and dancers. When she gets to the bar, Kim is standing in front of Mullin.

'Stay away from my sister,' Kim is saying to the heavily muscled man.

Before he can respond, Rose grabs Kim's arm and drags her away, steering her out the pub's front door.

On the verandah, a few people are smoking and chatting under a glowing yellow lantern.

Rose pulls Kim into the shadows.

'What?' Kim says defiantly.

'This isn't your business.'

'You have to stand up to bullies,' Kim insists.

'I have to live in this town,' Rose tells her.

'But—'

'Let me handle this my own way, Kim.'

George comes out with their coats and bags as the smokers go back inside.

'Thanks, George,' Rose says, as he helps her into her coat. 'Sorry about that.'

'Don't be sorry—I was ready to leave anyway,' he says. 'I'm quite tired.'

'I think we all are,' Rose says, with a knowing look to Kim.

They say their goodnights and head for home.

'I'm sorry, I should have kept my mouth shut,' Kim says.

'It's hard to know how to handle a situation like this.'

Rose and Kim are on the couch in front of the fire, drinking camomile tea, with Bob curled up between them.

'Anyway, it was dumb of me to confront him.'

'I just don't want to provoke him further,' Rose says. 'He's a violent man. And with everything that's been happening . . .'

'Of course,' Kim says. 'I don't know about you, but this tea is not doing the trick. Whisky?'

'Maybe one.' Rose hopes it will blur the image she can't get out of her head: Ray Mullin's cold stare.

ELEVEN

On Sunday morning, before Kim heads back to the city, Rose takes her to Manna.

'This is not an entirely hideous experience,' Kim says, wrapping a blanket around herself as Heidi brings her a plate of perfect eggs Benedict and puts a croque monsieur in front of Rose.

'See?' Rose says. 'I'm not missing anything down here.'

'And you're not lonely?'

'Not at all. Well, sometimes a little.'

'At least you're meeting people. There's George, your hot detective . . . Ray Mullin.'

Rose chuckles, shaking her head.

'Too soon?' Kim asks.

'At the moment, I think being alone is the safest option.'

Kim mulls this over as she savours her breakfast. 'No,' she says, swallowing a mouthful of perfectly poached egg. 'You should find someone. You have so much love to give, Rosie. Surely there's someone out there who deserves you.'

'Look who's turned into Pollyanna.'

Rose dips a corner of her toast into Kim's hollandaise. 'What about you? Are you still looking for love?'

'I have no love to give,' Kim states matter-of-factly. 'Except to you and Bob, and George maybe.'

'Are you sure you can't come to lunch?'

'I have lesson plans to prep before a staff meeting tomorrow at the crack of.'

'Are lesson plans for six-year-olds that complicated?'

Kim shrugs. 'Private school. Although,' she says, looking around the charming cafe, 'I'm tempted to chuck it all in for a nice simple job around here.'

'Really?'

'Sure. I could marry George. And if George won't have me, I'll marry Bob. We'll be one big happy family.'

Rose smiles as Kim gives a grateful Bob a bit of ham dripping in sauce.

Rose is grateful that the invitation to lunch included Bob, and as she drives to Moss Vale, the dog seems as excited as she is to see where George and Cordelia live. She has no idea what to expect, and when she parks where the map says the house should be, she's a bit surprised to find that it's on a main road, not far from a service station and a supermarket. From the car, all she can see of the property are trees and a weathered wooden fence.

She lets Bob out, keeping him on the lead while she looks for a way in through the fence. Not finding a gate at the front, she walks down a driveway, and as she passes a stand of trees growing thick, untended, Rose is beginning to think she's in the wrong place. But the drive leads through an open gate to a green lawn and a large colonial sandstone house with white wooden trim and a deep wraparound verandah, shaded by soaring gum trees. Rose thinks it might be the most beautiful house she's ever seen. A carved stone panel next to the front door bears the name *Threave House*.

The wide front door opens and Cordelia streaks out past George, who's wearing a navy jumper, forest-green pants and a black-and-white-striped chef's apron which hasn't a mark on it—classic George.

'Welcome!' he says expansively as Rose makes her way to the front door past Bob and Cordelia, who are frolicking on the vast lawn.

'This is exquisite!'

George smiles, nodding. 'That's what Stella said when we saw it.'

'How long have you lived here?'

'About fifteen years. We bought it when I retired and we fled the city. Never looked back.'

Rose gazes out over the grounds at the edges of the lawn—overgrown with native shrubs and wildflowers.

'I'll close the gate,' he says, and heads off to swing it closed. 'It's fenced all the way around, so the dogs can have the run of the place.'

'Fantastic. And your house has a name. I love a house with a name. Threave House is Scottish, isn't it?'

'It is! Now, come in out of the cold, we'll open a bottle of something and you can tell me what you're reading.'

Rose loves the fact that they usually start their conversations by asking each other what they're reading, suggesting that books are more important than their health, the weather or any of the other usual conversation starters.

He leads her inside and Rose instantly feels the enveloping warmth. 'Oh wow, it's so nice and toasty!'

'Yes, I'm afraid I'm being very environmentally unsound. I have a roaring fire in the main fireplace as well as the central heating blasting away. Not to mention the oven on high.'

Rose takes off her coat and gives it to George, who hangs it on a carved antique stand in the grand entrance hall. She touches the delicately turned wooden hooks. 'Wow, this is gorgeous.'

George proudly leads her into the spacious lounge room, which is filled with a heady mix of mint-condition antiques and modern art.

'Wow,' Rose says, adding, 'I'm afraid I'm going to be saying "wow" a lot.'

George chuckles. 'Stella had a great eye for furniture. She made some impressive finds at garage sales, junk shops. Never paid too much.'

Rose is drawn to a large abstract expressionist painting in blues and greys over the fireplace. 'I love that.'

'I'm glad. She let me choose the art. I prefer modern to old, but for Stella the older the better. And working on the furniture made her happy,' he says wistfully.

'She restored it herself?'

'She did. She could spend an entire day on the leg of a chair and love every moment. Personally, I'd rather read a good book.'

'I'm with you, but I admire people who can do things with their hands.'

'I do too. And I liked the smell of all the varnishes and oils she used.'

'It was probably the paint stripper, George, and you were getting high as a kite.'

He laughs. 'Probably right. Come with me—I need to check the chook.'

Rose groans happily. 'I thought that was roast chicken I could smell.'

They enter a country kitchen with a large central butcher's block island strewn with vegetable peelings, sprigs of fresh rosemary and thyme, and a bowl of garlic bulbs.

'It's only us, but I always find two people can do a lot of damage to one roast chicken.'

'You're a man after my own heart.'

George opens the oven door and Rose can see a large bird, its skin browning as vegetables around it sizzle and crisp.

'Getting there,' George says.

'I didn't know what wine to bring so . . .' She hands him a bottle of Glenmorangie single-malt whisky in a gold-trimmed gift box.

George's eyes widen. 'Now it's my turn to say wow.'

'I'm actually relieved it's just us. I thought you might have some local dignitaries or publishing people over too,' Rose says. Then, realising how ungracious that sounds, she adds, 'Which would have been great!'

'God, no,' George says as he puts the whisky aside. 'I have a confession to make.'

'Go on.'

'I don't actually like people. At least, not most people.'

Rose raises her eyebrows.

'You're surprised,' he says.

'I guess I'm surprised I'm one of the ones you *do* like.'

'Rose, one of these days you're going to realise how special you are.'

Slightly embarrassed, Rose turns away to peruse the array of cookbooks in an old-fashioned hutch. *Larousse Gastronomique*,

99

The Margaret Fulton Cookbook and Julia Child's *Mastering the Art of French Cooking*.

'Not into nouvelle cuisine, George?'

'I believe butter makes everything taste better.'

Rose laughs. 'You'll get no argument from me.'

George opens a bottle of fancy-looking chardonnay, and Rose watches as he fills two dainty, etched-crystal wineglasses. He hands her a glass and they clink.

'Welcome to my home,' George says. 'And to my life.'

'Aw, George, thank you!' She gives his arm a squeeze. 'What can I do to help?'

'You can pick out some music. There's a cabinet with records—'

'Vinyl?'

'Yes. In the lounge room, behind the bookcase. And if you know how to work a mid-century turntable, you can play DJ all afternoon.'

'George, you are officially the coolest guy I know.'

Rose takes her wine into the lounge room and sees a large bookcase, its shelves open at the front and back, which had been set up as a room divider between the lounge and a little reading nook. In the nook is a comfy chair, a lamp and a long, low cabinet beneath a large window. She looks outside and sees Bob sniffing in the undergrowth as Cordelia snoozes on a frayed dog bed on the verandah.

She opens the cabinet and is dazzled by the sight of hundreds of records. She kneels on a worn Persian rug and flips through them. Like the furniture, the records are all in mint condition. Classical, jazz, fifties and sixties rock, a bit of folk music . . . and Prince's *Purple Rain*. George is full of surprises.

She's deciding between Ella Fitzgerald and Nina Simone when she senses someone behind her. She turns, expecting to see George,

But no one is there.

She stands up and walks around the bookcase to the lounge room. 'George?'

The rattle of pans tells her that her host is still busy in the kitchen. But Rose can feel the flutter of air that passes through a room when someone has just walked by. She looks out the window again. Both dogs are in view.

Probably just the draughty old house. She tries to shake it off, but the feeling that someone was in the room with her lingers. She puts Nina on the turntable and hurries back to the kitchen.

Rose and George are sitting at the dining table, the late afternoon sun slanting through the windows, the remains of the chicken and vegetables on the serving platter. They had talked about books, their childhoods, their children, Celtic Britons and American jazz. In fact, they'd talked about everything except the death of Anna Taradash and the disappearance of Maria Aboud.

'Shall I open another bottle?' George asks.

'Oh no,' Rose says. 'Not for me—I won't be able to drive home.'

They sit for a few moments in silence. Rose likes it when people are so comfortable with each other they can keep each other's company without filling the air with words when none are needed. She's looking at the bookshelves that run from one end of the room to the other.

'We have so many of the same books,' she says. 'But you have nice hardcover first editions, and I have crappy old paperbacks.'

'But the words inside are the same,' George points out.

'Yes, they are.'

In another small silence, Rose's mind goes back to the feeling she'd had earlier—that she wasn't alone.

'George, do you mind if I ask how Stella died?'

'Of course not. It started with a cold. A nasty one—the sort that hangs on. It turned into bronchitis, and when they X-rayed her lungs to check for pneumonia, they found cancer.'

'Oh, George, I'm so sorry.'

'She had been a smoker. Loved smoking. It was part of her glamour.' He smiles.

'Was she sick for a long time?'

'Too long. It was awful watching her . . . disappear.'

Rose treads carefully towards what she wants to know. 'Was she in a hospice at the end?'

'No, she never wanted to leave this house.'

'So, she died here?'

'Yes.'

Rose wonders if what she was feeling earlier was an echo of Stella. Although she sometimes felt glimmers from a place's past, Rose had never encountered what people call ghosts.

'That's how I met Grace,' George says. 'When Stella was very ill, she delivered meals to us, before I learned to cook—or had the will to.'

'I'm sure Stella died very peacefully in this house, with you here by her side.'

George smiles. 'I'm glad you used the word "died" rather than "passed" or some other piss-weak euphemism.'

Rose smiles. 'I learned with Mum and Dad that it felt better to talk about what happened in real terms. Death is such an important part of our histories. Why tone it down or dress it up as something less than momentous?' Rose had told George about how her parents died shortly after they met. She never shied away from bringing it up if she felt someone would want to know.

'Well said. Now, to more mundane matters, would you like some coffee? Tea?'

'Coffee would be great.'

'Good. It will go well with the chocolate cheesecake Heidi made for us.'

Rose laughs. 'George!' But she's pretty sure she'll have room for a small slice.

She helps him clear the table and bring the dishes to the kitchen.

'Which way to the loo?' she asks.

He hesitates for a second then says, 'Down the hall, second door on the left.'

Rose goes down the hall, pausing to look at the framed photos on the wall. One was obviously taken on George's wedding day— he's young, handsome and beaming like a king as he stands next to Stella, a striking woman with dark wavy hair and very large dark eyes, in a simple white chiffon dress, no veil, holding a small bouquet of lilies-of-the-valley. Rose would have liked to know her.

She finds the second door on the left and enters a large bathroom with pale green tiles, a claw-foot tub and embroidered white linen curtains with matching guest towels.

It's a pretty room, but freezing cold, and Rose wishes the central heating reached this far. After she flushes, she's washing her hands at the sink when she catches a glimpse of movement behind her in the mirror.

She spins around. There's nothing—no one—there. But she's sure she hadn't imagined it. The feeling she'd had earlier in the lounge room is there again; a disturbance in the air as if someone had just walked past.

Then she notices a heating vent in the wall. She feels the air in front of it. A steady stream of heat is being pumped through and the room suddenly feels cosy and warm, as though it had been warm all day.

Back in the kitchen, Rose slices the cheesecake while George makes the coffee. She decides not to say anything about the spooky feelings she'd had. It would be rude, Rose thinks, especially on her first visit, to suggest to her host that his house is haunted by his dead wife.

TWELVE

The following afternoon, Rose is at her desk researching the origins of the Australian ballad 'Waltzing Matilda' for a television producer who wants to make a documentary about it.

Like most Australians, Rose had thought the song was written by the beloved bush poet Banjo Paterson, but it turned out he'd only been responsible for the lyrics. The melody was inspired by an old Scottish ballad Paterson had heard played on an autoharp by Christina Macpherson, a young woman whose family Paterson was visiting. She had rewritten the tune, putting her own spin on it, and if anyone should be credited with composing the melody, it was Christina. Rose hopes that if the true story is included in the documentary, she will have helped another woman forgotten by history to stake her claim.

Rose makes herself a cup of tea. Then, before delving back into the history of the song, she decides to check the *Southern Highland News* online.

The death of Anna Taradash is still one of the lead stories, and an article written by a Jasmine Nolan mentions that Anna was a friend of missing woman Maria Aboud. As far as Rose is aware, this is the first time the connection between the two women has been made in the media, and she fears it will trigger a wave of conspiracy theories. Anna's cause of death had still not been determined, the article continues, but the investigation was 'ongoing': *A person of interest who visited Ms Taradash in her home two days before her body was found is being questioned by police.*

Rose gasps. The article is referring to her!

She calls Blackmore, who picks up straight away. 'Rose?'

Trying to sound calm, Rose says, 'Detective, I've just read an article in the *Southern Highland News* that refers to me as a "person of interest".'

'Were you named?'

'No, but the journalist seems to be uncomfortably well informed. She even knew I'd visited Anna before she died.'

'Sorry . . . small town.'

'Did that information come from the police?'

'Probably.'

She waits, but it seems that's all he's offering.

'*Am* I a person of interest? Isn't that a euphemism for "suspect"?'

'You're not a suspect at this point—'

'*At this point?!*'

'You were the last person to talk to Anna that we know of, and you did produce pictures of a missing person . . .'

'I didn't "produce" them,' Rose protests.

'Rose . . .' Blackmore sounds weary but not unfeeling. 'I'll let you know if we need to talk to you again.'

Wow, loud and clear—he does not want or need her input.

'Okay.'

Ending the call, Rose is not in the right frame of mind to return to 'Waltzing Matilda'. Maybe she and Bob could use some air.

As Rose follows Bob around the dog park, it occurs to her that, other than the police, the only person who knew she wanted to talk to Anna Taradash was Irish Dave. On her way home, she stops at the real estate agency.

'I'm sorry to bother you,' she says, as Dave ushers her into one of those tiny claustrophobia-inducing rooms used for signing leases. 'But I saw you at Anna's funeral.'

He closes the door and they sit at the small table.

'No bother at all, Rose,' Dave says. 'I'm glad you came. What an awful business.' His accent makes even sad words sound like they've been sprinkled with fairy dust.

'Yes, it is. Did you know Anna well?'

'Not *well*. I'd been to a few of her exhibitions, and I got to know her better when she put the cottage up for sale. She was so full of life!'

'Yes! Maybe that's why it's so shocking.'

'But not surprising,' Dave adds.

Rose stares at him. 'What do you mean?'

'Well, some of us have been after National Parks and Wildlife to put up a railing at that lookout, but other people argue that it'll ruin the view. And now they have to consult with the Indigenous elders and all that palaver.'

Rose bristles. 'I think "all that palaver" is way overdue.'

'Fair point, I didn't mean to be insensitive. But it's a matter of safety.'

'Which lookout was it?'

'Long View—it was on the news just now. It's just a big flat rock you can stand on to look down into the valley. It's stunning but also bloody dangerous.'

'So, you think it was an accident? You think she fell?'

'I think it's likely.'

Rose nods, but adds tentatively, 'I suppose she could have jumped . . .'

'Well, I hope not. But whatever happened doesn't change the outcome.'

'No, you're right.'

'Is there something else?'

'I wondered if you told anyone I wanted to talk to her. Like a journalist?'

'No, Rose! Of course not! I would never do that.'

'Thank you. So, did you know many of Anna's friends?'

'No, she and her crowd were a bit arty for me. I always feel a bit clueless around arty people.'

'Me too.'

'No! A woman with your style?'

Is he flirting? It's been so long since someone flirted with her, Rose doesn't know what to say. She just sits there for a second smiling at him. He's smiling back.

She gets up. 'Well, I won't take up any more of your time.'

Dave stands and opens the door for her. 'Let me know if there's anything else I can help you with, Rose.' He takes her hand and holds it for a moment before letting go.

'Thanks, Dave.'

As she walks back to her car, Rose feels the flutter of excitement that comes after an encounter that might lead to something else. She thinks she might tell Kim about it—then, recalling how her sister had teased her about Blackmore, thinks again.

THIRTEEN

The next day, Rose drives into the national park. It had rained overnight and the sharp smell of damp earth and wet leaves is in the air. Nearly all the colourful foliage has gone now, leaving behind bare trees and the subtle greens of Australian natives. She steers down a gravel road and parks near a van covered in camping stickers.

She strikes off on the bush track in search of Long View Lookout, her hands in the pockets of her coat, where she carries Maria Aboud's photos. Before winter closes in, she'll have to buy a pair of gloves—her first since her gap year in Scotland. She'd found out how cold her hands could get when she was caught in a storm on a hillside outside Inverness, complete with howling winds and horizontal rain. And that was in midsummer.

As she gets further into the bush, Rose realises it was barely a week ago that she'd had that bad experience when walking alone. The same day Anna's body was found. But that was an unmarked trail, she reminds herself, and she'd told George where she was going when she saw him at the dog park that morning.

The police haven't ruled out the possibility that Anna was murdered, but even if she had been, surely the murderer wouldn't still be hanging around, hunting for fresh victims. On the other hand, Ivan Milat did just that. Rose is still haunted by the story of the truck driver who, for years, had picked up hitchhikers as they travelled through the Southern Highlands and sexually assaulted, tortured and killed them. In the mid-nineties, he was convicted of the murders of seven people, but police believed there were more victims. The bodies were all found in the Belanglo Forest, just outside Berrima. Milat died in prison, but his crimes echo through the Highlands to this day, a reminder that beautiful scenery can't hide our darkest sins.

But Rose does not feel those echoes as she walks through the bush, and in spite of what's happened recently, she's determined not to surrender to fear. Life offers so many things to be afraid of, but if you let them rule you, you'll never get out of bed in the morning.

Every once in a while, Rose stops to compare Maria's pictures with the landscape around her, but so far she hasn't found a match. She turns up her collar against the wind.

She's pleased to discover that the trail is dotted with descriptive signs about the First Peoples who'd lived here. She takes pictures so she can reread them at home, and one of them she plans to post on Instagram:

The Gundungurra people continue to travel through this country. Traditionally they had numerous pathways and many reasons to travel, such as gathering seasonal food, hunting, trading and ceremonies. Aboriginal people sometimes travel to re-enact the journeys of their Dreaming Ancestors. Along each route are landmarks which are part of sacred knowledge. To demonstrate respect, permission is required from the custodians of each specific land area to be crossed.

Rose is worried by that last part. Should she have asked for permission to walk here? Or did the park administrators seek permission on behalf of all bushwalkers? Or were the park administrators Indigenous? She offers a silent thanks to the Gundungurra people for letting her walk through their country.

As she passes giant termite mounds and ferns more than three storeys high, she marvels at how lucky she is that all of this is only a few minutes from her home. She's keeping her eyes peeled for scarred trees where bark has been carved away to make coolamons, as described in one of the signs, when she nearly trips over the sign for Long View Lookout.

An arrow points to a smaller path, which Rose follows, surprised not to have encountered anyone else who, like her, is curious about recent events. But Rose is alone.

Up ahead, she sees a flash of colour and movement, and as she gets closer she recognises the blue-and-white-checked crime scene tape used by the police. A long strand of the tape rises and flaps in the wind.

Rose passes the tape and finds herself standing on a large flat rock. Ahead is a deep valley that stretches to the horizon. She steps closer to the edge of the rock and looks over, but she can't see the valley floor. She inches closer still, peering over the edge, wanting to see how far down it goes.

There's a sound behind her and Rose spins around, losing her balance.

A hand reaches out, grabs her. She shrieks.

'What the hell are you doing?!' Blackmore bellows as he pulls her back from the edge of the cliff.

'I . . . I wanted to see if this was where the pictures of Maria were taken.' She takes the photos out of her pocket to prove it.

The detective is looking at her like she's insane. He shakes his head. 'Jesus, Rose, one woman is missing and another is dead. There might be a killer—'

'So, I'm not your prime suspect?' she says, raising her voice over the wind.

'No. But if you try to solve this yourself, I'll find a reason to lock you up. I don't want to go to another funeral.'

'I'm touched,' she says, only half-joking.

He looks at her, as if trying to figure her out. 'Tell me again why you got two sets of prints?'

'I always get two sets—it's only a dollar extra.'

'Even though it wasn't your film?'

'I started doing it when I travelled, so I could have a set for myself and send the other one home to my sister.'

'Huh.' He seems somewhat mollified.

'When I became a researcher, I'd take pictures of artefacts or pages of manuscript, and I'd give a set of prints to whoever I was working for and keep a set for my files.' Her voice fades; she's unsure if she's made her point. 'It's good to keep your own archives.'

A gust of wind nearly knocks her over. Blackmore takes her by the arm and leads her off the rock, back to the trail. 'I'm taking you back to your car.'

Rose follows Blackmore back along the trail, occasionally having trouble keeping up. He turns every once in a while to make sure she's still there, and at one point she imagines what it would be like if they were just strolling through the bush and he was telling her what all the plants were called.

She catches up to him. 'So, you don't think Anna fell?' she asks. 'That's what people are saying: that it's always been a dangerous—'

'What people?'

'Well, Dave said—'

'Dave who?'

'Dave O'Neill, the real estate agent.'

'Ah, the well-known criminologist.'

'So you think there *was* a crime?'

Blackmore stops and looks at her. 'I *think* you should find a new hobby.' He walks off.

Rose is having uncharitable thoughts about arrogant detectives, so she's unprepared when she sees uniformed police near her Honda, peering into the windows of the camper van.

And too late, she sees a young guy with a man bun and a fancy digital camera taking pictures of her and Blackmore as they emerge from the bush.

'So much for staying anonymous,' Blackmore says, implying with his tone that she has only herself to blame.

As the photographer continues to snap pictures, a young woman with thick glasses wearing a motorcycle jacket over a Lizzo T-shirt steps up to Rose with her phone held out like a microphone.

'Can I get your name?' she asks.

Rose looks at Blackmore for help, but he's talking to the other cops.

'May I ask yours?' Rose asks.

'Jazzy Nolan with the *Southern Highland News*.'

So this is Jasmine Nolan, whose by-line was on the article referring to Rose as a 'person of interest'. To Rose, Jazzy doesn't look old enough to have a driver's licence much less a degree in journalism.

'I'm Rose McHugh. I've been out bushwalking.'

Rose heads to her car as the photographer keeps snapping. Jazzy follows. 'Is it true that you were the last person to see Anna Taradash alive?'

Rose pretends she hasn't heard the question and, after fumbling with her keys, she unlocks her car and gets in.

Jazzy shouts through Rose's closed window, 'What do you know about the suspicious death of Anna Taradash?'

Aghast, Rose lowers her window. 'I don't know any—'

'Leave her alone, Jazzy,' Blackmore says.

Disappointed, the young reporter lowers her phone and walks off towards the police officers as the photographer takes pictures of Rose's car. She sees him pointing the lens at her numberplate. Then Blackmore barks something at him and he scurries off.

Rose starts the car and is about to leave when Blackmore comes over.

She sighs, sure she's in for another scolding.

He leans in close so the others can't hear. She can feel heat coming off him, even though there's a cold bite to the wind. 'Promise me you will not go bushwalking alone again.'

'Fine.'

'Did you get those security cameras?'

'Not yet.'

'Do it.'

'Yes, sir.' She revs the engine. 'Miss Marple signing off.'

As she drives away, she looks in the rear-view mirror and sees Blackmore still watching her.

FOURTEEN

'Such an attractive couple,' Kim says the next day. She had been following the stories on Anna's death in the *Southern Highland News* and had phoned when she saw the colour photo of Rose and Blackmore walking out of the bush.

'That joke is wearing thin, Kim. Anyway, no one would believe we're a couple with the way I look.'

'What do you mean? You look gorgeous!'

'I look homeless. It looks like this handsome detective found me sleeping under a tree, eating ants and worms. Look at my hair!'

'You look . . . romantically windswept.'

'And how is my muffin top visible through my coat?! I'm throwing in the towel. Stained trackies from now on.'

'Don't you dare! You look fabulous and I bet your boyfriend has this picture taped to the inside of his locker.'

'I don't think he has a locker. He has a desk.'

'Wow. Big-time detective.'

'And now that I've been named as the person helping the police with their inquiries, every man and his dog will think I'm part of this.'

'Well, you kind of are.'

'Only tangentially. And accidentally.'

'Do you still have Maria's photos in your bag?'

'No comment.'

'Ha. Anyway, a little notoriety never hurt anyone.'

When she hangs up, Rose thinks about the article that had accompanied the picture. It was surprisingly well written, in spite of two grammatical errors, and Rose promises herself she'll stop making assumptions about people based on the fact that they look young enough to need a babysitter. She was also impressed by how much Jazzy Nolan had managed to find out about her. Details about Rose's work, her move to the Highlands and even her regular appearances at the dog park had been noted. Rose didn't mind that she was referred to as a 'prominent historian'—although she could have done without the mention of her recent divorce. Social bloody media. Rose knew it wouldn't take Sherlock Holmes to follow the digital breadcrumbs if someone wanted to find out about her ex-husband and his new wife.

She decided to glance at the Instagram account of Child Bride and immediately regretted it. Even though Rose had been the one to decide her marriage to Peter was over, she couldn't suppress a pang of jealousy when she saw pictures of him smiling with the much younger woman. And once she started, it was impossible to stop doomscrolling—picture after picture of Peter and Child Bride making pasta, dancing (when the hell had Peter ever taken Rose dancing?) and laughing it up as they decorated what was no doubt going to be the room for the baby. There was even a selfie with a caption saying how excited Child Bride was to become a 'yummy mummy', a term Rose had always hated.

Putting both Child Bride and Jazzy Nolan's article out of her head, Rose immerses herself in work, but she hasn't been at it long when Bob starts to bark at the front door. Rose looks through the window and sees a white van marked *Aboud Estate Wines* pulling up in front of the cottage.

A man in his early fifties leaps out and charges up the front path.

Rose goes to the door, telling Bob to shush and, holding him by the collar, hoping he looks bloodthirsty rather than excited to make a new friend, she opens it.

'Rose McHugh?' He's big, aggressive, and enters her house without being invited.

Rose backs up a step and says, in what she hopes is a commanding tone, 'Please don't come any further.'

He suddenly realises what he must look like. His shoulders sink, the fight draining from him. 'I'm Nick Aboud. I . . . I want . . . what do you know about my wife?'

Rose looks at Nick, his desperation. She doesn't think he came to hurt her.

'Would you like a cup of tea?' she asks.

Bob sniffs around the back garden while Rose and Nick sit at the kitchen table with cups of tea.

'It was pure chance that I was digging where the film was buried,' Rose tells him.

'But who buried it? And why?'

Rose realises the question isn't rhetorical; he expects an answer. 'I have no idea. All Anna said was that the film must have been Maria's. I don't think she knew any more than that— about the film, at least.'

She takes a sip of her tea, notices he hasn't touched his. He seems at a total loss—for what to think, what to say.

'Did the police show you the photos?' she asks.

'Yes.'

'And you weren't the one who took them?'

'No.'

'And you don't know who did?'

'No.'

She can see he's embarrassed by this.

'I only got a quick look at them—the police said they needed them as evidence. But evidence of what?'

His anguish is plain. Rose makes a decision that she knows, even as she's making it, might be a mistake.

'I have a set of the prints—I always order two. It's only a dollar extra,' she adds pointlessly.

His eyes widen. 'May I see them?'

Unsure if she's doing the right thing, but aware that it's too late to refuse now, Rose gets her bag from the back of the door and takes out the now well-worn envelope. She puts it on the table in front of Nick.

He stares at the envelope for a few seconds before slowly opening it and taking out the photos with his big, callused hands. Rose watches as he goes through the pictures of trees and birds and trails, searching every corner for clues as to where they were taken, and by whom.

When he comes to the picture of Maria standing on the trail smiling seductively at the camera, he stops breathing. He's clenching the photo so hard its edges bend.

Rose lays her hand gently on his arm and he starts to breathe again. He can't tear his eyes away from the picture.

'Nick,' she says softly, 'maybe this isn't such a good—'

He draws his arm away and straightens his back.

'These were taken around the time she disappeared. That's the way she wore her hair then.'

'Did you tell the police that?'

'Yes.'

He continues looking through the pictures, seeming calmer now.

'So, you don't know where they were taken?' Rose asks.

He shakes his head. 'I mean, it looks like somewhere in the Highlands—the vegetation, the light . . . Could be Morton . . . Bangadilly.'

Rose nods.

'But where *exactly* this is . . .' Nick shrugs. 'There are hundreds, maybe thousands of trails through the bush around here.'

When he's finished going through the photos, he straightens them into a neat pile, then slides them back into the envelope with something like reverence.

He looks into Rose's eyes. 'Thank you for letting me see them.'

'Of course.'

He finally takes a sip of his tea and watches Bob through the kitchen window.

Rose feels as though he's opened a door. She takes a chance on stepping through. 'Have you always lived in the Highlands?'

'No, I'm a Newcastle boy. I worked at a vineyard in the Hunter one summer and got the bug. I finally scraped up enough to buy a patch of land down here, before every man and his dog came down. I love it,' he says, as if trying to convince himself, 'but no one tells you how hard it'll be.'

'Did Maria work in the vineyard?'

'For a while. But her family raised horses. I reckon she thought nothing could be harder than that . . . until she saw what happens to grapes in a drought or a late frost. You know how many kinds of fungus a grapevine can get? Compared to grapes, horses are a walk in the park.'

'So if she didn't work in the vineyard, what did she do?'

'She worked in a pub for a while. The Irish pub in Berrima?'

'Oh yes,' Rose says. 'I was there recently. I think Anna's brother works there.'

Something in his eyes sharpens for an instant before he looks away.

Rose lets the silence widen a bit. But after a few moments she ventures another question. 'Nick . . . do you know if Maria was thinking of leaving?' She purposely doesn't specify whether she means leaving the area, or leaving him.

Her candour catches him off guard. He seems disarmed by it, and clearly decides to be candid in return, but he lowers his voice almost to a whisper. 'I think she was having an affair. She talked about leaving me for a while. And then something changed. She said she'd "settled something". She was going to stay. I swear to God.' He looks at Rose, as if pleading with her.

'I believe you,' she tells him. 'And you told the police all this?'

'Yes!'

Rose waits for him to go on.

'She was full of plans. She even said she wanted to turn the tasting rooms into a function centre—you know, for weddings and stuff. And then she disappeared. It doesn't make sense that she picked up and left after we'd talked about giving it another crack! Running away without saying goodbye—it doesn't make any sense.'

'No,' Rose hears herself agreeing. 'It doesn't make sense at all.'

When he's finished his tea, Rose walks Nick outside.

He turns to her before getting into the van. 'If you find out anything, could you let me know?'

'I will.'

She doesn't tell him she's been warned by the police to let them do their job.

Rose watches as he gets in the van and drives off, wondering if she really will tell him if she uncovers anything new. She's not sure what to think about the man. She is fairly certain he doesn't know what happened to his wife—but then again, she hasn't always been the best judge of character when it comes to men.

She does believe Nick loved Maria.

Which doesn't mean he didn't kill her.

FIFTEEN

The outdoor heater isn't on at Manna, so Rose and George are shivering as they cling to their coffee cups for warmth. The dogs, fast asleep under the table, seem oblivious to the arrival of winter.

'Do you think we should ask Beth to turn it on?' Rose asks.

'Is that her name? The new young lady with the elaborate tattoo on her neck of a dagger dripping blood?'

Rose smiles. 'Yes, Heidi's about to have the baby and she said she's training Beth to help out for a while. She's a local girl. We ought to give her a chance.'

'Of course we should.'

'But,' Rose suggests, 'maybe we should tell her that Heidi usually turns the heater on.'

'Be my guest.'

Rose laughs. 'You ran a publishing company, George—I'm sure you've stood up to scarier people.'

'*I'm* not.'

Beth, a scrawny young woman in her late teens, comes out with a cinnamon bun on a plate. She bangs it on the table without eye contact or a word and stomps back to the kitchen.

'Glad we stood up to her,' Rose says as she cuts the cinnamon bun in half. She takes a bite. It's cold. 'And George, thank you again for lunch at your place. It was such a special day.'

'It was for me too,' he says.

Rose has been trying to figure out a way to bring up what she felt in the house, but she doesn't want to put ideas in his head if they're just figments of her imagination. 'Do you know much about the history of Threave House?' she asks, trying to sound casual.

'We were told that the main house, the sandstone bit, was built in 1864, then they added the wooden extension in 1915.'

'Wow, it doesn't feel like an add-on. It has such good flow.'

'It does, doesn't it?'

'So,' she goes on, 'do you know anything about its history . . . the people who lived there before?'

George hesitates for a beat. Is he trying to remember? Or is he deciding how much to tell her?

'Not really. Apparently the man who had the house built was a wealthy landowner. No doubt guilty of all manner of crimes against humanity.'

Rose decides to do some digging of her own later. Changing the subject, she says, 'So, I had an unannounced visitor yesterday.'

George is immediately intrigued. 'Oh?'

'Nick Aboud.'

His eyes widen.

She describes their exchange, then asks George if he knows Maria's family, but before he can answer, a voice rings out, 'That better not be the last cinnamon bun.'

Grace sweeps up to the table in her purple coat, breathing on her hands. 'Fuck, it's cold!' She leans into the door to the kitchen. 'Hey, Beth, how's your nan?' She listens, then says, 'That's no good. Tell her I'll pop round soon. Meantime, could I get a flat white and a cinnamon bun, hot—and could you turn this heater on? We're freezing our balls off out here.'

Rose and George laugh as Grace pulls up a chair. 'What?' she says.

'You've just given us a small but important life lesson,' says George.

'Well, you don't get anything without asking for it.'

Not only does Beth light the gas heater, she brings them each a blanket, and by the time Grace's coffee and hot cinnamon bun arrive, they are positively cosy. Rose and George order second coffees from Beth, who now looks them in the eye and even gives them a wan smile.

George says to Grace, 'You know Maria Aboud's family, don't you?'

'A bit. Why?'

'Rose is doing some digging into the whole affair.'

'Oh God,' Rose interjects quickly. 'Don't tell her that, George. I shouldn't.' She turns to Grace. 'In fact, your husband told me to let the police do their job.'

Grace waves dismissively. 'Oh don't worry about him. Anyway, he told me he thinks you're smart.'

'A smart-arse, more likely,' Rose says, but secretly she's pleased that he doesn't think she's a complete idiot. 'He told me not to be a Miss Marple.'

'What a dickhead,' Grace says, her mouth full, icing sugar sticking to her lips.

Rose laughs, shaking her head. 'No, he's right. I should stay out of it.'

'On the other hand,' George says, 'you are quite intimately involved in the case. I read as much in the local paper.'

Grace had read the article too, but George fills in the blanks for her, including how Rose had found the film and met with Anna, and the phone call the day before Anna died.

'You poor thing,' Grace says to Rose. 'No wonder you want to do some digging. You didn't choose to be, but you *are* involved.'

Rose feels vindicated.

'It's such an awful tragedy,' Grace says.

'Yes. Did you know Anna well?' Rose asks. 'I saw you at the funeral.'

'I wouldn't say "well", but we were friendly acquaintances. I'd bought one of her pieces ages ago.'

'Do you think there could have been something between her and Maria?'

'You mean romantically?'

'Yes.'

'I don't know. I mean sure, it's possible. Have you talked to Anna's brother Brett?'

'No. And I'm sure I shouldn't.'

'Didn't Nick Aboud ask you to find out what you could?' George asks.

Grace's eyes widen. 'You talked to Nick?'

'After my name was in the paper, he came to my house. Actually, George, he asked me to tell him *if* I found out anything. He didn't tell me to go out and look for new information.' She tells Grace about Nick's visit.

'From what he said, it sounded like Maria had been having an affair but it was over. She had decided to stay in the marriage. At least that's what Nick thought. But then she disappeared. I haven't told your husband that Nick came to see me, by the way.'

'Don't worry, we don't talk shop.' Grace is staring at Rose the same way her husband does, as if she can peel away all the layers of Rose with her eyes. For some reason, Rose isn't offended by it.

'All right, young lady,' Grace says to Rose point blank, 'what's your theory?'

'Well . . .' Rose is reluctant, but Grace is looking at her expectantly. 'I think it's possible that when Maria broke off the affair, her lover might have been angry, jealous, and could have killed her. I hate to say this, but I guess it could have been Anna.'

She pauses for a response, but George and Grace are silent, waiting for her to go on.

'Then, when I showed Anna the photos, it stirred up her guilt. Maybe she thought it was only a matter of time before it all came out and so she took her own life.'

George looks at Grace, waiting for her verdict.

'Hey, it's possible,' Grace says. 'You should talk to Tony, Maria's brother. He's a mechanic up the road—the place that looks like a front for a meth lab. He and Maria were really close.'

'What do you think?' Rose asks George.

George considers carefully. 'Well, I don't want to sound like your big sister . . .'

'She's a bit overprotective,' Rose interjects for Grace's benefit.

'But I'm getting a little worried for you,' George continues. 'One woman is dead and another one is missing. There may be no connection between their deaths, but you *are* a link. I would hate to lose you just when we had become friends.'

A chill slides down Rose's neck and runs the length of her spine. She squeezes George's hand. 'Thanks.'

'Jesus, George, don't be so melodramatic,' Grace says. 'We're not going to lose her if she talks to Tony. He's a sweetheart—*and* an honest mechanic. And cheap as chips compared to the guys down the road.'

Rose sighs. 'I don't think DI Blackmore would be very happy about me playing Miss Marple again.'

'Fuck him,' Grace says, smiling as she pops the last piece of cinnamon bun in her mouth, and Rose tries not to think of the different ways she could interpret that. Grace goes on, 'Don't break the law and he can't do anything.'

'My sister said I have to find out what I can, if only to clear my name. She thinks I'm a suspect.'

'Well, until they find out who's responsible,' says George, 'I suppose you are.'

Not entirely sure she's doing the right thing, Rose walks up the driveway to the garage, a single-storey brick building just off the main road. She goes into the cramped front office and asks if Tony is available. A white-haired man in grimy overalls directs her through to the back.

Rose enters and sees a man in his early thirties, also in overalls, but surprisingly neat and clean, looking up into the underside of a car raised on a hydraulic lift.

'Excuse me—are you Tony?'

He turns. 'Yeah?'

He has Maria's colouring—brown eyes, dark-blond hair— and is as beautiful as she was.

'I'm Rose. I wonder if I could grab you for a quick chat sometime—I just need a few minutes.'

Tony wipes his hands on a rag and shouts into the office, 'I'm takin' my break.' To Rose he says, 'You mind me smoking? We can talk out back.'

He leads Rose out behind the building, where there's a small table and a few chairs under a gnarled, leafless tree. Tony doesn't seem to feel the cold as they sit on the metal chairs. He takes out a pouch of tobacco and papers and deftly rolls a cigarette.

'You're the one in the paper, yeah? In the article about Anna?'

'Yes, that's why I'm here. Grace Blackmore suggested I talk to you.'

'Tell Grace that shit box of hers needs a service. She drove by the other day and her engine was knocking so loud it must've woke up half the Highlands.'

Rose smiles. 'I'll tell her. Meantime, I wanted to ask you about some pictures—well, some film—that I found in my back garden.' She gets the envelope out of her bag. 'I've given a set of prints to the police, and the thing is . . . your sister Maria is in them.'

Tony nods as he takes a drag on his rollie. 'They showed them to me.'

Rose is disappointed—another person close to Maria who can't offer anything new.

'So, you don't know who took them?'

'No idea.'

'Or where they were taken?'

'No. As I said to Joe Blackmore, it could have been anywhere around here. But I wouldn't mind having another look.'

'Of course.' She hands Tony the photos.

He smokes as he looks through the pictures. Like everyone, he stops when he reaches the one of Maria. 'She sure was pretty.'

'Yes, she was. Or *is*. I mean, she's still a missing person, right?'

'Nah. I'm sure she's dead.'

Rose is surprised at his bluntness.

'If she was alive,' he says, 'she would have called me. She didn't get along with Mum and Dad. They didn't want her to marry Nick—thought he was too old for her. They wanted her to marry someone "suitable", whatever that means.'

'So, nothing here looks familiar?'

His eyes are still on the photos. 'Nah. There's a million trails like these.'

'Sorry. I'm taking up your break.'

'It's okay—it's nice to see Maria looking happy.'

Rose decides he doesn't mind her taking up his break, or talking about Maria.

'You grew up around here? On a horse farm?'

'Yeah. Not wild about them, though.'

'Horses?'

'They're unpredictable. Not like an engine.'

Rose nods in agreement, as if she knows anything at all about either horses or engines.

'You said you and Maria were close?'

'Very.'

'Did she ever talk about going away? Travelling, I mean?'

'Sure, when she was younger—just outta high school. She used to talk about going overseas.'

'To . . .?'

'New York. Paris. The usual spots.'

'But then she married Nick.'

'He swept her off her feet with all his big ideas about organic wine and that. He loved her but I don't think he knew what to do with her.' He pauses to suck on his cigarette. 'I think she was fooling around.'

Rose waits for him to say more, but he doesn't.

'Do you know who with?' she prompts.

'No. But I could tell she was hiding something. She was cagey about where she was going, who she was with. I mean, why would she be like that if she didn't have something to hide? Her mate Anna probably knew.'

Rose tries to tread carefully. 'Could she and Anna have been involved?'

He looks at her sharply. 'Like, sexually?'

'Yeah.'

He shakes his head. 'Maria wasn't into that. At least, I don't think she was.'

Rose changes tack. 'What was it like growing up here? I used to come down here with my family when I was a kid—thought it was paradise.'

'I guess it was. Maria and I pretty much ran wild. We used to go into the park and pretend we were in Middle Earth.'

'I wouldn't have picked you for a Tolkien fan.'

Tony smiles. 'I got glandular fever when I was a kid and missed a lot of school. Mum wouldn't let me watch TV so I started reading. Have you read *Lord of the Rings*?'

'A long time ago.'

'It's really good.'

'Yes, it is.'

Rose likes Tony. She lets him run with his memories.

'Maria was always Galadriel, and I wanted to be Aragorn, but she made me be Frodo—or *Sam*!'

Suddenly, an idea occurs to Rose. 'Where in the park was your Middle Earth? Was there a special place?'

'Yeah, come to think of it.'

Rose nudges the pictures back towards Tony and he picks them up, going through them more slowly from the beginning. Then he stops, takes a closer look at one of the pictures.

'Whaddya know . . .'

He scrapes the butt of his cigarette against the leg of the chair to put it out, then carefully puts it in his pocket instead of tossing it on the ground.

130

'This one.' He picks up one of the shots of the bush and holds it out for Rose to see.

There's a rocky outcrop with a tree growing on top, its branches dangling below the rock, obscuring whatever might be behind it. Kangaroo vines are tangled with the branches of the tree.

'Do you recognise it?' Rose tries to keep the excitement out of her voice.

He taps the photo with his finger. 'It's changed . . . but it could be the place.'

'Tell me about it.'

He looks back at the photo. 'If this is where I'm thinking of, there's a little cave behind the vines. We used to play there for hours.'

Rose bites her lip. 'Do you think you could show me where it is on a map?'

'Sure.'

Tony leads her into the front office. The white-haired man is still sitting behind the desk, and he watches suspiciously as Tony goes to an old wire rack full of maps. He selects one and opens it, spreading it across the desk. He takes a ballpoint from a chipped mug and marks a spot on the map.

Rose leans in to look.

'This is us, yeah?' he says.

Rose nods.

He draws a line along the road to a turn-off, follows a few twists and turns until he's deep in the heart of the forest.

'See this? It's a fire trail. Goes to Gunrock Creek. If there's still a trail here, follow it till you get to the overhanging rock. If there's cave behind those vines, you've found it.'

Driving home, Rose decides not to call DI Blackmore and tell him what Tony told her. She doesn't want to get a blast of his outrage when he hears that she harassed a member of Maria's family whom he had already questioned. And she suspects that an airy-fairy story about childhood make-believe games would only make him roll his eyes. The more she thinks about it, the more fanciful it seems. What Tony had told her wasn't evidence; it was a nice memory about his missing sister. And as all the studies about witness testimony showed, memories can be wildly distorted by time and emotional needs.

Rose decides not to follow up Tony's lead. And to reward her extraordinary self-restraint, she stops at the Gumnut Patisserie in Berrima and buys one of their chocolate eclairs. You can only restrain yourself so much.

SIXTEEN

The next morning, Rose is trawling through State Library of New South Wales records on behalf of a director for a documentary about Antarctic explorer Ernest Shackleton. Not for the first time, she is reminded of how lucky she is to be able to access the archives online. Before they were digitised, she would have had to spend days at the library, pressuring overworked librarians and navigating an out-of-date card catalogue to find one measly fact.

She soon finds what she's looking for: a crewmember's diary of Ernest Shackleton's ill-fated Antarctic expedition on the ship *Endurance*, in 1915. The diaries have been transcribed, but the record also contains photos of the actual diary pages, written in the man's own hand, there at the click of a mouse. Rose likes reading the text that way, sensing the hardship in the handwriting—the gradually increasing pressure of the crewmember's pencil as things on the ship go from bad to worse, and the journal's abrupt end when the ship is consumed by the ice.

Even though Rose has been asked to find information solely about Shackleton and that voyage, she finds herself reading more than she needs to, feeding her hunger to find out what happened to the people at the periphery of big historical events.

When she stops mid-morning to make a cup of tea, Bob gives her his let's-go-to-the-park look. She'd wanted to get more work done before heading out, but she finds it hard to say no to Bob.

She pulls on her coat, grabs Bob's lead, and is reaching into her bag for her car keys when she feels the envelope of photos. She opens it and looks at the top picture—the one that might be where Tony and Maria used to play *Lord of the Rings*. Last night, Rose had convinced herself that it couldn't have been the same place, that Tony was projecting fond memories onto a random bush scene. There was nothing to investigate—and if there was, she should leave it to the professionals.

On the other hand, what if there *is* a cave behind the kangaroo vines and it *is* a place that Maria knew and loved? Maybe she took someone there and that someone took the pictures. Maybe it was Anna. And if so, maybe there was some trace of them in the cave that could lead to answers about what happened.

As she gets in her car, Rose ignores Blackmore's voice in her head telling her not to interfere, and persuades herself that she's just going for a walk in the great outdoors.

With Tony's map on the seat beside her, Rose drives along the route he sketched and parks at the entrance to the fire trail leading to Gunrock Creek. She grabs the map and lets Bob out. She had promised Blackmore she wouldn't walk alone in the bush, and she's not: she has Bob.

'Sorry, fella, I need to keep you close. It is a national park, after all,' she says guiltily as she attaches the lead to his collar.

It's a cold, grey day, but the bush feels alive as Rose and Bob set off along the dirt track. She has the map open and the photographs out, looking for a match between the pictures and the wilderness around her.

Bob yanks on the lead occasionally when he catches a whiff of something enticing like possum poo, but Rose keeps him at her side. They've been walking for around twenty minutes when she stops.

Off to the left is a vista including a distinctive tree branch with an unusual twist running parallel then down to the ground. She thumbs through the pictures, finds the photo. She hadn't noticed it before, but there it is: the tree branch with the unusual twist pointing downwards. Pushing away the thought that there are doubtless thousands upon thousands of branches in the park with unusual twists, she allows herself to hope that this tree could be the one in the picture. Rose's heart beats a little faster.

Sensing her excitement, Bob bounds ahead, Rose accelerating to keep pace. After a while, she slows down. 'Hold on, Bob.' He stops and sniffs at a mound of busy ants. She checks the map. It shouldn't be much further—the rocky outcrop, the vines, the cave. She keeps walking, carefully checking the photos and her surroundings.

According to Tony's map, the outcrop is off to the right, and he'd said it should be visible from the trail, but that was twenty years ago. Rose and Bob walk on until they reach the edge of a cliff—the end of the track.

Rose keeps Bob well back from the edge and looks out at the view. In distant valleys she can see farmland and a winding road with what from her vantage point looks like a toy truck following its curves.

'I think Tony's Middle Earth cave must have been somewhere else, Bob. Thank God I didn't tell Blackmore about it and make an even bigger fool of myself.'

She puts the map and photos into her pocket and nudges Bob around for the walk back. This time, Rose has her phone out, taking her own pictures. Giant tree ferns, eucalypts, banksia and bottlebrush are all home to birds that seem more vocal than usual, probably warning each other about the human on the loose accompanied by a large, silly-looking dog.

Rose stops to take pictures of a black cockatoo with yellow tail feathers perched regally on the branch of a young gum. She inches closer, snapping away, and when she gets too close, the bird lifts off the branch and flies away through a tangle of kangaroo vines. Rose looks at the picture she took. She likes it, with the bird slightly blurry as it flew from the branch.

And then she looks again at the scene behind the bird. She looks up to where the cockatoo sat on the branch. The surrounding tangle of kangaroo vines obscures a rocky outcrop that wasn't visible when she was walking from the other direction. But now, heading back, the new angle gives her a view she didn't have before. She takes out the photo from the envelope and holds it up.

She's found it.

Her heart hammering in her chest, Rose is deciding what to do when Bob suddenly bolts. His lead is torn from her grasp as he races away through the vines.

'Bob! *No!*'

Terrified that Bob will disappear into the bush, Rose fights her way through the kangaroo vines, struggling against the amazingly strong hold of the twisting, bending stalks that seem to leap from the ground, clinging to higher and higher branches.

'Bob, come!'

But she still can't see him as she reaches the rocky outcrop that looms above her. She stops. Listens. Hears a scraping sound.

Then Rose steps around the outcrop and there it is: the cave.

It's small but dry and protected, and Rose can imagine that to children like Maria and Tony it was big, inviting, mysterious.

Bob is at the deepest recess, digging in the dirt—the scraping sound she'd heard.

Rose enters the cave, grabs his lead and tries to pull him back from whatever has tantalised him, but he's resisting, which is unusual.

'Leave it, Bob!' she orders.

She seizes him around the chest to pull him back, then looks down to see what he'd found so interesting.

With his front paws, the dog has dug a small trench. Peering more closely, she realises that besides dirt, there's something in the trench.

It looks like fabric.

Rose can't move, can't breathe. It's only Bob struggling to break free that gets her moving. She wants to run, but she needs to be sure. Maybe it's not fabric, but a leaf or a feather. She drags Bob out of the cave and ties his lead to a scribbly gum.

'Sit! Stay.'

He stays, but he's not happy. And he's not sitting.

Rose finds a sturdy stick and goes back into the cave. With the end of the stick, she carefully scrapes the dirt from whatever it is in the trench.

It *is* a scrap of fabric—faded blue. It might be denim.

With the stick, she peels the fabric aside, revealing something hard beneath. It's pale yellow. And then she realises what it is.

Rose stumbles out of the cave and takes out her phone. She hits Blackmore's number but nothing happens. She stares at the screen. No reception.

Bob starts to howl; he can feel Rose's distress. She unties him and they scramble back through the vines to the trail. And then they run.

Rose is shivering when she reaches the car. She opens the rear door and lets Bob in. He watches from the back seat as she looks at her phone. One bar. She calls Blackmore. It rings a while before he answers, sounding like a man whose patience has worn thin.

'Hello, Rose.'

'I found something. I found the place . . . in the pictures of Maria.' Her voice is trembling, the words tumbling out too fast. 'There's some fabric, and what might be . . . a bone.'

'Where are you, Rose?' he asks urgently.

She tells him.

'Get in your car, lock the doors and wait. I'm on my way.'

It seems to Rose that it takes forever, but eventually Blackmore and Constable Tran arrive. Rose gets out of her car and Blackmore goes to her.

'Are you all right?'

'Yes, I'm just . . . it's a shock. Do you think—'

'Rose,' Blackmore interrupts, his voice calm, 'I want you to take me through what happened.'

'Okay.' Rose explains about meeting Tony, his story of playing *Lord of the Rings* with Maria as kids, Bob digging in the cave, and what she'd found. She hands him the map and the photograph, apologising for having done all this herself.

'It's okay, Rose. I'm going to ask Constable Tran to drive you home now.'

Rose looks at the young constable with relief. 'Thank you. I'm not sure I'm up to driving.'

'We'll get a statement from you later,' Blackmore tells her.

'Okay.'

'For now, I need you to keep this to yourself. I'm sure you understand.'

'Of course.'

Deb smiles reassuringly at Rose. 'Why don't you give me your keys?'

Rose tries to stop the keys from rattling as she places them in the constable's small but steady hand.

'Are these heated seats?' Deb asks.

It takes a moment for Rose to disconnect from the mental image of the yellowed bone protruding from the ground.

'Sorry?'

'These seats? Are they heated?'

Deb must be trying to distract her from what she found in the cave, Rose realises. 'Yes, Constable.'

'Deb.'

'Yes, Deb. They're heated.'

'So you lived in Sydney before this?'

'Yes,' Rose says. 'In Glebe.'

'I'm from Cabramatta.'

Something stirs in Rose. Curiosity. 'Really? Were you born there?'

And as they wind their way back through the bush to the main road, Rose learns all about Deb's family and their journey from Vietnam after the war. It's a fascinating story, but every once in a while Rose's mind drifts back to the young woman buried in a cave where she once pretended to be Galadriel.

Rose is relieved to get home, but when she lets Bob out of the car she is reminded of him digging in the cave, the fabric, the bone. She shivers.

'Would you like a cup of tea?' she asks Deb, reluctant to be alone.

'Sure. I have to wait for someone from the station to pick me up anyway.'

Rose is glad the cottage is still warm. She lays another log on the embers of that morning's fire and turns on the lamps.

'Do you want me to make the tea?' Deb asks.

'No, thanks, it'll do me good to keep busy.'

Rose makes a pot of strong tea and brings it into the lounge room, where Deb and Bob are playing tug-of-war with one of Rose's slippers.

'Bob's awesome,' Deb says.

'Yes he is.'

Rose pours the tea into mugs and they sit back and watch the fire.

'It's so quiet here!'

'I know. Everyone thinks I'm crazy to live out here on my own.'

'I think it's great,' Deb says. 'I live in a share house. Never lived alone. It sounds like heaven.'

'Yeah—no one to fight with over the remote.'

'Or whose turn it is to buy milk!'

'Yes! But sometimes it gets a little lonely.'

'I bet,' Deb says, and Rose likes her matter-of-fact appraisal of things.

Deb is looking around the cosy room appreciatively. 'Have you read all these books?' she asks, gesturing to the bookcase.

'Yes. You're welcome to borrow some, if you like.'

Deb gets up and scans the shelves. 'I like stories about murder.' Then she covers her mouth with her hand and turns to Rose. 'Shit, sorry.'

'That's okay. I like stories about murder too. When they're fictional.'

Rose gets up and goes to stand beside Deb at the bookcase. She takes out a mystery set in the Shetland Islands and gives it to the constable.

'If you like it, I have the other seven books in the series.'

Deb gazes at the book cover. 'This looks cool!'

Rose smiles. 'It is.'

Deb's phone pings, and she glances out the window. A police van is waiting.

'You gonna be okay?' she asks.

'Yes, and thank you for keeping me from falling apart.'

It's dark by the time Rose feeds Bob and pours herself a glass of wine. After a few steadying sips, she calls Kim.

'Feel like a few days in the country?' Rose asks, trying to sound normal when her sister answers.

Kim reads her right away. 'What's happened?'

Rose suddenly feels tears welling up. She can't speak.

'Rose? Rose!'

When Rose finds her voice, it sounds strangled. 'I'm okay.'

'What's going on?!'

Rose takes a deep breath. 'I'm not supposed to tell anyone.'

'Fuck that—I'm not anyone.'

'Of course you're not.' And Rose tells Kim about Tony, and the cave—and the bone.

'I'm coming down right now,' Kim declares.

'No, honestly, you don't need to do that. I'd rather have a day or two to myself to . . . to absorb it all. And if you're coming on the weekend, it'll give me something to look forward to.'

'Do you really?'

'Do I really what?'

'Look forward to me coming down?'

'Of course I do!'

'Good. Sometimes I think you see me as a massive pain.'

'Well you are, Kimmie, but that doesn't mean I can live without you.'

Later that night, Rose is nestled in bed under the doona with Bob lying at her feet. It's an especially cold night, and her little bedroom is the furthest room from the pot-bellied stove, so she really feels it. She's thinking of buying an electric heater, just for really cold nights. She had hoped to see out the winter with just the wood burner, but remembering how cosy George's place was with its central heating *and* a raging fire in the fireplace, she suspects she'll need something to supplement her little stove. And winter has only just begun.

She's losing herself in an Adam Dalgliesh mystery when her phone rings and she jumps a foot in the air. She looks at the screen. It's Joe Blackmore. She answers.

'Rose, I hope I'm not ringing too late. I wanted to check on you and also let you know where we're at.'

'Thank you.' Rose is surprised and touched. 'Constable Tran was wonderful.'

'She's a good cop. Listen, you need to come into the station tomorrow to make a statement. You'll be meeting with a homicide detective from Goulburn, Detective Chief Inspector Al Addison.'

'Will you be there?' Rose could do with his moral support.

'Yes, I'll be working under the DCI,' he says. 'We believe you found the remains of Maria Aboud. The remnants of cloth appear to match what she was wearing when she was last seen.'

'My God.'

'Her family has been notified,' Blackmore says, 'but not the public—although the media know that human remains were found.'

Rose feels a sudden urge to confess. 'I told my sister.'

There's a pause.

'Okay,' he says at last. 'But don't tell anyone else. Not until we've taken your statement.'

'I promise.'

'And we probably won't be able to keep your name out of the news,' he warns.

'Shit. Can't you say the . . . the remains were found by a dog walker? Isn't that what they always say? And it's true!'

'Rose, I'm afraid you were seen by someone when Constable Tran drove you home. The guy told Jazzy Nolan. Apparently, they're mates.'

'You're kidding.'

'I'm not.'

Rose sighs, suddenly more exhausted than she's ever been in her life.

'So, can you come to the station at nine?'

'I'll be there.'

SEVENTEEN

Rose doesn't get much sleep, and what she does get is shallow and unnourishing. In the morning, she feels battered and drained. She turns on her phone and sees two missed calls from Sam. She FaceTimes him and he picks up right away.

'Mum!'

'Sweetheart, sorry, my phone was off.'

'Auntie Kim told me—'

'She wasn't supposed to tell anyone!'

'Are you okay? You must be freaked out.'

'I'm fine, just *really* tired.'

Rose gets out of bed and heads to the kitchen. She sits the phone on the bench as she makes a cup of tea.

'You're in shock.'

'It was so awful. That poor woman.'

'I know I already asked, but do you want me to come home?'

'What? No! Kim's coming down on the weekend. And finding the . . . remains was actually a good thing.'

'Really?'

Rose explains what Blackmore told her: that they were most likely Maria's. 'At least her family can stop wondering whether she's alive and had abandoned them.'

'I guess.'

144

'And I'm not an expert like you, but from what I saw, she was buried in that cave a long time ago. It's not like it just happened and the killer is hanging around.' Unless he is, she adds mentally.

'So I shouldn't worry.'

Rose takes a sip of tea. 'No, that's my job.'

Sam's face relaxes into a lopsided grin.

'Speaking of your expertise, how's it going?' Rose asks.

'Good. I love going on the digs. Getting filthy, the suspense. You know: will this be a Viking crown? It could be!'

Rose smiles. 'So then, nothing's changed since you were five.' She remembers how much he loved getting dirty as a kid. Finding 'treasure', even if it was just an old bottle cap.

He laughs. 'Exactly.'

Rose sees the time on her phone.

'I should go—I have to be at the police station at nine to make a statement.'

'Let me know how it goes.'

'I will.'

'Love you, Mum.'

'I love you too, Sam.'

When she hangs up, she realises she feels better for having talked to her son. With all the energy she had spent over the years taking care of him, she hadn't realised how much he could give back just when she needed it.

Rose takes a short, hot shower, gets dressed and decides she'll have enough time to take Bob to the dog park before meeting DCI Addison. She hopes he's as accepting of her amateur sleuthing as Blackmore seems to have become.

Bob isn't on the lead when they leave the cottage, so she's unprepared when he bounds off towards Jazzy Nolan and the photographer with the man bun, who are waiting in the front garden.

'Bob!' Rose calls out, too late, as he jumps up playfully, knocking Jazzy flat on her back. Rose runs to grab the dog as the photographer helps the young reporter to her feet.

'I'm so sorry,' Rose says. 'Are you all right?'

Jazzy is brushing dirt off her leather jacket. She asks the photographer, 'Did you get that?'

He looks at her sheepishly. Jazzy flashes him a dirty look.

'Bob was excited,' Rose says. 'He's harmless really.'

'Not if he knocks people over.'

Rose suddenly realises she has the upper hand here. 'Well, you were trespassing, and as my guard dog, Bob was making sure you hadn't come here to attack me.'

Jazzy blinks. Rose can see she knows it's a stalemate.

The reporter puts on a smile. 'Look, Rose, we're just here to find out what happened in your own words. We want your take on things.'

Rose gets her keys out and unlocks her car, letting Bob climb on the back seat.

'I'm not allowed to say anything,' Rose says, adding a sarcastic, 'Sorry.'

The photographer snaps away as Rose gets in the car, until Jazzy punches his arm to make him stop.

A needle-like sleet is keeping most dog owners at home, so Bob has the park almost to himself. They only stay for a little while, but he gets to zoom up and down the hills like he owns the place. He's become a bit wary of some of the cattle dogs who come to the park and seem to mistake him for a sheep, nipping at his hindquarters as he runs away, but today he's free to tear around the park with impunity.

At five minutes to nine, Rose pulls into the police car park and leaves Bob snoozing in the back seat, the windows open just enough to let in some of the frigid air. She looks up at Blackmore's window, but no one's there.

As Rose hurries up the steps to the sliding doors, a couple of photographers who'd been lurking outside start snapping pictures. She tries to keep her head down without looking too much like the accused.

When Rose enters the police station, she sees an unfamiliar constable behind the counter dealing with a woman in tears. Rose doesn't want to interrupt, but it's close to nine and she is worried about making a poor impression on DCI Addison. Rose has just taken out her phone, thinking that she'll call Deb or Blackmore to tell them she's here, when she feels a hand on her back.

'This way, Rose.'

Blackmore steers her past the desk and into the inner sanctum. The pressure of his hand on her back is comforting. And more. She's forced to admit that in spite of her efforts *not* to be attracted to this man, she is. It's hard to fight chemistry, even though she's sure the chemistry only goes one way.

'DCI Addison will be here shortly,' Blackmore says as they enter an interview room.

'I hope he's nice.'

'I'm not here to be nice to you, Ms McHugh—you're here to be nice to *me*.'

A white-haired woman in her late fifties with gold-rimmed glasses and a sharp suit has followed them in and sits in the chair opposite Rose. She lays a thick file on the table.

'I'm DCI Addison.'

'Oh, sorry, I wasn't . . .' Rose falls silent as Blackmore, sliding into the seat beside his superior, subtly shakes his head.

'Expecting a woman?' Addison finishes. 'Sorry to disappoint.' She speaks very fast, as if trying to make the most of her time, suggesting that this interview is probably a waste of it.

'No,' Rose goes on, 'I'm not disappointed, in fact I'm—'

'What?' Addison snaps. 'Glad I'm a woman because I'll go easier on you?' Her look says she won't. 'Full name and address?'

'Rose Mc—'

'You don't mind if we record the interview, do you?'

'No, that's fine.'

Addison nods at Blackmore, who turns on the recorder and states the date and the names of those present. Rose feels nervous, guilty, confused. Addison and Blackmore are staring at her.

'Address?' Addison asks.

Rose gives her address and phone number.

'Why did you move to the Southern Highlands?' Addison asks.

Rose is thrown. She glances at Blackmore.

'Don't look at him, he doesn't know why you moved here.'

'Well, it started with . . . the foliage. We used to drive down from Sydney to look at the autumn leaves when I was a kid.'

Addison is looking at her as if that's the dumbest thing she's ever heard.

Rose feels a rising anger and it gives her clarity. 'I've always wanted to live here. I like it. I live with my dog and I work from home.'

'Why did you buy Anna Taradash's house?'

'Because it was perfect—just outside Berrima, in the bush, on a little creek. It has a pot-bellied stove and wooden floors and—'

'I get the picture,' Addison says, making no attempt to keep the condescension out of her voice, as if Rose's chocolate-box fantasy is pathetic. 'So you didn't buy the house to gain access to the garden?'

Rose isn't sure what she means. 'No. I mean, I like the garden, but it's actually a lot of work, and—'

'Or what was buried in the garden?'

Rose looks back and forth between Addison and Blackmore. 'You mean the film?'

'That's right, Rose.' Like she's an idiot. 'The film that conveniently led you to the body of a woman who's been missing for six years.'

'There was nothing convenient about it.' Rose has developed a profound dislike for Addison in an incredibly short amount of time. 'I just happened to find the film when I was replanting after—'

'Yes, yes, I've read the report.' She extracts a piece of paper from the thick file in front of her and glances at it. 'You claimed that someone unknown put newspaper into your plumbing system, so the garden had to be dug up. Were you hoping the plumber would find the film and, when he didn't, you had to keep digging?'

Rose is speechless. She looks at Blackmore for help but his expression tells her he has little power to intercede.

'We believe the damage to my plumbing system was caused by Ray Mullin.'

'Ah yes.' Addison nods, and reaches into the file for another report. 'Mr Mullin made a complaint, claiming that you ran into him and then verbally abused him on a main thoroughfare.'

Rose's eyes widen in outrage. 'Look, DCI Addison, I don't know where you're getting your information, but—'

'From an eyewitness,' the police officer says smoothly. 'A Mrs Wilczynski, who was passing on foot at the time.'

'If that's the old lady with the shopping trolley, she ran off! Mullin must have found her later and pressured her to back up his story.'

'Or, you were familiar with Mr Mullin's criminal record and thought he'd be the right man to run into and claim for damages.'

'Do I need a lawyer?'

'You tell me, Rose: do you think you need a lawyer?'

Rose takes a deep breath and decides the best way to handle this is with reason, if she can muster it.

'I do not need a lawyer because I have done nothing wrong except try to help a police inquiry that was going nowhere.' She tries not to look at Blackmore, hoping she hasn't burned that bridge. 'I found the film accidentally and was curious about what was on it, so I had it developed. As soon as I found out there were pictures of a missing woman, I took them to the police.'

Addison appraises Rose and nods, seeming to accept this version of events. For now.

'All right,' she says. 'What made you go to see Anna Taradash before the police had a chance to interview her?'

Rose sighs, realising she's going to be here for a while.

When Rose finally returns to her car two and a half hours later, Bob is sitting up in the back seat looking concerned. Or maybe he just needs to pee. Rose lets him out and he relieves himself on the nature strip. She looks over her shoulder to make sure

DCI Addison isn't watching through a window, intent on busting her for having an unleashed dog.

'Back in the car, Bob.'

Bob obediently hops back in and Rose makes her escape. Which is what it feels like as she drives home slightly over the speed limit, relieved to be out of that stifling little room and away from DCI Addison's questions.

The chief inspector had made Rose describe every single incident in her life that was even remotely connected to either Anna Taradash or Maria Aboud. And things that weren't connected. She asked about Rose's work, about her income, about her 'contacts' in the Highlands, as if she were part of some criminal network that used national parks to hide the bodies of its victims.

On the other hand, Rose can't blame her. Both Anna and Maria's bodies had been found in the park. But the absurdity of Rose being involved or responsible for any of this seemed to be lost on the DCI.

The thing that bothered her the most was the warning implicit in Addison's final words. She had said Rose must not interfere *any further* in police investigations. How could it be described as interference when she helped the police with a cold case?

Unless they thought Rose wasn't entirely innocent.

As the day progresses, the weather closes in, the sleet falling hard and steadily on the corrugated-iron roof. It sounds like someone dumping buckets of nails overhead.

Rose is watching TV in the lounge room under a yellow mohair blanket that was a house-warming present from Kim. Bob is asleep next to her, his chin resting on her knee.

Rose is immersed in a mystery series set in Northumberland whose hero is a frumpy female detective with a past full of demons and no time for bullshit.

Her phone rings. She almost doesn't bother to look at the caller ID, having just spoken to Kim and filled her in, but when she sees George's name, she answers.

'Hi, sorry, I should have called you.'

'Don't apologise! I just wanted to see if I can do anything.'

'Thanks, George, but no. I assume you saw the news?'

'Yes, and I was asked to go in and speak to that DCI Addison. Very unpleasant woman.'

Alarm bells start clanging in Rose's head. 'What? Why did she want to speak to you?'

'To find out what I knew about your movements.'

Rose is shocked into silence for a second then she bursts out laughing.

'Rose?'

But Rose can't stop laughing no matter how hard she tries. Finally, she gets control of herself.

'Sorry! It's the exhaustion,' Rose says. 'It sounded like they were asking what you knew about my bowel movements.'

Now George is laughing and it sets Rose off again. By the time they calm down, Rose is feeling better.

'I'm too tired to talk now, George, but let's get a coffee tomorrow and debrief.'

'Good plan. Sleep well.'

Rose turns her phone to silent, and watches as the TV detective delivers a devastating comeback to a suspect who thought he could intimidate her because she was a woman. Rose decides to prepare some devastating comebacks in case she ever comes across Al Addison again.

EIGHTEEN

The next day, Rose and George huddle next to the heater at Manna, their hands wrapped around mugs of coffee, discussing their close encounters with the DCI.

'Apparently her first name is Alice,' George says, 'but she goes by Al.'

'Do you think she enjoys acting so tough?'

'Possibly. But she's probably had to become tough in what is no doubt an aggressively male environment.'

'You're right. But I'm not going to feel sorry for her.'

'No. Maybe it's all a performance and she just plays bad cop to get people to confess to every small sin they've committed in their lives.'

'Well it didn't work with me. I found myself wanting to hide things from her. I wanted to say it was none of her business why I moved here or why I dug up my garden or why I had those pictures developed.'

'I was the opposite,' George says. 'I was ready to tell her that when I was twelve I took a pound note from my mother's purse to buy cigarettes. But she didn't ask.'

Rose smiles.

Beth comes out to check on them. She has been unfailingly friendly ever since Grace broke the ice. 'You guys want another coffee?'

'Not for me, Beth,' Rose says.

'No worries.' She begins to clear a nearby table. 'And don't listen to the trolls, Rose,' she says over her shoulder. 'They're losers.'

Rose stares at her. 'What trolls?'

Beth sets the plates and cups back on the table and, taking her phone from her pocket, opens Instagram. She goes to Rose's account, which she'd started following after Rose left a big tip when Beth started heating up the cinnamon buns.

She holds out her phone to show Rose's latest post: the sign in the park about the Gundungurra people.

Rose takes her phone and reads the first few comments.

White women are dead and you post pictures about abos, you cunt
Fucking moll
See you in jail

Rose gasps. 'I didn't see these.'

'You must have notifications turned off,' Beth says. 'Don't read them.'

But Rose can't help herself.

Very convenient you knew where the bodies were buried

Dumbfounded, Rose looks up at George and Beth, her eyes wet with tears.

'What do I do?'

'Delete them,' Beth says. 'Block the trolls.'

'But how—'

'Give me your phone,' Beth orders.

Rose gratefully fishes her phone out of her bag and hands it to Beth, who starts tapping the screen.

'I'm making your account private, but you should go through your followers and delete any that look dodgy.' She hands Rose's phone back to her. 'Social media's a shitshow.'

'Thank you, Beth, I hadn't even thought . . .'

'No worries.'

Beth scoops up the dishes from the other table and whisks them into the kitchen.

'I can't believe this,' says Rose.

'And you wonder why I don't like people,' George says. He leans down and strokes Cordelia's head. 'Animals are the only innocents.'

As if sensing Rose looking at him, Bob's head pops up from under the table and he tolerates her urgent hug with his usual good nature.

Rose makes it through the next couple of days by busying herself with work, trips to the dog park and bingeing British mysteries on TV.

She's relieved when Friday comes. Having left the city straight after school, Kim arrives in time for dinner.

The kitchen is lit with candles, and a Bach cello suite is playing on the radio. Bob is snoozing in the corner. Rose tosses steaming spaghetti in pesto sauce while Kim opens a bottle of wine and fills their glasses. When Rose takes a steaming, crispy loaf of garlic bread out of the oven, Kim moans.

'I'm going to eat that entire loaf.'

'Are you sure it's good enough for you?' Rose teases. 'I bought the bread locally.'

'Now, now. I've conceded the point that you can get decent food down here. It's the psychotic killers you have to worry about.'

Rose sighs.

'Sorry,' Kim says, and it's clear from her voice she means it. 'But just to get the subject out of the way, is there any update?'

They sit down.

'All I know is that the . . . the remains are definitely Maria's. But they haven't made an arrest, or George would have told me.'

'How is George connected?'

'He's not, but he's filtering the news for me. I can't face it.'

'Good idea. I wish someone would do that for me. All I want to know is whether JLo is still with what's-his-name.'

Rose smiles as she serves the pasta.

Suddenly Bob's head pops up, on alert. Rose and Kim look at him. He gets up and trots out of the room. Rose and Kim look at each other.

There's a knock at the front door.

'Are you expecting anyone?' Kim asks in a low voice.

Rose shakes her head. She gets up and doesn't stop Kim when she gets up too, just in case the social media trolls have decided to visit her at home.

Bob is waiting at the front door as Rose arrives, Kim close behind her.

'Who is it?' Rose asks through the closed door, trying to sound tough.

'It's Joe, Rose . . . Joe Blackmore.'

Rose and Kim exchange a quick look before Rose opens the door.

'Come in.'

Blackmore enters and greets Bob. 'I called and you didn't answer, so I—'

'You were worried,' says Kim, stepping forward. 'I'm Kim, Rose's sister.'

She extends her hand and Blackmore shakes it.

'Nice to meet you, Kim.'

'I turned my phone off,' Rose explains to Blackmore. She turns to Kim. 'Why don't you get started?'

'Sure.' Kim heads off to the kitchen.

'I'm sorry to interrupt your dinner,' the detective says.

'That's okay, it's just spaghetti.'

'Don't say "just spaghetti" to an Italian.'

'You're Italian?'

'On my mum's side. I wanted to thank you for finding Maria. If you hadn't got Tony reminiscing, we wouldn't have found her in a million years.'

'I like getting people to tell their stories.'

'You should be a cop.'

'I think people open up to me because I'm *not* a cop. I'm the least scary person alive.'

'I don't know about that. You gave Al Addison a run for her money.'

'But I didn't scare her.'

'I don't think anything does.'

Kim appears from the kitchen. 'Are you sure you wouldn't like a bite to eat, Detective? Rose makes a mean pesto.'

He smiles. 'Does she?'

'I add chilli,' Rose babbles. 'Lemon zest . . .'

Blackmore nods, impressed. 'It sounds great, but I'm afraid I can't join you.'

He turns towards the door.

'Thank you for coming, Detective.'

'Please, call me Joe. Goodnight, Rose.'

And he's gone.

Rose closes the door behind him, and she and Kim return to the table.

157

'I knew he was hot,' Kim says, 'but I didn't know he'd be like, God of Thunder hot.'

Rose laughs as she tears off a piece of garlic bread. 'It's the voice. But he's a happily married man, so nothing will ever happen. I'll have to start looking further afield.' Unexpectedly, Irish Dave, the real estate agent, pops into her head. He'd flirted with her the last time she saw him, and she'd wondered if he might call to ask her out. Hadn't there been a little spark? Maybe he'd decided that it would be inappropriate since she'd been his client.

Kim, meanwhile, is still focused on DI Blackmore.

'And you really like his wife?' she probes.

'She's kind, smart, fun.'

'How's her health?' Kim asks.

'Don't even joke.'

'Sorry. You know me. I see a line, I cross it.'

Rose shakes her head but laughs. 'I would be sorry if you didn't.'

'I hope you mean that.'

Rose and Kim polish off a bottle of wine then sway off to their respective bedrooms. That night the temperature plummets.

The next morning, just before dawn, Rose is asleep under the doona, Bob lying at the end of the bed across her feet, when Kim comes tearing into the room, waking them up.

'What's wrong?' Rose asks, her voice croaky from sleep.

Kim slides under the covers and snuggles close to Rose. 'What's wrong is it's fucking freezing!'

Rose remembers. 'Shit. I forgot to put some wood on the fire before we went to bed.'

Kim is shivering, teeth chattering. 'Why don't you just turn on the heat?'

'I don't have a heater.'

'You *what*?! You live in fucking Antarctica and you don't have a heater? Thank God I'm here.'

Later that morning, after strong coffee and bacon and egg rolls at Manna, Rose and Kim head to a hardware store to look at heaters.

Kim has her eye on a big, fancy one with a remote control, while Rose is looking at a humbler version. 'What's wrong with this one?' Rose asks.

'It's sad.'

'But that one's two hundred dollars more.'

'And worth every cent,' Kim says.

Rose is considering the fancier option when Kim taps her on the arm.

'Isn't that . . .'

Rose looks up just as Grace, who's further down the aisle, sees her.

'Grace!'

'Rose,' Grace says warmly as she comes towards them and gathers Rose into a hug. 'I'm so sorry you had to go through that awful experience.'

'Thanks. When I close my eyes I keep seeing the cave and—'

'I meant being interviewed by Al Addison. What a piece of work that woman is. Good at her job, apparently, but a massive bitch.'

Kim laughs appreciatively and Grace turns to her. 'I'm Grace. And from the resemblance, I'm guessing you're Rose's sister.'

'Yes. Kim.' They shake hands. 'I've heard wonderful things about you.'

'Rose is far too glowing in her assessments of other people.'

'Always has been,' Kim says.

'We're picking out a heater for my place,' Rose says. 'Kim doesn't think my old wood burner is up to the job.'

'I'm sure she's right,' Grace says as she looks back and forth between the two heaters under consideration and points to Kim's choice. 'This one. The other is a bit sad-looking.'

Kim laughs and nods at Rose.

'I'm getting some paint,' Grace explains. 'I've been meaning to do the bathroom for the last ten years or so. The mould is finally starting to talk back.'

'Well, I'll see you at Manna soon,' Rose says. 'We'll grab a coffee.'

'And cinnamon buns. Lovely to meet you, Kim.'

'You too,' Kim says sincerely. She turns to Rose. 'What a delightful woman.'

'I know, right?' Rose says.

'Hate to say this, Rosie, but that is stiff competition.'

'I'm not competing.'

'But if you were, you wouldn't stand a chance.'

'Thanks for your support.' Rose leans down to pick up the expensive heater and heads to the check-out.

That night, Rose and Kim have George over for dinner. Rose is excited: it's the first time she's entertained someone other than Kim at the cottage. She bakes salmon and asparagus in lemon and butter, with potatoes dauphinois (she suspects all that butter and cream will be right up George's alley), and for dessert serves a lemon tart she bought from Gumnut. Kim had insisted on supplying the wine, which turns out to be several bottles of a fancy Italian pinot grigio. With a roaring fire and good music in the background, the cottage has never looked more welcoming, and Rose is gratified by George's appreciative comments as she shows him around.

By the time George is picked up in a taxi close to midnight, Rose is feeling happy and has pushed the grim events from earlier in the week to the back of her mind. She's washing up while Kim dries, having agreed that it would be too depressing to face dirty dishes in the morning.

'I don't know if this is the right time . . .' Kim starts. 'But maybe it is.'

'Oh God,' Rose says. 'I couldn't drink a whisky, Kimmie.'

'No,' Kim says, slurring slightly. 'Not that. I was gonna say, have you thought about coming back to Sydney?'

'Actually,' Rose says, 'I want to see that exhibition at the little gallery in Paddington. You know, the one with the bird photographs.'

'No, Rose, I mean, with everything that's happened . . . come on. You've given it a red-hot go.'

'What are you talking about?' Rose asks, pretending she doesn't understand what Kim is driving at.

'Rose, I know you love this cottage, but it's in the middle of nowhere.'

'Stop—'

'Within a month of moving here you were the last person to talk to a woman who was found dead the next day—'

'Two days later,' Rose corrects her.

'—and then you found the remains of another woman,' Kim continues, her voice growing louder, 'who had been murdered in a bloody cave!'

Bob, agitated by the raised voices, comes in and starts to bark. Rose stares at Kim, then goes to Bob and gives him a scratch. 'It's all right,' she says in a soothing voice. 'Aunty Kim has had too much to drink.'

Kim's expression hardens. 'Jesus, Rose. That's not the point.'

'Isn't it?'

'I'm sorry,' Kim says, her voice softer now. 'But I care about you.'

Rose puts the last of the wineglasses on the dish rack and turns to Kim.

'I'm not moving back to the city. And you drink too much.'

She walks away, leaving her sister standing in the kitchen with a wet tea towel in her hands.

The next morning, Rose is dreaming that she's in a shop, looking for a new dress, but they don't have the one she wants in her size. This is one version of a recurring dream in which she doesn't have enough money to buy the dress she wants, or they don't have it in her size, or the shop is about to close. Rose suspects this is not her subconscious mind telling her she needs a new dress, but rather it's an expression of the fact that, deep down, she never feels quite worthy, quite prepared.

She's still looking for that elusive dress when the dreamscape changes and suddenly the shop has an espresso machine. Rose can smell the strong, rich coffee.

She opens her eyes and flinches at the sight of Kim sitting at the end of the bed, hair wet from a shower, holding out a steaming mug.

'I didn't mean to scare you,' Kim says. 'I *did* mean to do something nice for a change, bring you coffee in bed, say good morning!' Kim smiles broadly in an uncharacteristically jolly way, and hands Rose the mug. 'Good morning.'

'Thank you,' Rose says, not mentioning that she prefers to start her day with something gentler, like tea. But the first sip of coffee changes her mind, and she's even more grateful when Kim puts a glass of water and two Panadol on the bedside table. 'Thank you,' Rose murmurs again.

'I'm sorry I told you to leave the Highlands.'

'I'm sorry I said you drink too much.'

'Well, I accept your apology, even though you were right: I do drink too much. But you were a bit mean about it.'

'I was, wasn't I? I was drunk too.'

'Maybe, but I think you were pissed off that I think it's my place to tell you how to live your life. I mean, if you want to live in some godforsaken, freezing-cold den of psychopathic killers, it is totally your right.'

Rose shakes her head. 'Please don't make me laugh—I'll spill coffee on the doona.'

'Anyway, I turned on the heater and there was still wood burning from last night, so the place is very toasty.'

'Jeez, you're chipper.'

'I'm excited. We're going to an antiques place in Bundanoon I heard about.'

'Are we?'

'Yeah, so take your Panadol, have a shower and get your arse in gear.'

'Actually, I wouldn't mind spending the day in bed reading and nibbling on leftovers.'

'Yeah,' Kim says tolerantly, 'but that's not gonna happen. C'mon, Rosie. It's a big world out there!' She swans out.

Rose is happier to get up than she thought she'd be, perhaps buoyed by Kim's apparent acceptance of Rose's choices. She hopes that someday, Kim will even celebrate those choices. Not everybody gets to live the life they've always dreamed of.

NINETEEN

The weeks pass, and winter officially has the Highlands in its jaws.

Rose now brings the heater into her room at night and leaves it on—very low, but just enough so that she won't be found dead, frozen like a plank under the doona, in the morning. She isn't thrilled about running the heater all night, because electricity isn't cheap, but firewood isn't either. And Kim was right—the heat from the stove isn't enough.

The trees that had so recently gleamed orange and red are now bare, their skeletal branches trembling in the cold wind from the south. The ground hardens overnight, the frost on the grass crunching under foot in the morning, and later, under the weak sun, melting into mud. Visits to the dog park these days end with Rose towelling Bob off vigorously before he's allowed to get into the car, and at home she rushes him straight into a bath, which he whines about as if she's skinning him alive.

After one particularly cold and muddy trip to the dog park, Rose is on the verge of going straight home when she is tempted instead by the prospect of a hot, frothy flat white and a cinnamon bun. George wasn't at the park, and the cold has cut the number of people willing to sit outside, but when Rose arrives at Manna she's happy to take a table alone next to the blazing heater.

After ordering from Beth, who's wearing a pink beanie and an oversized puffer coat, Rose glances at the noticeboard the cafe has recently put up. There's a flyer inviting locals to join the Moss Vale Seniors Choir, one for knitting classes, and a notice advertising an auction of the sculpture of Anna Taradash.

'You should come.'

Rose turns to see Grace, her red hair backlit by the winter sun, looking glamorous in her purple coat.

'Hi!' Rose says. 'Are you staying for coffee?'

'I will if you let me sit with you near the heater.'

'Of course! I already ordered. I got a cinnamon bun, which I am happy to share.'

Grace orders a coffee from Beth while Rose pulls Bob closer to give Grace more room.

'I really should go easy on the cinnamon buns,' Rose says. 'I tried to get into my skinny jeans last week and couldn't get them over my thighs.'

'Ah, but you see, the fault there lies with the jeans, not your thighs.'

'If only that were true.'

Rose looks back at the notice for Anna's art auction. 'I think I *will* go. I only saw a few of her sculptures the one time I went to her house, but I thought they were fantastic.'

'Yeah, she was a talent. Her family is donating part of the proceeds to a group that helped Anna when she was starting out. It supports emerging artists. Which I guess is a euphemism for artists who are not yet making money from their art and probably never will.'

'In that case, I'll definitely go, and if I can afford to, I'd love to buy something.'

Beth brings their coffees and one cinnamon bun, with a knife and two plates. Rose cuts the bun down the middle and serves Grace a portion.

'I'm so glad you talked me into this.'

'I'm actually being selfish,' Rose says. 'You're helping me feel less guilty.'

'Catholic?'

'Lapsed.'

'Like Joe.'

'He doesn't strike me as a man tormented by guilt.'

'You'd be amazed,' Grace says, taking a gulp of frothy coffee. 'I ran into George the other day—he said he had a fabulous night with you and your sister a couple of weeks ago.'

'Yes, it was fun.' Except, Rose thinks, for the disagreement she and Kim had afterwards. 'George is such an old-school bon vivant. I wanted to reciprocate after he had me over to his house for lunch.'

'Ooh, you *are* one of the privileged few!'

Rose is suddenly worried she's unintentionally offended Grace. 'I'm sorry, I thought you'd—'

'Don't worry, he's had us over.'

'It's a gorgeous house.'

'Isn't it?'

Rose decides to test the waters. Ever since her weird experience at Threave House, she's wondered whether there was something to it. 'It has a . . . a funny vibe in places.'

Grace pauses, the cinnamon bun halfway to her mouth. 'What do you mean?'

'Oh, nothing, it's just . . .'

'It's not nothing, I can tell.' Grace's eyes are alight.

Rose tells Grace about the eerie feeling she'd got when she was looking through George's records, and then again, more intensely, in the bathroom.

'Have you ever had feelings like that before?'

Rose doesn't tell everyone about her feelings, as people either tend to think she's nuts or begging for attention, but she suspects Grace will be receptive. She tells her how she can sometimes tune into the history of a place, whether good or bad things happened there. When she describes what happened at Echo Lake, Grace is riveted.

'I've heard about that place. I've never been there and I don't intend to go.'

'I don't plan to go back.'

'So, would you say you're psychic?'

'No—well, I don't know. I think we all have levels of knowing, or awareness or intuition, that are under-utilised or ignored. But I always paid attention to those feelings because I'm fascinated by the past. Or maybe it's *why* I'm fascinated by the past. For me, the past is alive. History has echoes, but we're often too busy to hear them.'

'Wow,' Grace says, sounding awed. 'That is so cool. But I imagine it can also be . . . disturbing.'

'Yeah, like at George's. There we were, having a lovely time, and then suddenly I'm wondering if a ghost was watching me pee.'

Grace laughs. 'Have you seen a ghost before?'

'No. This was the first time I actually thought someone was there in the room with me.'

Grace shivers theatrically. 'It sounds terrifying.'

'It was . . . unsettling.' Remembering what George had told her, Rose steers the conversation to Stella. 'George said you were delivering meals to them when Stella was sick.'

'Yes, poor things. He was devoted to her.' Then Grace realises why Rose is asking. 'Do you think it was Stella's ghost?'

'Maybe. I did get the feeling, especially in the bathroom when it was icy cold, of . . . terrible sadness.'

Grace thinks about this. 'Of course, Stella would have been sad to be sick, sad to be facing death. But I think that, towards the end, she was in a morphine haze most of the time.'

'I'm sure George would have kept her as comfortable as possible.'

'For sure,' Grace agrees.

Rose decides she will have to look beyond George and his wife for whatever it was she felt in Threave House. Either that or dismiss her feelings as nothing more than an overreaction to a cold toilet seat.

When Rose gets home, she is still thinking about how hard it must have been for George to adjust to living alone at his age, and she has a sudden urge to reach out. She calls him and he picks up after one ring.

'We've missed you at the dog park,' Rose says.

'I've been going a bit later in the morning when there's a chance it's warmed up.'

'Good thinking. Listen, would you like to come with me to an auction of Anna Taradash's work? It's on Saturday after-noon at the Burrawang pub. We could go early and have lunch. My shout.'

'What a brilliant idea! I haven't been to the Burrawang for years.'

'I've never been.'

'It's legendary. It's where good reputations go to die.'

Rose laughs. 'Well, I might as well kill off what's left of mine. Shall I pick you up at midday?'

'Lovely.'

TWENTY

The Burrawang turns out to be Rose's dream pub. On the main street of one of the Highlands' most charming villages, it still has some of its original nineteenth-century sandstone features within a handsome 1920s brick structure, filled with warming fires and long wooden tables, with antique botanical prints on the walls.

She and George find a table next to a fireplace in the main dining room, and both decide on the fish and chips and a glass of locally made craft beer.

They talk about what they've seen in the news about Maria Aboud's murder, which is surprisingly little. Apparently, the police were following up on some encouraging leads, which could mean anything or nothing. Rose is relieved that she hasn't had anything further to do with DCI Addison. And after being warned off, she hasn't done any more digging of her own. Her Miss Marple days are officially over. But she hopes the police will be able to make an arrest soon, as all the unanswered questions about Maria, Anna and of course who took the pictures are nagging at her like an itch.

After lunch, Rose and George make their way into the bar with its long, wooden horseshoe counter lit by simple brass hanging lamps and another fireplace. The walls are white, with

171

a cosy adjoining snug painted forest green. Rose can imagine spending several hours here with a good bottle or two of red. The pub has a profoundly nice vibe. Next time she comes, she decides she'll call an Uber.

She and George snag a couple of spots at the end of the bar, where there's a small stage set up with a microphone and a stool. George orders another beer, and Rose a soda and lime.

The room is filling up with a mix of cashmere-and-pearl-wearing matrons and younger people colourfully dressed or in black from head to toe. Rose doesn't feel like she fits in any of these groups, whereas George, in his velvet trousers and black beret, would be welcome in all of them.

When Rose sees Grace and Blackmore enter, she gives them a small wave, and Grace eagerly makes her way over with her husband trailing behind.

'Are we drinking?' Grace asks as the swelling crowd forces her and Blackmore to press in close to Rose and George.

'George is, but I'm designated driver,' Rose says wistfully.

Blackmore leans closer to her and sniffs. 'I'm afraid I can smell beer on your breath, Rose. You'll have to come with me.'

Rose looks at him, aghast, until the others burst out laughing.

'Joe, that is so mean,' Grace says. 'Did you see the look on Rose's face?'

'I confess,' Rose says, playing along. 'I did have one beer, but an hour ago. With lunch.'

'Well, *I'm* drinking,' Grace declares as she orders a bottle of pinot noir from the barman.

'Who's the auctioneer?' Rose asks.

As if in answer, Anna's brother steps up to the microphone and switches it on.

'Hello, art lovers!'

The now-packed bar falls silent and everyone turns towards Brett, who looks at ease on the small stage.

'Thank you all for coming. Anna would be thrilled that we managed to fill the Burrawang in her honour.'

A sudden solemnity settles over the room.

'But we're not here to mourn—we're here to celebrate her fantastic work and pay lots of money for it, so I suggest you get very drunk and very generous.'

Laughter restores the room's sunny mood.

'As you may know,' Brett goes on, 'half of the proceeds will go to the Highlands Art Hub, which connects local artists with city and regional galleries as well as art buyers. Anna was a big believer in the Hub, and she would want you to support it too. Now, for our first piece . . .'

Rose leans in to Grace, who's at her elbow. 'He's a confident speaker, isn't he?'

'When he's not bartending he's a DJ and an MC for hire. And quite good-looking.'

A woman wearing a T-shirt with the Aboriginal flag carries a delicate sculpture to the stage. Brett helps her place it on the bar stool.

Similar to the one Rose saw on Anna's verandah, the sculpture is of an elegant, stylised sapling with tiny wrought-iron leaves, loose and dangling.

'Are you thinking of buying anything?'

Rose turns to see Irish Dave, looking casual and relaxed in a fisherman-knit jumper and jeans.

'I'd love to,' she says, 'but I'm on a budget. You?'

'I wouldn't know what anything's worth, although don't they say a thing is only worth what someone will pay for it?'

'True,' she says, smiling back at him in response to the twinkle in his eyes.

'I'm just here to show my face,' he says. 'Maybe scoop up some new clients. I heard there would be some heavy-hitters here.'

'Well they're not hanging out with me, Dave.'

He laughs but says, 'More's the pity,' before wandering off to chat up an older couple who look like they've stepped out of the pages of *Horse & Hound*.

Brett taps the microphone and the chatter in the bar subsides.

'Okay, guys, what do I hear for this beautiful tree?'

There's a silence.

Rose looks around, slightly embarrassed in the way she always is at an auction until someone makes the first bid. She's thinking of putting her hand up when a voice from the back of the room calls out, 'Five thousand.'

Gasps and hoots of appreciation erupt from the crowd and Rose is astonished.

'I had no idea,' she says.

'For better or worse,' Grace replies, 'Anna's death made her work more valuable.'

On the stage, Brett is beaming. 'That's the spirit. Do I hear *six*?'

By the end of the auction, they've raised over thirty thousand dollars, most of Anna's pieces selling to art dealers or wealthy Bowral collectors. Rose never stood a chance. She wonders if the frenzied bidding was due to Anna's mysterious death, and the fact that it's been linked with another woman's murder.

But despite her lack of success at the auction, Rose had a good time and loved discovering a new pub and a new village in the

Highlands, confirming her love for the area and her decision to stay. And running into people she knew, like the Blackmores and Irish Dave, made her feel like she belonged.

She's always enriched by spending time with George, and she thinks she and Grace are becoming real friends. As for Blackmore, she's over her teenage crush, though she wouldn't deny that there's something about his pheromones that affects her. Bloody chemistry.

On their way home, George thanks Rose for inviting him along, and for being designated driver. But Rose can tell there's something else he wants to say.

'What's on your mind, Georgie?' she asks, her tone light.

He hesitates. 'I was thinking . . . you should be stepping out with an eligible man your own age, not some fusty old fart.'

Rose can't help but laugh. He stares at her.

'Sorry, George, but you're about the least-fusty old fart I've ever met. I have more fun with you than with just about anyone else.'

George smiles, looking a little embarrassed. 'That's very flattering. But you know, single young men might be more likely to approach you if you're not on the arm of an ancient relic.'

'Good point. I hear Ray Mullin is single. I should really make myself more available.'

George laughs.

Rose is pulling into George's drive when he asks, 'Are you going to Maria Aboud's memorial service next Saturday? Joe mentioned it.'

'Are you?'

'No, I didn't know her.'

'I didn't either, of course . . . but I do feel so bound up in all of this.'

'But you need to protect yourself,' George reminds her. 'If nothing else, from those awful trolls.'

'God, yes. And there was Addison's warning to steer clear or else! I think I'll give it a miss, as much as I'd like to pay my respects.'

'I'm sure you can figure out another way to do that,' George assures her.

TWENTY-ONE

At the dog park the next morning, as she looks at the deep-green conifers on the far horizon, Rose decides that a good way to remember Maria might be to plant a tree in the garden—an evergreen that, even in winter, will be vibrant and alive.

Rose drops Bob back at the cottage before going to the plant nursery on the other side of Berrima. She doesn't want him to go digging up some expensive tree she'd have to pay for. Her plan is to buy a plant for Maria, and maybe one for Anna, to put in her garden as a kind of memorial. Even if Anna was somehow connected to Maria's death, Rose could tell that she'd suffered, that she loved her friend.

She parks on the street, then walks through the gates and along a gravel driveway to the entrance, where *Berrima Green* is carved into a rough-hewn wooden sign above a slightly crumbling stone verandah wrapped around a squat, colonial building. To the left and right are rows and rows of plants—banksias, grevilleas, eucalypts and other natives, as well as exotics like the bare, thorny shrubs that will be dripping with roses come spring.

A woman is watering a row of small shrubs with a hose, and Rose recognises the woman from the dog park who reminded her of Georgia O'Keeffe, with her long grey plait and beautiful, weathered face.

Rose walks along the aisle between the plants towards the woman, who turns and smiles.

'Good morning, may I help you?' she asks in a throaty, smoker's voice.

'Yes,' Rose says. 'I'm looking for a couple of small evergreens for my garden. I was thinking some sort of conifer.'

The woman sets down the hose.

'Why not get an Australian native? We have heaps of shrubs and small trees that stay green all year round.'

'Oh, I hadn't even thought.'

'No. Most people don't. They think of the Highlands as some sort of little Britain with its foul weather and all the bloody roses. They want to plant things that fit with their fantasy. And the autumn foliage? Don't get me started.'

Rose suddenly realises this must be Joe Blackmore's mother, and now the comments he'd made about foliage tourists when she first met him make sense. This woman is clearly passionate about restoring the Highlands' native flora, and she probably preaches her cause to every customer who comes to the nursery. But Rose isn't yet willing to completely renounce her nostalgic attachment to a mostly European garden.

'Well, the autumn foliage *is* beautiful,' she argues.

The woman regards her with suspicion.

'But,' Rose adds, 'let's look at some natives.'

The woman leads her off through the labyrinth of plants. 'You'll want something that'll stand up to drought *and* frost,' she says over her shoulder.

'For sure.'

'What sort of light will they get?'

'I'd like to put them where they'll get full sun, at least for part of the day.'

The woman pauses, as if deciding which path in the maze to take. After a moment, she leads Rose along a row of shrubs with long, thin leaves and spidery blossoms in a range of colours, fluttering in the cold breeze.

'Grevilleas—flowering and evergreen,' the woman says.

'I love these.'

'Natives. Can't beat 'em.'

'It's amazing they still flower in the cold. They look so . . . fragile.'

'Looks can be deceiving. They're tough as nuts. And bisexual.'

'Wow,' Rose says. She doesn't know exactly what it means for a plant to be bisexual, but she promises herself she'll look it up. 'They're beautiful.'

'They have to be to survive—that's how they attract birds like honeyeaters. And, of course, bees.'

Rose smiles. Blackmore and his mother are alike in the way they share information about plants. They're not showing off; these things are important to them. Rose is struck by the realisation that the proliferation of European plants in the Highlands is another form of colonisation, of invasion. She decides to buy the natives.

After perusing them, she settles on one with pale, creamy blossoms, and another with dark crimson flowers.

'I like these two.'

The woman picks up the crimson one by its black plastic pot and places it in the centre of the aisle so Rose can see it on its own, then pulls out the creamy white one, gently untangling its branches.

'I think I've seen you at the dog park,' Rose says.

The woman stares at Rose exactly the way Blackmore does. 'I thought I recognised you.'

'You're Joe Blackmore's mother?'

'Yes. Donna.'

'I'm Rose. Your son helped replant my garden after the police had to dig it up.'

Rose watches as Donna puts the pieces of the puzzle together, realising that Rose is the woman on the fringe, if not at the centre, of recent events—the woman who found the roll of film in her back garden that led to the remains of Maria Aboud.

'I'm planting these in honour of Maria and Anna,' Rose says.

Donna nods. 'That's a nice idea.'

'Your son told me he learned about plants from you.'

'And then he became a cop.' She smiles sardonically.

'But he still loves plants. In fact, he pointed out that I was putting mine in the wrong spots.'

'That'd be right.'

Rose realises she's taking up this woman's time. She looks down at the two grevilleas.

'I'll take them.'

'Good.'

Donna squats, taking care not to strain her back as she picks up the crimson-flowered plant. 'Can you get the other one?'

'Sure,' Rose says, more confidently than she feels. She squats, picks up the white one, and follows Donna back through the labyrinth. Rose tries not to huff and puff audibly as the other woman, who must be at least seventy, carries the plant easily, as if it's as light as a feather.

Donna sets the grevillea down at the base of the steps to the colonial building. Rose sets hers down as well.

'Do you need them delivered, or will you take them with you?'

'I'll take them with me.'

There's something about this woman that makes Rose want to appear capable—to *be* capable. Rose follows Donna up the steps and across the stone verandah into the shop, which is fragrant with flowers and herbs.

On white display shelves are scented candles and organic soaps as well as hand-painted ceramic pots and vases, gardening gloves, aprons and packets of seeds. Bamboo baskets on the floor and hanging from the ceiling are filled with gardening tools, picnic rugs, sun umbrellas.

Rose is drawn to the soaps. She loves that they have no packaging—they're just rectangles of soap, coloured by whatever herb or flower they're infused with. She picks out a lavender soap and one that's very pale yellow, scented with what the sign says is lemon myrtle.

She brings the soaps to the counter, where Donna is rummaging in a drawer. She extracts a small brochure and hands it to Rose.

'Care instructions for the grevilleas.'

'In case your son doesn't come around again,' Rose jokes, then immediately regrets it.

'And the soap?' Donna asks, unfazed.

'Yes, please.'

Donna rings up the purchase, and Rose takes out her debit card and taps the EFTPOS machine. They wait for the transaction to be approved, but instead the screen says that it has been declined.

'We'll try it again,' Donna suggests. 'Sometimes the machine makes bad judgement calls.'

Donna re-enters the sale and Rose taps her debit card again. Declined.

'Sorry,' Rose says. 'Let me check my account. But I'm sure . . .'

She opens her banking app and stares at the screen. She has less than twenty dollars in her debit account. She moves some money from her savings and tries not to feel alarmed by how often she's been dipping into her savings lately.

Donna enters the sale a third time, Rose taps her card, and to her relief the transaction is finally approved.

'Thank you, Donna. You have a beautiful shop. And nursery.'

'Thanks, I hope you'll be back.'

'I'm sure I will.'

Outside the shop, Rose realises she can't carry both plants to her car at once. She considers going back inside to ask for Donna's help, but decides instead to carry the plants one by one to her car.

When she finally has both grevilleas on the floor of the back seat and gets behind the wheel, Rose is sweating in her duffel coat.

On the way home, she worries about her finances. Ever since she struck out on her own, she'd been managing all right, but she has hit a dry patch, as is often the way with freelance work. She can't deny that she took married life with its two incomes for granted. Living on one much smaller income is going to be hard.

After spending most of the divorce settlement on the cottage, she still has a bit of savings left—enough to keep her going for a while, as long as she lives frugally *and* maintains her income. But if the freelance work dries up any further, she'll have to get a job: a proper, regular job, which she hasn't had since she was a check-out girl at the local supermarket in high school.

Rose isn't sure what jobs might be available for a historical researcher in the Southern Highlands. Years ago, she'd thought of doing a teaching degree, which would have come in very handy right now—good teachers are always in demand. But it never happened. She's picturing herself stocking shelves at the supermarket as she turns into her street, so she nearly doesn't notice the other car coming down the road towards her from the direction of her house.

A blue BMW.

Before she can tell if it's Ray Mullin, the car turns the corner and heads off towards town.

Now worried about the cottage, her plumbing and Bob, Rose accelerates towards home. She pulls into the driveway so fast she has to slam on the brakes to avoid running into the fence.

She leaps out of the car, and when she lets herself in the front door is relieved to find Bob sitting on the couch in front of the still-warm stove. She gives him a hug, then goes from room to room, making sure everything is in order: no fires started, no flooding in the bathroom.

She goes out to the back garden, where everything looks as it should, and then goes to the side wall, where the pipes had been stuffed with newspaper on Mullin's last visit. It all looks undisturbed. She's about to go back inside when she notices the old shed. She goes over and peers into the darkness through its half-open door. She can't see anything. She moves closer, yanks the door open, and jumps when a brush turkey comes barrelling out.

On her way back to the house, she looks up and sees the security camera. Taking Blackmore's advice, she had one installed to cover the back garden and the side wall, and another one facing the front yard and driveway.

Rose goes inside to her laptop, opens the link to her security footage, and goes back ten minutes, first from the camera at the back. She watches. Leaves blow in the wind. Then nothing for a bit. She starts when a branch falls, hitting a rosebush on its way down. She rewinds and watches it again to make sure it dropped and wasn't thrown. But it looks like a natural event.

She switches to the camera facing the front of the cottage, rewinds ten minutes and watches. There's nothing and no one on her front lawn. The street is quiet. No cars. No movement.

And then a car drives past. It could be the BMW. Did it slow down slightly as it passed her house? Rose rewinds, watches it again. She can't be sure whether it slowed. She keeps watching, and in a few moments the same car comes from the other direction, and this time it slows to a stop in front of Rose's house. Rose feels her stomach drop. She keeps watching. It's impossible to see who's at the wheel; the picture is too grainy. After a few moments, the car moves on. She couldn't read a numberplate, but she's pretty sure it was a BMW.

Ray Mullin had just been to her house.

TWENTY-TWO

Rose thinks of calling Blackmore, but he has his hands full with the murder investigation and other actual crimes. But he had said to let her know if Mullin approached her again. She decides that rather than calling him, she'll send him a text. It will sound less desperate and he can get back to her when he has a chance.

She types out: *Hi, Detective, it's Rose McHugh here. Ray Mullin just came to my house—well, he drove by then came back and stopped for a moment and . . .*

Rose realises this is way too wordy. She deletes it all, types: *Rose here. Mullin just did a drive-by of my house. For the record.*

She sends the text, then looks at it again, decides it sounds brusque. But maybe brusque is good.

Her phone rings. It's Blackmore.

'Hello, Detective, I didn't mean to interrupt your—'

'It's okay, Rose, and call me Joe.'

'Joe.'

'What happened exactly?'

She tells him.

'Do you check your security footage regularly? From whenever you've been out, and overnight?'

'No.'

'Probably a good idea to start doing that. Will you be at home after five?'

'Yes.'

'I'd like to review the footage. We need to take this guy seriously.'

'Okay, thanks.'

She has a few hours before five, so after reading the care instructions that Donna gave her, Rose plants the two grevilleas in the back garden, in a spot that will get lots of light. She decides that the crimson one is for Anna, and the creamy one—called 'Moonlight', according to its tag—is for Maria. They're significant additions to her garden, steering it on a course towards native flora and away from exotic invaders. She'll have to show Joe. Or not.

Bob is intrigued by the new additions, sniffing curiously until he decides they're okay, and pees on the freshly packed soil at the base of the red grevillea.

Inside, Rose puts the lavender soap next to the bathtub, then stokes the fire and makes herself a cup of tea. She brings the tea into her office, which she's unhappy to discover is exceptionally cold. She drags the heater in from her bedroom, turning it up high. Which might not be the smartest thing to do considering her finances, but surely hypothermia would curtail her ability to work.

As the room warms up, she drinks her tea and decides to email some of the authors and TV producers she's done research work for in the past, saying hello and reminding them that she's still available for work even though she's moved out of Sydney.

And then a troubling thought occurs to her. A lot of her clients were contacts she'd made through Peter. She wonders if the divorce and her subsequent flight from the city have alienated them.

Rose wasn't surprised when some of their couple friends stopped calling her when she and Peter split up, and in most cases she wasn't sorry. Her best friends over the years were always Kim and Peter, and Sam when he came along. And, of course, all the rescue dogs. But now she worries that she's paying the price for being a bit of a lone wolf.

Even though their interactions were painful after their marriage imploded, she and Peter are still on speaking terms, so she decides to give him a call.

'Rose, are you okay?' Peter asks, sounding concerned.

This is classic passive-aggressive Peter, Rose thinks. His worried tone implies that she can't take care of herself without him. Or maybe she's being harsh.

'I'm fine. Why?'

'Well, I read about the . . . incident . . . down there.'

God, she hates euphemisms. 'You mean the dead body I found?'

'Yes.'

'I'm surprised you didn't call me if you'd heard.'

'I should have,' he says. 'But boundaries can be confusing after a divorce.'

'Well, I'm fine. I'm glad I was able to help the police. The woman had been missing for six years. At least her family can have some closure.'

Rose hates everything about what she just said—the way she big-noted herself, using the death of a woman to make herself sound important. And she despises that use of the word 'closure'. She doesn't believe you can ever close the door on grief.

'That's a good thing, then,' he says.

'Yeah, look, the reason I'm calling is that, while I usually have enough work lined up, things are a bit slow at the moment.'

'Oh, if you're short of money . . .'

'No, no, I'm fine. I just wondered if you thought any of your mates might be giving me the cold shoulder because you and I split up.'

'I'm sure that's not the case. But I do know that during Covid university budgets were decimated and they haven't recovered. And advances for books, even textbooks, have shrunk to nothing. We're being forced to do our *own* research.'

'God forbid!' she says.

'Poor students!'

'You'll have to make it up as you go along.'

They both laugh and Rose is reminded of the banter that used to enliven their evenings as they had dinner or did the dishes together. At one time, they were pretty good at making each other laugh.

There's a pause as they're both lost in a haze of nostalgia. Or maybe Peter's looking at his watch.

'What about those TV people?' he asks.

'Yeah, they've been great. But it's inconsistent. Nature of the beast, I guess.'

'Well . . . I *do* have a little job I wouldn't mind some help with.'

'God, Peter, I'm not *that* hard up.'

He laughs. 'It's right up your alley—I'm looking into writing a book about Pytheas's trip to Britain in the third century BC.'

'A Greek?'

'Yes. I've barely got started, what with all the . . .'

'Renovations, getting ready for the baby?' Rose suggests, trying not to sound as if she's needling.

'Yes.'

'Sorry, I should have asked before now. How's it going?'

'Good! We're still waiting for new taps for the kitchen, but—'

'I meant the pregnancy.'

'Oh, good. Great, in fact. We're having a girl.'

For a moment, Rose can't speak. She would have loved a little girl. 'That's lovely,' she manages, hoping he couldn't tell she had to force the words out.

'So, do you want to look into Pytheas?' Peter asks.

'Sure. Email me what you have and what your angle is, and I'll see if we can spin it into a book.'

'If anyone can, Rosie, you can.'

Him calling her Rosie is all it takes to start the tears flowing after they hang up. But she's quick to remind herself that nostalgia is a trap. It could persuade her that the best thing about the marriage was being together: the banter, the lovemaking. In reality, she'd cherished all those nights when Peter was out, supposedly at conferences. She'd loved being alone or with Sam, doing their own things. And the sex had long since become perfunctory.

It's getting close to five, and Rose is about to pour herself a glass of wine. Then she thinks better of it. She doesn't want Blackmore to think she's a day drinker.

She's in the lounge room reading when Bob goes to the front door and sits. Rose knows it must be Blackmore, because Bob likes the detective, and he only waits at the door without barking when it's someone he likes.

Rose opens the door.

'Hi, Rose,' Deb says. Then, seeing the disappointment in Rose's face, 'Sorry, is now a bad time?'

'Not at all, come in.'

'The boss couldn't make it.'

Bob nuzzles Deb's hand and she scratches him obligingly.

'That's fine. Can I get you anything?'

'No, thanks. So, Mullin was back?'

Rose explains what happened and takes the constable into her office, which she kept warm with the heater going. She and Deb sit at the desk and Rose opens her laptop.

They look through the security footage for the last couple of weeks, but don't find any other visits from Mullin. In fact, the only car that appears is Rose's, and she's the only human caught on video. It's hard not to think that this woman who comes and goes with only her dog for company looks a bit pitiful.

After Deb leaves, Rose dwells on her isolation, felt more keenly now that she's seen the stark reality of it on film. But she reminds herself that for the first time in *decades* she's making friends completely separate from both Peter and Kim. George is a friend, and she thinks Grace is one too. And she feels like Joe might become one.

By the time Rose makes herself some linguini with garlic, oil, spinach and cheese, and settles in front of the TV with Bob at her side, she's feeling better. A warm fire, Hitchcock's *Suspicion*, and an obscene amount of parmesan. What more could a woman want?

The next morning, Rose reads through Peter's submission and is instantly hooked.

Pytheas was a geographer, explorer and astronomer from the Greek colony of Massalia—the ancient Greek name for the French city of Marseilles. Around 325 BC, he travelled to what is now Great Britain and Ireland, but, sadly, his account had not survived. What was known about his journey came from the writings of others.

The consensus is that Pytheas was the first scientific explorer from the Mediterranean to meet the Celtic and Germanic tribes. A lot had been written about him, but Peter was looking for a new angle. This is just the sort of challenge Rose loves—digging for information and insight in both recent sources and the fragments and rubble of ancient texts and artefacts.

Rose mentally rubs her hands together as she starts to comb the web for the most obvious resources, and realises that Sam might be able to help her gain access to university and museum archives in the UK. Hoping it's not too late, she calls him.

After several rings, she's about to hang up when he answers, his lopsided grin and deep green eyes filling the screen.

'Mum!'

'Sweetheart! How are you?'

It looks and sounds like he's in a noisy pub and he has to shout to be heard. 'Hold on!'

Rose can tell he's a bit tipsy. And happy. In fact, he looks ebullient. He goes outside, where it's darker and quieter, but she can still see him in what must be the late evening gloaming of the English summer.

'I should let you go,' she says. 'You're out on the town!'

'No, it's fine. You okay?'

'Yes, all good. I just called because I'm doing some research for your dad and thought you might be able to help.'

She sees his smile flicker and fade. Ever since he found out about the circumstances that led to his parents' divorce, Sam has been angry at his father, and although she understands his reasons, Rose doesn't want their rift to deepen to the point where it can never be bridged.

'How can you work with him? As if he hasn't been a massive arsehole.'

'Sam, I know you're angry—'

'*You're* the one who should be angry.'

'I was, but being angry is exhausting. And I'm happy now. Truly. And don't forget, it was my decision to leave. Your father isn't perfect, but he's the only father you have. You'll regret it if you don't forgive him.'

'What if I can't,' he says: a statement, not a question.

'Get back to your friends. I'll email you about the research.'

'Okay, Mum.' He smiles again and her heart swells. 'Love you.'

'I love you, Sam.'

Rose marvels at how mature she is when giving advice to Sam about Peter, but how immature she is when dealing with her ex herself. As all parents know, when it comes to their children, the message is, *Do as I say, not as I do.*

After lunch, Rose is feeling restless and decides to take a drive to the Fitzroy Falls visitors centre. She's been meaning to go ever since that day she wound up at Echo Lake, and it will make a nice outing. There's a cafe and gift shop, and a small museum. Rose has a special fondness for regional museums and the people who run them—invariably locals who are proud of the history of their area.

She hasn't been through the bush, even in the car, since the day she found Maria's remains, and as she leaves the open farmlands and enters the national park, she tries not to feel anxious. The last thing she wants is to be too afraid to go for bushwalks in the park, much less drive through it.

The dense canopy blocks out the light and she switches on her lights. As she approaches the turn-off for the fire road that leads to Echo Lake, the memory of what happened makes her a little queasy. Or maybe whatever disturbance she sensed can reach her all the way out on the road.

As she comes around a bend, she sees a car driving about fifty metres ahead of her.

It's the blue BMW.

Rose slows down, not wanting to catch up to the car, surprised that he's not going faster. But she understands why when she sees his brake lights and he turns onto the fire road—the one leading to Echo Lake.

Rose keeps going, and as she passes where he turned off, she looks for the car, but all she can see is a cloud of dirt.

Later, after having a look through the small museum, she is sitting in the cafe outside the gift shop with a pot of tea and a lemon tart. As she sips her tea, Rose wonders what Ray Mullin could have been doing on that fire trail. Maybe he takes his dog there to have a run and a hunt? It would be just like him. She pities any wildlife that gets in their way. But why there? Was Mullin drawn to the terrible atmosphere of the place? Or was he the one who turned it into a place that seemed to pulse with menace?

Rose is doing the dishes that night—another advantage of being single is that washing up is so easy—when Joe Blackmore rings.

'Hi, Rose. I wondered if I could drop in for a minute?'

'Yes, of course.' Rose thinks what a wreck she looks: hair up in a messy bun, no make-up, trackpants, and her grubbiest, comfiest jumper. 'Er, how long will you be?'

'I'm at your front door. I meant to call before I left the station, but once I was on the road . . .'

Rose is positive she's never looked less attractive, but it doesn't matter. 'Be right there.'

She walks to the door and finds Bob sitting patiently. She opens it to Blackmore, who has never looked more handsome—wavy silver hair, five o'clock shadow, warm smile.

'Sorry to drop in.'

'It's fine,' Rose assures him as she leads the way to the lounge room.

'I just wanted to let you know where we are with the investigation.'

'Have a seat.' Her glass and the half-empty bottle of red wine are sitting on the coffee table. 'Would you like a drink?'

'I shouldn't.'

He sits down, and Rose pushes her glass aside, as if she wouldn't like to refill it. Bob hops on the couch between them and puts his head in Blackmore's lap.

'Sorry,' Rose says half-heartedly, hoping he doesn't mind.

'You should stop saying you're sorry for stuff you don't have to be sorry for.'

'Easier said than done. So, the investigation . . .'

His expression becomes sombre. 'We found evidence in the cave that implicates a suspect. It also means that we're treating the death of Anna Taradash as a homicide.'

'Holy shit.'

'I can't be more specific, but I wanted to reassure you that we do not believe Ray Mullin is responsible.'

'You mean,' she says, jokingly, 'you don't need me to do any Miss Marpleing?'

He smiles. 'What I mean is, I don't want you to worry for your own safety.'

'Well, I guess that's something.'

'Have you seen him again?'

'Today, actually. I was driving to Fitzroy Falls and he was on the road ahead of me. He turned off onto that fire trail—the one leading to Echo Lake.'

Blackmore mulls this over and Rose pours herself some wine, takes a gulp.

'At this point, there is no connection between Mullin and the murders,' the detective says. 'We hope to make an arrest soon. But please don't tell anyone—not even your sister.'

She nods. 'Okay.'

'I wanted to tell you, since you were the one who broke the case.'

'Thank you. But can I ask . . . has Ray Mullin ever been arrested for assaulting a woman?'

'No. He likes to beat up other men. With women, he just destroys their property.'

'A true gentleman.'

Blackmore smiles at her irony 'Yup. Well, I'll be off.'

After he's gone, Rose feels lighter. She decides she's going to stop living in fear.

She calls George.

'Rose! What a nice surprise,' he says.

'Let's go to the Irish pub tomorrow night.'

'What's tomorrow? Thursday?'

'Does it matter?'

George laughs. 'Absolutely not. Is it a special occasion?'

'It is the dawn of a new era. The era of not living in fear. Of not wanting things I can't have. Of not *regretting,* of not *apologising* for everything!'

'I love this era! It will rival the Renaissance as the greatest era of civilisation.'

'And we shall ring it in with whisky and wine.'
'Sounds like we'll be Ubering.'
'*Oh* yeah. Let's start early. Meet you there at five?'
'Counting the hours.'

TWENTY-THREE

There are only a few other patrons in the pub when Rose enters, wearing her red dress under her duffel coat, her hair a bit wild and free, almost no make-up. She'd considered going without, then looked at herself in the mirror. A smudge of colour on her cheeks and a quick swipe of mascara made all the difference. At least, it made her feel better.

She looks around but George hasn't arrived yet. Brett is behind the bar. A little self-conscious, she takes a stool. She's about to take off her coat, then suddenly decides the red dress is a bit brash for a Thursday afternoon.

'Hey,' says Brett as he wipes the bar in front of her.

'Hi.'

'What would you like?' Brett asks.

'Is it too early for whisky?' Rose asks.

'Never,' Brett says, as if it's common knowledge. He gestures to a long shelf with dozens of varieties. 'They're mostly Irish, but we have a few from Scotland as well. And some very nice local product.'

'What do you recommend?'

'What style do you like?'

'I don't like the ones that smell like nail polish remover.'

Brett laughs. 'The peaty ones.'

'If you say so.'

'Let's start you off with some Redbreast. It's smooth and soft on the palate—won't burn a hole in your throat.'

'Sounds excellent.'

As he pours a generous shot of dark, cherry-gold whisky, he says, 'You didn't buy anything at the auction.' He slides the glass in front of her.

Rose is surprised he'd noticed she was there. 'I was priced out after the first bid!'

'All charity auctions should be held in pubs.'

'Definitely—you did really well.' Rose picks up the whisky, smells it. 'Ooh, that's nice.' She takes a sip. 'That is dangerously easy to drink.'

Brett smiles, picks up a bar towel and polishes a glass. 'I'm Brett Taradash.'

'I know. I'm Rose McHugh.'

'I know.'

'So, you know I bought your sister's house?'

'And the rest.'

Rose feels exposed. She keeps forgetting that she's been in the news. 'I wouldn't want to keep a secret in the Highlands.'

'It's not really an option.'

'I'm so sorry for what happened.'

'I think I'm still in denial about Anna. But I'm glad you found Maria.'

'I heard she worked here?'

'For a while.'

Rose wants to tell him that the police are homing in on a suspect. She doesn't even know if he's been told that they think Anna was murdered, and that it wasn't suicide or an accident. But she promised Blackmore she'd keep it to herself, so she says nothing.

'I hope you've told Brett that we're ushering in a new era.'

George slides onto the bar stool next to Rose and they hug warmly.

'Ah yes,' she says. 'A fresh start, a new beginning. An era of not living in fear.'

'I like the sound of that,' Brett says.

George points to Rose's glass. 'To quote the line from that film, I'll have what she's having.'

Brett nods and pours George a hefty shot.

'I can only have one,' George tells Rose. 'There was no Uber available, so I drove.'

'Oh no, I could have picked you up in mine.'

'That would have been a very expensive detour.'

'There aren't enough drivers in the Highlands,' Brett says, as if it's an affront to civilised society, before heading off to serve another customer.

'Maybe that's what I'll do,' Rose muses.

'Become a bartender?'

'An Uber driver. I'm a little short on work at the moment.'

'That's no good.'

'I resorted to taking a job from my ex-husband. It's what set me off on this idea of a new era. I'm determined to stop beating myself up for my mistakes.'

'Is that how you see your marriage? As a mistake?'

Rose thinks it over, taking another swig of whisky. 'No,' she admits. 'For most of those years, it worked. I mean, in spite of the secrets and lies, it worked for me. And we have Sam. Nothing about him is a mistake.'

George raises his glass to Rose's and they clink.

'Speaking of new eras, I'm about to enter a new decade,' he says. 'I'm turning eighty soon.'

'No way! Oh George, we have to have a party.'

'My daughter has already planned one for Saturday fortnight. You must come, of course. And invite Kim.'

'She'll love that! How exciting. Where will it be?'

'At the house.'

'Of course.' Rose was thinking it would be at a restaurant or bar, a party venue—not the house that she's worried is haunted.

George glances at Brett at the end of the bar. 'I might ask him if he's free to bartend.'

'That's a great idea. He seems like a good guy.'

Rose orders another whisky and George switches to water as they trade party stories from their personal histories—funny, weird and embarrassing—for the next hour. She's starting to feel warm, and takes off her coat, setting it on the stool next to her.

She doesn't realise how effective the whisky has been until she goes to the toilet. Swaying a little as she washes her hands, she looks in the mirror. 'Fuck it.' She reminds herself to drink some water before having another whisky.

When she returns to the bar, she finds George talking to Irish Dave, who has taken Rose's stool. He's wearing a navy blazer over a pale blue Oxford shirt and jeans. And boots, of course. With his Black Irish colouring, he looks downright handsome. Or maybe it's the whisky.

He gets up when he sees her coming.

'Evening, Rose.'

'Dave!' she says a little too enthusiastically. 'How's it hangin'?'

She sits on the vacated stool, wondering why she used an expression she's never used in her life.

Dave smiles. 'All good, Rose, all good.'

George says, 'I've just invited Dave to my party.'

'Great!' Rose tells herself to stop gushing.

'But I don't believe this young lad is turning eighty,' Dave says.

'I know.'

Perhaps George had noted the flicker of interest in Rose's eyes as she looked at Dave, because he says to the other man, 'Why don't you join us?'

'Oh, I don't want to intrude,' Dave says.

'Don't be silly,' Rose tells him.

Dave pulls up a bar stool and Brett comes to take his order.

'Looks like it's a whisky night,' Dave says.

'We're on the Redbreast,' Rose says, and Dave and George both laugh. She glances down and realises she's wearing red. Her cheeks burn.

'Redbreast it is,' Dave says. 'And another round for my friends.'

'Ohhh . . .' Rose can't decide whether this is a good idea or not.

George stands up. 'Not for me, I'm afraid—I'm driving. I'm going to love you and leave you.' He gives Rose a quick hug and whispers in her ear, 'Stay and have some fun.'

Rose realises that George is leaving her alone with Dave on purpose, and she's not entirely miserable about it. 'Thank you.'

George wraps his green scarf around his neck and says, 'To the new dawn.'

Rose smiles. 'The new dawn.'

'I will see you both at my birthday party, if not before.' He taps his beret in a farewell salute and leaves Rose and Dave at the bar.

'What a nice man, and so stylish,' Dave says.

'He was my first friend in the Highlands.'

Dave feigns offence. 'I thought I would have that distinction.'

'Aw, that's true.' Rose touches his arm and then mentally tells herself to stop touching him. 'Brett, may I have some water?'

Brett brings them a carafe of water and two glasses, and Dave fills a glass for her.

'No water for you?' she asks.

'Never touch the stuff,' Dave says, deadpan.

Rose chuckles.

'I'm glad I ran into you,' he says. 'I wanted to say how sorry I was that you've had such an . . . eventful time since moving to the Highlands.'

'Thank you. It has been strange. And very sad. You've met my sister, Kim—she thinks all the killing and vandalism is par for the course down here!'

'Vandalism?'

She tells Dave about her run-in on the road with Ray Mullin and her sabotaged plumbing.

'Mullin's handiwork for sure,' Dave says.

'Do you think?'

'Oh yeah. He used to install air-conditioning units, and I think he also did some basic plumbing and handyman-type stuff. That would be just his style.'

'For a while, I even wondered if Ray Mullin might have been the man who killed Maria Aboud. He seems so full of rage.'

'You say "for a while"—does that mean you no longer think it was him?'

Rose realises she's in danger of giving the game away, even after swearing to Blackmore that she'd keep her mouth shut. She drinks half a glass of water. 'I don't know. Maybe it could be. But he's only ever been arrested for violence against other men. And he never killed anyone.'

'That we know of.'

Rose shivers.

'Sorry, this is terrible talk,' Dave says.

'I don't mind. I mean, human behaviour . . . there's no point pretending there isn't a lot of darkness there.'

'That is true.'

'Do *you* think Ray Mullin is capable of killing someone?'

Dave takes a sip of whisky, giving it some thought. 'I think everyone is capable of murder given a good reason.'

'Do you?' Rose asks, sceptical.

'Take you, for instance . . .'

'Me?! I don't even like killing mosquitoes. I mean, they have lives too . . . tiny little souls.'

Dave looks at her and then, realising she means it, he grins. 'Fair enough. But let me ask you: do you have children?'

'A son.'

'And if someone threatened to kill him,' Dave says, 'and the only thing you could do to stop them was to kill *them* . . .'

Rose has thought about this before and knows she would do anything to protect Sam. 'You're right. I could definitely kill someone.'

'And you'd cover it up to get away with it, because it was justified—some evil person was threatening your innocent child.'

Rose looks at Dave. 'Jeez, things must be pretty vicious in the real estate game.'

Dave laughs and finishes his whisky. 'Luckily, the real estate game—here in the Highlands, at least—is nice and tame, just the way I like it.'

'How long have you been here?'

'Over twenty years.'

'Dave doesn't sound like an Irish name.'

'It isn't. The Irish version is Daithi.' He pronounces it *Da-hee*. 'Dave is a bit easier for Australians.'

'So have you always sold real estate?'

'I've done a lot of things. There was a bit of wildness in my twenties.'

Rose smiles. She can imagine him being wild in his twenties. 'Where in Ireland are you from?'

'Bantry. In south-west Cork. Do you know Ireland?'

'Not well. I was a tourist there back in *my* twenties.'

'So, not that long ago,' he says.

'Very funny. So what brought you to Australia?'

'Sorry to be predictable, but . . . a woman—an Australian lass I met on holiday in Spain. We had what they call a whirlwind romance, got married. But it didn't stick. In the real world, she wasn't as nice as she was on Ibiza. I'm sure I wasn't either.'

Rose nods knowingly. 'It wouldn't be the first holiday romance to fizzle out.'

'But I fell in love with Australia. And when I came to the Highlands, I felt like I belonged—maybe for the first time ever. So I stayed.' He's looking at her, smiling.

She smiles back. 'I felt the same way.'

'Now I see why you're in with the coppers,' he says. 'You're good at getting people to talk. I don't know when I've talked like that.'

'I'm not sure I'm *in* with the coppers,' she protests, thinking of DCI Addison.

He points to her empty glass. 'Another round?'

'No, no, I should get home.' As if on cue, her phone chimes to say her Uber is outside. 'I was smart and prebooked a car so I wouldn't be tempted to stay and close the place.'

Dave smiles. 'Well, your first friend in the Highlands would have been happy to drive you home.'

'Thank you—maybe next time.'

'I hope there is one.' He helps her into her coat, making her feel pampered, protected. It's been a long time since she felt that way.

'Me too. Anyway, I'll see you at George's party.'

'Lovely.'

Rose gives him a little wave goodbye and tries not to wobble as she walks out of the bar. At the door, she turns briefly.

Dave is watching her go, smiling.

When she gets home, Rose drinks a large glass of water and makes herself a cheese toastie, while Bob inhales his late-arriving dinner. She's looking forward to this toastie, for which she's used two cheeses and a mix of butter, mayo and Dijon mustard. She hopes her mother isn't watching from heaven, if there is such a place.

She brings the toastie into the lounge room, where she'd left enough embers glowing before she left to start a new fire the moment she got home, and calls Kim, who complains for a while about the new principal.

'But we're sorting him out,' Kim says. 'The art teacher's going to break his kneecaps.'

'Well, that's all right then.'

'Are you okay? It's late for you to call.'

'It's nine-thirty.'

'Exactly.'

Rose tells her about seeing Irish Dave at the pub. As always, Kim cuts to the chase.

'So was it a drink-drink—a "let's ply each other with liquor and fuck like rabbits" drink? Or a "we're both here so we might as well have a drink together" drink?'

Rose has to think about that. 'Somewhere in the middle?'

'Are you seeing him again?'

'Yes—we're going to meet up at George's party.'

'What party?' demands Kim, who loves a party.

'It's his eightieth, and you're invited, so you can be an eye-witness to however I disgrace myself.'

'Great. When is it?'

'Two weeks from Saturday. You can come down and—'

'Damn! I'll be on a dumb team-building retreat. I'd skip it, but we're being paid for it, and it might be when they break the principal's kneecaps, which I don't want to miss. Anyway, maybe you'll be better on your own.'

'What do you mean?'

'I think sometimes you *behave* around me, maybe more than you would otherwise. Let's face it, Rose: you need to start mis-behaving.'

'I wasn't very well behaved tonight.'

'There you go. And I wasn't there.'

They say goodnight and, afterwards, Rose thinks about what Kim said and realises it's true: she *does* tend to behave more when Kim is there. She just didn't realise that Kim knew it too.

TWENTY-FOUR

For the next two weeks, Rose works on the Pytheas project, takes Bob to the dog park, and wonders if it can get any colder. It can.

Even with the heater on high and the fire roaring, Rose has a hard time keeping warm, especially in her office. She's resorted to wearing fingerless gloves while she types, which makes her feel like Bob Cratchit in *A Christmas Carol*, even though Kim told her to pretend she's Madonna in the eighties. Rose also keeps a hot-water bottle in her lap or against her back. She decides to buy an extra one so she can do both.

Rose also scours the media for any further news about Maria's killer. To her surprise, there is none. She'd had the impression from Blackmore that the police were on the verge of making an arrest. Perhaps it was taking longer than they'd anticipated to build a case.

On the Saturday of George's party, the frost stays on the ground all day and the sky is leaden. Rose tried to book an Uber or a taxi for the night, but none were available. She should have thought to book earlier, knowing there would be a lot of people going to Threave House. She thinks about getting in touch with Irish Dave, maybe suggesting they go together, then decides that would be presumptuous. She knows Grace and Blackmore are going, but the idea of sitting in the back seat like their overgrown child makes her feel pathetic.

She resigns herself to driving. Maybe it's better that way. She'll have one drink when she gets there, two at the most, and then drink lots of water. No matter what happens with Dave, it won't be because she's under the influence. It makes her feel very grown-up and sensible.

Her favourite part of going out, she reflects that evening, is the ritual of getting ready. She puts on some music, pours herself the smallest glass of wine (white, so her tongue doesn't stain red) and opens her wardrobe. But its contents are hardly inspiring.

She calls Kim, who answers after a few rings.

'I'm dying of boredom,' Kim moans.

'Hello to you too.'

'It shouldn't be called team-building—more like team-*destroying*. Who came up with this shit? Hey, shouldn't you be getting ready for George's?'

'Yes, and I need your advice.'

'Thank God, my life has purpose.'

'I don't want to wear the red dress again, because George and Dave saw me in it at the pub a couple of weeks ago, but other than that all I have is the black one I wore to Anna's funeral. Or I suppose I could wear my black pants and—'

'Not pants! Jesus, Rose. Go with the black dress. No one saw it at the funeral; you kept your coat on. But tart it up. Do you still have those suede heels?'

'The stilettos?'

'Yes.'

'I do, but—'

'Do you have some sheer black tights?'

'I might.'

'Great. Okay, so the black dress, tights, stilettos. Wear your chunky bracelets. All on one arm. Do red lips, smoky eyes.'

'Where do you get this stuff?'

'Fluff your hair out, tease it at the crown.'

'Seriously?'

'Yes. How are your nails?'

'Unpainted and staying that way.'

'You'll still look super-hot. Start now. Put the dress on first so you don't smudge everything. Have you poured yourself a glass of wine?'

'I have.'

'White?'

'I wasn't born yesterday.'

'Good girl. Now get out there and shake your tail feathers.'

'Well, I can't shake them too hard. I couldn't get a taxi so I'm driving.'

'Shit! No, wait, that's actually better. Get a little tipsy and Dave will have to drive you home.'

'I don't want to force the guy against his will.'

'Trust me, it will not be against his will.'

'We'll see.'

'Call me tomorrow and let me know if he was a decent shag.'

Rose laughs. 'What about you? Thinking of sleeping with any of your colleagues?'

'Believe it or not, I have my eye on the principal.'

'What?'

'But it might be against some sort of departmental guideline.'

'I'd imagine so.'

'Gotta run—we're about to start the team-building drinking. There's hope yet. Love you!'

'Love you too.'

Rose looks at herself in the mirror, wondering if she has enough time to effect the transformation that Kim had in mind. Where were fairy godmothers with their magic wands when you needed them? Rose pulls her black dress from the wardrobe, determined to make a stab at it.

As she puts herself together, sipping her white wine, Rose's spirits lift. She has successfully managed not to worry about the strange feelings she had when she went to Threave House last time. She has talked herself into believing she simply had a chill.

She looks good, feels good, her best friend in the Highlands is having a birthday party at his lovely home, and she will know other people there, including a single Irishman who just might turn out to be a date.

Rose turns into George's driveway and parks inside the gate, where there are already a number of cars. She carefully picks her way across the gravel in her stilettos, which seem to be a size smaller than when she wore them last, and wonders for the thousandth time what evil bastard invented high heels.

At the front door, her stomach flutters with nerves. Big parties have never been her strong suit, and she hates walking in alone. She rings the bell.

The door is opened by a young man in white shirt, black pants and gold nose ring with an air of formal good cheer. 'Welcome to George's eightieth!' He ushers her in. 'May I take your coat?'

Rose is happy that, once again, George's house is heated to a tropical degree, and she hands the man her coat.

She walks into the lounge room, where it seems half the town is already making themselves at home amid the soft candle-light and white orchids perched on side tables. She recognises a number of people whose names she doesn't know, though there's no sign of the Blackmores or Irish Dave.

'*There* you are!'

Rose turns to see George, arms outstretched, in a royal blue jumper and dark green velvet pants. 'Thank God you're here,' he says. 'Madeleine invited all these people I barely know. She doesn't think it's a real party unless there's a queue for the loo.'

'Happy birthday, Georgie,' Rose says. 'You look fabulous!'

'What about you?! You look like Rita Hayworth and Jean Shrimpton rolled into one.'

'I don't know who Jean Shrimpton is but I'll take it as a compliment.'

'Showing my age,' George says. 'She was an English model back in the sixties. I met her once at a party—it was the only time Stella ever got jealous. Let me get you a drink. Brett has concocted a punch that's already claiming lives.'

George leads Rose to a bar that has been set up in the dining room. Here, too, candles and orchids combine to make the space feel elegant and intimate. Brett stands behind the bar looking dashing in a black-on-black brocade vest.

'Good evening, Rose, would you like some punch?' he asks. 'Or will it be your usual whisky?'

'No whisky tonight. I'll try the punch. What's in it?'

'Whisky.'

Rose laughs.

'But don't worry,' Brett says. 'There's also fruit juice, herbs, spices and black tea.' He gestures to a crystal punch bowl where slices of orange and sprigs of fresh thyme float atop the amber liquid. Dipping a ladle in, he fills a glass to the brim.

'It sounds amazing,' she says as she takes the glass and sips. 'Mmm, that's delicious! Do I taste cloves?'

'Good call.'

'Now,' George says, 'I want you to meet my daughter. I've been raving to her about you.'

Rose is relieved that George isn't leaving her on her own just yet.

Back in the lounge room, they sidestep a waiter with a tray of canapés in sculptural shapes, and George leads Rose to a woman around her own age who bears a striking resemblance to the photos of Stella in the hall. She's wearing a white sheath dress and a large, complicated necklace of the type that fashion magazines refer to as a 'statement piece'.

'Rose, this is my daughter, Madeleine. Madeleine, this is Rose.'

The two women shake hands.

'Lovely to meet you,' Rose says, detecting a slight stiffness in the woman's manner. 'When I was little, I wished my parents had called me Madeleine—like the children's books.'

Madeleine forces a smile. 'You're thinking of Made*line*.'

'Oh, right. Well, either one would have been more exciting than Rose.'

Madeleine looks at her as if she's deeply stupid. Rose looks to George for help, but he's distracted by some new arrivals. 'Excuse me,' he says, 'I should play host—at least till everyone's had enough punch to stop caring.' He walks off.

Rose looks back at Madeleine, whose fake smile has evaporated.

'My father tells me you've been spending a lot of time together,' she says, as if daring Rose to deny it.

'Yes,' Rose responds lightly. 'We often meet at the dog park then grab a coffee. He's a wonderful man, and he's been very generous—'

'I'm sure he has.' Madeleine's tone is chilly.

'And I think he enjoys hanging out with me and Bob.' Rose doesn't know why she's trying to justify the time she spends with George.

'Bob?'

'My dog.'

Madeleine blinks to cover a subtle eye roll, and Rose is sure that Bob's lack of pedigree would not be to the woman's taste. Rose takes a gulp of her punch, surprised to find that she's at the bottom of the glass.

'I know what you're doing,' Madeleine says in a whisper.

Rose can't work out if she means in life, or right now at the party. 'I'm sorry?'

Madeleine elucidates. 'Don't imagine for a second that you'll get anything out of this.'

'What are you—'

'I know all about women like you: divorced, lonely, move down here to find a rich widower. It's been tried before. It won't work.'

'Madeleine,' Rose says with all the earnestness she can muster, 'if anything has given you the impression that I—'

But Madeleine turns and walks off.

Rose stares after her, stupefied. Then she looks around, wondering if anyone else had heard their exchange, but everyone seems to be immersed in their own conversations, chatting enthusiastically over the music.

Rose takes her empty punch glass back to Brett and lets him refill it. Then she moves to a corner of the dining room, keeping her eyes peeled for Dave. Hopefully Madeleine will see them together and realise that Rose has someone other than George in her sights.

Rose breathes a sigh of relief when Grace and Joe Blackmore enter. Grace has her red hair piled on top of her head like a film star and she's wearing slim black tuxedo pants, a billowy white blouse, dark red lipstick. Blackmore looks slightly ill at ease but still handsome in a smart suit, dark shirt, no tie.

'Hi!' Rose greets them as Grace stands back, admiring Rose's ensemble.

'You look sensational,' Grace says. 'Doesn't she, Joe?'

Joe nods and Rose waves the compliment away. 'You've got to try this punch,' she says. 'It has cloves in it.'

Joe holds two empty glasses out to Brett, saying, 'I hope that's not all it has in it.'

Grace loops her arm through Rose's and steers her off down the hall. 'Have you met Madeleine?'

'Oh my God, what is the deal with her?'

'What did she say?'

'She thinks I'm out to get George's money.'

'Oh God, I probably should have warned you, but I didn't want to gossip about George behind his back.' Grace looks over her shoulder to make sure Madeleine isn't lurking nearby and lowers her voice to a whisper. 'Madeleine is paranoid—but not without reason.'

'Tell me,' Rose urges.

'After Stella died, George was vulnerable to say the least, and he was quite lonely. He met a woman whose husband had gone off with someone else and left her with nothing. She made a play for

George, who couldn't see what was happening. Anyway, it all got a bit messy, and since then Madeleine sees it as her job to prowl the perimeters of George's social life, making sure no one gets in.'

'No wonder. But you'd think she'd give people the benefit of the doubt. At least at first.'

'I think she believes in the pre-emptive strike.'

They stop. They're standing in front of the door to the bathroom.

'Is that the bathroom where you saw the ghost?' Grace asks.

'I don't know if it was a ghost. But yes, this is the one.'

Grace shivers dramatically. 'Remind me to use the other one.'

'I didn't actually *see* anything. All I had was . . . a sad vibe. Maybe it was left over from Madeleine's last visit.'

Grace laughs as they head back into the lounge room. 'Come on, who don't you know? Who do you *want* to know?'

Rose looks around for Dave but doesn't see him. 'I sort of made a plan to meet up with Dave O'Neill.'

'The real estate agent?'

'Yes.'

'Did you now?' Grace says, delighted.

'We had a . . . moment a couple of weeks ago.'

'Excellent news.'

'Well, we'll see if—'

'Grace?'

They turn to see Madeleine. 'Can you help me with something in the kitchen?'

Grace says to Rose, 'I'll be right back.'

Rose is sure Madeleine has called Grace away to isolate her, and sure enough, she's left standing on her own in the middle of the room. She's about to head off on some pretend mission when a woman in her early sixties approaches.

'I've seen you at Manna,' the woman says, extending her hand. 'I'm Violet, but everyone calls me Vi.'

Rose shakes the woman's hand, realising that she has seen her at the cafe. 'Hello, I'm Rose.'

'I own the Highland Fling—the soft furnishings shop next to Manna.'

'Oh yes.' Rose always smiles at the riot of clashing tartans on everything from cushions to curtains to tea towels and lamp-shades. 'I've been meaning to stop in.'

'Well, why haven't you?' Vi demands, outraged. Then she howls with laughter.

Rose smiles politely. 'Have you had the shop for long?'

And with that one simple question, Rose uncorks an elaborate history of Vi's life in retail that spans four decades and is as complex and momentous to Vi as the Norman conquest is to Rose. With no Dave in sight, Rose lets herself be dragged off to a corner, where Vi regales her with amusing anecdotes about cutthroat suppliers and shifty shoplifters. At least, they're amusing to Vi. Rose tries hard not to seem bored, and Vi doesn't seem to need a response beyond the occasional, 'Oh really?' But when Vi talks about tartan patterns being 'ancient clan identifiers thousands of years old', Rose is compelled to speak up.

'Actually,' Rose says, 'it wasn't until the late seventeenth or early eighteenth century that families started using particular tartan designs to represent clanship.'

Vi stares at her as if Rose has just thrown a drink in her face.

'I'm sorry,' Rose says. 'It's just that I'm a historian and Scotland is a particular area of study . . .'

'I see.' Vi suddenly lights up, as if she's had a eureka moment. 'Wonderful. You can be my consultant. I'll put you on my website. What's your name again?'

'Rose. Rose McHugh.'

'*Mac*Hugh? Scottish?'

'No, sorry, it's *Mc*Hugh. Irish.'

Vi waves this off. 'Close enough. So, as I was saying, tartan, which the Americans call *plaid* for some ungodly reason . . .'

Over Vi's shoulder, Rose sees Dave enter the party, and before she can stop herself she says, 'There's Dave!'

Vi turns and sees Dave just as he sees Rose. He waves.

Both Vi and Rose wave back.

He makes a drinking motion and points towards the bar and Rose nods, relieved and excited to see him.

'Where was I?' Vi says. 'That's right—so *plaid*, which is what the Americans call tartan, is actually a piece of tartan used as a kilt or a shawl. We have them in the shop, and—'

'Excuse me, Vi, I'm sorry to interrupt, but I must go to the loo. Too much punch.'

'Of course! Here I am, babbling away. Off you go—we'll catch up later.'

Rose hopes not. Vi seems harmless enough, but Rose is exhausted from the short time she's spent with her. Kim called people like her vampires: they sucked the life out of you, giving nothing back, leaving you limp and bloodless.

Rose edges her way through the crowded lounge room, carefully circling around Madeleine, who's complaining to Donna Blackmore that her agapanthus didn't look as purple this year. At last, she reaches the dining room. She looks around and spots Dave looking very relaxed in a corner with a stylish young Bowral Blonde.

Rose stands there for a moment but he doesn't look up, and she doesn't want to just barge up to them. She decides it would be a good idea not to appear too eager anyway, so she wanders through to the hall.

As she looks at the pictures of George's family, a man who appears to be a hundred and twenty, wearing a regimental blazer and leaning on a walking stick, comes out of the bathroom. He holds the door open for Rose, assuming she was waiting to go in. So she does.

Rose closes the door behind her and stands there, looking around warily, waiting for the unsettled feeling. But the room is warm and feels completely normal. She looks at herself in the mirror. The reflection gazing back is a bit uninspiring. She brushes her hair, remembering to tease it at the crown, and re-applies her lipstick.

When she comes out of the bathroom, she's about to head back down the hall when she sees Vi heading her way. She quickly turns and heads in the other direction. At the end of the hall, there's a door on the right. It's closed. She grabs the doorknob, hoping it isn't locked. It's not.

She goes in.

The room is dark. Rose feels around for a wall switch, but she can't find one. She takes out her phone and turns on the torch, shining it around the room.

There's a single bed and, next to it, a small table and lamp. Rose makes her way slowly over to the lamp and turns it on. The watery light barely illuminates what looks like a spare bedroom. The few sticks of furniture are old, at least pre-war, but not lovingly restored like the pieces in the rest of the house. These seem neglected.

Rose's eye is caught by an old photograph on the wall. Not of George and Stella when they were young. This one is from further back. It's a picture of what looks like a newborn baby in an old-fashioned wooden cradle. There's something strange about the baby. The baby's eyes are closed. And then . . . they open.

Rose can't move. Can't breathe. And then, when she exhales, she can see her breath. The room is suddenly very cold. She looks again at the photo of the infant but the eyes are closed. It must have been a trick of the light. Maybe headlights shone through the window when someone entered the driveway, creating an illusion.

She practically breaks her neck getting to the door. The doorknob is like ice.

Rose hurries back to the dining room and the bar. She looks around but she can't see Dave.

'Can I get you a refill?' Brett asks.

'Yes, please. Thank you, Brett.'

He hands her a glass of punch and she realises she wants to stay with him for a bit. He's friendly, familiar.

'Nice party,' Brett says, but then, as if aware that she's less than comfortable, he whispers conspiratorially, 'Personally, I think parties are overrated.'

Rose whispers back, 'I agree. And I don't think I'm very good at them.'

'I think the only people who *are* good at them are people capable of pretending they like everyone. But who likes everyone?'

'Exactly!' Rose looks around again for Dave, but he's nowhere in sight. 'So, have you worked at parties here before?' she asks him.

'No, I don't think George has had a big party for a while. And at the last one Maria did the bar.'

'Maria Aboud?'

'Yeah. She would have loved this—all the candles and flowers. All the frou-frou stuff. Before she . . . you know . . . she was talking about starting her own event-planning business.'

'I didn't know George knew Maria.'

'Oh, I don't know how well they *knew* each other, but sure—
I mean, it's the Highlands. You can't fart without everyone else
knowing about it.'

A well-heeled couple approaches Brett with empty glasses, so
Rose takes her punch into the lounge room. She glances around
and her eyes find Dave.

There in the corner where she and Vi had been, Dave and the
Bowral Blonde are deep in conversation, their foreheads nearly
touching. Maybe he's been trapped like she was with Vi. Or maybe
he's found a better option than Rose. She looks around and sees
George across the room. He catches her eye and waves, beckon-
ing her over. Thank God. She's dying to ask him about Maria
being in his house, which she's quite sure he never mentioned. In
fact, she's certain he'd said he didn't know her.

Rose is making a beeline for George when there's a blur of
white—Madeleine—who steps in between them, bringing a
drink to George, whom she then sweeps across the room to talk to
an expensively dressed cluster of Highlands notables. Rose looks
around for Grace, or Blackmore, or even Vi, but she's drowning
in a sea of strangers.

Spotting the large bookcase, she walks purposefully towards
it, then saunters casually around the back to the reading nook.
There she slumps into the comfy chair and peruses the books.
George has every P.D. James mystery in hardcover, in order,
and Rose can't imagine anything better than taking off her
ridiculous shoes, putting her feet up and taking one of them off
the shelf.

As she's skimming the titles, she peers at the party through
the gap between the books and the shelves above. It's a perfect
spot to spy from.

The Bowral Blonde is now touching Dave's chest. He does not recoil.

Madeleine has her arm protectively around George, whose eyes are a bit glassy from the punch.

Blackmore is standing next to Grace as she laughs at something the one-hundred-and-twenty-year-old in the regimental blazer is saying. A strand of her hair comes loose, and Blackmore reaches over and tucks it behind her ear. Without turning to look at him, Grace touches his arm in thanks.

Rose closes her eyes, willing the tears not to come.

'She's only been here a few months,' a voice says.

Rose opens her eyes and sees that Vi is talking to a rake-thin woman on the other side of the bookcase. It's clear they don't know Rose is there.

She stays very still and listens.

'Beth said she's from Sydney,' Rake-thin says. 'I heard she's a historian.'

Rose perks up a bit. 'Yes, she tried to tell me some nonsense about the history of tartan. Can you imagine? *Me?!* She's one of those people who thinks she's an expert on everything.'

Rose is horrified. The women are talking about *her*!

'I hate those people,' Rake-thin says.

'She's been sticking her nose in everyone's business, including the police.'

'Really?'

'Yes. And would you believe it, I just saw her throw herself at Brett!'

'*There* you are, Rose,' Grace says.

Rose turns, her face a map of misery.

'What's wrong?' Grace asks.

Vi and her friend have fallen silent and are looking at Rose through the gap in the bookcase. Now they'll think she was spying. Which she was.

Rose leaps up and rushes straight past Grace, mumbling, 'Sorry.'

She doesn't stop until she gets to the front door, where the young man with the nose ring is still on duty.

'Do you want your coat, madam?'

Rose nods, not trusting herself to speak.

When he hands her the duffel coat, she pulls it on and heads out into the night.

TWENTY-FIVE

The cold hits Rose like a smack, and as she teeters down the driveway in her heels, it occurs to her that she's not entirely sober after a few glasses of punch. She barely touched the last one, though, she reasons, and there was as much fruit juice as whisky in it.

She fishes out her keys and has to concentrate to find the right button to unlock the car. She gets in and turns on the engine to start heating it up. But she's almost enjoying the cold—it's a distraction from her humiliation and shame.

Was that really what people thought of her? That she was a know-it-all who stuck her nose into police business and tried to seduce young bartenders? And what the hell was going on with Irish Dave? Did he get a better offer? Was he ever really interested in meeting up with her? Come to think of it, it was George who'd made Dave have a drink with Rose at the pub, and Dave hadn't called her afterwards, which he could have, to suggest they go to the party together.

She covers her face with her hands and is grateful to find that it's too cold to cry.

Rose just wants to get home, but she suspects she's over the limit. Not by much, but enough. She shouldn't drive. She takes her phone out and tries to summon an Uber, but the next available pick-up isn't for hours. She calls a cab company and the number rings out. Saturday night in the Highlands.

She remembers she filled her water bottle before she left, and there it is, sitting in the cup holder. Small mercies. She chugs half the bottle and takes some deep breaths. This is going to be okay. 'You can do this,' she says out loud.

She turns on the headlights, puts the car in gear. 'Slow and steady, slow and steady.' She backs out and manages to turn the car around without side-swiping the other parked vehicles. She feels triumphant, wants to share the moment, and decides that talking to someone on the way home might help her to stay alert.

She hits Kim's number on her phone, puts it on speaker, then pulls out onto the main road. It rings and rings before Kim finally answers.

'Rosie-Rose!'

Great. Kim sounds pissed too.

'How's your principal?' Rose asks. 'Not that you have any—ha!'

'Did you just make an insulting pun?'

'I mustn't be pissed if I can pun.'

'*Or* you're *completely* pissed. What's going on?'

Rose nearly misses the turn for Berrima, but makes it with only a small screech of her tyres.

'What's going on is I swear never to go to a party again.'

'What happened?'

'What a *stupid* idea parties are. I mean, who invented them?'

'Are you driving?'

'There's too much pressure—to look good, to have fun, to say the right thing, to get laid. To *mingle*! Where the hell do you learn how to mingle?!'

'What happened to Irish Dave?'

'He was with some woman with shiny blonde hair in a really pretty outfit. And Madeleine accused me—'

'Who's Madeleine?'

'George's daughter. She accused me of trying to get George's money!'

'Pull over, Rose.'

'I'm *fine*. I'll slow down.'

'Jesus, Rose.'

'I only had two or three drinks, and they were mostly fruit juice. And tea! And the roads are *dead* quiet.' It occurs to her that the use of the word 'dead' is unfortunate.

'Rose ...' Kim says, with the sort of gravity reserved for discussions about their parents' death—which was caused by a drunk driver.

Wip-wip-wip!

Rose looks in the rear-view mirror. A police car, its blue lights swirling, has driven up behind her.

'Call you later!' Rose hangs up, pulls over and stops.

She waits, wondering what the police could want with her. She wasn't speeding, her lights are on, she is sure she was driving in the proper lane without swerving. They couldn't possibly know she'd been drinking.

A police constable approaches. Rose rolls down her window. She smiles when she sees Constable Tran and tries to speak without slurring. 'Hi, Deb!' she says, too brightly.

'Hi, Rose.'

Deb looks into the car, sees the phone on the passenger seat, but she doesn't point it out.

'Do you have any idea why I pulled you over?'

'No, Deb, I do not.'

'You were driving incredibly slowly.'

Rose frowns. 'Is that against the law?'

'It can be dangerous, especially at night.'

Rose processes that. 'Well, I wanted to be careful in case the roads were icy.'

'Have you had anything to drink, Rose?'

'Oh, just one or two, but ages ago.'

'You were at George's party, weren't you?'

'Sorry, weren't you invited? It was a shit party anyway.'

'It's okay. I heard the boss talking about it. And I know you're a friend of George because he came in to talk to DCI Addison.'

Rose smiles. 'About my . . . movements.' She tries not to, but bursts out laughing.

'Rose, do you consent to a breathalyser test?'

'Yes. I'm confident it will show that I am . . . relatively sober.'

'Wait here.'

Deb goes back to the police cruiser and Rose grabs the bottle of water, guzzles the rest of it and chucks the bottle on the floor of the car.

Deb holds a small instrument in front of Rose's face. 'Count to ten slowly.'

Rose complies.

Deb looks at the meter. She sighs. 'Rose, it's right on the line.'

'I am fine to drive. But if you like, I will stay here and sleep in the car.'

'You'll die of hypothermia.'

'Why don't I just keep going very slowly?' Rose suggests.

Deb looks around, makes a decision.

'Here's what's gonna happen. We'll wait a while and then I'll breathalyse you again. Once you're under the line, you will drive very carefully home and I will follow to make sure you get there in one piece. Otherwise, who's gonna look after Bob?'

'Bob!' Rose is suddenly emotional.

'Okay?'

'Yes, sir.'

Deb returns to the police cruiser, and Rose sits behind the wheel, trying not to count the number of ways she has been humiliated tonight.

Back home, Rose kicks off her stilettos, noting that the only people more foolish than the designers of high heels are the people who wear them. Once she's in her pyjamas, she snuggles on the couch next to Bob, calls Kim and fills her in on her tragic performance at the party and her close shave with the law.

Kim's night wasn't much better, with the principal explaining to her over a pitcher of margaritas that relationships with teachers are not permitted and, in any case, he's gay.

After she hangs up, Rose contemplates making a cheese toastie but decides she doesn't have the energy. If only she'd eaten some of those postmodern canapés. Instead she fills her hot-water bottle and takes it to bed.

As she's falling asleep, Rose suddenly remembers being in the spare bedroom at George's house—the icy cold, the eyes of the infant in the cradle—and the thought pushes sleep away. To distract herself from the memory of the creepy baby picture, she sifts through the various conversations of the night, and gasps when she remembers Brett saying that Maria bartended for George at his house. But George had said he didn't know Maria. Was he lying? Or did he just forget? Was it possible that he got involved with Maria after Stella died? Is Maria one of the reasons Madeleine is so protective of him? Could George have had something to do with Maria's death? Is it her spirit that haunts his otherwise lovely home?

When Rose finally falls asleep, she dreams of her house in the city, where Peter is now married to a beaming, pregnant Maria.

TWENTY-SIX

The next morning, Rose sleeps later than usual and when she wakes, she realises something is different. The sound. Usually, she can hear leaves whooshing, branches creaking, birds calling, the subterranean hum and chirp of insects.

She looks out the window, and at first she can't believe her eyes.

Snow.

The back garden, the shed, the trees, are covered with a layer of pure white snow like icing on a wedding cake. The sky is pale grey, almost white.

She had heard that it snows every few years in the Highlands, and she's seen pictures, but she didn't expect to see it herself in her first winter. It fills her with wonder and dispels at least some of the residual embarrassment from last night and her worry that George may be a murder suspect.

Next to her, Bob is sitting on the doona, looking out at the strange new world. 'What do you say, Bob? Shall we venture forth?'

Rising, Rose pulls on some warm clothes and a woollen beanie, then pauses theatrically at the back door. Bob has no experience of snow, and she has no idea how he'll react. He looks at her, confused by the big production she's making out of his morning routine.

'You ready, boy?'

She opens the back door. Bob runs out into the garden then stops.

Rose walks over and pats him reassuringly. 'It's okay, Bob—it's snow.'

The dog sniffs the white stuff at his feet, perplexed, disturbed, before running around the garden, picking his feet up as if they're on fire.

'Bob, it's okay!'

He whimpers and seems to be panicking.

'Oh, Bobby, come here. Come!'

Bob obeys, but he's not happy.

Rose picks up a handful of snow and lets him sniff it, then throws it in the air. 'See? It's fun!'

Bob tears off again, still lifting his feet high, trying not to touch the ground as he runs. Rose tries to put herself in his shoes, so to speak. Everything he once knew about the world is a lie. The ground is no longer hard and dark but light and fluffy. And cold as ice. No wonder he's freaking out.

By the time they get to the dog park later that morning, Bob has not only got used to the idea of snow, he's decided it's the best thing since liver treats. He and the other dogs are ploughing trails through it, and the temperature stays low enough to keep the ground from turning to mud. Rose looks around for George and Cordelia, but they're probably sleeping in.

Rose is on her way back to the car, marvelling that the bagpiper is out and playing his pipes, when her phone rings. It's George. She decides not to bring up Maria over the phone. The idea of him being a murder suspect is one that should be broached in person.

'How about this snow?' she asks.

'Isn't it fantastic? But poor Cordelia doesn't think much of it.'

'Bob wasn't too sure at first, but now he's a fan. How are you feeling today?'

'Well, reports of my death have been greatly exaggerated, and Madeleine and the cleaners have finally left, thank God. Tell me again why I agreed to a big party?'

'I'm probably the wrong person to ask.'

'I'm sorry I didn't get a chance to spend more time with you—I was busy dealing with people I couldn't care less about!'

'The burden of being the star attraction.'

'I wondered if you'd like to meet me for an early meal tonight at the pub. After all those fancy hors d'oeuvres, I need something greasy, with a crumb coating.'

Rose laughs. 'Yes, please! Shall we say six?'

'Perfect.'

The pub is unusually crowded for a Sunday night, with a festive atmosphere because of the snow. It reminds Rose of her one Christmas in England, just before Sam was born, when the old inn she and Peter were staying in was wrapped in snow like a glittering present under a Christmas tree.

'I felt like a kid, playing with Bob,' Rose tells George. 'As if the rules of the adult world don't count on a day with snow.'

'I know what you mean. It's one reason I couldn't wait to get rid of Madeleine. She saw the snow as a damn nuisance.'

All the tables were full when they arrived, so Rose and George are perched at the bar sipping soft drinks, elbow-to-elbow with other patrons, preventing the kind of intimacy required for a conversation about Maria. What she saw and felt in the spare bedroom is also weighing on her mind. But she doesn't want to dampen what is turning out to be a much better night than the one before.

'One burger and fries, one chicken schnitzel,' Brett announces as he sets their plates on the bar.

'Thank you, Brett,' Rose says. 'Just what the doctor ordered.'

Rose was surprised she didn't feel more awkward when she saw that it was Brett working tonight. He put her at her ease right away, saying that she was wise to leave the party when she did, as some of the other guests got a bit rowdy. Rose wanted to ask who, but restrained herself with some effort.

George makes Rose feel better too. When she tells him about her embarrassing brush with Vi, he says Vi was the one who should have been embarrassed and Brett chimes in, saying that Vi is a well-known cow.

'I normally wouldn't name names,' Brett says, 'But as it happened in front of everyone . . .'

'Go on, Brett,' George says. 'People will be talking about it for years, so Rose might as well hear it from an eyewitness.'

'Vi started pawing Joe Blackmore in front of everyone.'

'No way,' says Rose, trying to contain the schadenfreude blooming within her.

'He tried to let her down politely, of course, but she started to make a scene and Grace had to steer her off down the hall.'

Suddenly Rose feels terrible for Vi. 'I hope someone took her home.'

'Yes,' George says. 'And hopefully today she has no recollection of what happened.'

Rose thinks about the human mind's capacity to protect itself from bad or embarrassing things. Sometimes we can erase what we've done, or what has been done to us, from our conscious memories. But these things have a way of appearing in our dreams or our behaviours, where they can blow up in our face.

Rose casually asks George if he knows the woman Irish Dave was talking to, but he hadn't noticed them.

'Are you interested in him?' George asks, matching her casual tone.

Rose stops pretending it doesn't matter. 'I *was*. But I think I've changed my mind. Kim keeps telling me an important quality in a man is that he should want me desperately—I shouldn't have to run after him.'

'I agree. If Dave isn't beating a path to your door, he's crazy.'

'Thanks, George.'

She's halfway through her burger, thinking about how often our expectations are turned on their heads, when the room goes quiet.

Rose looks around.

Everyone has turned to the door, and Rose sees that DCI Addison, Blackmore and two uniformed constables have entered the pub. Addison is looking around, searching the crowd. When she spots Rose and George at the end of the bar, she starts walking straight towards them, the other police following.

As they get closer, Rose looks at George. She feels sick to her stomach. Can it be true? Have the police come for him?

But Addison walks straight past Rose and George, and goes behind the bar.

'Brett Taradash,' Blackmore says, 'we are arresting you on suspicion of the murder of Maria Aboud. You have the right to remain silent . . .'

Rose barely hears the rest of Blackmore's speech as she watches Brett, who is staring at the police, incredulous. 'Is this a joke?' he asks.

But Blackmore continues the mandatory spiel, which sounds like something out of a bad movie. Addison nods at one of the constables, who places Brett's wrists behind his back and cuffs them. The click of the handcuffs is surprisingly loud in the silence of the pub.

Rose and George look at each other, stunned.

Brett is led away, and he gives Rose a fleeting look as he passes. Of innocence? Remorse? Defiance?

She replays it in her mind over and over, but she has no idea what it meant.

TWENTY-SEVEN

Rose calls Kim when she gets home and tells her about the arrest.

'Anna's *brother*?!' Kim says.

'Yes. And George and I had just been talking to him. And I talked to him quite a bit last night at the party. He seems like such a lovely guy.'

'They wouldn't have arrested him without a strong case.'

'No, of course not. It certainly makes me question my judgement, though.'

Kim sighs. 'Rosie, you have always been a shit judge of character.'

'No, I haven't,' Rose says without conviction, remembering that until Brett was arrested, she had even wondered if George could be guilty of Maria's murder.

'And what about his poor parents?'

'I know. Can you imagine? First they lose their daughter, and then their only surviving child is arrested for murder. They'd be destroyed.'

After Rose hangs up, she thinks about her own son and has a sudden need to talk to Sam.

'Mum!' he says, his crooked smile beaming from her phone. 'What's up?'

She decides not to tell him about the arrest. She doesn't want anything to spoil what will probably only be a few minutes of connection. 'Nothing special, sweetheart. How are things over there?'

'Good. I'm just going to breakfast. Is everything okay?'

She reassures him and they agree to talk again soon. But just as she's hanging up, she hears another voice on Sam's end. It's a man, his tone teasing, intimate. She wonders if it's the same boyfriend he's had for a while.

Rose feels an awkward mix of joy and fear. She's happy for Sam if he's found someone to love and to love him. But what if that someone convinces him to stay in England for good?

The next morning, Rose checks the Sydney papers online, knowing the arrest will have made the national news. According to the lead article in the *Sydney Morning Herald*, police found evidence with Maria's remains, as well as in the suspect's home, linking Brett Taradash to her murder. They were also questioning him about his sister's death and were expecting to lay formal charges soon.

At George's party, Brett had told Rose that Maria wanted to start an event-planning business. Maybe he and Maria were close—maybe more than friends. Nick Aboud believed his wife had been having an affair. He said Maria virtually admitted as much. But he'd also been convinced that she'd ended the relationship and was recommitting to the marriage. If Maria had been having an affair with Brett and she ended it, maybe he became angry and killed her. Rose supposed it was possible that Maria had told Anna about the affair, or Anna had found out.

Maybe the photographs that Rose showed Anna compelled her to confront Brett, and he killed her to keep her quiet. It all added up. On paper, at least.

But it didn't ring true.

When Maria was murdered, Brett was in his mid-twenties. Even now, he was still fresh-faced. He seemed so innocent. On the other hand, killers weren't all moustache-twirling villains. They were students, politicians, priests, bank tellers, boyfriends and husbands. Women sometimes killed, but not often. As Rose discovered when she did the research, only between five and ten per cent of murderers were women.

Rose is desperate to know what evidence the police have against Brett, but she can't call Blackmore. He wouldn't tell her, and she'd get an ear-bashing for asking. She'll have to wait, along with everyone else, until more information comes out in the media. Or in court.

It's just as well. Rose has sworn off amateur sleuthing, and she intends to let the professionals get on with it. She has more pressing matters to attend, chief among them her floundering career.

After delivering her report to Peter, explaining that she had unearthed nothing about Pytheas that hadn't already been thoroughly raked through in published histories, she was yet to receive any new research jobs. She had been hoping there might be a book in what she dug up, but as she told Peter, unless Pytheas's own account of his time with the Celtic tribes in the third century BC turned up in someone's attic, it was a dead end.

So she's back where she started, wondering what jobs there could possibly be for a historian in the Southern Highlands.

237

After their trip to the dog park, Rose decides it will be easier to face her future with something from the patisserie.

She's turning on to the Old Hume Highway heading into Berrima when she notices the Highlands Area Museum. The small regional museum is housed in a green barn-like structure and has the Australian flag with its Southern Cross constellation and Union Jack flying proudly out front. Rose wonders why they wouldn't also have the Aboriginal flag flying. A banner declaring that the museum is open hangs above the entrance. She pulls off the road and parks.

Rose visited the museum when she first moved to the Highlands, and enjoyed its quaint displays of war memorabilia, local arts and crafts, and an Edwardian wedding gown on a decidedly twenty-first-century mannequin. As with many regional museums, a few of the displays have a slightly homemade quality, but some aspects suggested that whoever ran it was astute and passionate about local history.

Rose enters and wanders around, immediately drawn to a replica of an early twentieth-century kitchen, complete with Bakelite radio, wooden icebox and vintage toaster with dropdown sides. She suspects a lot of the artefacts were collected from local garage sales and junk shops, and wishes there were more.

'Can you imagine all the house fires those toasters started?'

Rose turns to see a short, plump woman in her late sixties wearing a turquoise twin-set over grey pants. Her glasses have mauve frames, and the name tag pinned to her cardigan tells Rose that her name is Susan. Rose isn't sure the line about house fires is the way she'd introduce a visitor to the display, but to each her own.

'I'm sure you're right,' Rose responds. 'I love the Bakelite radio.'

'It's not Bakelite, it's Plaskon. Bakelite was dark brown or black. It wasn't until they introduced a new technique in plastic-making that they could make it in that beige-y colour. It was called Plaskon.'

Susan says this with such authority that Rose is inclined to believe her, but when she gets home she'll check the history of Bakelite and Plaskon online.

'Are you visiting the area?' Susan asks.

'I live nearby.'

'Having a day off?'

Is there something judgemental in her tone? As if anyone who comes to a museum on a weekday must be a slacker?

'Just taking a break. I work freelance—I'm a historian.'

If Rose had expected Susan to look impressed, she's disappointed. In the awkward silence that follows, Rose wanders to the next exhibit.

In a glass case, antique cameras sit incongruously next to a teapot commemorating the wedding of King George V and Queen Mary.

Rose decides to bite the bullet. 'In fact, I wondered whether you might ever have need of a historical researcher.' She turns to Susan, putting on her best job-interview smile.

For a few moments Susan just stares at her, frozen, and Rose fears the woman has had a stroke. But Susan suddenly springs back to life.

'We would *love* to have someone like you at the museum. There's always loads of work, researching and cataloguing. If you want to email your curriculum vitae, I'll take a look and have a word with the board.'

Rose is stunned: Susan has said exactly what she was hoping to hear. For a split second, she worries that the woman is being sarcastic, but she doesn't seem the type. 'Great!'

'I'll get a brochure with our email address.' Susan goes off through a door marked *Staff Only*, while Rose looks around, envisioning how she might create future exhibitions that will be the talk of the town, maybe even drawing crowds from the city.

To celebrate her potential new job, Rose buys a lime tart for now *and* a chocolate croissant for the next morning. After all, you only live once. Even if it means dying at fifty from heart failure.

She's pretty sure she'll pass muster with Susan and the board. Her degree, her experience and lofty academic references should be more than enough to get her over the line. Even if it doesn't pay much—even if it's minimum wage—and the job is only part time, it will give Rose that extra bit of security she needs.

Back home, she looks up the history of Bakelite and Plaskon and discovers that Susan was right—another point in the woman's favour. Rose sends her CV, saying she hopes she'll have the opportunity to work at such a well-run museum dedicated to local history. Rose imagines herself moving from research to curating exhibits, maybe writing a guide to local history. Or even a book.

Her phone rings, and for a moment she wonders if Susan was so impressed that she has decided to ring Rose straight away to arrange an interview, but when she looks at the caller ID she sees it's Irish Dave.

She stares at the screen in surprise. Unsure of what she'll say—or what *he'll* say—she waits a few rings before picking up.

'Dave,' she says brightly, but not too brightly.

'Rose,' he says, his voice gentle with remorse. 'I'm so sorry I didn't catch you at George's party.'

'That's okay, you were tied up,' she says, as if it couldn't have mattered to her less.

'I was indeed. A woman I sold a house to a few years back is thinking of selling and she basically wanted a detailed report on the property market. I told her to call me at the office, but you know how it is: some people are hard to escape from.'

Rose remembers Vi and how she'd commandeered Rose's attention for far too long. 'I do.'

'And by the time I'd extricated myself from her clutches, they said you'd gone. I felt like a right idiot.' He pronounces it *eejit*, and Rose smiles.

'That's all right. I'm not a huge fan of parties—they're not really the place to get to know someone.' She realises she's implied she wants to get to know him. Well, what the hell—she does.

'I couldn't agree more. I was wondering if you'd be free for a coffee soon? Have you discovered Manna yet? It's a wee cafe with the best freshly baked—'

'—cinnamon buns in town,' Rose finishes, and they both laugh.

'Great minds.'

'I know it well. And the cinnamon buns, to my regret.'

'Oh, Rose, you've nothing to regret.'

They make a date to meet at the cafe later in the week. Dave might not set off fireworks inside her the way Blackmore did for a while, but maybe that's for the best. Relationships shouldn't be about explosions and flames, but a slow-burning warmth that can sustain itself longer than a spark.

Wow, Rose thinks as she ends the call. New guy, new job— her life is suddenly full of possibilities. She phones Kim.

'If you don't have any team-building events or margarita marathons this weekend, feel like a visit to the sticks?'

'Sure! Any big parties on?'

'No, thank God. Anyway, we *are* the party,' Rose says.

'You're in a good mood.'

'I just got a lead on a job.'

'Ah, something in farming? Animal husbandry? I can see you with your arm up a cow's vagina.'

'Yes, in fact I have my arm up one right now.'

'Nice.'

'I also have a coffee date with Irish Dave.' She recounts their conversation and Kim agrees it's worth giving the guy a second chance.

Before they hang up, Rose tells her to wear comfortable shoes.

'Why?' Kim asks, suspicious.

'Because I've entered you in a nude cross-country run.'

TWENTY-EIGHT

A few days later, Rose and Bob arrive at Manna just before ten o'clock for her date with Dave. She'd thought about leaving her dog in the car—it's not really the done thing, she suspects, bringing your dog on a date—but then she'd decided that she and Bob were a package. And if she ever had to choose between a man and Bob, well, it would be no contest.

Bob is slurping from the water bowl at her feet when Dave enters the courtyard. Rose half gets up as he approaches, and they greet each other a little awkwardly with air kisses. Dave gives Bob a vigorous scratch behind the ears, for which the dog is audibly grateful, groaning for more when Dave stops.

'Sorry,' Rose says. 'No manners.'

'That makes two of us. I apologise again for—'

'Please, you don't have to.'

'Well, anyway, I also wanted to explain why I hadn't called you sooner, even though I wanted to.'

Before he can say more, Beth comes out to take their orders and turn on the heater. Rose notes that Dave calls Beth by her name, a small but important act of recognition that people often don't bother with. When she leaves, Dave goes on without being prompted.

'To be perfectly honest, I wanted to call after you bought the cottage, but it felt . . . inappropriate, since I'd met you doing business. It's tricky these days. I can't seem to keep up with the rules.' He gives Rose a rueful look. 'Then, when I ran into you at the pub, I thought enough time had passed, and you seemed to be . . . well, to be open to the idea of getting together socially.' He pauses, looking slightly embarrassed. 'Am I talking too much? Ma always said I talk too much.'

Rose smiles. 'It's refreshing. Most men don't talk *enough*! And certainly not as candidly.'

He nods. 'The other thing is that I had Covid last year, and even though I'd been vaccinated, I've had a touch of what they call long Covid. I'm fine for a few weeks and then I get really bloody tired. I can't go out as much, and I can't stay out late. How the mighty have fallen.'

'Oh, Dave, I'm sorry,' Rose says. 'I had Covid too but barely had symptoms. I hear long Covid can be a nightmare.'

'It is. So I've been hesitant about starting anything until I feel a hundred per cent—if I ever will again.'

'Oh, I'm sure you will.'

Beth brings out their coffees and the mandatory cinnamon buns, steaming in the cold air.

'They're coming up with new treatments all the time,' Rose says. 'Anyway, thank you for telling me all this. To be honest, I *was* disappointed that we didn't hang out at George's, but as I said, parties aren't really my thing.'

Dave takes a long drink of his coffee and nods. 'That's good. I mean, not that I disappointed you, but . . .'

'That's okay, Dave. I get it.'

They pass the next half-hour talking about local personalities they both know and new places that Dave might show her in the future. But they agree that, for now, he needs to look after himself and take things slowly. Rose reassures him that she isn't going anywhere anytime soon.

Driving home, she calls Kim and tells her about the 'date' with Dave. It wasn't exactly a Cinderella moment, but Kim thinks that might be a good thing. She points out that Rose has always fallen for alpha males—guys like Peter or Joe Blackmore, who are dominant in their fields; forceful personalities who made Rose feel safe and protected. Or who created that illusion, at least. Maybe it was time to go for a beta male, Kim suggests. Someone like Dave—slow, steady and, in the end, more supportive. Rose agrees there might be something in this.

She has often wondered whether she was searching for a father figure—someone to replace the man she'd lost at such a young age. It was perhaps no accident that Peter was nearly twenty years her senior. She guessed that Dave wasn't more than five years older than her, so maybe she was finally ready for a relationship on a more equal footing. She looked forward to seeing what developed between herself and the Irishman.

TWENTY-NINE

When Kim arrives on Saturday morning, she's wearing ballet flats over sheer stockings.

'I said to wear comfortable shoes,' Rose says.

'I am.' Kim gestures to her feet. 'Aren't they chic?'

'Very. But not quite right.'

Minutes later, Kim is trying on a pair of Rose's old Reeboks. 'A bushwalk,' she says with disgust. 'I'd rather drink paint.'

'Don't worry, the trails are well worn.'

'So am I.' Kim looks at herself in the mirror. 'They won't go at all with my leather trench coat.'

'No one will see you,' Rose says.

'It's not about who sees me—it's about how I see myself. These sad, smelly old things make me feel . . .'

'Like me?'

'No. Sad and smelly.'

Rose chuckles and pulls on her duffel coat.

As they drive through the countryside, spying small patches of snow lingering in shady valleys, Kim is still complaining.

'Why can't we wait until spring for a bushwalk? When it's warmer?'

'Because it'll be *too* warm. It's easier to hike in the cold.'

After parking at the visitors centre at Fitzroy Falls, they head into the gift shop. Kim considers some gold earrings in the shape of gum leaves as Rose asks the park ranger at the till—a woman in her thirties with a beautiful tattoo of a platypus on her forearm—if they have a book on the history of the park.

'No, sorry. We have maps and some brochures, but all our books are about plants and wildlife and stuff like that. You could look on the National Parks website.'

'I did, but I didn't find what I was looking for. Maybe you can help me,' Rose says. 'I was hiking in a place called Echo Lake, and I felt a bit . . . frightened. Do you know the place I'm talking about?'

'It's a weird place, all right,' the ranger says. 'The one time I was there, I didn't want to hang around.'

'Do you know if anything . . . odd . . . happened there?' Rose asks.

'No. I mean, not that I've heard. But the Gundungurra people lived in this area for at least forty thousand years before white settlers came. Who knows what happened over the millennia?'

Rose thanks the ranger and Kim buys the earrings.

Outside, they consult the large map mounted on a sign at the start of the trail.

'What's the big deal with bushwalking today?' Kim asks. 'You go all the time, don't you?'

'I did . . . but with everything that's been happening, I've become a little uneasy about walking alone. Last time I came here, I never made it past the cafe.'

'So I'm your bodyguard?'

'Or an eyewitness to my murder.'

'Don't even joke. Now I *really* don't want to go.' Kim looks around at the shadows deepening, heavy clouds gathering above the trees.

Rose reassures her, 'I just want to walk as far as the lookout to the Falls.'

'It's just water, Rose; it falls. And speaking of which, it looks like it could rain.'

'I don't think so. Come on.'

Rose strikes off along a wide, manmade walkway with green railings on either side. And just as they're crossing the bridge over Wildes Meadow Creek, the sun breaks through the clouds.

They stop to watch the dappled light dancing on the water as leaves flutter in a gust of wind.

A whipbird calls out. A magpie answers.

'Ohhh,' Kim says. 'It's magical.'

Rose smiles, nodding. 'Isn't it?'

'And it *smells* so good. What *is* that?'

'Eucalyptus, wattle and a lot of other flora I can't name. And, of course, the soil, the river, the animals, the air . . .'

'Wow,' Kim says, as if getting it for the first time. 'This is *really* nice.'

Rose laughs, pleased that Kim finally feels the attraction. 'We'll make a bushwalker out of you yet.'

They head along the path, with Kim gaping at the distant canopy above, the now-blue sky visible between the treetops. Rose has to grab her arm when her sister nearly trips over a fallen branch. 'Look where you're going,' she cautions.

'I didn't know ferns could get that tall!'

Rose smiles but stays silent, letting Kim's awe of nature blossom on its own.

After walking for another ten minutes or so, they arrive at the lookout. On the left side of the gorge, water rushes over the edge of the sandstone escarpment, tumbling to the reservoir in the Yarrunga Valley hundreds of feet below. The valley floor is dense with subtropical rainforest, framed on either side by golden cliffs, hazy plateaus in the distance, a sapphire sky above.

Rose breathes it all in, feeling like she's making peace with the bush again.

Kim pulls out her phone and hands it to Rose. 'Can you take a picture of me with the falls in the background? And make sure you crop out the shoes.'

Rose laughs and obliges, and then Kim pulls her close for a selfie with the two of them in frame, the valley behind them.

'Send that to me, okay?' Rose says. 'I don't have many pictures of us together.'

'I'll show the kids at school—they won't believe Ms McHugh went bushwalking.'

'Shall we keep going?'

'Absolutely!'

As they walk deeper into the forest, the trees and shrubs become bigger, older, wilder. They stop to marvel at a massive tree whose broad trunk is covered with gnarled knobs that make it look like something out of a Brothers Grimm tale.

'I can't decide whether that's beautiful or hideous,' Kim remarks.

'It just . . . is what it is,' Rose says.

Further along, they pass a head-high mound of tightly packed yellow earth.

Kim stops. 'What is *that*?'

'A termite mound.'

'No way.'

'Wow, you really don't get out much, do you?'

Rose walks on as Kim snaps pictures. 'I'd love to bring the kids here. Their brains would explode.'

Rose feels a sudden swelling of love for her sister. 'You're a real softie at heart—you love those kids.'

'Me? Nah! They're a bunch of ratbags.'

But Rose knows that the children Kim teaches fill her life and her heart with the kind of connection and joy that every one of us needs.

Half an hour later they're still walking, and haven't seen any other hikers since the lookout at the falls. The clouds have returned, and even though it's late morning, it's as dark as dusk under the dense canopy. The cold wind from the south reminds them that it's still the dead of winter, and spring is a long way off.

'We should head back, think about lunch,' Rose says, surprised that Kim hasn't wanted to bail sooner.

'Yeah, okay.' Kim checks the time on her phone. 'God, I completely lost track of time.'

They turn and head back along the trail. Rose loses her footing on a loose rock but Kim grabs her elbow.

'Thanks! It's hard to see,' Rose says. They keep their arms linked as they make their way carefully down the track. They come to a fork in the path.

'Which way?' Kim asks.

'Umm . . .' Rose doesn't want to admit she has no idea. 'It must be this one. The valley's to the right, yeah?' She looks at Kim.

'Don't look at me!'

'It's this one.' Rose tries to act sure of herself.

They walk for a while, the bush around them a drab greyish brown without the sun to bring out its colours.

'I don't recognise any of this,' Kim says.

'That's because we're seeing everything from a different angle.'

But Rose is nervous, wondering if they could have taken a wrong turn. She knows Kim is thinking about the same thing she is—the bodies found in the park. But they keep walking.

And then, from behind them, footsteps. Far off at first, but getting closer. They're coming fast. Louder, closer.

Rose and Kim have backed up to the edge of the track, looking behind them, but they can't see anyone.

'Fuck,' Kim says, panic in her voice as she and Rose huddle closer.

And then, from around a bend, there's a blur of pink lycra, and a woman streaks past, out on her late morning run.

Rose and Kim look at each other and burst out laughing. They are still chuckling about their brush with a crazed killer when they reach the car.

THIRTY

'Let's have a drink before Grace gets here,' Kim suggests.
'Sure,' says Rose. 'Might as well take advantage of having a designated driver.'

When George heard that Kim was coming down for the weekend, he invited the sisters over to Threave House for a casual dinner. He also asked Grace and Joe, but DI Blackmore had to work. Brett Taradash had been formally charged with the murder of Maria Aboud and was being investigated for the murder of his sister. The detectives were working day and night building the case against him. Rose was relieved that the whole matter was completely out of her hands. But her curiosity lingered.

Grace is on antibiotics and not drinking, so she offered to ferry Rose and Kim to and from George's so they could imbibe.

Rose enters the bathroom where Kim is applying eyeliner with the steady hand of a brain surgeon. 'It's just a casual dinner,' Rose says.

'Doesn't mean I shouldn't look my best.'

Rose looks at Kim's outfit—a tailored burgundy dress with lace-up high-heeled boots. 'Maybe I should change?'

Kim regards Rose's outfit in the mirror—a black silk shirt over jeans and her suede boots with the little heel. 'No, you look great. But add a bracelet or two. Unless you're planning to birth some calves tonight.'

Silver bangles clinking noisily, Rose gets in the back seat and Kim gets in front with Grace.

'You are very kind to do this, Grace,' Rose says, buckling up.

'Well, I can't drink anyway—bloody UTI—so I might as well be a good Samaritan.'

Rose remembers how early in her relationship with Peter she used to get urinary tract infections all the time. Her doctor said it was due to frequent, vigorous sex. Rose tries not to think about Grace and Blackmore having frequent, vigorous sex.

'Anyway, I'm being selfish,' Grace says. 'I wanted time alone with Rose to find out if she left the party because she saw the ghost.'

'What?!' Kim's head whips around to look at Rose, who shrinks in the back seat like a naughty child.

'Oops, sorry!' Grace looks in the rear-view mirror at Rose. 'Can't keep my mouth shut drunk *or* sober,' she says.

'That's all right,' Rose says. 'I hadn't mentioned it to Kim, what with everything else going on.'

'Mentioned what? What ghost?' Kim demands.

Rose sighs and recounts everything, from the feeling she was being watched in the lounge room and bathroom, to the infant whose eyes seemed to open for a moment. And the cold—the bone-chilling cold.

'Holy shit,' Kim says, digesting Rose's account of her last visit to the house she's now staring at through the windscreen.

Grace turns off the engine.

'I haven't said anything to George,' Rose says.

'Maybe you should,' Kim suggests. 'You know what I think about your feelings.'

Rose tells Grace, 'Kim thinks there's always an entirely unmysterious explanation for whatever it is I sometimes feel.'

'Well, I'm not sure,' Grace says. 'But it might be a good idea to ask George about it.'

The front door opens, and warm light spills onto the drive around George's silhouette, momentarily dispelling the idea that this comfortable, elegant home could be haunted.

'I thought I heard a car!' he says.

Rose and Kim are drinking red wine while Grace makes do with something fizzy pretending to be a cocktail as they stand around the island bench in the kitchen. George is checking on the lasagne in the oven.

'Another few minutes, I think. I like it when the cheese is really brown and the edges are almost burnt.'

'George, you are the perfect man,' Kim says. 'I would ask you to marry me if I wasn't uncomfortable with my husband having a harem.'

George chuckles, and refills her wine.

'It's true,' Grace says. 'Don't you have any men friends?'

'One or two,' he says. 'But they're not as interesting as women.'

George glances at Rose. She's been quiet since they arrived. 'And what about you, Rose? Kim is suggesting you're part of my harem.'

The others look at Rose and she realises they're talking to her. 'Sorry, what? I was off with the pixies.' In fact, ever since she stepped through the door, all Rose could think about was what echoes she might feel tonight.

'Fretting about the ghost?' Kim asks, not at all innocently.

'Oh, Kim.' Rose is mad that her sister has forced her hand, but she doesn't want to ruin the night by showing it.

'Don't be angry, Rose,' Grace says. 'I can't stop thinking about it either.'

They all turn to look at George, expecting him to appear confused, but instead he looks like a man whose darkest secret has suddenly been exposed.

'You know what we're talking about, don't you?' Rose asks.

George sighs. 'Yes. Let's get dinner on the table and I'll tell you what I know.'

In the dining room, lit by candles left over from the party, the women savour the lasagne, garlic bread, green salad and red wine while George tells his story.

'Stella and I fell in love with Threave House the moment we saw it, and for years we didn't notice a thing. Then, when she got sick and started chemo, she was on medication that made it hard for her to sleep. She said rather than keep me up half the night, she'd move into the spare bedroom at the back.'

Rose and Kim exchange a look, which George intercepts.

'You know the room I mean?' he asks Rose.

'I do.'

'I said I should be the one to move—I wanted her to keep the main bedroom—but Stella insisted, said the back room was darker, quieter. So we fixed it up a bit and got her settled, but on the first night, I woke up to find Stella standing over my bed, shivering. She said the back room was too cold, so she got in bed with me, and we stayed up the rest of the night, talking about how we met . . . our favourite songs . . . the fabulous clothes she bought on Carnaby Street. Nobody wore them better.' George blinks back tears.

'George,' Rose says, 'you don't need to . . .'

'No. This is good. It's important.' He takes a sip of wine. 'The next day, I checked the room for draughts, but it was airtight. Even though the central heating seemed to be working fine in the room, I brought in a space heater and we put an electric blanket on the bed. That night, I waited up to make sure she'd be okay. I was reading in the lounge room when Stella came out, shaking, and said it wasn't going to work. And it wasn't just the cold.'

Rose takes a deep breath. 'Go on.'

Grace moves to top up George's wineglass, but the bottle is empty.

'She said there was something strange about the room,' he continues. 'The next day, I spent some time there. I brought a book and sat in a chair to see if I could pick up on something. I didn't get the cold feeling, but my eyes kept being drawn back to a photo on the wall.'

Rose says in a whisper, 'The baby in the cradle.'

George's eyes widen and he nods. 'The baby in the cradle.'

'Nobody say another thing until I get back,' Kim orders. 'We need another bottle. Come with me, Grace, I'm totally chicken shit and I'm not walking around this house alone.'

'Let's make it two bottles,' Grace says as she gets up.

'Stay where you are,' George commands.

Everyone freezes.

George gets up and slides opens a door in the sideboard to reveal dozens of bottles. 'There's some lovely wine right here.'

In unison, Kim and Grace say, 'Thank God!' and everyone laughs.

But Rose doesn't want George to lose the thread. He's getting close to what she wants to know. 'Keep going, George.'

He sits back down while Kim opens the wine and refills glasses.

'I didn't know where the photograph came from, but it looked old. I assumed Stella had picked it up in a garage sale. But she said no, it was here when we moved in. She never particularly liked it, but for some reason she was reluctant to let it go. She felt compelled to leave it on the wall, where she found it.'

Rose shivers.

'I suggested we get rid of the photograph, but Stella was adamant that it should stay where it was. But she was equally adamant that she could not sleep in that room. In the end we decided to stay together in the main bedroom. I assumed that her feeling cold in the back room was because of the chemo, or it was her way of wanting to be near me. But I flattered myself. Over the years, other people have suggested I turn the room into a study or something, but if they spend any time there they soon change their minds. Somehow it's not the kind of room that invites people to linger. Madeleine thinks I should knock down the wall the photograph is on to extend the lounge, but I can't bring myself to do it. Whether out of loyalty to Stella, or some sense that the room should remain untouched, I have no idea.'

'When I went in during the party, I thought I saw the baby's eyes open,' Rose tells him.

'That's it!' Kim says. 'Enough. I'm putting on some music. Something fun.' She gets up. 'Coming, Grace?'

Grace laughs. 'As long as I get first pick.' She follows Kim, leaving Rose and George alone at the table.

'So, did you ever look into the history of the house to find out about the baby?' Rose asks.

George nods. 'I did a bit of digging, but didn't come up with much. Someone thought the photograph must have been taken in the early part of the twentieth century, but that's as far as I got. I'm sorry if you were frightened. Forgive me for not saying anything sooner, but no one else has had the kind of experience you've just described—at least, not that they've told me about! And I didn't want to scare you away.'

'I understand.'

'Rose . . . do you think I have a ghost?'

'I have no idea. I don't even know what a ghost is, or if I've ever encountered one.'

She tells him about the feeling she had of being watched, the cold in the bathroom.

'In the past, in other places,' she explains, 'I've picked up on sort of . . . I call them "echoes" of things that happened there before. Most people would just call them vibes.' She shrugs. 'I have no idea what it means—whether I'm psychic or whether time is circular and there is no past, only the present. I've heard some First Nations people refer to time as the Everywhen. I like that. It makes sense to me. But this was the first time I had a sense of a . . . a soul, actually in the room with me, watching me.' She looks at George. 'You must think I'm crazy.'

George sighs. 'Far from it. I believe there are more things in heaven and earth . . . Nothing would surprise me.'

Rose nods. 'I wonder . . . would you mind if I did some research into the house? About the previous inhabitants?'

'I would love that. It would be nice to get some answers.'

The moment of gravity is interrupted when the opening notes of 'Into the Groove' blare from the lounge room.

Rose raises her eyebrows. 'Madonna?'

'I am a man with more than one dark secret.'

Rose smiles, hoping George has no more surprises in store.

THIRTY-ONE

At the dog park on the following Monday, Rose is glad she wore her gumboots as she sloshes up the hill after Bob. The snow had melted and when the dogs tore around the park, a layer of mud inches thick was churned up.

Rose gets to the crest of the hill and is admiring the view through the bare trees towards the escarpment, with its trimming of eucalypts at the base and top, when her phone rings. She answers.

'This is Susan Callahan, from HAM—the Highlands Area Museum?'

Bob chooses that moment to do a poo, so Rose scurries over with a plastic bag while trying to sound professional. 'Hello, Susan!'

'I spoke to the board and we'd love you to work for us at the museum.'

'Oh wow, that's fantastic,' Rose says, tying a knot in the top of the bag.

'We were thinking two days a week?'

'Great! Um, we didn't talk about money . . .'

'Money?'

'Yes . . . um, how much the position pays.'

'Oh, nothing—it's volunteer!' Susan says this as if it's the best news ever.

Rose's heart sinks. 'Ah . . . okay. Well, I—'

'Can you start this week? Thursdays and Sundays, from ten to four. I'll be with you for your first day, to show you the ropes. We have a few tour groups coming through on Sunday, so it'll be good for you to get your sea legs on Thursday.'

Rose is a bit overwhelmed.

'Rose? Are you still there?' Susan asks.

'Yes. Okay!' Rose is so taken aback she doesn't know how to tell Susan she actually needs a paying job.

'See you Thursday!' Susan says cheerily.

'Bye,' says Rose.

Rose looks at the bag of poop in her hand and wonders if she should have said no.

Back home, with the heater cranked up high and a fire roaring in the stove, Rose scours the media online, but there's nothing new about Brett or the case, only a rehash of the charges and the fact that he's pleading innocent.

As she's deciding what to do with the rest of her day, Rose's mind is drawn back to her personal worries. She will soon need an income. On the other hand, she has enough to live on for a while. Perhaps the smart thing to do is to lay the groundwork for something in her field. Maybe through the Highlands Area Museum—or HAM, the acronym Susan used, as if it's up there with MOMA and MONA. Rose takes a deep breath and resolves not to get too stressed about everything. She's a lucky woman with a gorgeous cottage, a wonderful dog and a bright future.

Remembering that she'd told George she'd look into the history of his house, she makes another cup of tea and brings it back to her office. The photograph of the infant in the cradle looked early twentieth century, so she decides to start by finding out who the owners of Threave House were between 1900 and 1930. It doesn't take long browsing public records archives online to find the name of the Grayspence family, who had made a development application for the house in 1927. Digging a bit deeper, she discovers that the house had been in the Grayspence family for forty-nine years before that.

Rose checks the electoral rolls and finds the names of over a dozen adult Grayspences, men and women, who were registered at Threave House in that period, and makes a list of the women in the house. She's looking for someone who may have been the mother of the baby in the picture. She searches for women of child-bearing age in records of births, deaths and marriages, and discovers that on 16 March 1919, Mary Grayspence, who had married the oldest son of the house, died at the age of twenty-one. Rose gasps when she sees that their child, an infant named Margaret, had died less than a week earlier, on 11 March, at the age of two weeks.

Immediately Rose thinks that both mother and child probably died from complications during labour, but there's nothing explicit in the records. Maybe she can find their obituaries. Rose spends another hour or so trawling through the Highlands newspapers of the time—the *Southern Mail*, the *Mittagong Express* and the *Moss Vale Record*—but she can find no mention of the deaths of Mary Grayspence or baby Margaret. In the Highland Family History Society archives, there is a listing for the burial of the child, but not the mother.

Rose goes back to the early March 1919 *Moss Vale Record* and scans its front page. One of the lead articles describes fears that pneumonic influenza, also known as the Spanish flu, had broken quarantine in Sydney.

Rose has heard about the awful toll taken by the Spanish flu, and there were many comparisons during the Covid pandemic, but her working knowledge is thin. She goes back through the archives and is surprised to find that in 1918 the Australian government was confident that they had contained the virus through mask-wearing and free inoculations. But in January 1919 there was an outbreak at Sydney Quarantine Station, and shortly afterwards, a returned soldier suffering from the flu was admitted to hospital, where the infection quickly spread to the staff.

In spite of precautions, the Spanish flu made its way south to the Highlands, and many locals were taken ill or died. But as far as Rose could tell, everyone who died from the flu had an obituary in one of the local papers. So, if poor Mary had died of the flu, or from complications in labour, why was her death not acknowledged publicly?

Rose is so absorbed that she jumps when her phone rings. It's Kim. Rose tells her what she's discovered.

'Keep digging,' Kim says. 'Not in George's garden, of course. I don't want you to find any more bodies or rolls of film.'

'Please don't joke about that stuff.'

'I'm not.'

'Maybe I'll ask my colleague at HAM.'

'What's HAM?'

'The Highlands Area Museum, of course.'

'You got the job!'

'Yup.'

'Woohoo! Well done, Rosie. Have you negotiated your salary? Don't sign a contract until I have a look.'

'Salary? Oh no, it's a voluntary position. But I'm excited.'

'I thought you needed a job-job. You know, one that pays money?'

'Not right away. Anyway, I figure I'll make some good contacts through the museum with people in the local historical scene, and perhaps pick up some research work. I start Thursday.'

'Okay.'

'It feels like a new beginning, a fresh start. I can't wait!' Rose says, trying very hard to believe it.

THIRTY-TWO

On Thursday morning at 10 am, Rose is standing next to Susan in the doorway of the HAM storeroom, looking at a stack of dusty cardboard boxes on one side, dented file cabinets on the other, and a trestle table with an ancient computer under a small window overlooking the car park.

'I just haven't had the time,' Susan says, waving at the cardboard boxes.

'So, they're family records?'

'Mostly from deceased estates, and stuff that didn't get sold at garage sales,' Susan says. 'But I'm sure there's gold in there.'

'I'm sure there is.' Rose means it. To her, some of the most valuable but underrated historical artefacts were to be found in household paperwork—the letters, bills, shopping lists and memorabilia that people stashed away through their lives, and which showed where they travelled, how they spent their money and what was important to them.

'Most of it will be junk,' Susan says. 'But if you find anything that isn't, enter it into the database and then file it in whichever folder seems to make sense. With your qualifications I'm sure you'll sort it out. I'll show any visitors around this morning, and then this afternoon we can do it together.'

'Great. Thank you, Susan.'

Rose is secretly glad she got the backroom job, at least for the morning, as she suspects she'll prefer it to showing tourists the commemorative George and Mary tea service.

By one o'clock, Rose has worked her way through half a box. There was a lot of junk, much of it illegible scraps of paper, but there were a few nuggets. A young soldier named Ted Heery, stationed in the Finisterre Range of New Guinea in 1944, wrote a letter to his girlfriend Mabel in Moss Vale asking her to marry him if he got out alive.

Rose also found a photograph of a 'Women's Liberation' rally in 1974 in Leighton Gardens, in the centre of Moss Vale, with one woman holding a sign that said: EQUAL PAY FOR EQUAL WORK! Rose shook her head—fifty years later and it still hadn't come to pass.

But Rose's favourite find is a handwritten note from a child to her mother, apologising for eating the bowl of icing intended for the Victoria sponge that was cooling on the windowsill.

After logging the letter from Ted Heery in the database, she checks to see if he and Mabel got married, and sure enough, there is a record of Ted's marriage a year later, but to someone named Jean Wilson! Rose laughs out loud.

'Find something funny?' Susan asks.

'Actually, yes.' Rose is about to tell her about the love triangle involving Ted, Mabel and Jean, but Susan looks preoccupied.

'If you want to grab something for lunch,' Susan says, 'now would be a good time. I have to scoot off—my mum has had a fall.'

'Oh, I'm sorry. Do you want to leave now? I brought my lunch.'

'That would be great.'

'So . . . will we keep the museum open?'

'Yes, you'll be fine—most of the exhibits are self-explanatory, and we don't get many visitors during the week. I'll come back as soon as I can.'

'I hope your mum's okay.'

'I'm sure she is. She's in a nursing home, but I want to check on her.'

'Of course. See you later.'

Rose props open the door to the exhibition room while she sits at the trestle table and eats her cheese sandwich. She's a little worried that she won't know what to do or say if visitors come in, but she'll manage somehow.

She's about to turn off the computer when she realises there might be something in the database about Threave House or the Grayspence family, and when she looks them up, she's rewarded with a reference number to a file. She goes to the filing cabinet and locates a folder with several entries, including an article from the *Moss Vale Record* about the return of the eldest son, John Grayspence, from World War I. He'd survived the Battle of Fromelles in 1916 and served another year before coming home. Rose knows from her earlier research that he and Mary were married early in 1918. There is also a notification from the local hospital that pneumonic influenza had been detected in at least two of the inhabitants of the household. The date is February 1919.

This probably explains the deaths of Mary and her baby, but not why the young mother's death was unacknowledged.

After lunch, Rose walks around the museum, absorbing the information on the wall plaques and taking pictures so she can do more research from home. She's looking at some pottery by a local artist when she hears the door open behind her.

Rose turns, putting on her best welcome face.

Three older women enter, chatting away. Rose is aghast to realise one of them is Vi of the Highland Fling.

They haven't spotted her yet and Rose is tempted to hide in the storeroom, but then Vi glances her way.

'Hello, Vi,' Rose says in as neutral a tone as she can muster.

Vi just stares at her, saying nothing. Rose can't believe the woman is actually going to snub her.

'I'm sorry,' Vi says, sounding genuinely puzzled, 'have we met?'

Rose relaxes, realising Vi doesn't remember her—thanks to the punch, no doubt. 'At George's party. We spoke about . . . your shop. I'm Rose.'

'Rose! Yes, I met so many people that night, and I'm afraid I didn't recognise you out of context. I'm showing the local sights to some friends from the city.'

'Lovely,' Rose says. 'Let me know if you have any questions, and I'll try to help.'

Rose lingers near the replica kitchen, staying out of their way as the women make their way from one exhibit to another. They pause at the pottery.

One of the friends asks Vi, 'Is this Indigenous?'

'No, they have their own galleries.'

Rose stiffens. What does *that* mean? But now that Vi mentions it, Rose hasn't seen anything in the museum or the archives that relates to the First Peoples of the area—the people who have the longest history in the Highlands.

'We're quite proud of our treatment of the Aborigines here in the Highlands,' Vi goes on. 'There was never any trouble. The local tribes were very friendly, which of course wouldn't have been the case if they'd been treated badly.'

Rose can't help herself. She walks up to the small group. 'Actually, we know that one of the first white explorers raped a Gundungurra woman and was later speared and died.' She had read everything she could find about early white settlement in the Highlands, and was not surprised that its history was sometimes grim and bloody.

The three women look horrified.

'And there was a massacre halfway between here and Sydney,' Rose continues. 'Governor Macquarie ordered soldiers to kill Indigenous people who resisted their advances. Women and children were shot at and chased by dogs over a cliff. Fourteen of them died. Colonisation is never "friendly".'

There's a long silence, then Vi says, '*Now* I remember you.' Her eyes narrow. 'You were the one trying to tell me about *tartan*.' As if nothing could be more absurd.

Rose sees the Plaskon radio and has a sudden urge to throw it at Vi's head. Instead, she says, 'That was me.'

Vi turns away and her friends scurry after her, whispering as they head to the exit. At the door, Vi stops and turns to regard Rose, giving a disgusted shake of her head.

After they've gone, Rose looks around the empty museum, wondering if she should stick to research. But the more she thinks about it, the angrier she gets. The myth of peaceful colonisation—an oxymoron in itself—is alive and well in the Southern Highlands. Why *shouldn't* she try to set the record straight? Surely she has an obligation to expose the lies of the past that still linger—lies that breed a sense of white entitlement.

On the other hand, Rose wonders if she needed to be so abrupt, so intentionally shocking. Could her tone have had something to do with the fact that Vi insulted her to the other woman at George's party? Or the fact that Vi had hit on Blackmore, however clumsily? But Rose remembers feeling sympathy for the woman after hearing what happened, and decides that her outrage at Vi's ignorance wasn't personal. But she knows she handled the situation badly. It was Rose's job to educate the women, not rub their noses in their ignorance.

Susan doesn't make it back to the museum before four o'clock, but she phones to tell Rose where there's a spare set of keys so she can lock up. When Susan asks how her afternoon went, Rose assures her that all was well.

That night, Rose is curled up on the couch with Bob and a bowl of chive-butter popcorn, watching *A Room with a View*. Miss Honeychurch and her cousin have just moved into their Florentine rooms with views when Rose's phone rings.

It's Susan.

Rose pauses the movie. 'Hi, Susan, how's your mum?'

'Better, thanks.' Then her tone hardens: 'I had a call from a visitor to the museum who was quite upset about stories you were telling about rapes and massacres.'

'Yes?'

'I was wondering what motivated you to tell such stories.'

Rose takes a deep breath and, trying to keep her voice even, says, 'If you mean *true* stories about the history of the Highlands, then I'm sorry the visitor was upset, but not as upset as the Gundungurra people whose lives and land were stolen.'

A silence ensues, which Rose refuses to fill.

'Rose,' Susan says sweetly, 'our exhibits display artefacts relating to colonial life in the Highlands. We're not what you'd call . . . political.'

Rose stares at the frozen face of a young Helena Bonham-Carter on the screen.

'Yes, but I was exposing a lie she told about our *social* history. Isn't it wrong to pretend that no violence was perpetrated against Indigenous people? We're a history museum, not Disneyland.'

Another silence.

'I'm sure it's hard for someone like you,' Susan says in an unctuously caring way, 'to adjust to the way we do things at a small, regional museum, and it was only your first day, so . . . we'll let it go.'

Rose is seconds from telling Susan to take her non-paying job and shove it, but she knows her best chance of changing things at a place like HAM is from the inside.

'Thank you, Susan. But I'm not going to lie if a visitor asks me a direct question about what happened.'

'Fair enough. So you can open up on Sunday?'

'Yes.'

'Great. Be sure to wear your Mickey Mouse ears.'

A beat.

'That was a joke,' Susan says. 'Disneyland?'

'Sorry,' Rose says. She didn't know Susan had it in her.

A short while later, Rose has reached the part in the movie where Lucy Honeychurch finds George Emerson on the Tuscan hillside in a field of red poppies—her favourite scene—when her phone rings again.

It's a landline number she doesn't recognise and she's tempted to let it go to voicemail, but her curiosity gets the better of her.

'Hello?'

'This call is from Long Bay Correctional Complex,' a recorded male voice says, 'with a call from . . .'

'Brett Taradash,' says Brett, sounding like a beaten dog.

'If you do not wish to accept the call,' the recorded voice goes on, 'hang up now. If you stay on the line, be advised that this call will be monitored and recorded.'

Rose is freaking out. But before she can decide whether or not to hang up, Brett's voice comes on the line. 'Rose?'

'Yes.' She realises she's whispering.

'Thank you for not hanging up.'

Rose doesn't know what to say, but manages, 'That's okay . . . How are you?'

'Fine.' He sounds shattered.

'Brett, what—'

'Can you come see me? I need to talk to you.'

'Me? But . . . why?'

'I need to tell you what happened.' He pauses, then seems to realise what she must think. 'I mean, I didn't do it. Any of it!' He sounds like he's falling apart.

'I—I can't help you, Brett. I'm not a lawyer or a detective or a—'

'But you found Maria. The cops couldn't find her, but you did.'

'I got lucky, Brett. Finding those pictures—'

'But then you talked to Tony and he told you about the cave. Please—just come and see me, and I'll explain. I promise you, I didn't do it.'

Rose thinks for a second, looking at the TV screen, where the young lovers are frozen in a field of poppies backlit by the golden sun. 'All right.'

'Thank you. You need to call and make a booking to visit.'

Jesus, what is she getting into? But she agrees to schedule a visit as soon as she can.

When Rose tells Kim about Brett's call, she's ready for her sister to tell her not to go, so she's surprised when Kim offers to go with her. Then she thinks about why that might be.

'I don't think so, Kim. I can see you dressing up in your trench coat and heels, pretending you're in a Raymond Chandler novel.'

'Damn. I've always wanted to visit someone in prison.'

'I'm sure it's not like the movies.'

'I bet it is.'

'I would love to take you, but I have to do this alone.'

'So what are you going to wear?'

'I don't know. Does it matter?'

'Of course it matters. There are rules.'

'Really?'

'Look it up. You can't just waltz in wearing your Dead Kennedys *Too Drunk to Fuck* T-shirt.'

'I loved that T-shirt. Didn't I lend it to you?'

'Lost it. Look up the rules, Rose. You don't want to be turned away.'

So, Rose goes onto the New South Wales Corrective Services website and discovers that there is, indeed, a strict dress code. How did Kim know this stuff?

When visiting an inmate in jail, you are not permitted to wear midriff tops, short skirts, scarves, hoodies, hats or anything low-cut. No clothing with offensive words or messages, and no gang colours, signs or logos. And no jewellery.

On the morning of her visit, Rose dresses in a white shirt over black pants, flat shoes and her navy duffel coat. No make-up, her hair pulled back in a ponytail. When she looks in the mirror, she realises she looks like a junior detective who's just been suspended for her insipid fashion sense. Perfect for Long Bay jail.

THIRTY-THREE

On the drive up to Sydney, Rose tries to figure out what Brett thinks she can do for him. Presumably he has a lawyer. She doesn't know if his parents are being supportive, or whether they believe he's guilty. He might be completely isolated. He must think she can exonerate him, but the only sure way to do that would be to find the real killer. But if the police believe Brett is a murderer, why shouldn't she?

The sun is shining when Rose gets out of the car and breathes in the briny air coming off the ocean. It's a glorious day for mid-winter, and she's suddenly overwhelmed with nostalgia for warm Sydney winter days like this, with the smell of the sea and fish and chips, and a permanent holiday vibe. In her haste to turn her back on her old life, she'd forgotten how much of it was lovely. She feels a pang in her heart for Sam, and the countless times they went to the beach at Bronte, where he rode on the kiddie train and got an ice cream afterwards. She doesn't remember Peter joining them on many of those excursions. He must have been 'working'.

Reluctantly, Rose turns to face her destination: Long Bay Correctional Complex. Surrounded by rolling green lawns, waving palm trees and a warm yellow brick wall, the prison looks, if not inviting, then at least as good as a prison could look. There are watchtowers at the corners and a high chain-link fence topped with coils of barbed wire around the grounds, but it's still not as bad as she'd expected.

She heads to the visitors gate and joins the queue, where she realises she's the only person not wearing a tracksuit. The other visitors look at her as if she's the enemy, and she regrets not wearing something to blend in. Even Kim's trench coat and heels would have been better than looking like a cop. Rose tries smiling at the wiry young woman behind her, but the woman looks like she wants to plunge a knife into Rose's carotid artery. Rose stops smiling.

After a long wait, Rose is ushered through a heavy door that clicks shut ominously behind her. The sensation of being locked in is something she has never felt before. She feels fear but, more than that, an unexpected wave of depression.

She tries to distract herself by reading the signs. DO NOT BRING IN GUNS, KNIVES, DRUGS, ALCOHOL OR SYRINGES. The signs aren't helping. She's told by a stony-faced guard that cigarettes and mobile phones must be put into a locker, for which she needs a one-dollar coin. After scrabbling around in her bag, she finds a coin and locks her phone away, putting the locker key in her pocket. She is told to stand with her arms out while someone uses a hand-held scanner to search her. She's then herded into a small space where a guard with a dog on a sturdy lead walks up to her. The dog sniffs Rose for drugs and explosives.

Rose feels like a lump of meat. No one has looked her in the eye or smiled or said anything that wasn't a command. She can't imagine life in this place. And she's just visiting. Her depression deepens as she enters the visitors room. It's large, low-ceilinged and windowless, with round stools and tables bolted to the floor. There doesn't seem to be any ventilation, and the smell of stale breath and sweat hangs in the air.

Rose is led to an empty table and told to sit on one of the white stools. It's only then that she realises there are four white stools at each table and one black, the latter reserved for the inmate. What look like mostly families are filling up the other tables. Rose is startled when a child laughs.

It feels like an eternity before Brett is brought into the room. Rose tries to arrange her face into a smile. He starts to sit down next to her.

'Black seat!' barks a guard, charging up to them, and Brett's whole body spasms. He shuffles over to the black stool and sits. The guard retreats to stand by the wall.

Brett has a fresh bruise on his right cheekbone, and his lower lip is red and puffy where it was recently split. He's lost weight and his eyes are watery and bloodshot. He doesn't look like the same person.

'Are you all right?' Rose knows it's a stupid question, but it's what comes out.

Brett has the grace not to answer it.

'Thank you for coming, Rose.'

'Not at all.' She doesn't want to ask the next question, but it's important for her to know. 'Have your parents been to visit?'

'Once. Mum fell apart when she saw me, so I told them not to come anymore. We talk on the phone, but Mum always starts crying.'

Rose pictures Sam in prison and shivers. But she's relieved that Brett's parents have visited; it suggests they probably don't think he's guilty. 'I'm sure it's hard for them,' she says. 'And what about your lawyer? Do you have a good one?'

'She's some big shot from the city. But she doesn't know the Highlands.'

Rose can hear the despair in his voice. 'What can I do, Brett?'

'You know the cave? Where you found Maria?'

'Yes.'

'We used to go there. Me and her.'

'When?'

He takes a deep breath.

'For a long time. We used to hang out there in high school, smoke weed and stuff. Then, when she was working at the pub, we kind of . . . got involved.'

'Did her husband know?'

'I don't think he knew it was me. The thing is, the police have physical evidence that I was in the cave. And I carved our initials there, in the rock. Plus there were some texts on my phone.'

'What kind of texts?' Rose asks, not sure she wants to know.

Brett grimaces. 'You know—like, making plans to meet up. Some sex stuff.'

Rose sighs. 'Was this around the time she disappeared?'

'Not long before.' He looks directly at Rose for the first time and lowers his voice to a whisper. 'But I didn't kill her. And I didn't kill my sister.' He looks like he might cry; Rose wants to take him in her arms but knows it's not allowed.

'Tell me the truth, Brett. Did you take those pictures, the ones I found?'

'No, but the police don't believe me. That's one of the reasons they think I killed Anna—they said I had the opportunity to bury the film at her house and then she confronted me after you showed her the pictures.'

'Oh God.'

'Someone else took those pictures.'

Rose waits for him to go on.

Brett lowers his voice. 'There *was* someone else.'

'Someone Maria was involved with?'

'She mentioned a guy who wanted to take her away. I got the impression he had money. I think she was tempted.'

'Did you tell the police all this?'

'Of course. They think I made it up. There are no phone calls or texts to suggest Maria was seeing anyone else. No other DNA. Nothing in the cave.'

'Brett, I am terribly sorry you're in this situation, but I don't know what I can do.'

'You're smart. You're a good listener. People tell you things. You can find stuff out. The police have decided it was me. They're not looking for anyone else. *No one* is looking.' His head drops forward and he covers his face with a hand.

Rose looks away, pretending she can't see his devastation.

He looks up at her and, in a low voice, he says, 'I don't think I'm gonna last very long.'

Again, Rose wants to reach out and touch him, but, as if he can read her mind, the guard sends her a warning look.

'Brett, the police have told me to stay out of this. They think I'm a busybody . . . or worse.'

She waits for him to say something, to let her off the hook, but he just stares at her, hopeful.

Rose takes a deep breath, her nose filling with the smell of rancid sweat. 'If I find out anything that might help your case, I will let you know, but I am going to have to tell the police first.'

Brett's face lights up. 'That's fine, that's great!'

'Please don't get your hopes up.'

'Too late!' he says and smiles, then winces as his split lip reopens. He wipes the blood on his sleeve.

Rose stands up, suddenly feeling as if she might faint if she doesn't get out of there.

'I'll let you know,' she says.

'Thank you.'

Rose watches as Brett is escorted through a door and back into whatever hell is on the other side.

When Rose walks through the door of the jail to the outside world, she is almost in tears. Not just for Brett, but for herself—tears of relief that she's free, that she isn't stuck inside, where chance or fate or circumstances might land you.

Rose is heading to her car when she notices a blue BMW parked nearby. It couldn't be, but it looks like Ray Mullin's car. Was she being paranoid? What were the chances of him being here at the same time she is? Maybe he was visiting a friend in prison. She hadn't seen him inside, but, like most people, she had gone out of her way to avoid eye contact with others. She looks around. She can't see anyone other than the armed guards in the watchtowers.

Rose goes around the back of the blue car to look at the numberplate. Her breath catches in her throat. It's Mullin's car. Rose hurries back to her Honda, gets in, guns the engine and roars out of the car park.

On her way back to the Highlands, she thinks about why Ray Mullin might have been at Long Bay. She has never been a fan of coincidences. Could he have followed her there? Could he be connected to Maria's murder? He has a history of violence. And he has money. At least, she assumes he does if he drives a new BMW. Could Ray Mullin be the mystery man Maria told Brett about? The one who wanted to take her away?

As she drives up the long incline into the Highlands, Rose feels the temperature drop. She turns on the car heater, and it's only then that she thinks again of George—how he never mentioned

Maria tending bar at his house. George has money, too. And his daughter seems to think he's in danger of having his head turned by a younger woman. Could he have had a relationship with Maria? The age difference seems too great, but it wouldn't be the first time a young woman had become involved with a much older man, for any number of reasons. And there's the persistence of sad, even scary echoes at George's house. What if she's on the wrong track with her theory about Mary Grayspence? Although she had dropped her suspicions about George when Brett was arrested, Rose wonders now if the lost soul in Threave House belongs to Maria Aboud.

It's late afternoon and getting dark by the time Rose gets home. She lets Bob out in the back garden while she gets a fire going in the stove and pours herself a whisky.

After she lets Bob back in, she curls up on the couch and FaceTimes Sam.

'Hey, Mum,' he says, yawning.

'Sorry, I know it's early.'

'It's okay, what's up?'

'I'm just calling to say that I'm happy you're living your best life, and if you're in love and decide to stay in the UK, that's fine with me—I couldn't be happier for you.'

'Mum!' Sam interrupts her. 'What's going on?'

Rose tells him about her trip to Long Bay, and that it made her realise how lucky she is that her son isn't in prison on a double murder charge.

Sam laughs. 'Thanks. Anyway, I can't imagine wanting to stay here forever, even if I am in love.'

'Are you? It's great if you are.'

'I don't think so, Mum. At least not yet,' he says, pausing to yawn. 'It must have been weird at Long Bay.'

'It was . . . I don't think Brett did it.'

'Then his lawyer will get him off.'

'It wouldn't be the first time the cops got the wrong man.'

'Maybe you should stay out of it.'

'I don't know if I can.'

He yawns again and brushes his hair out of his eyes—sea green in the rosy English dawn.

'So what's new in the world of archaeology?' she asks, to change the subject.

He thinks for a moment, then his face lights up. 'Get this—an Australian mathematician worked out that some ancient hunk of Mesopotamian clay showed that they were using geometry a thousand years before the Greeks!'

'Was the clay a recent find?'

'No, that's the insane thing! They dug it up in 1894 and it's been sitting in some museum in Turkey ever since.'

'Just goes to show you—sometimes the truth is right in front of us.'

After they hang up, Rose thinks about what she's said, and how she should apply it to her suspicions about George. Sure, he has money, and he likes women, but she's been forgetting the truth that's right in front of her: George is a good man. She knows she should have asked him by now about Maria bartending at one of his parties, but she's been afraid that his answer will shake her conviction that he is innocent of her murder.

THIRTY-FOUR

When Rose and George find each other shivering at the dog park the next morning, they agree to regroup at Manna.

They enter the cosy courtyard to find its heaters going, blankets folded over the backs of chairs, and Grace starting on a coffee and cinnamon bun.

'Join me,' she says. 'Just don't ask me to share.'

After they order, Grace says casually, 'Tell me something new—my life is feeling like *Groundhog Day* at the moment.'

Rose imagines how awful that must be—waking up every morning with Joe Blackmore, then looking in the mirror and realising how gorgeous and kind and smart you are. Rose says, 'I did something new yesterday.'

She has their attention.

'I went to Long Bay jail—pardon, Correctional Complex.'

George and Grace stare at her.

'Why?' George demands.

'Brett Taradash asked me to visit him.'

'Holy fuck,' says Grace.

George looks dismayed. 'Oh, Rose.'

Rose says to Grace, 'I'm sure your husband already knows— they keep tabs on who visits accused murderers in prison.'

'Yes,' Grace confirms. 'I'm sure they do.'

'It's okay. I mean, it was horrible. But I'm glad I went.'

Their coffees arrive and Rose looks at her friends, takes a deep breath. 'I think Brett is innocent.' She describes her visit in detail, including Brett's split lip, his plea for help, and then finding Ray Mullin's car near hers in the car park.

'You guys have known Brett a lot longer than I have—'

'But not well,' George interjects.

'Do *you* think he did it?' Rose asks.

George and Grace look at each other.

'I don't,' George says. 'But the police do.'

'I'm sorry,' Rose says to Grace. 'I shouldn't put you on the spot. I'm sure this is some kind of conflict of interest.'

'I don't care.' She ponders for a moment. 'Brett has always *seemed* to be an unlikely killer,' she says.

'So, what are you going to do?' George asks Rose.

'I'm not sure. I don't know where to start.' Then she decides it's finally time to ask George the question that has tormented her. 'How well did you know Maria?'

George seems surprised. 'I didn't.'

Rose isn't happy to contradict him, but she knows she must. 'Brett said she tended bar at one of your parties before she disappeared.'

Grace's eyes widen as George seems to think back, then nods.

'What I meant was, I knew her by sight, but I never *knew* her. That party was organised by Madeleine. I had nothing to do with Maria, beyond saying thank you for getting me sozzled.'

'Did Madeleine know her well?' Rose asks.

'I don't think so; she probably heard about her through one of her event-giving friends.'

'Would you ask her?' Rose says.

'Why don't you ring her?' George suggests.

Rose looks down for a second.

'What?' George says.

'Nothing,' Rose says, too late. She sees the perplexed look on George's face. 'I'm not sure I'm her favourite person, that's all.'

Realisation dawns on George's face, and his cheeks flush with anger. 'Did she say something?' he demands.

'It was nothing—she was being protective.'

'And it's a good thing she is,' Grace jokes to George. 'Rose is obviously after your dosh.'

Rose can see that George is embarrassed, but he feels the need to explain. 'There was a woman years ago, after Stella died, and I—'

'George, you don't need to tell me,' Rose assures him.

'I already have,' Grace admits.

'Wonderful,' George says. 'My humiliation is public and complete.'

'Stop it, George,' Rose insists. 'We've all been fooled by people. And I respect Madeleine for looking out for you.'

'She just doesn't have to be such a bitch about it,' Grace adds.

They all laugh—even George, Rose is relieved to see.

'Anyway, George, if you could discreetly ask Madeleine whether she knew Maria at all, and if she knows anything about who Maria might have been seeing, that would be great.'

'I will. But I won't mention that some sleazy gold-digger put me up to it.'

Grace howls with laughter and the dogs look up from their spot under the table, as if wondering what the hell these humans find so funny.

Instead of going straight home, Rose decides to do something she's been tempted to do since their first run-in—have a look at where Ray Mullin lives. It would be interesting to see if he might be the mystery man with money that Brett mentioned. Especially now that she's convinced George is in the clear.

She finds the photo she took of his driver's licence and checks the address. He lives on a road off the highway not far outside Moss Vale—ten minutes away. Surely if he's free to drive down her street, she has the right to drive down his.

When Rose turns on to Mullin's road, she slows down, looking for house numbers. It's a new development, and the houses are big with few trees but very expensive-looking cars.

She's keeping her eyes peeled for the blue BMW when she reaches Mullin's address. She slows to a stop and looks at the house. It's an architectural dog's breakfast—a bloated, mock Tudor McMansion with Greek Revival details. Rose wonders if she sees the house as unattractive because she knows who lives there, but she's pretty sure it's objectively ugly.

The driveway is empty and there's no movement in the windows, but security cameras are positioned around the house. Uh-oh.

'Can I help you?' a voice behind her booms.

Rose turns to see a heavy-set man in an expensive but too-tight suit walking up to her window. She's not game to roll it down. She says through the glass, 'I'm thinking of buying a house on this street.'

'This one's not for sale,' he says, and walks back to the Porsche which had pulled up quietly behind her. He gets in and drives around her into the driveway of Mullin's house.

Rose hits the accelerator and speeds away. Shit. The guy looked like Mullin. His brother? He'll tell Mullin she was there.

Fuck. What was she thinking? Putting herself at risk while trying to help Brett could be the dumbest thing she's done in a while. But it does look like Mullin has money, so maybe he *is* Maria's mystery man.

That afternoon, Rose is in the back room at the museum going through boxes, feeling like a goldminer panning for something bright and shiny amid the rubble. It's not her day to be working, but she didn't have anything better to do and she was a little uneasy at home alone. Plus it gave her an opportunity to check the database for anything that might be relevant to Maria, Anna, Brett and Ray Mullin or their families, though this proved to be a dead end.

Susan sticks her head in the door. 'I'm heading off, Rose. Can you lock up?'

'Sure. Hey, before you go, may I ask you a historical question?'

Susan opens the door wide and walks in, seeming flattered that Rose asked.

'Of course. Although it wouldn't be culturally appropriate for me to comment on Indigenous matters . . .'

Rose smiles weakly, rolling her eyes. 'I'm wondering, if someone died back in the early 1900s of something like the Spanish flu, and they were a member of a prominent family, is there any reason why an obituary wouldn't be published?'

Susan's brow furrows. 'Hmm . . . maybe the person was disgraced somehow, or their death was a scandal. But even so, there should be an obituary. They've always been a popular item in the papers.'

'That's what I thought. So, there wouldn't be a reason to cover it up if they died from the flu?'

'Heavens, no. Thousands here died of the Spanish flu. It unfolded just like Covid. They thought they'd contained it but it jumped quarantine, and before they knew what they were dealing with, it had run through entire families—and right after the war! Soldiers who had survived Gallipoli came home and died of the flu. I guess when your number's up . . .'

'So sad,' Rose says.

'You might try going through the archives of the Family History Society.'

Susan goes to the computer and shows Rose how to access their archives online. 'You need to have an account, which we do.'

'Amazing. Thanks, Susan.'

After Susan leaves, Rose dives into the Family History Society archives and finds everyone in the Grayspence family, including Mary and Margaret. The dates of their deaths are there, but not the cause of death. But she also finds a family tree that's been updated by someone in the Grayspence family who has an account with one of the ancestry websites.

Rose is able to click on a link and follow the Grayspence family descendants all the way to the present day. John Grayspence had a younger brother who married a woman in 1933. They had several children, the youngest of whom was a daughter, Helen, born in 1939. Helen Grayspence is listed as the account holder who most recently updated the family tree. There is an option to contact her. Rose feels the thrill she gets when she is close to solving a puzzle.

She sends Helen a message, explaining that she's doing research on the Grayspence's ancestral home, Threave House, and would love to chat.

The woman might not write back. She would be in her eighties now, and might even be dead. On the other hand she might be alive and know something about George's house, and tales of her ancestors who lived there long ago.

Rose starts when her phone rings. It's Grace Blackmore.

'Hi, Grace!'

'Rose! Forgive me, I am a first-class idiot.'

'Why? What have you done?'

'I told Joe I saw you at the cafe and that you think Brett is innocent.'

'It's all right, Grace. I don't mind if he knows. What did he say?'

At that moment her phone beeps to signal another call coming in. Checking the caller ID, Rose sees that it's Blackmore.

'That's him calling now,' Rose says. 'I should go.' She is sure she can feel his fury surging through her ringing phone.

'Sorry, I hope I didn't put you in the shit,' Grace says.

'Don't worry, I'm good at doing that myself.'

They hang up and Rose answers the detective's call, trying to project calm.

'Hello, Joe.'

'Rose?' She's not surprised he's one of those people who goes quiet when he's mad.

'Yes?'

'What are you doing?'

'If you mean my visit to Brett Taradash, then I was visiting a friend who invited me.'

'Rose, we have gathered, and are *continuing* to gather, a mountain of evidence—'

'Circumstantial.'

'—proving that this man has killed two women.'

'Do you have a smoking gun?'

'This isn't a film, Rose.'

'And I wonder if you can tell me why Ray Mullin's car was at Long Bay when I was visiting Brett.'

'What?'

Rose is glad that this comes as a surprise. 'I wonder if he followed me *again*. Seems like an awfully big coincidence that he happened to be there when *I* was. And it's interesting that he has a history of violence, he was in the Highlands when both murders were committed, and he has money, like the man Brett told you about—the one Maria said wanted to take her away. What if Mullin followed me to make sure I don't find out the truth?'

She hears Blackmore sigh.

'I will talk to Ray Mullin to establish his reason for being at Long Bay. I don't like coincidences either. But, Rose, I cannot warn you forcefully enough to stay away from this case.'

Rose thinks carefully about what she should say.

'Rose?'

'As long as it's not against the law for me to talk to people about the case, I will. I promise not to put myself in danger. And if I find out anything, I'll tell you before I tell Brett.' Rose wonders who this woman is, speaking with such authority and clarity— who doesn't babble or backtrack, and who stands her ground.

'Did he tell you that he and Maria argued just before she disappeared? We have a witness,' Blackmore counters.

'No.' Rose's poise wavers for only a moment. 'But if we suspected everyone who has an argument of murder, we'd all be in jail.' How is she coming up with this stuff?

'Will you do me a favour, Rose?'

'That depends.'

'Be careful.'

She can hear the weight in his words.

'I will.'

As she hangs up, Rose wonders why Brett hadn't mentioned arguing with Maria. Maybe he didn't know they'd been seen. Or perhaps there was no argument, and the so-called witness made it up to divert suspicion from himself, because *he* was the person who actually killed Maria? Rose is tempted to call Blackmore back to ask him who this witness was, but she decides not to press her luck.

THIRTY-FIVE

The next day is bone-chillingly cold, with dark clouds threatening to burst, and after a muddy slog around the dog park, Rose craves the comfort of a coffee at Manna. She feels a twinge of anxiety and realises she's been a little nervous about passing the Highland Fling and running into Vi ever since the episode at the museum.

But it's not enough to keep her away from her favourite coffee spot. And it's still early enough that Vi might not have opened the shop.

Rose walks briskly past the Fling, and when she enters Manna's courtyard she finds that Grace has arranged the market umbrellas in such a way that, even if the rain comes, she can still sit outside.

'Why aren't you inside with the sensible people?' Rose asks. 'You don't have a dog.'

'Because this is my favourite time of year—it reminds me of summer in Glasgow.'

Rose laughs as she sits down opposite Grace, marvelling at how she can look like a *Vogue* cover model on a wet, miserable day.

'No park today for George and Cordelia?' Grace asks.

'I think the weather kept them closer to home.'

'I'm so sorry about yesterday,' Grace says. 'I sometimes forget what's a secret and what isn't.'

'Me too. But I didn't say it was a secret, so you're off the hook.'

Bundled in layers of woollen jumpers, Heidi comes out looking about ten months pregnant.

'I thought you'd stopped working,' Rose says.

'I had, but Beth didn't show up today. Coffee and a cinnamon bun?'

'Just coffee,' Rose says. 'I'm trying to limit myself to one buttery, sugary treat per week.'

'Hey, speaking of treats, there's an exhibition coming up of Fiona Hall's work at the MCA in the city,' Grace says. 'Do you want to come? I can't take Joe to museums. He gets antsy and makes me rush. Says rude things about artistic pretension.'

'I'd love to,' Rose says.

'Great. We could go on a Saturday and invite Kim. We'll have a girls' lunch somewhere overpriced with a view.'

Grace must see the hesitation in Rose's face, because she says, 'What? Bad idea?'

'It's just, sometimes Kim can kind of . . . take over. She's always been more outgoing than me, and I tend to retreat when we're with other people. Does that make sense?'

Rose's coffee arrives and she wraps her cold hands around the warm cup.

'Of course it does,' Grace says.

'Do you have siblings?'

'Six.'

'Whoa!'

'I love them—well, most of them—but it's complicated.' She gets a faraway look. 'The only person I ever *really* wanted to kill was my brother, Stuart. He was three and I was four. I would

293

have done it, too, if Mum hadn't wrestled the bread knife out of my wee hand.'

Rose laughs. 'Stories like those are why I should be happy I only had one child.'

'But you're not? Happy?'

'I would have liked more children.' Rose sees this as her opening to raise a subject she's been curious about. 'You and Joe don't have kids?'

'No. We tried. For years. Went down the IVF road, but many tears and many thousands of dollars later, it never happened.'

'I'm so sorry. You would have made wonderful parents.'

'Anyway, there are benefits. I just can't think what they are right now.' Grace smiles, but Rose can see how much it hurts.

'I'll tell you one of them,' Rose says. 'Not lying awake every night of your life worrying. I think I worry even more than most mums because of what happened to my parents.' She tells Grace how her parents died and how she and Kim coped in the aftermath. 'I'm sure that's why Kim can be overprotective and sometimes overbearing with me.'

'What a terrible thing for girls so young. Did you have other family around?'

'Not in the area. And I think Kim wanted to prove she could look after me alone. It gave her a kind of mission—a way to rise above the trauma.'

At that moment Rose's phone rings. It's Kim. Rose holds up her phone for Grace to see. 'It's like she knows I'm talking about her.'

'Go ahead, take it.'

'No,' Rose says, trying out a bit of assertiveness as she sends the call to voicemail. 'I'll call her back later.'

By the time Rose leaves the cafe, a dense fog has settled over the icy roads—not a moody, romantic fog, but a can't-see-your-own-hand-in-front-of-your-face fog. She has her headlights and emergency blinkers on as she inches forward along the road. Bob is sitting up on the back seat whimpering as he looks out the window at the curtain of pale grey.

Around a bend, the fog seems a bit thinner, so Rose speeds up—she doesn't want to be hit from behind by a sixteen-wheeler—when out of nowhere, an old woman with wild white hair appears in the middle of the road. Rose hits the brakes and Bob is flung against the back of the front seat.

'Sorry, Bob!' she says, as she pulls off the road and stops. She checks Bob, who seems to be okay. Then she looks out her window, wondering if it was an apparition.

But there she is—a very old woman in an old-fashioned nightgown, standing in the fog.

Rose leaps out of the car and approaches the woman slowly.

'Why don't you come off the road? It's dangerous here.'

The woman clutches the collar of her nightie and starts to back away. Rose is worried they're both going to be killed. Bob, watching from the car, starts to howl, and the old woman's eyes widen in fear.

'It's all right, let's get off the road.' Rose puts her arm around the woman, and is relieved when she yields, seemingly comforted by Rose's touch. Standing near the car, the woman starts to shiver. Her feet are bare.

Rose takes off her duffel coat, wraps it around the woman, and helps her into the passenger seat of the Honda. Bob stops howling when Rose gets behind the wheel, and she buckles the woman in, turning the heated seat on high.

'Can you tell me where your house is?'

But the old woman just looks at her, and then smiles. 'I like your seats.'

Rose smiles back. 'I do too. Now let's find out where you live, shall we?' She suspects the woman has some form of dementia or is affected by medication—or both. At least she seems content to be in the warm car.

Rose drives to the next house, where a young woman with a crying baby on her hip says she's seen the old woman wandering the streets, and she thinks she lives in a blue house off the next side road.

Rose gets back in the car to find the woman has turned towards Bob in the back and is letting him lick her hands.

'He likes you,' Rose says. 'What's your name?'

But the woman just smiles at Bob.

'Well, I'm Rose.' And she drives on through the fog, eventually pulling up in front of a small, rundown house with flaking blue paint and an overgrown yard. The front door is wide open.

Rose helps the woman out of the car and into the house. The small lounge room is dusty and cold. Two worn easy chairs, each with a TV tray, face a boxy television set which is too big for the table it's sitting on.

'Hello?' Rose calls out.

Nothing.

She sees a small electric heater at the foot of one of the chairs. She turns it on and steers the woman into the chair. 'Let's get you warmed up!' Next to the chair is a pair of worn pink slippers. She slides them onto the woman's feet.

'Put the telly on,' the woman says, as if Rose isn't moving quickly enough.

'Yup.' Rose finds a remote and turns on one of those morning shows with a trim blonde host demonstrating a home

facial system. The old woman is instantly engrossed. Rose finds
a thin blanket on the floor and spreads it over the woman's lap,
tucking it around her.

Rose does a quick tour of the rest of the house—dirty dishes
in the kitchen, clothes on the floor, a general sense of neglect. The
two bedrooms at the back each have single beds with sheets that
need changing. In one of the rooms, she finds a framed picture
of the old woman with her arm around Beth, the waitress from
Manna, her blood-dripping neck tattoo poking out from under
her collar. She remembers that Heidi said Beth hadn't shown up
at work today.

Rose goes back into the front room. 'Do you know where
Beth is?'

The woman looks up. 'Who are you?'

'I'm Rose.'

'Beth didn't bring the tea.'

'Shall I make us a cup?'

The woman is momentarily distracted by the blonde host on
TV as she rolls a facial massage device over her cheeks. Then
she looks back at Rose. 'Tea and toast,' she says sharply. 'With
marmalade!'

Rose goes into the kitchen, takes out her phone and calls the
police, asking to be put through to Constable Tran if she's there.
When she tells Deb what happened, the constable asks Rose if
she can wait with the woman until someone gets there.

'Of course.' Rose hangs up and is looking for tea when her
phone rings again—Kim. Her sister always expects Rose to pick
up no matter what. Slightly annoyed, Rose sends the call to voicemail and puts the kettle on. She finds the teabags, washes out a
mug. As the slightly stale bread is toasting, she looks in a drawer
and finds an unopened electricity bill addressed to Gail Devlin.

She opens the fridge and recoils at the smell of rotting vegetables and spoiled milk. She hopes Gail doesn't take her tea white.

A few minutes later, Rose and Gail are sitting in the easy chairs, watching a dashing chef demonstrate how to make pasta.

There's a knock at the door. Rose gets up and opens it to Deb and Blackmore.

'Oh, I didn't—' Rose says as Blackmore walks past her and looks around the room.

'Come with me,' he says to Rose. 'Constable, stay with Mrs Devlin.'

Rose follows him into the back rooms and he asks her to repeat everything she told Deb over the phone as he makes a preliminary search. Rose adds, 'I had a coffee this morning at Manna and Heidi said Beth didn't show up for work.'

Blackmore stops going through Beth's wardrobe and turns to stare at Rose.

'But she didn't seem overly alarmed,' Rose adds.

Blackmore says, 'Her clothes are still here. And her phone.' He picks up a mobile on the dresser. He heads off to the bathroom, and Rose follows. There are two toothbrushes in a cup on the sink.

'Maybe Beth just needed some time out,' Rose says. 'Caring for someone with dementia isn't easy.'

'Or we have another missing woman,' Blackmore says grimly.

Just as Rose pulls into her driveway, her phone rings. Kim again.

'Hi,' Rose says, getting out of the car. 'Sorry, it's been a crazy morning.'

'I've been worried, Rose.' Kim sounds a bit angry.

Rose would normally try to soothe her sister, but she isn't in the mood. 'Well, that's not my fault.'

Kim sputters, confused by Rose's response. 'What's going on?'

Rose unlocks the door and enters the warm cottage, irritated that Kim has interrupted the relief she felt at getting back to her safe haven. Rose quickly recounts the events of the morning.

'So who's going to look after the old lady?' Kim asks.

'I don't know. Look, Kim, I'm in the middle of something. Can we catch up later?'

'Sure. Why don't I come down this weekend and we can hit the pub?'

'Actually, I have some stuff on.'

A pause.

'What stuff?'

Rose hesitates. 'I'm going to an exhibition of work by Fiona Hall.'

'At the MCA?'

'Yes.'

'Well'—Kim sounds increasingly confused—'do you want to come here first?'

Rose feels sick. She knows this is going to hurt Kim. 'Grace invited me.'

'Oh . . . so you were going to come to the city and not see me?'

'I don't know, I hadn't thought. We just made the plan over coffee this morning before the whole thing with the old woman happened.'

'I see. And do you think it's healthy, cosying up to the wife of the man you're in love with?'

'What?! First of all, I'm not in love with him, and second, I'm not "cosying up"; Grace and I are friends. Am I not allowed to have my own friends? Or am I fourteen again and everything I do has to be approved by you?'

'Rose, that's—'

'You still try to control me. And it's not healthy the way you live your life through mine!'

'What are you talking about?' Kim sounds outraged.

'I'm talking about how you always pushed in—with Sam, with Peter, with George. You tried to stop me from coming to the Highlands, and now you're jealous because I'm forming a friendship with someone outside your sphere of influence.'

Silence.

Rose is trembling with the rush of saying things she's wanted to say for years but never had the nerve. She's also feeling guilty for making Kim the target of this onslaught. Her first impulse is to apologise, but she stops herself.

'Everything I have done,' Kim says, her voice shaking, 'has been for you. To protect you.'

'Well, maybe that's the problem,' Rose says, she hopes not unkindly.

Kim hangs up.

Rose stares at the phone, wanting to call Kim back and invite her to lunch with her and Grace on Saturday. But she doesn't. She knows she's hurt Kim, and hates feeling this way. But it's time.

Rose had been excited when a small research job for a TV producer arrived, focusing on the role of women in the Australian gold rush of 1851 for a possible mini-series. But now, sitting at her desk, she can't concentrate, her mind going back to her conversation with Kim, picking through it for signs of hope that they haven't crossed a line they can't come back from.

Rose is staring at the bare tree outside the window when her phone rings. She grabs it, hoping it's Kim, calling to have a heart-to-heart that will end with laughter and a plan for Kim to come down to the Highlands soon.

The number is blocked.

'Hello?'

'Hi, Rose.' It's Deb Tran's voice. 'DCI Addison needs you to come into the station right now.'

'What's it about, do you know?'

'I'd better not say.'

The fog isn't quite as thick as Rose drives back to Moss Vale, but if anything, the air is colder, and she's not looking forward to meeting with Addison. At least the prospect has distracted her from her fight with Kim, which has made her feel like there's a large, cold stone in the pit of her stomach. She's also ravenous, not having eaten breakfast or lunch.

Rose assumes Addison knows about her visit to Long Bay, and wants to tell her off. She had hoped that Blackmore might have deflected another lecture from the DCI, but she knows that might be hard with someone like Addison.

When she gets to the police station, Rose asks Deb about Gail, and Deb explains that the woman, who is Beth's grandmother, is now being looked after by Grace. Gail and Beth used to be Meals on Wheels clients, before Beth got old enough to do the cooking and go to work, so Grace is used to dealing with Gail. Rose smiles, imagining Grace and Gail sitting in the easy chairs, watching some soapy daytime TV movie. Hopefully Gail doesn't panic when she realises that her granddaughter has disappeared.

'You're telling me it's a *coincidence* that you were the last person to speak to Anna Taradash alive,' Detective Chief Inspector Addison says, '*and* you found Maria Aboud's remains, *and* you just happened to find a woman wandering the streets who turns out to be the grandmother of a woman now reported missing?'

Rose wants to climb into a hole and go missing herself. 'Well, the first two aren't a coincidence,' she says. 'One led to the other. But yes, I happened to be driving home when I found Gail on the road.'

Addison seems to be waiting for more, so Rose goes on.

'Moss Vale isn't that big a town. It may be a coincidence, but it's a *plausible* coincidence.'

Rose risks a glance at Blackmore, but he's looking at a file on the table. Rose isn't sure if this is the same interview room as last time, but it seems smaller. And there's no air. She feels queasy, sweaty.

Addison says, 'When Constable Tran interviewed Mrs Devlin, she said you just appeared in her lounge room and Beth was gone. She denied being found wandering the streets.'

'Gail Devlin has dementia, Detective Chief Inspector. And even if she *did* remember wandering the streets, which I doubt, she would probably deny it for fear of Social Services sticking her into a state nursing home. Ask the woman with the baby on Throsby Street. I stopped there to find out where Gail lived, and she saw Gail in my car and said she had seen her wandering the streets. She was the one who directed me to the blue house, where Gail and Beth live.'

Addison looks at Blackmore with an unpleasant smirk. 'Do you find it convenient, DI Blackmore, that the witness who contradicts Ms McHugh's account is demented?'

Blackmore looks at Addison, then at Rose.

Rose tries to speak but she suddenly feels nauseous. And she can't find her breath. She has to get out of this room. She stands up abruptly.

And then everything goes dark.

There's a loud thump as something hits the edge of the table.

Rose is sitting in Blackmore's office holding an icepack to her upper lip while blood seeps from a small gash between her nose and mouth. Deb hands her a paper towel to soak up the blood, then Rose presses the icepack back in place.

'Well, that was a first,' Blackmore says.

'First what?' Rose asks, wincing at the pain above her mouth.

'The first time someone ended an interview with Addison before she wanted to end it.'

Deb chuckles, but stops when she sees Blackmore's look.

Rose moves the icepack aside and takes a long drink from a can of some sugary soft drink.

'Are you sure you don't want to go to hospital?' Blackmore asks. 'Your face hit the table like a sack of cement.'

Rose shakes her head slowly, swigs more soft drink, then puts the icepack back on her lip.

'I fainted because I haven't eaten. I used to faint when I was a kid—in church, when we had to fast before communion. This'll be enough to get me home.' She holds up the drink can.

'I'm sure stress was part of it,' Blackmore says. 'I'm sorry about that. We wouldn't have raised the alarm so soon, but with recent events, we need to make sure Beth's disappearance isn't connected.'

'I understand,' Rose says, her words muffled by the icepack.

'What if you need stitches?' Deb asks.

Rose gets her phone out and looks at her wound in the camera. It's half a centimetre, and the bleeding has stopped.

'I doubt it,' Rose says.

Deb hands her a small bandage and Rose smooths it gently over the cut. 'I must look like I have a moustache.'

Deb laughs as she collects the bandage wrapper and bloody paper towels.

'I have to get home to Bob,' Rose says as she stands up carefully.

Blackmore takes her elbow. 'I'll walk you to your car,' he says.

'Thank you.'

Rose actually feels better when they get outside in the cold air. She gets into her car. 'Will you let me know if Beth turns up?'

'I will,' the detective promises. 'You sure you're okay to drive?'

'Yes . . . I'm sorry I've been so much trouble.'

'Don't worry,' he says with a small smile in his husky voice. 'You keep me from getting bored.'

She tries to smile back but flinches at the pain above her lip.

Her head is throbbing as she drives away, and all she wants is to be cocooned in her little cottage, in front of the fire next to her dog, wrapped in a blanket, shutting out everything dark and disturbing in the real world.

THIRTY-SIX

As soon as Rose wakes up the next morning, she grabs her phone from the bedside table to see if Kim has called. She hasn't. In the past, whenever they had a fight, Rose has been the one to make the first move, to extend the olive branch, but she's determined not to be that person this time. She doesn't want to cave in again. But she's weakening. She misses her sister.

Rose thinks back to the first time they visited the cottage together, when Kim tried to dissuade her from buying it. Unlike her sister, with her heavy-handed arguments against the purchase, Irish Dave merely stood back and allowed Rose to decide for herself. Maybe it was just his effective sales technique, or maybe he saw what Rose needed—to stand on her on two feet.

She's tempted to call Dave and tell him what's been going on in her life, but they had agreed to take it slow. She hasn't heard from him since that day at Manna, and she would have hoped he'd call by now, but she needs to respect his boundaries. It must be awful, living with a long illness, chronic fatigue, and she mustn't add to his burdens by sharing her own.

She lets Bob outside, makes a cup of tea and brings it back to bed along with her laptop so she can check the news.

The headlines scream, ANOTHER WOMAN MISSING, and on the front page of every media outlet are pictures of Beth, smiling and happy, her neck tattoo prominent, presumably so she, or her remains, can be easily identified. Questions are raised about a possible serial killer, and the spectre of Ivan Milat is raised. Editorials question whether the police are holding the wrong man in Long Bay. An anonymous resident of Bowral helpfully suggests that Beth's will be the third body to turn up in local bushland.

Perhaps the only person who wouldn't find this news distressing is Brett, Rose muses. If something had happened to Beth, it's possible the same person who killed Anna and Maria is responsible. Maybe Brett would be proved innocent. And while Rose certainly doesn't hope Beth met with 'foul play', if someone else is responsible, her belief in Brett wouldn't feel so absurd.

Rose finds it all too upsetting, so she opens her emails, hoping for some good news. Instead, one email is from the TV producer who had hired her to investigate the role of women in the gold rush to let her know that he won't be needing her services after all—the project's funding fell through. What?! Rose had already got started, even though, if she's honest, she didn't get very far. But she had started to think about it—to immerse herself in the migration boom that followed the discovery of gold in the mid-nineteenth century, when families were hungry and desperate to find ways to scratch a living out of the land. She's tempted to bill him for half a day's work, but doesn't want to get a reputation for being a diva.

The other email is her electricity bill for the last three months—her whole tenure in the cottage—and she gasps aloud at the amount due. Apparently it's called bill shock, and is increasingly common. When she looks at the monthly usage, she sees that it skyrocketed once she got her little space heater.

Rose has to face the truth: she's going to have to get a proper paying job. She finds the job ads for the Highlands and scrolls through.

A stud farm in Wildes Meadow is looking for a farmhand whose duties included the handling of young thoroughbreds. Rose pictures herself wrangling a frisky horse and the image is both frightening and laughable. She keeps going.

A construction firm is looking for a site foreman for a large commercial development in Bowral. Rose in a hard hat ordering builders around is no less ridiculous than her working with horses. She scrolls down.

There's an opening for an Uber Eats driver, but she'd have to ride a bike or scooter. Suicide.

The McDonald's in Sutton Forest is looking for a 'crew member', but she's no doubt too old for the position, and can't see herself in one of those funny hats.

She perks up a bit when she sees an ad to work with Donna Blackmore at the nursery, but applicants 'must have know-ledge of plants', which Rose does not, and she also can't imagine working outside through the winter.

The last job advertised is for a check-out person at the Aldi in Moss Vale, for twenty-five hours a week. Out of all the listings, it's the only job she might be able to do, even though her previous experience was nearly thirty years ago, and no doubt the tills are very different now. It might be fun if she were sixteen years old, but she's looking down the barrel of fifty, and the thought is deeply depressing. On the other hand, most people don't have 'fun' at work and she'd be lucky if she could get the job.

Rose checks her phone again, making sure the sound is turned on, but there's still no call or text from Kim. She looks out to the back garden at Bob, who seems to have adjusted to the Highlands a lot better than she has. Maybe Kim was right. Maybe life in the country was a silly fantasy that hadn't materialised and was not financially sustainable.

And it wasn't safe. A third woman had disappeared, and Rose is weirdly linked to all of them. Her only two friends are a much older man whose daughter hates her, and a woman whose husband is the unattainable object of her lust. She has made several enemies, including a man who served time for assault and a local businesswoman who thinks Rose is a know-it-all. What a mess. She should sell the cottage and go back to the city.

She's sinking deeper into her pity party when an email pops into her inbox. It's from Helen Grayspence, with the subject heading *Threave House*.

Rose can't open the email fast enough.

Helen apologises for not getting back to her right away, explaining that she doesn't check the ancestry account too often. She'd be happy to talk to Rose, and gives a phone number. Rose decides it's too early now, but she'll phone right after the dog park and cafe. She gets out of bed, excited to have a mission that will distract her, at least momentarily, from her dead-end life in this cold and dangerous place.

As they stand shivering at the dog park while Bob and Cordelia chase cockatoos, Rose and George discuss Beth's disappearance as well as the email from Helen Grayspence. George jokes that it's a good thing Rose *doesn't* have a job. When would she find time to solve everyone else's mysteries if she did?

They agree to meet at Manna, and on the short drive there Rose wonders if she actually *could* become a private investigator. She decides to look into what it would entail when she gets home, just for the hell of it. Kim would *love* the idea of her becoming a 'gumshoe', and she feels a sharp pang of longing for her sister.

Rose is surprised to find Manna unusually crowded, before realising it's full of reporters and curious locals following the irresistible scent of the Highlands' latest horror. She orders a takeaway coffee from Heidi, who says she still hasn't heard from Beth and is now worried sick about the girl. Rose intercepts George on her way out of the cafe, warning him of the crowds and saying she'll call him tonight. Hopefully she'll have something to report about the history of Threave House.

On her way to the car, Rose nearly bumps into Vi, who purposely blocks the footpath, so Rose has to walk around her. Rose hopes the day improves.

As she lets Bob into the back of the car, her phone rings, and she snatches it out of her pocket hoping it's Kim. But it's Grace.

'Hi, Grace.'

'Where are you?'

'Leaving Manna—it's packed with reporters.'

'Can you come over to Gail Devlin's?'

'Okay.'

'Don't tell anyone where you're going.'

Rose can't imagine why Grace wants her there—she'd sounded quite urgent, not to mention cryptic.

As Rose pulls up in front of the little blue house, she sees both Grace's car and Blackmore's. She suddenly feels sick, hoping they haven't found Beth's body in the basement. Rose will probably be the prime suspect.

She opens the windows a crack for Bob, who's happily snoozing on the back seat, and goes to the front door. She knocks gently, and is surprised when it's opened by Constable Tran.

Rose enters the small lounge room, which is now warm and cosy, with Gail and Grace happily ensconced in the easy chairs watching the morning show. Grace smiles at Rose. 'Someone wanted to see you.'

'Hi, Rose.'

Rose turns to the voice behind her.

It's Beth, coming out of the kitchen. Rose impulsively scoops up the girl in a bear hug. Beth hugs her back.

Blackmore emerges from behind Beth, carrying a tray with a pot of tea, mugs, fresh milk and a plate of biscuits.

'I'm so sorry,' Beth says, looking deeply remorseful.

'Are you okay?' Rose asks, still confused.

'Yeah, all good.'

'Well, she will be when we organise some help for her and her nan,' says Grace. 'Sorry I didn't tell you over the phone, but'—she glances at her husband—'we didn't want you to give the game away. Beth and her mum shouldn't have to deal with reporters right now.'

Rose is embarrassed that they thought she might have told everyone at Manna the good news that Beth was home safe. On the other hand, she might have done exactly that.

'We'll leave you to it,' Blackmore says, holding the door open for Deb before casting a last look at his wife. They smile at each other, and then he's gone. Rose isn't sure that any man has ever looked at her that way. She isn't sure Peter ever did.

Beth perches on a small stool next to Gail and takes her grandmother's hand while Grace pours tea into mugs.

'Beth,' Grace says, 'didn't you have something else you wanted to say to Rose?'

'Yes!' Beth says, suddenly remembering, 'Thank you for finding Nan and bringing her home. I don't know what came over me.' She looks down, then at Grace, who nods encouragement. 'It was just . . . the night before last, Nan had me up all night, fetching this and that . . .'

Rose glances at Gail, who is completely riveted by what's on TV and isn't listening to Beth's narrative.

'When I got up yesterday morning I was so tired,' Beth says. 'We didn't have any food in the house, and I was supposed to work and . . . I just *snapped*. It's really hard sometimes.'

'Of course it is,' Rose agrees.

'I went to Liam's place down the road, and we got wasted and fell asleep and . . .' She shrugs.

'You were in a house down the road the whole time?' Rose asks.

'Yeah. I mean, I thought Nan would be okay for a while. I didn't mean to stay away so long. When we woke up this morning, Liam looked at his phone and he had about a million texts from people saying I was dead or something.'

'Oh, sweetheart,' Rose says.

'We spoke to Social Services,' Grace says, 'and they're going to get Beth some help looking after Gail.'

'Mrs Blackmore says we're eligible for financial assistance!' Beth says, wide-eyed. 'I didn't even know.'

'Well, Beth,' Rose says, 'I'm so happy you're all right and you're going to get some help. You should have my number, too, in case you just need to talk, or get out of the house. I'd be happy to hang out with Gail. Does she like music?'

'I guess,' Beth says.

'What sort does she like?'

'I dunno. Old music.'

'Frank Sinatra?'

Beth shrugs.

Rose finds a song on her phone and presses play. A big band version of 'The Way You Look Tonight', with Frank on vocals, booms out of her phone and Gail's head whips away from the TV. And then Rose starts to sing along with Frank, not well but with spirit, and Grace joins in, and then Gail starts singing too, remembering every word. They're all singing in different keys but having the time of their lives.

Beth stares at them like they're crazy.

When the song has finished, Rose explains that her grandmother had dementia and couldn't remember her own name, but when Frank or Bing Crosby or Dean Martin started to croon, she came back to life and remembered lyrics verbatim. Gail might like listening to that sort of music from time to time, Rose suggests. Beth is dazzled, and thanks her, as Rose says her goodbyes and leaves.

She finds Bob snoring away in the back of the car and muses about how nice and uncomplicated life as a dog must be. Maybe Rose will come back as a dog in her next life, if she's lucky.

When she gets home, Rose calls Helen Grayspence, trying not to get her hopes up that this woman will have anything significant to say about her ancestors or the photo of the baby in George's house.

'Hello?' The voice that answers is strong and clear.

'Hello, this is Rose McHugh. Am I speaking to Helen?'

'Yes—hello, Rose.'

They chat amiably as Rose explains that she's a historian looking into the background of Threave House on behalf of her friend George, the current owner. Helen is as anxious to hear about George and what he's done with the house as Rose is to hear about its past, and she invites Rose to come to her place in Kangaroo Valley.

'Certainly,' Rose says, thrilled that the woman is happy to meet face to face, which might make it easier to raise the subject of ghosts. 'What day would suit you?'

'Well, I'd like to say I'm a busy woman, but my days are fairly empty. If you're free this afternoon, you could come by at three?'

'Perfect.' Rose notes down Helen's address. Between Beth's return and the conversation with Helen, things are looking up.

This is Rose's first trip to Kangaroo Valley since moving to the Highlands, and she can't remember the last time she was there; it may even have been as a child, when her father was driving.

The winding road, with its hairpin turns along the escarpment, takes her by surprise. It's a windy day, and she imagines the swaying, creaking trees dropping their massive branches on top of her car or on the road in front of her, forcing her to swerve off into the guardrail and plunge over the edge. She slows down and is grateful there isn't a hoon in a ute behind her, nudging her faster than she wants to go. Even driving at a crawl, it takes all her concentration to stay on the road, but every once in a while she gets a glimpse of the magical valley off to the side. How nice it would be if someone else were driving and she could look out the window and take in the view. She thinks, not for the first time, that as happy as she is on her own, there were certain perks to being married. Although, if the main reason to be with someone is so they can occasionally take the wheel while you look out the window, it isn't enough.

Rose breathes a sigh of relief as she comes off the mountain into the valley, driving past farms with rolling green pastures and gum trees hundreds of years old. She stops at the General Cafe, which she decides she will return to with Kim—if they're ever on speaking terms again. The menu is a creative fusion of modern Australian and Japanese cuisine, and she buys two slices of cheesecake to take to Helen.

A few minutes outside the town, she finds Helen's house—a small but perfectly formed mid-century stone, wood and glass hideaway. Rose parks out front and is met by Helen at the front door.

The older woman is tall and thin, with shoulder-length silver hair, striking blue eyes and a wrinkled face that's a wonderful map of her life experience. She's wearing a quilted black and pink kimono top over black pants and white high-top sneakers. Nothing about Helen Grayspence is what Rose expected.

'Come in, and welcome,' Helen says warmly.

Rose enters the split-level house to find the entire back wall is a giant window overlooking the Kangaroo River and surrounding bush. Rose is entranced. It would be like living in a treehouse. She hands Helen the cheesecake and is drawn to the glass wall, staring down at the water rushing over mossy stones under the windswept trees.

'It's like a magnet, isn't it?' Helen says.

'I'd never get anything done if I lived here. I'd just sit all day and watch the river.'

'Some days that's exactly what I do.'

Helen sets out the cheesecake on two plates. 'Thank you for this. How did you know I love cheesecake?'

'Well, you sounded very reasonable over the phone, and what reasonable person doesn't like cheesecake?'

Helen's laugh is like a tinkling bell. Rose doesn't ever want to leave.

'What would you like to drink? I could make tea, black or herbal, or coffee. I'm actually going to make myself a martini, and I'd love you to join me, but with the drive back . . .'

'Oh God, I cannot tell you how much I would *love* a martini, but you're right—I'd never make it back up the mountain. Black tea with milk would be great, thanks.'

While Helen is making tea for Rose and a martini for herself, complete with cocktail shaker and James Bond martini glass, Rose warms her hands in front of the floating fireplace in the centre of the open, high-ceilinged room.

'One of the benefits of retirement is that you can drink martinis whenever you want,' Helen says.

'What work did you do?'

'I was a doctor. A GP. I had a clinic in Mittagong for years, then, when my husband and I retired, we bought this plot of land. He's an architect. He didn't believe anyone had ever improved on mid-century style, and I tend to agree with him, so he designed this.'

Rose gets the feeling Helen lives alone and is curious about her referring to her husband in the present tense. 'So, is he still . . . with us?'

'He's alive, if that's what you mean. We were divorced a year after we built this place. Once we were alone together, we realised we didn't have a lot in common—or even like each other very much. I think for forty years we were both so busy with careers and children that we hadn't noticed.'

'Did he stay in the area?' Rose asks as Helen sets the drinks and cake on an oval coffee table and sits on a modern ochre couch.

'He moved to California. He's teaching at some prestigious university, having his ego fed by adoring undergrads. Please, have a seat.'

Rose sits down in an Eames lounge chair at an angle to the couch, so she can talk to Helen and take in the view. 'My ex-husband is a professor of ancient history at Sydney Uni. We met when I was his student.'

They exchange a look that says they share a working know-ledge of academia's complex romantic entanglements.

Rose suddenly realises she could happily chat away for hours with this woman, and decides that's all the more reason she should be completely honest about why she's here.

As Helen sips her martini, Rose recounts her experiences at Threave House, from the feeling of being watched, to the cold in the bathroom and then the icy terror of the back bedroom and its strange portrait of an infant on the wall. She describes Stella's experience and her own search through the records for the identities of Helen's deceased ancestors, and the mystery of the missing obituary.

Throughout, Helen stays silent, giving Rose as much time as she needs to explain how her investigations have led her here.

When Rose is finished, she asks Helen, 'So, does any of this make sense to you?'

Helen gazes out at the river, remembering.

'I'm sure it's why I prefer modern houses. Growing up in Threave House was hell.' She gets to her feet. 'Would you mind if I refresh my drink?'

'Not at all,' Rose says, desperate to hear what Helen has to say. Helen returns with a fresh martini and the teapot. She pours Rose another cup and resumes her seat on the couch.

'I'm a doctor—a scientist. I believe in hypotheses that can be tested and proved or disproved through the systematic gathering of data. But contrary to everything I believe as a scientist, I know there is a ghost at Threave House. And I know who it is.'

Rose takes a moment to absorb this. 'I want to hear everything you have to say, but only if you're happy for me to pass it on to George.'

Helen nods. 'It's time I told someone. This has been our family's shameful secret for too long.'

'Thank you.'

Helen takes a swig of her martini. 'I shared a bedroom with my older sister until I was nine and she was thirteen. She'd been nagging my parents for her own room, so I was given the back bedroom. Until then, it had been a guest bedroom, but we rarely had guests. The first night I spent there, I kept getting up, begging my parents to let me go back to my old bedroom. But I was returned to the new room and told not to leave until morning.

'The room was cold. But, worse, it was . . . the best word I can use to describe it is sad. Horribly sad. I cried myself to sleep night after night, and we all thought—I as well as my parents—that it was because I missed my sister, or simply didn't want to be alone. But my reaction was, to say the least, disproportionate. I became hysterical, beyond consoling. And I had nightmares. Mum wanted to let me move back in with my sister, but my father wouldn't hear of it. He said I was spoiled.

'And that picture of the baby . . .' Helen shivers theatrically.

Rose nods.

'I hated it,' Helen says, 'but my father wouldn't let me take it down. He said it was his niece and this had been her room. He didn't tell me anything else. One night, I think I was about eleven or twelve, I woke up suddenly out of a deep sleep and knew someone else was in the room. I looked around, and there in the corner, in the dark, was a woman—standing perfectly still, facing me. I couldn't make out her features, but I could tell she was wearing a floor-length nightgown.'

Rose feels the terror the girl must have felt and realises she's holding her breath. She forces herself to breathe as Helen goes on.

'I tried to call out for Mum, but no sound came out of my mouth. I pulled the covers over my head so the thing in the corner couldn't see me. I stayed like that for God knows how long and must have fallen asleep. The next morning I told Mum and Dad there was a woman in my room, and they told me to stop making up stories.'

'You poor thing,' Rose says, wishing she was drinking Helen's martini.

'It wasn't until my sister got married and moved away that I was allowed to reclaim her bedroom. I was fifteen. Even though I wasn't sleeping in the back room anymore, I would occasionally feel like the woman was somewhere in the house, watching me. My father was at work one day when my mother saw me staring at something in the hall. "You can see her, can't you?" she said, and then she told me what had happened.

'In 1918, my uncle John and his new wife Mary were living at Threave House with his parents. He had survived the so-called Great War and they were expecting their first child. The Spanish flu had been running rampant, but by January 1919 the authorities thought they had it contained. Sound familiar?'

Rose nods, 'Just like Covid.'

'Mary was eight months pregnant that February, when she started feeling ill. John was also unwell, as was his father and my own father, John's younger brother. When they realised it was the

Spanish flu, the family was quarantined. Pregnant women were dying at a far higher rate than other infected people, and the family was afraid they'd lose Mary and the child. But miraculously, Mary survived, and a month later she gave birth to little Margaret.'

'The baby in the picture?' Rose asks.

'The baby in the picture,' Helen confirms. 'Margaret lived for two weeks, but she was weak from the flu. The virus was not kind to babies whose mothers had been sick. The baby died, but Mary could not accept it. She was insane with grief. John tried to comfort her, promised her they'd have another, but Mary wanted Margaret back. A week after they lost the baby, Mary lay down in the bed in the back bedroom and cut her wrists. John was devastated, and angry. There was no obituary because suicide was a sin, and it would have brought shame to a family whose son had been decorated in the Great War. They could have lied and said she died from the flu, but they blamed her instead.'

Perhaps it's the way that Helen brought this story to life, or the effect of her own recent experiences, but it takes a moment for Rose to realise they're both quietly crying.

It's dark as Rose drives back up the mountain, and it's actually easier to see cars coming because they have their headlights on. But it's harder to see the road, which is completely unlit. Rose grips the wheel, trying to anticipate the sharp curves under the trees that seem to lean over the road with malicious intent.

Once she's back in the high country, driving long stretches through bush and farmland invisible in the dark, Rose goes over Helen's story in her head. She had assumed the dead mother and child had succumbed to the flu, but Mary's grief and subsequent suicide go further, perhaps, towards explaining why her presence is still felt in the house. Rose has heard the theory that a spirit haunts a place if the person died suddenly or violently, or for some reason left unfinished business. If Mary was unable to accept the death of her baby, and her own death was unacknowledged because it was considered shameful, then it's not surprising that her soul might be unsettled, floating restlessly in the house where she last held her child.

Rose wonders about Anna and Maria, and whether their spirits somehow inhabit the forests where their bodies were found—and whether there's anything she can do to bring them peace.

'My God, the poor woman,' George says over the phone.

Rose is nestled on her couch in front of the fire. She has told George everything she learned from Helen, and he is as moved as she was.

'I know,' Rose says. 'Maybe we should do something to recognise Mary. To acknowledge her life—and her loss.'

'What do you have in mind?'

'I don't know, but let's think about it. Maybe I can find out more about her from Helen. If she was a devout Catholic, for example, we could have a mass said in her honour.'

'Although I believe the Catholic Church still considers suicide a mortal sin.'

'Christ, you're right. Well, let's think of something that might be meaningful to her, not just to us.'

After they hang up, Rose longs to tell Kim what's been going on—with Helen, with Gail and Beth, all her weird Highland adventures. But she'd promised herself she wouldn't be the one to call. On the other hand, hearing about Mary's grief and the terrible disease that killed an infant, a loss whose echoes were still felt to this day, she realises how pointless a promise like that is. She calls her sister.

The phone rings a few times and she's starting to fear Kim won't answer when finally she hears a guarded, 'Hello?'

'You sound like you don't know who it is,' Rose says. 'I hope you haven't deleted my phone number.'

'Thought about it. And a lot of things that I guess I'm still processing.'

'Me too. But in the meantime, can we just be friends again?'

'Oh my God, I was hoping you'd say that. I tried talking to one of the other teachers at school about something vaguely deep and meaningful and she looked at me like I had fruit bats flying out of my nose.'

'What were you talking about?'

'Who knows? It wasn't important.'

Rose laughs.

'But you would have got it,' Kim explains. 'So, I saw in the paper that the missing woman was found.'

'Beth, yes—she was never really lost. But I got questioned again by the police.'

'Ooh, did your hot detective tie you up and interrogate you?'

'Yes, that's the way they do things now. And afterwards he came to my rescue when I fainted and slammed my face into the table.'

'What?!'

'I have a scar that looks like a pencil moustache.'

Kim laughs.

'Don't laugh.'

'I can't help it!'

When Kim has calmed down, Rose fills her in on the latest developments, including her visit to Helen Grayspence.

'Wow,' Kim says. 'My life is so dull in comparison. Guess I'll have to head down to the Highlands soon for some excitement.'

'I think you'd better. I'm clearly becoming unhinged on my own. I even looked into becoming a private detective.'

'Stop it, that's fabulous! You should do it.'

'I don't think so. It turns out most freelance detective work is spying on people who have made workers compensation claims.'

'Well, that doesn't sound very Sam Spade. Clearly I need to intervene to handle your career.' Then she seems to remember what they'd fought about. 'Or not! You should do whatever you want, of course. I didn't mean—'

Rose laughs. 'It's okay, Kim.'

'So, shall I come the weekend after next?' Kim asks almost timidly. Rose notes that she doesn't suggest this weekend, when Rose has plans with Grace.

'Perfect.'

'Meantime, don't hold any séances or find any dead bodies without me.'

'Promise.'

'Love you, Rosie.'

'Love you, too!'

For the first night in ages, Rose sleeps soundly.

THIRTY-SEVEN

With Beth home safe, the consensus is once again that Brett Taradash killed Anna and Maria. But Rose remembers what he looked like when she visited him in jail—desperate and beaten but, above all, innocent. Could she be so bad a judge of character as to be completely fooled by him? Kim reminded her that Ted Bundy seemed like a nice guy too, but from the footage of Bundy in interviews, Rose doesn't think he presented as anything like Brett. Bundy had a certitude, a swagger and a coldness, none of which Brett has ever displayed. If Brett really is a psychopath, then he's also the greatest actor of all time.

Thinking about what other paths might lead to still buried truths, she wonders how Nick Aboud feels about the arrest, and she decides to approach him. When he came to her house, he'd asked Rose to let him know if she found anything, and she'd ended up finding his wife's remains. He might not want to speak to her at all. On the other hand, it's worth a shot—who knew where it might lead? She rings the number listed for the vineyard.

'Nick Aboud speaking.'

'Hello, Nick, this is Rose McHugh.'

A pause, then, 'Rose, I've been meaning to call you. I wanted to thank you.'

'Oh, you don't owe me any thanks,' Rose says, flustered.

'No, I do. I can't tell you how grateful I am.'

Rose is thrown—grateful that she found his wife? Or that her discovery led to the arrest of someone other than him?

'At least now I know she didn't run away,' he clarifies.

'Well, I'm glad I could do something. And there are a couple of things I wanted to ask you. Is now a good time?'

'Actually, I'm about to show a prospective buyer around—I'm selling up. Why don't you come here and see the place?'

'All right.'

They make a plan for Rose to drop by the next day, and she is struck by the difference between the man on the phone and the one who came to her house. The Nick Aboud she'd first met was almost paralysed with heartache. Now he sounded lighter, as if relieved of a great weight.

Rose is still mulling over Nick's transformation as she drives to the vineyard outside Sutton Forest the next day. It makes sense that, after Maria's remains were found, he was finally able to move on. Before then, not knowing where she was, whether she was dead or alive, he must have been going insane. On the other hand, wouldn't he have hoped that she was alive? If he loved Maria, wouldn't it be better to have discovered that she'd left him, rather than that she was dead? Was he relieved because someone else had been charged with her murder, she wonders. Was Nick in high spirits because he'd got away with it?

Rose shakes off a momentary twinge of nerves as she drives through a wide metal gate and passes row after row of bare vines in neat rows, their spindly trunks and leafless, bony branches clinging to the wire fence in the winter wind. She parks next to

Nick's van in front of a cluster of low buildings. She gets out, and as she approaches a modern wood and glass building with a sign reading CELLAR DOOR, Rose asks herself if it's wise to be visiting Nick Aboud alone. If Brett is innocent, does she have something to fear from this man?

'G'day!'

Rose turns to the voice behind her. Nick is gripping large pruning shears, which he raises in a wave as he approaches.

'Hello, Nick.'

'Been trimming the vines.'

'I didn't realise you did that in winter. The vines look so . . . dead.' Rose regrets her choice of word the second it's out of her mouth, but Nick doesn't notice.

'Yeah, they look that way, but you have to prune in winter to tell the vine how many bunches of grapes you want next season.'

'So you might be staying on?'

'No, but the bloke who came yesterday might want to make a go of it, so I'll keep things going—at least till he makes an offer. Or doesn't.' He takes a step towards her. 'Let's go inside, have a tipple.'

Rose steps back and lets him lead the way into the building. They enter a small boot room, where he puts his shears in a tool basket before taking her into an elegant space—a sleek wooden interior with polished concrete floors and large picture windows looking out over the vineyard. Simple wooden tables and chairs are spaced comfortably around the room, and against one wall is a bar and shelves displaying the different Aboud Estate wines.

Nick gazes out the windows at what he's about to give up. 'Everyone else likes the view when it's green, but I like it now. The vines are still busy, getting ready for all those tasty grapes that'll develop in the heat.'

Rose hears his passion, but also a note of regret.

'Have a seat.' He gestures to a table, where an open bottle of pale pink wine and two glasses are waiting.

'This is a beautiful room,' Rose says, sitting down.

'Maria did it. She was great at that stuff.' He pours the wine. 'Know much about rosé?'

'Nothing, I'm afraid.'

He picks up his glass, swirls it and then sniffs. 'This is a pinot noir rosé. Our star performer. It has a reputation as a difficult grape but it grows really well here. Loves the cold and wet.'

Rose takes a sip. She hadn't thought she'd be drinking—it's not even midday—but she doesn't want to refuse Nick's hospitality, especially as he's so excited about his wine. 'Mmm, that is delicious,' she says, immediately taking another sip.

'Thank you.'

'So, you're selling up?'

He nods. 'Yeah, now that I know Maria's not coming back, I can't stay.'

'I guess not. Where will you go?'

'Back up to Newy. Mum and Dad are getting on, and it'll be nice to look in on them more often.'

'Well, I'm glad you can . . . move on.' Rose is treading lightly, not wanting to suggest that he's happy with the way things have worked out.

'Yeah, I hadn't even realised how . . . *frozen* I was—not knowing if Maria was alive or dead. I had bad depression. And I'm ashamed to say it, but I was glad when I found out she hadn't left without telling me.'

'Don't be ashamed. It's understandable.' Rose finds herself empathising with this man, who, only moments ago, she'd thought of as a murder suspect. She worries fleetingly that she always seems to believe the last person she talked to.

'But it's driving me crazy,' he says. 'I want to believe that the argument she had with that young bloke was about her saying she wasn't going to leave me. But if that's true, then that's probably why he killed her.' He gasps at the thought before collecting himself.

Rose has to remind herself why she's here. 'So, you're convinced he's responsible?'

Nick looks at her sharply. 'Aren't you?'

'Well,' she says, backtracking, 'apparently the evidence is circumstantial. You always want there to be . . . you know, undeniable proof.'

'I reckon the undeniable proof is they used to go to that place in the bush—the cave where you found her. Then someone saw them fighting. It all adds up.'

'Yes, it does,' Rose admits. 'Do you know who it was who saw them arguing?'

'No.'

Rose suddenly pictures Ray Mullin reporting the argument to the police to cover up his own actions. But there's no reason to think it was him. And surely Blackmore wouldn't trust his word.

Nick raises his glass. 'Anyway, thank you, Rose.' He waits for her to raise her glass in return, and they clink.

As Nick waxes lyrical about pinot noir grapes, Rose slowly sips her wine. She can tell he's lonely and enjoying her company. But when he starts to pour another glass, she stops him.

'Thank you, Nick, but I'm driving. I should get going.'

'Fair enough. Do you want to see Maria's office before you go?'

'I'd love to.'

Rose isn't sure what to expect when he leads her into a small room behind the bar, but she discovers a space that's more like a cosy den than an office. There are interior design and entertaining books on the shelves and a day bed strewn with cushions and lifestyle magazines.

'She was going to run her event business out of here. I guess I can finally pack it up. Thanks to you.'

Rose is turning to leave when her eye is caught by a wooden ball on a shelf. It's about twenty centimetres in diameter and its intricate inlaid pattern is identical to the wooden pyramid that Anna had, and the cube that Rose bought in Bowral.

'May I?' Rose asks, pointing to the ball.

'Be my guest.'

Rose picks it up and examines it, feeling the tiny wooden pieces shift under her touch. 'I have a cube like this. And Anna had one in the shape of a pyramid. Did you give it to Maria?'

'No.'

She replaces it on the shelf. 'Do you know if she bought it? Or maybe Anna gave it to her?'

'No idea.' Nick looks at Rose. 'You should have it,' he insists.

'Oh, no, I couldn't.'

'I'm serious. I want you to have something of hers.' He picks up the wooden ball and holds it out to Rose.

She takes it.

'Thank you, Nick.'

At home, Rose carries the wooden ball to the bookcase in her lounge room, repositioning her cube to sit at the opposite end of the same shelf. The ball has a small, flat base so it sits without rolling away. She stands back and admires the symmetry, thinking about how we're comforted by things being in balance—small things that we surround ourselves with in our homes that seem to repel the chaos outside.

But she's nagged by the question: does it mean anything that both Maria and Anna—and she herself—had one of these pieces? Or is it just another coincidence?

Rose is still pondering this question the next day, as she wheels her shopping trolley down the health food aisle at the super-market. This aisle is usually deserted, especially this early in the morning. She got into the habit of shopping right after opening time during Covid to avoid crowds, and she still likes to come when it's quiet. She's bobbing her head to a song playing on the sound system—'Everybody' by the Backstreet Boys, which two-year-old Sam used to bounce along to—when she hears a voice behind her.

'Crazy old bag.'

She turns to see Ray Mullin carrying a shopping basket. She glances into it and doesn't know why she's surprised to see fresh fruit and organic cereal.

'I thought you were just a crap driver,' he says. 'Then I hear you came to my house.'

Rose feels the flight instinct rising within her, and she's about to turn and leave when something makes her stop.

'But you came to mine,' she says. 'Twice. At least.' She stands her ground and glances up, hoping to see security cameras hanging from the ceiling, but there aren't any over the health food aisle.

He takes a step closer and lowers his voice to a whisper. 'No one's gonna miss you when you're gone.' He walks away.

Rose realises her hands are sweating as they grip the trolley handle, and the Backstreet Boys tell everybody to rock their body right.

Should she let the police know that Mullin made another implied threat? In her head, he fits the profile of a man who could do harm to women, and there's a chance that he knew Maria Aboud. They're both locals and he'd been to the pub where she used to work.

But Mullin was right—Rose did go to his house. No doubt he would spin it into a story about a crazy hormonal woman who'd rammed him with her car then stalked him at home. And now she was spreading malicious rumours connecting him to two murders of which he is innocent.

Rose pictures herself being led away from her cottage in handcuffs or a straitjacket and decides to keep the encounter to herself.

THIRTY-EIGHT

Rose thoroughly enjoys her trip to the city with Grace, fending off the occasional pang of guilt when she thinks about how much Kim would enjoy it too. After seeing Fiona Hall's beautiful miniatures of tin trees at the museum, they had lunch at Cafe Sydney, a restaurant perched on the rooftop of Customs House overlooking Circular Quay. Rose was in awe of the postcard view of the harbour, the bridge and the gleaming white cruise ships. And she was at first too dazzled by the menu to choose, but then the barramundi had her at 'caper lemon burnt butter'. Grace had the tandoori-roasted salmon and they swooned as they tried each other's selections.

The best part of the trip was actually the drive up to Sydney and back, and Rose can't remember the last time she spent hours just talking with someone other than Kim or Peter or Sam. She and Grace traded stories about their families, their childhoods, their careers. Grace had been an idealistic young journalist, working for a left-wing newspaper in Glasgow that no one read, and longed to do something meaningful. She started volunteering as a 'big sister' to women leaving prison, and now also ran a program for victims of domestic violence as well as Meals on Wheels in the Highlands. Rose suggests that her own service to the community has been terribly inadequate in comparison, but Grace points out that Rose is trying to help a young man whom she believes is innocent to escape from a murder charge.

They feel the temperature drop as they drive back into the Highlands, and finally get around to talking about their marriages, Rose listening avidly as Grace describes how she met Joe.

'I was in Sydney on holiday with a girlfriend from Glasgow. She was turning thirty and she was determined to marry an Australian. I kept her company while she prowled the streets—literally. One night, we ended up at the Opera Bar and were on our third margaritas when she spotted two blokes—and I had to admit, there was something about them.'

'Joe?' Rose asks.

'And his brother.'

'Joe has a brother?'

'Eric, a couple of years younger. They could be twins. Anyway, we all got flirting—they'd been at a bucks' night and were even more blootered than we were. Long story short, my friend went back to Glasgow empty-handed, and I got lucky.'

'Aw, that's lovely. But I feel bad for your friend.'

'Don't. She ended up with a gorgeous woman who's making her a lot happier than Eric would have.'

They both laugh.

'And what about Eric?' Rose asks.

'Bloody Eric. He's going through his second divorce. He's his own worst enemy—always picks the wrong women. Or they pick him.'

As they approach Berrima, Rose tells Grace about her visit to Kangaroo Valley. Grace is riveted, as much by the description of

Helen Grayspence and her fabulous mid-century-style house as the sad tale of her aunt Mary.

'We must find a way to recognise Mary properly,' Rose says, and Grace agrees.

THIRTY-NINE

Rose is making her way through the boxes at the museum, having unearthed more intriguing nuggets of family history which she has dutifully logged and filed. She wonders if anyone will ever need or want access to the information. Maybe there's a book in it. Ever since she received her blood-curdling electricity bill, she's been aware that she has to find paying work.

'Are you busy, Rose?' Susan is standing in the doorway. Today she's wearing a mauve twin-set and the grey pants. Like Rose, she seems to have a uniform.

'Just deciding whether to file an 1897 photo of an unnamed woman on a horse under pets, hobbies, stud farms or women's history,' responds Rose.

'Livestock. There's a young lady here to see you.' Susan lowers her voice. 'She's very pushy.'

'Oh,' Rose says, bemused. 'I'll be right out.' She files the photo under 'Livestock', wondering what pushy young woman might want to talk to her, hopeful that it's someone who is so desperate to pay for her services as a researcher she has sought Rose out in person.

But when Rose enters the main museum space, it's Jazzy Nolan in her leather jacket, peering at the old radio in the kitchen display. Jazzy looks up as Rose approaches. 'I love this old Bakelite radio.'

'It's Plaskon,' Rose says. 'What do you want?'

'I want to do a feature story on Rose McHugh,' the reporter says, spreading her hands as if she's framing a banner headline. 'The woman at the heart of the Highlands' great mysteries.'

'No,' Rose says, turning around and heading back to the storeroom.

'You haven't heard my angle.' Jazzy follows her straight into the back room, even though Rose makes a feeble attempt to close the door.

'I don't need to. I'm not at the heart of anything.'

'Oh, but Rose, you are! Beth Devlin told me you were the one who found her grandmother, wandering the streets, crazed and—'

'She wasn't crazed, she was cold.'

'She was cold, that's good,' Jazzy says, speaking into her phone, apparently recording.

'Please don't,' Rose says as she sits back down at the ancient computer.

'And you found photos of a missing woman and then found that woman's remains yourself! Our readers want to know: are you psychic? Do you use astrology? Tarot cards? What's your modus operandi, Rose?'

'Is this girl bothering you?' Susan asks from the door.

Rose sighs. 'I'll take care of it, Susan.'

But Susan just stands there, unwilling to miss any part of the show.

Jazzy starts to thumb through the box of mementoes. Rose gets up and takes the box away, sliding it under the desk.

'Jazzy, you really have to leave,' Rose says. 'I'm not interested in becoming any more notorious than you've already made me.'

Jazzy speaks into her phone. 'Notorious . . . that's good . . . it's got a Hitchcock vibe.'

'No, Jazzy. I mean it.'

Jazzy finally seems to be getting the message. She lowers her phone. But there's a steeliness in her stare. 'What did you and Brett Taradash talk about when you visited him at Long Bay?'

Rose gasps. 'Who told you—'

'What exactly is your connection to the crimes? Did you and Brett plan—'

'That's it,' Susan says, as she hustles Jazzy out through the door. 'This area is closed to the public.'

Jazzy calls out from the exhibition space, 'You were seen several times with the accused, including the night he was arrested. I'll get to the bottom of this, Rose. Whatever you're hiding, I'll find out!'

Susan steers her out the front door. When she returns, Rose is sitting at the desk, shaken.

'Don't worry about her,' Susan says. 'It's a slow news day.'

'But do you think she—or anyone—really thinks I had anything to do with . . .' Rose shudders.

'I don't know. They will find it interesting that you visited an accused double murderer.' Susan leans closer. 'Is it one of those things like when women fall in love with serial killers and start writing them letters in prison?'

'No! I had met Brett a few times and he seemed . . . he just . . .' Rose is about to explain that he'd asked for her help, but she stops herself, realising that whatever she tells Susan could be on the Highlands grapevine in minutes. 'He's just very . . . isolated.'

'Well, I should hope so. He's a double murderer.'

'Alleged,' Rose says weakly.

FORTY

The next day, Rose has to run some errands in Moss Vale, and she walks along the main street with her head down like a convicted felon. After her latest encounter with the Highlands' most shit-stirring journalist, Rose is afraid of appearing in the media as an accessory to murder and being confronted in the street by an angry mob.

She's passing the real estate agency when an ad in the window catches her eye. She stops.

Beautiful colour photos of the Aboud Estate vineyard are the centrepiece of the display, and Rose marvels at how different the vines look just before harvest, dripping with grapes and lush with green leaves in the warm summer sun.

'Hello, Rose.'

Rose turns to see Dave coming out of the office, pulling on his puffer coat, his breath visible in the cold, moist air. 'Hi,' she says. 'How are you?'

'Not too bad. Getting there.'

'I'm glad.'

He sees that she was looking at the ad. 'Thinking of buying a vineyard?' he asks jokingly.

'No, thank you—Nick told me about all the things that can attack the grapes!'

'You know Nick?'

'Not well.'

'There's a lot of interest in the place,' Dave says. 'People love the fantasy of having a vineyard. No idea how bloody hard it is.'

'I feel bad that Nick has to leave. It was his dream.'

'Yes, but I can understand why he can't stay.'

'I know. But I think there are still some unanswered questions about the case.'

'There always are, Rose,' Dave says with a cheeky grin. 'Anyway, maybe we can have that dinner soon?'

'That would be great.'

'Fantastic. I'll ring you.'

As she walks away, Rose hopes he really means it.

That night Rose is curled up on the couch in front of the fire, Bob's head draped over her thigh, as she tells Kim about running into Dave.

'So, do you like him?' Kim asks.

'I do. I'm not what you'd call . . . infatuated, but maybe that's a good thing.'

'Yeah, you're much more likely to be a doormat for someone if you're infatuated.'

'Do you think I was a doormat for Peter?'

'Not a doormat . . . more like a bathmat—useful, but with a mind of its own.'

Rose laughs. 'Thanks.'

'So, what about Brett? Are you still planning to help him?'

'There's really nothing I can do.' But Rose knows she's trying to talk herself into being detached. She doesn't feel detached.

When they hang up, Rose looks up at Maria's wooden ball on the bookcase.

Standing, she takes it off the shelf and inspects its intricate inlaid pattern. She likes things that are both beautiful and useful, and this is merely beautiful. But that's true of all art, isn't it? Beauty is enough.

But there's something about this beautiful wooden object that's nagging her.

Rose presses the wooden inlay, feels the pieces shift. Why do the pieces move? Is it just for a textural, tactile effect? Or does the movement of the pieces suggest some utility? She takes her wooden cube off the shelf and sets it on the coffee table next to Maria's ball. Their geometric pattern is the same.

Rose picks up her cube and pushes against the pieces of inlay. Like the ball, they move ever so slightly. They feel like pieces of a puzzle that fit together.

And suddenly, Rose remembers a wooden pyramid she gave Sam for his tenth birthday. It was about the same size, maybe twenty centimetres high, and it was beautiful, intricate, with dozens, perhaps hundreds of moving parts. And it was designed to open up to reveal a secret chamber inside.

The pyramid was a puzzle box.

Sam was obsessed with figuring out how to open it and it took until late that night—way past his bedtime—but he finally worked it out, opening the secret chamber at the heart of the pyramid.

But surely if Rose's cube opened, the woman who sold it to her would have mentioned that it was a puzzle. On the other hand, maybe the woman didn't know, or couldn't be bothered explaining. Rose looks online, but the artist, Ned Petrovic, doesn't have a website, or a listed phone number.

Rose picks up her cube, trying to move the pieces this way and that, but they don't seem to want to come apart. She closes her eyes and tries to remember how Sam's pyramid worked. She can picture the pieces on one side—there may have been a piece that had a ridge or a notch in it.

Rose brings her wooden cube into the kitchen and turns on the overhead light. She turns the cube over in her hands, and just when she's about to give up, she sees one tiny piece that has a groove along one side. She hooks it with her fingernail and pulls.

The piece slides out like a tiny wooden tray. She turns it clockwise, like a key, and at first nothing moves, but after she gives it a jiggle as she turns, the top half of the cube slides across the bottom half. Another few twists, and the halves come apart completely, revealing a small hollow core.

Rose's cube is a puzzle box.

She races into the lounge room and grabs Maria's ball. It's trickier to examine, given its curved shape, but after searching every millimetre of it, she finds a tiny notch right near the base. She fiddles with it, but can't seem to make it budge. She looks at the other side near the base. There seem to be other random notches, and Rose realises they might just be stress marks from where the ball has been set down. She keeps looking and finally gives up. The ball doesn't seem to have any purposeful grooves or notches. She's tempted to get a hammer and smash it open. Or a saw to cut it in half—to see what, if anything, is inside. Then she imagines what Nick would say if he knew she was desecrating his gift that had once belonged to his beloved wife.

She's about to leave it and go to bed when something one of her university lecturers once said pops into her head: that the biggest mistake you could make was to get lost in the details. You needed to stand back to see the big picture.

Rose sets the ball on the kitchen table and stands back. Right away, she can see that it isn't a perfect, circular globe. It's slightly more pointed, narrower at one end, like an egg. She picks it up and jiggles the pieces so it's perfectly round again. She squeezes it back into an egg shape, this time revealing a notched piece, which she slides out. She turns it like a key and one half of the ball slides down. Rose feels her heart leap in her chest as she slides the opposite side up, and they open to reveal a hollow space at the very centre of the ball.

And in the hollow space, two words are engraved: *Mine forever*.

Rose blinks. She looks inside her cube. Nothing is engraved. Could 'mine forever' have been carved by Maria or whoever gave her the wooden ball? Could it have been her killer?

Tomorrow she will track down Mr Petrovic and find out everything she can.

Rose turns off her light and pulls the doona up around her chin. It's a cold night. Bob is sleeping soundly at her feet, keeping both of them warm. Ever since she got the dreaded electricity bill, she feels completely justified in allowing the dog on the bed.

As she's drifting off to sleep, the words 'mine forever' hover at the edge of her consciousness. Is it a deeply romantic message to one's beloved? Or a creepy threat in that 'Every Breath You Take' way?

FORTY-ONE

On her way to the dog park the next day, Rose has to wrestle with the steering wheel to keep the car from being flung off the road by the high winds. A vicious southerly had hit just before dawn, sending the temperature plunging and sweeping grey storm clouds over the Highlands. This kind of wind always puts Rose on edge.

She considers whether she should tell Blackmore about the puzzle boxes, and the inscription in Maria's—*Mine forever*—but decides he'd probably think that interpreting it as an actual clue was fanciful at best. She'd said she'd let him know if she uncovered anything *significant*, not annoy him with wild speculation. It would be better to wait until she can tell him who'd bought Maria's wooden ball. Maybe then she'd redeem herself with a lead that would set Brett free—or help to convict him.

As Bob and Cordelia cavort on the hills as if it's a summer's day, Rose and George stand rigid with their backs to the howling southerly. George isn't what you'd call frail, but he's thin and he's old, and Rose is afraid he'll be knocked over by a sudden gust.

'Any progress on behalf of Brett?' George asks.

Rose hesitates. 'No. Nick Aboud is convinced he did it, but I'm still keeping an open mind.' She decides not to share with George her half-baked theory regarding the wooden ball. She doesn't want the Miss Marple description to resurface, especially if she's wrong.

'And there was nothing else Nick said that might be relevant?'

Rose shakes her head. 'Not really. I just wish I knew who the mystery witness is.'

'Mystery witness?'

'The person who claimed to see Brett and Maria arguing.'

'You don't believe it?'

'I'm just thinking that, if Brett is innocent, then Maria's killer might have made up the story of an argument to implicate him.'

George looks off at the escarpment shrouded in swirling mist. Rose can tell something's bothering him. 'George?'

He turns to her. 'It was me. I'm the witness who saw Brett and Maria arguing.'

Rose is dumbstruck.

'It was behind the pub one night, not long before she disappeared. I have no idea what they were arguing about and I didn't think anything of it at the time. After she disappeared, I thought, like most people, that she had left her husband. But after Brett was arrested, I realised I had to come forward.'

Rose doesn't know what to think, except that she doesn't know George at all. 'Why didn't you tell me?'

'I should have. And I probably should have gone to the police at the time. But I'm not convinced the argument proves he killed her, and I didn't want you to think I was undermining your efforts to find out the truth—especially if Brett is innocent.'

Back at the cottage, Rose makes herself a cup of tea and tries to wrap her head around George's explanation for why he hadn't told her before now that he was the witness to Brett and Maria's fight. It was logical, but something about it didn't add up. Maybe it was *too* logical. She thinks back to him failing to mention that he knew Maria, that she had been to his house. And there was the story about how he'd fallen for a younger woman after Stella died. Could he also have fallen for Maria? Was he the man of means who wanted to 'take her away'?

George was a very sprightly eighty years old. Six years ago, he was seventy-four and doubtless even stronger. She tries to imagine him overpowering a healthy young woman. It's hard to picture, but not impossible, especially if he'd caught her by surprise. But Anna was murdered recently. Rose can't imagine George having anything to do with that. But he was the first person to know that Rose had found the pictures, and he knew she had gone to see Anna with them.

Rose is tying herself in knots, feeling guilty for entertaining the suspicion that he might be a murderer. He is her best friend in the Highlands. But she knows the only way to eliminate him as a suspect is to find out the truth.

She calls Long Bay jail to ask that a message be passed on to Brett to call her later, but the operator for Corrective Services tells her that it's not possible for her to pass a message to an inmate— they're not an answering service. Once again, Rose realises how naive she is, and how completely out of her depth. The operator explains that Rose will have to write to him, or book a visit, which means that an answer to her question could be days away, or even a week or more.

She doesn't know the name of the gift shop where she bought her wooden cube in Bowral, but it was right outside Dirty Jane's.

She calls Dirty Jane's and speaks to a very helpful woman who gives her the phone number of the shop.

'A what?'

'A wooden cube—it's actually a puzzle box . . . about twenty centimetres high,' Rose explains, 'with an intricate inlaid wood pattern.'

'Oh, I remember those, yeah. We don't have any left.'

'The woman who sold it to me said it was made by a local artisan—Ned Petrovic—but I can't find a number for him, and I wondered if you had it.'

'Wow, I have no idea.'

Clearly not, Rose thinks. 'Well, do you think you could ask someone? Perhaps the woman who runs or owns the shop?' Rose doesn't think she's being presumptuous in thinking that isn't the woman she's talking to now.

'Oh, she's out.'

'Well, could you leave her a message?' Rose asks politely, but wanting to reach through the phone and strangle this person.

'Sure. She went out for coffee at the little place down the road, so she shouldn't be long—maybe fifteen minutes or so.'

Too much information, Rose thinks, reciting her name and number.

'Have a nice day,' the woman says cheerily, and Rose hangs up, feeling guilty for being sharp with her. The poor woman is probably making minimum wage to be pleasant to demanding shoppers and annoying women wanting phone numbers that might lead to the identity of a killer.

Rose blames the wind. The wind makes her irritable.

Minutes later, Rose's phone rings and she grabs it, drops it and finally answers, breathless. The woman who owns the gift shop explains that Mr Petrovic never answers his phone, so she gives Rose his address in the nearby town of Robertson. Rose thanks the woman for her trouble, takes Maria's wooden ball off the shelf and leaves the warmth and security of her cottage to brave the wind once more.

Rose drives along the highway through sloping pastures in which cows are huddled in clusters, buffeted by the wailing wind. Rose is glad she's not a cow, especially on a day like today.

As she enters the quaint village of Robertson, she sees the sign for Sassafras Way and smiles, remembering how she and Kim thought the word was hilarious when they were kids. She passes the shops on the main road near the Big Potato, a ten-metre-long, four-metre-wide tuber built in the 1970s by a potato farmer who intended it as a Potato Information Centre. There turned out to be no call for such a thing, so now it sits abandoned in a park like a big brown turd. Although, as Rose passes, she sees a tourist standing in front of the potato, grinning into the wind as his friend takes a picture.

On the edge of town, she turns into a street imaginatively called the Old Road, and at its end finds a tidy fibro building with no sign, but with a window displaying beautifully carved and turned wooden objects. Rose parks, takes the wooden ball from the passenger seat and gets out, whipped by the frenzied wind.

She hurries to the door and turns the handle, but it's locked. She walks over to the window and peers inside. In between the hand-made objects, she can see a man with a bald head and horn-rimmed glasses bent over a benchtop, where he's slicing into a piece of pale wood with an X-Acto knife. His whole being is focused on the wood as he makes fine, shallow slices, picking up the pieces he cuts with delicate tweezers, and placing them on a small tray on the bench.

Rose doesn't want to interrupt him, but she's determined not to leave before she gets some answers. She knocks on the window.

The man pauses. Then, without turning towards the window, he goes back to cutting into the wood.

Rose takes a deep breath and knocks again.

This time, he stops, his shoulders hunching in frustration. He lays the knife on the bench and comes to the window.

'Mr Petrovic?' Rose shouts over the wind.

Petrovic glares at her and shakes his head, waving his hands in a shooing motion. The message is clear: *Bugger off, lady*. He turns back to his bench.

'I need to talk to you, Mr Petrovic!' Rose shouts louder.

He stops, his back to her. But he's listening.

'Please! It's important.'

He turns unhappily and goes to the door. Rose moves over to wait as he opens it.

'Thank you so much, Mr Petrovic, I wonder if you can—'

'Well come in,' he says, impatient.

As she enters the studio, which is barely warmer than outside, Rose wonders if the wind affects him too. 'I'm sorry to interrupt your work,' she begins. 'I'm a big fan, by the way.'

'What do you want?'

Not a people person, then.

Rose holds out Maria's wooden ball. He looks at it, then her, and frowns. 'Don't tell me you broke my concentration to ask me how to open it.'

347

'No, I figured it out.' She demonstrates by trying to pull on the wrong inlay and Ned rolls his eyes, but she finally gets the right one and opens the sphere into its two halves. She holds up the hidden compartment so he can see *Mine forever*.

'So?'

'I wondered if you were the one who inscribed or engraved the message.'

He shakes his head. 'You expect me to remember something I made years ago?'

Rose blinks. 'I need to find out who bought the piece, or who ordered the inscription. I think it came from here, when this used to be a shop.'

Ned scowls, remembering. 'People used to come in all the time.'

'How annoying,' Rose says, without a trace of irony.

'Couldn't get any work done.'

'Do you remember if it was a man or a woman who bought the piece?'

'Was a bloke.'

Rose tries to swallow, but her heart is in her mouth. 'Mr Petrovic, can you describe him?'

'Don't remember faces.'

'Or do you have any record of—'

'Why do you need to know?'

'It's a long story.'

'There's a surprise.'

'But it's important. Someone's life depends on it.'

Petrovic laughs sceptically and goes to the back of the studio, where there's a small office. Rose follows him as far as the doorway and watches as he scans a shelf with stacks of leather-bound notebooks. He grabs one, opens it, puts it back on the shelf, grabs another one, opens it, puts it back. He takes a third notebook, opens it, and starts flicking through the pages with his scarred and callused fingers.

He pauses on a page, runs his finger down a column. And stops. 'Here it is.'

Rose has to tell herself to breathe.

He holds the book open and shows her. A handwritten entry: *Round box, mine forever*, followed by numbers. Rose's heart sinks. 'No name?'

'No. But that's the bloke's phone number.'

Rose gets her phone out. 'Do you mind if I take a picture?'

Petrovic closes the book. 'What for?'

Rose doesn't want to give him any details, especially if there turns out to be no connection between the man who bought the ball and Maria's death.

'Please, Mr Petrovic. I know this sounds crazy, but it really is a matter of life and death.'

Petrovic sighs, shaking his head, but he finds the page and holds it open. Rose quickly snaps a photo before he can change his mind. 'Thank you *so* much!'

He puts the notebook back on the shelf and walks straight to the front door of the studio, holding it open for Rose.

'Sorry again for disturbing your work,' she says.

His eyes are already back on the piece of wood on his bench as he closes the door behind Rose.

She rushes to her car and gets in. She takes her phone out and scrolls through her contacts till she reaches George's mobile number, then goes to the photo she just took. The last three numbers are 693. It's not George's number.

Rose groans with relief. But wonders—what now? She could call the number in the photo, but then her own number

349

would show up, and she doesn't want the potential killer to have it—especially if it's someone like Ray Mullin. She realises it's time to hand over what might be crucial evidence to DI Blackmore.

She starts the car, turning the seat warmers up high.

FORTY-TWO

It's late afternoon by the time Rose enters the police station. She glances up at the New South Wales Police insignia and its motto: Punishment swiftly follows crime. She wonders who, if anyone, will be punished in this case. Maybe she holds the key to his identity.

She approaches the desk. A police officer who looks like he's still in high school, complete with teenage acne and patchy moustache, is scrolling through his phone.

'Constable Rumsey?' Rose says, reading his name tag.

He looks up, startled, as if caught trying on his father's police uniform. 'Yes, miss?'

'My name is Rose McHugh. I wonder if I could speak to Detective Blackmore?'

'I'll see if he's in.' Rumsey dials an internal number and mumbles into the phone.

Rose glances behind her and sees a young man sitting in the waiting area, looking at his hands. She's pretty sure it's the same guy who was there, his face bloated from drinking or drugs or a fight, when she first entered the station months ago. Maybe he's a frequent resident of the overnight cell, waiting for someone, hopefully his mother, to pick him up.

'He's out.'

Rose turns back to Constable Rumsey. 'What about Constable Tran?'

'She's with him. Can I help you?'

Rose hesitates to entrust potentially damning evidence in a murder investigation to a boy going through puberty.

'Thank you anyway.' She goes to a corner of the waiting room and calls Blackmore's number. It goes to voicemail.

'Hi, Detective, Rose McHugh here. I . . . I've found something that I think you might want to follow up. It's the phone number of a man who gave Maria a gift with a very, er, *possessive* message. If it's Brett's number, it's more circumstantial evidence against him. If not, it could belong to the killer. Maybe it's Ray Mullin's? Okay, bye.'

She hangs up and texts him the photo of the number that Ned Petrovic so grudgingly shared.

Fighting against the wind, she's hurrying to her car when her phone rings. She looks at the screen, hoping it's Blackmore, but she's pleased to see from the caller ID that it's Irish Dave. She gets into her car and slams the door shut against the howling wind before she answers.

'Hi, Dave. How awful is this wind?'

'I hate it,' he says. 'It's keeping people at home—I just had a viewing cancelled.'

'That's no good. How are you feeling?'

'Grand. That's why I thought I'd call you about that dinner.'

'That would be lovely. When—'

'What about now? Sorry, do I sound a bit excited?'

She laughs. 'That's okay. Being cool is overrated.'

'Isn't it, though? So what do you say?'

Dinner with Dave sounds like just the distraction she needs, Rose decides. 'Let's do it. I need to take Bob out first, though.'

'I'll pick you up from the cottage?'

'Why not? See you shortly!'

When she gets home, Rose lets Bob into the back garden and calls Kim to tell her about her impromptu date.

'I'm just getting changed so I look a little less . . . windswept.'

'You should wear that black dress with the spaghetti straps.'

'It's below zero! And I'm not accepting an Oscar, I'm going for a casual mid-week meal.'

'It's so hard to be beautiful *and* warm.'

'I'll call you later and let you know how it went.'

'Call me in the morning. You'll probably be too busy having toe-curling sex to call tonight.'

Rose is zipping up her boots when there's a loud thud in the back garden. She rushes to the window.

A huge branch from the tallest gum tree has fallen. She can't see Bob.

'*Bob!*'

Rose runs outside and finds her dog standing over the fallen branch, sniffing curiously. She throws her arms around his neck. 'Oh, Bob. Come inside, boy, it's freezing.'

She urges him back to the kitchen, the door slamming shut behind them as soon as they enter, pushed by a gust of wind.

'Jesus, what a day.'

Another bang. Rose jumps.

She looks out at the garden, but can't see anything. When there's another bang, she realises it's the front door. She goes to the door and opens it.

Dave is standing there, smiling apologetically. 'I'm sorry for knocking so loudly, but there was no answer and I thought maybe with the wind you couldn't hear me.'

'Come in,' she says, closing the door behind him. 'I was out the back. What my sister would call a widow-maker just fell.'

'Oh no!'

'Bob was out there, but it missed him.'

'You should get the tree doctor over to make sure you're not dicing with death.'

'Good idea.'

He looks around as Rose gets her coat. 'Wow, the place looks fantastic.'

'Thanks. I haven't done that much, but it's cosy.'

'It's more than that. It's stylish—and it's you. I could never get my place looking this good. Maybe I need a woman's touch.'

Rose smiles.

'You look very nice, too,' he says.

She had managed to throw on a green silk blouse, black pants and the suede boots with the heel.

'Thank you. So do you.'

'Well, now you're fibbing.'

She laughs.

They walk outside together, and Dave holds the door of his white Audi open for her. Rose sinks into the warm leather seat, excited to be on a proper date. In spite of the wind, maybe it isn't such a shit day after all.

Dave starts the car. The engine is incredibly quiet.

'Is this electric?' Rose asks, impressed.

'It is,' he says as he pulls onto the road.

'I didn't pick you for a greenie.'

'Oh, I'm full o' surprises,' he says playfully.

Rose smiles. 'Where are we going?'

'I thought we'd go to the Burrawang.'

'Fabulous. I was only there the one time, at Anna's auction, and I've been dying to go back.'

They make small talk as they drive through Moss Vale and then turn onto the road to Burrawang, heading through fields and farmland as the daylight wanes.

When they're about ten minutes or so from Burrawang, Dave turns off the main road onto a smaller one. Rose looks at him.

'Short cut,' he says.

But as they drive through denser, darker bushland, something changes—the air in the car, something in the atmosphere thickens, becomes heavy.

'I've never been this way,' Rose says, trying to keep her tone light. She waits for Dave to respond, but he's quiet.

Outside, the headlights catch the edge of the bush, the thick ferns and tall trees of Morton National Park closing in around them.

'I don't think this is the way.' She glances at Dave, his unsmiling face. He's driving fast.

Rose looks ahead. There appear to be no other cars in the park—not at this time of day, at the end of winter.

Her phone rings and she reaches for her bag, but Dave's hand flies out and grabs her wrist. 'Leave it,' he says.

Rose sits back and Dave lets go of her wrist. It hurts where he grabbed it. She rubs it, trying to process what's happening. Adrenaline is flooding through her now, her body getting ready for fight or flight. But this doesn't make sense.

She looks down to the compartment between their seats where Dave's business cards are stacked. They have a line drawing of a Highlands house, his name, and his phone number. It ends in 693.

Rose covers her mouth, stifling a whimper. She hadn't recognised the number because she'd put him in her phone as 'Irish Dave'.

'Let me out,' she says, trying to keep the quaver from her voice.

Dave says nothing, his eyes on the road. He doesn't slow down.

Rose looks out at the forest. A few rays from the setting sun flicker between the trees as they pass.

She rests her hand near the doorhandle.

'You'll break your neck.'

He's right.

Rose moves her hand back into her lap. She can taste bile at the back of her throat. This is what I get for chasing my fantasy of a rural idyll, she thinks. This is how I'm going to die.

Terror now has her in its teeth. She suddenly remembers this is how she felt when she was told of her parents' sudden death. A jolt of terror, followed by . . . nothing, as if it were happening to someone else. The denial was so strong, it held her apart, protected her from feeling pain that would have crushed her. At least for a while.

Now, Rose pushes past the jolt of terror, letting herself slip into denial, to a place where she can't feel the fear. Maybe she can speak. Maybe she can save herself.

'How?' she asks, her voice strangely toneless.

'I got a call from a local artist. He said a crazy woman wanted my phone number, and he gave it to her, but he wanted to warn me. Figured you for a stalker.'

'You were the other man—the man with money who wanted Maria to be yours forever.'

'She *is* mine forever!' Dave says.

Rose flinches. But she wants to keep him talking. As long as he's talking, he's not hurting her. 'But . . . Anna?'

She doesn't think he's going to answer at first, but then it seems he can't help himself.

'After you found those pictures, I had to make sure she didn't have anything else of mine tucked away.'

'She knew about you and Maria?'

'Not until I paid her a visit.'

Rose tries to think of something else to say. 'Do you really have long Covid?'

'Never had Covid—one of the lucky few.'

'So you were never interested in me; you just wanted to know what I knew.'

As if to confirm this, Dave slows to turn onto an unsealed road. As he does, Rose pops her seatbelt, grabs the doorhandle and flings herself out of the moving car.

She slams into the dirt, tasting gravel, and rolls through scrub that tears through her clothes to the skin.

Brakes screech behind her, the car skids on the dirt track.

She scrambles to her feet and runs blindly into the bush without looking back.

Rose runs deeper into the forest as the fierce wind makes the leaves shudder in the trees. She's never run so fast, zigzagging around trunks and fallen branches, slipping on moss-covered rocks.

Her coat gets snagged on a branch, so she peels out of it. There's barely any light and she gets tangled in vines, stumbling in her high-heeled boots. She stops, looks behind her. She can't hear anything over the trees groaning in the wind. She pulls off her boots and keeps running.

Branches rake her face, tear at her silk shirt as she trembles with adrenaline and the cold. Behind a broad gum tree, she slows to catch her breath. She touches a hand to her cheek and finds it wet with tears and blood. She stumbles on.

She fights through scrub, a tight cluster of banksia, and suddenly the ground drops away beneath her and she is falling.

She hits the ground hard.

Dragging air into her lungs, her knees throbbing, she gets to her feet and looks around. The light is nearly gone now but she recognises this place. She's been here before. Echo Lake.

The shadow descends, the sick feeling.

Then, behind her, his voice.

'What do the police know?' Dave asks.

'I texted them your number,' Rose says. Her heart is pounding hard and she struggles to catch her breath.

Dave comes closer, shaking his head slowly. She backs away, falls over a branch.

'If they had it, they'd have me,' he says.

Rose realises that her text to Blackmore might not have gone through. Had she hit send? If she had trusted Constable Rumsey with the phone number, the wooden ball, she might not be facing her death right now.

'I left a message,' she says. 'They'll find you.'

'Maybe. But at least I'll have made you pay.'

Nausea overwhelms her. She drops to the ground and tries to

scramble away but he's right behind her. He grabs her hair, yanks her head back.

'Too bad. Twenty years ago you'd have been almost fuckable.'

A spark of rage ignites inside her. She kicks out at his legs as hard as she can. He buckles but maintains his grip. With his free hand he punches her in the face.

She's stunned, goes limp, and the cut above her lip reopens, blooms with blood.

Lying on her back, she tries to clear her blurred vision but he kicks her in the ribs and flips her onto her stomach with his boot. He shoves her face into the ground, her mouth filling with dirt. The terror engulfs her. She feels something heavy on the back of her neck. It's his knee, pinning her down, grinding her into the earth. Dirt fills her nostrils. She can't breathe.

'Those American cops know what they're doing. Easiest way to subdue an animal.'

Rose's windpipe is being crushed from the back. She's suffocating. With the little strength she has left she squirms against Dave's grip but it's not enough. Rose is fading.

Suddenly she sees Sam's face, his lopsided grin, and it gives her the strength to turn her head and breathe. Dave presses harder against her neck with his knee, his full weight bearing down.

Out of the corner of her eye, Rose can see the trees swaying over what was once Echo Lake. A huge branch is bending in the freezing wind. The branch bends further; it looks like it could break. Suddenly Rose loves the wind, wills it to blow harder, to tear the branch and send it tumbling onto Dave as he bends over her, intent on killing her for discovering the truth.

The branch creaks and Rose takes as deep a breath as she can, letting the wind fill her. There's an almighty crack, and as Dave turns at the sound Rose twists out from under him.

The huge branch falls, hitting Dave on the shoulder, and Rose crawls away, but the searing pain in her ribs where he kicked her slows her down. Gripping his shoulder, furious, he comes after her. She clambers to her feet but he grabs her shirt and flings her to the ground. She clutches at what's around her, finds a rock. He kicks her ribs again and she feels something crack. He bends over her, wrapping his hands around her neck, his teeth bared. She swings the rock up and slams it into the side of his head.

He yells in pain and she rolls away, but he grabs her ankle and drags her back underneath him. The look in his eyes tells her that it's over. Her strength is spent. He picks up the fallen branch and presses it against her throat. Her eyes flutter closed. Rose pictures Sam and Kim as she's about to lose consciousness, saying goodbye.

Suddenly Dave lets go.

Dragging air into her lungs, her throat burning, Rose tries to see where he's gone, but she can't make him out in the gloom. She can hear grunting, though, thrashing in the dry leaves. She sits up, squinting into the near-dark.

And then she sees two shapes. She can't believe her eyes.

Bob is on top of Dave with the man's forearm in his mouth.

Dave punches Bob on the side of the head and Bob whimpers but he doesn't let go.

Rose staggers to her feet. She grabs a branch, swings it high and brings it down on Dave's face. Blood explodes from his nose and mouth. She brings it down, again, and again.

He tries to say something through broken, bloody teeth. She raises the branch again but someone grabs it in mid-air. She turns.

Blackmore.

'Enough, Rose.'

She drops the branch and collapses. Bob goes to her, licking the blood and tears from her face.

Wrapped in a blanket, Rose is sitting in the open door of Blackmore's car, which is parked next to the white Audi, as a paramedic cleans the cuts on her face and hands. He has trouble manoeuvring around Bob, but Rose won't let go of her dog.

She watches Dave being strapped down and loaded into an ambulance. Constable Tran climbs in after him.

'I'll bring Rose to the hospital,' Blackmore tells the paramedic. 'Why don't you get in the back seat with Bob, Rose?' Blackmore suggests gently.

She looks at him and nods, and he helps her into the back seat, tucking the blanket around her. Bob sits on the seat next to her and lays his head across her lap. She strokes his head, feeling the warmth of him under her hand.

Blackmore has been driving a while before Rose speaks, her voice thin and broken.

'How did you find me?'

Blackmore looks at her in the rear-view mirror. 'We don't have to do this now, Rose.'

'Please.'

Blackmore relents. 'I got your text with Dave's number. When you didn't answer your phone, Constable Tran and I went to your house but you were gone. I called George and he said to call your sister. She said you were on a date with Dave.'

'But how did you find us?'

'Don't be mad, but Kim installed a tracking app on your phone.'

Rose doesn't know whether to laugh or cry, so she does a little of both.

'She's been worried about you. When we saw you were in the park, I thought Bob could help find you. Not strictly by the book, but'—he shrugs—'it worked.'

Rose strokes Bob's head as, through eyes blurred with tears, she looks out the window into the darkness of the bush.

FORTY-THREE

'So, you've forgiven me?' Kim asks.

'For saving my life?' Rose says. 'I'm working on it.'

They smile. Kim selects a log from the basket and lays it on the fire. She sits back on the couch where Rose is snuggled under a blanket with Bob snoozing by her side.

Kim picks up the bottle of red wine from the coffee table and fills their glasses. Rose takes a sip, wincing, and gently touches the bandage over her mouth.

'I don't know why they call it a coffee table,' Kim observes. 'It should be a red wine table. Or a cheese toastie table.'

'Ooh, that's what I feel like tonight.'

'That's good, because it's all I know how to cook,' Sam says, coming in from the kitchen. After Kim had called him, he caught the next plane home.

'Is that what you live on?' Rose asks, her voice still raw from being strangled.

'No—two-minute noodles are a good back-up,' he says cheerily as he sprawls on the rug in front of the fire.

Rose smiles, comforted by Sam's presence. And Kim's. She'd spent a few days in hospital, but there wasn't much they could do for broken ribs and a bruised neck, so she'd been released that morning.

Kim and Sam had picked her up, and they went straight from the hospital to Blackmore's house, where Bob had been spoiled by Grace with grilled lamb chops and other delicacies. Now, with Bob, Sam and Kim by her side, a bottle of red, and a fire in the stove, Rose is feeling pretty good.

There's a soft knock at the door.

Sam gets up and answers it. Rose tries to see who it is, but winces when she turns her head.

'This looks comfy,' Blackmore says as he enters.

'I'm never getting off this couch,' Rose replies.

'I'll get the toasties started,' Sam says.

'I'll slice the cheese,' Kim adds, leaving her sister and the detective alone—though she is no doubt listening from the kitchen.

Blackmore sits next to Bob and scratches him behind the ears. He looks at the large bouquet of native flowers in a vase on an end table. 'Nice flowers.'

'From Al.'

His brow furrows with a question.

'My good mate, Al Addison,' Rose clarifies.

Blackmore laughs softly, then becomes serious. 'I wanted to let you know that Dave has been charged with your attempted murder, and the murders of Anna and Maria.'

Rose takes a long, slow breath. 'Has Brett been released?'

'Yes. He wants to come and thank you, when you're up to it.'

Rose nods.

Blackmore goes on. 'We found evidence at Dave's house connecting him to both crimes, including the wooden pyramid sculpture you saw at Anna's. We think he hit her with it when he went to see her, before dumping her body off the cliff. Her blood was still on it.'

'And he kept it?' Rose asks, horrified. 'I don't suppose there was a message inside?'

'*From your best friend, Maria.*'

'Wow.'

'He must have thought he'd never be caught,' Blackmore says.

'He didn't count on Miss Marple,' Rose croaks.

'He did not. We also found other photos of the bush near the cave, and the camera he took them with.'

'So, who buried the film in my garden?'

'We don't know. It could have been him.'

'I think it was Maria,' Rose says in a whisper. 'She wanted to end it with Dave, but she also wanted to leave something of their affair behind—with a picture of her near the place she used to bring him. Buried in a safe place, at the home of her friend.'

'As good a theory as any.'

'I can't believe I went out with the guy.'

'He fooled all of us, Rose. And you did manage to break his nose and most of his front teeth.'

'Good,' Kim says from where she's hovering in the kitchen doorway.

Rose turns and smiles at her.

'I guess you don't feel very good about the Highlands any-more,' Blackmore says. 'Even with the autumn foliage.'

'On the contrary,' Rose says, glancing at Kim. 'I still love it here. I have a pretty good feel for places—I'm just shit at judging people.'

Blackmore smiles. 'I won't take that personally.'

Rose smiles back, then looks up at Kim, who is wiping away her tears.

FORTY-FOUR

A week after her release from hospital, Rose calls Jazzy Nolan, who picks up on the first ring.

'Rose McHugh?' the reporter says, excited. 'How are you? I'm so glad you called! I—'

'Jazzy, I'd like to meet,' Rose says.

'Absolutely. Name the time and place.'

'Good,' Rose says. 'I have a story to tell.'

A few weeks after that, on a cold but windless sunny day, Rose drives to Threave House. She arrives before the others to help George get things ready. They open a few bottles and set out some food, but this isn't a party.

It's a farewell.

Kim arrives with Grace; she had declared it was her turn to be the designated driver. The Girls from Galway and Helen Grayspence arrive shortly after.

Jazzy Nolan's article in the *Southern Highland News*—about Mary Grayspence, a young wife and mother whose story had never been told—has been framed and sits in the centre of the table. Jazzy had been disappointed when she realised Rose wasn't going to tell the story of her date with a psychopath, but when she heard Mary's story, and how her death had been swept under the carpet and lost to history, she threw herself into the assignment with zeal. Helen had found out more about her aunt, including her love of Irish and Scottish folk songs, which she sang to Margaret during the baby's short time on earth.

After the article was published, people wrote in about their own friends and relatives whose memories had been sullied or ignored due to the conservative mores of the time. Jazzy told Rose she was thinking of doing a monthly column about forgotten people of the Highlands, and asked Rose to be her historical consultant. Rose suggested they should start by having descendants of the local Indigenous people tell their stories.

Rose fills their glasses with wine, and they take them into the back bedroom, which has been freshened with some new furniture and a thick rug. Next to the picture of tiny Margaret in her wooden cradle is a photo of Mary and John on their wedding day, supplied by Helen. Next to it is an empty hook, where Rose hangs the framed article, in lieu of an obituary, to honour Mary's life and death.

George raises his glass. 'To Mary and Margaret and John.'

Rose, Kim, Grace and Helen raise their glasses and echo his toast.

And then the Girls of Galway sing a song of farewell.

Of all the comrades that e'er I had
They're sorry for my going away
And all the sweethearts that e'er I had
They would wish me one more day to stay
But since it fell into my lot
That I should rise and you should not

I'll gently rise and softly call
Goodnight and joy be to you all
So fill to me the parting glass
And drink a health whate'er befalls
Then gently rise and softly call
Goodnight and joy be to you all.

Rose is looking at the picture of Mary as her eyes fill with tears. And just as the song ends, Rose feels something like a soft wind passing through her. She turns to look behind her, to see where the draught is coming from, but the door and windows are closed. She looks at the others. They're all shedding tears, but none of them seems to have felt the wind.

FORTY-FIVE

Spring has come to the Southern Highlands. Flowers in pink, yellow and white bloom on trees and shrubs in gardens and parklands. The fragrance of rose and jasmine makes Rose giddy with joy. As much as she loves the cooler weather, she has never been so happy for the seasons to change.

A straggly-looking tree in her front garden that she had never been very fond of has become a frenzied cloud of white blossoms. She decides to take a picture and show Donna at the nursery to find out what it is.

Rose is scattering native grass seed in the areas of the back garden that are still bare after being dug up by the police earlier in the year, while Bob wrestles with a stick under the ash whose bright green leaves seem to have emerged overnight.

Her phone rings. It's Susan from the museum.

'Hi, Susan, how are you?'

'I'm fine, Rose, but I'm sorry to say that my husband is unwell.'

'Oh, I'm so sorry to hear that.'

'It means I can no longer manage all my duties at the museum.'

'What a shame,' Rose says, afraid this means someone else will take over—someone who won't see the point of keeping Rose on, especially since she's finished logging the memorabilia.

'It is. Anyhoo, I wondered if you'd be interested in taking over. It'll mean running the museum, but also administering the archives and looking after the Family History Society. It's a paid position. Not much, but it'll keep you out of trouble. Actually, knowing you, it probably won't.'

Rose is overwhelmed. 'Oh, Susan, thank you. I would be honoured to take the position.'

'Good. We need to run it by the board, but don't worry— they're all relatives.'

'Seriously?'

'Yes, Rose, this is the Highlands.'

Rose laughs and thanks Susan, wishing her and her husband the best. She hangs up and looks at Bob, who is now snoozing under the grevilleas Rose had planted for Maria and Anna. They're still blooming, thriving in their place.

With the sun filtering through the lush, green trees, Rose is grateful that she has found her slice of paradise in the Highlands, and that she has made good friends. She has so much to look forward to, especially Christmas, when Kim will be coming down. And Sam will be here too, bringing his English boyfriend with him.

But when she closes her eyes and feels the sun on her face, Rose sees Echo Lake—a place that has yet to give up its secrets. She may never know if something terrible happened there in the past, or whether the sick feeling was a premonition of her own dance with the devil.

She opens her eyes and breathes in the smells of spring, of her small patch of land. If she listens closely enough, maybe she can hear its memories, like echoes from the past.

ACKNOWLEDGEMENTS

I acknowledge the traditional owners of the Southern Highlands, including the Gundungurra and Dharawal people, past and present.

The Southern Highlands towns, parks and some of the shops and pubs mentioned in this book are real, but some locations are imaginary, including Echo Lake, which was inspired by an experience I had at another place, far away.

Many people helped this book see the light of day, first and foremost Ruby Cottle, my toughest critic. Good friend Deb Callaghan provided both moral and practical support. Jo Cave, my botanical expert, supplied insight into the ongoing war between natives and exotics, and she was also an astute story critic. David and Sarah Champtaloup generously provided detail. I have taken expert advice only as far as it suits the plot, and any inaccuracies are mine alone. Any similarities to real people are purely coincidental.

I owe a huge debt of gratitude to Jane Palfreyman at Allen & Unwin for taking a chance on a first-time novelist and for her incisive notes on the manuscript. Thanks also to editors Rebecca Starford, Angela Handley and Ali Lavau for their insight and advice, Katri Hilden for her meticulous proofreading,

Aleksander Potočnik for his map of the Southern Highlands and Luke Causby for his atmospheric cover design.

Finally, I'd like to thank the team at Cameron's Management, including Jane Cameron, Chelsea Thistlewaite, Lisa Fagan and Anthony Blair, who have stood by me for so many years.

ABOUT THE AUTHOR

Born in New York, Joan Sauers is a screenwriter, producer and author who worked in London, Los Angeles and New York before settling in Australia. She has lectured in screen-writing in Sydney, London, Paris, Berlin and Casablanca and has had fourteen books published in Australia, the United States, India and Japan. She was script editor on films including *The Babadook* and TV shows, *Rake* and *The Principal*, and has written many screenplays. Most recently, Joan was a writer on the ABC series *Wakefield*, which also aired on Showtime in the US. She is currently writing the TV series *Ladies in Black* and a sci-fi romance created by her daughter. Joan divides her time between Sydney and the Southern Highlands, and has one daughter and two grandsons.